CRUSADE

Stuart Slade

Dedication

This book is respectfully dedicated to the memory of
Brigadier General Paul Warfield Tibbets

Acknowledgements

Crusade could not have been written without the very generous help of a large
number of people who contributed their time, input and efforts into confirming
the technical details of the story. Some of these generous souls I know personally
and we discussed the conduct and probable results of the actions described in
this novel in depth. Others I know only via the internet as the collective
membership of The History, Politics and Current Affairs Board yet their
communal wisdom and vast store of knowledge, freely contributed, has been truly
irreplaceable.

In particular, I would like to acknowledge the assistance of Shane Rogers who
provided irreplaceable insight into the engineering problems that result from the
destruction of Germany. In addition, Shane provided analyses of South East
Asian and Australian politics and history that were of extreme value. A note of
thanks is also due to Ryan Crierie who willingly donated his time and great
expertise in producing the artwork used for the cover of this book.

I must also express a particular debt of gratitude to my wife Josefa for without
her kind forbearance, patient support and unstintingly generous assistance, this
novel would have remained nothing more than a vague idea floating in the back
of my mind.

Caveat

Crusade is a work of fiction, set in an alternate universe. All the
characters appearing in this book are fictional and any resemblance to
any person, living or dead is purely coincidental. Although some names
of historical characters appear, they do not necessarily represent the
same people we know in our reality.

Copyright Notice

Contents

Previous Books In This Series
Available From Lulu Press

The Big One	(1947)
Anvil of Necessity	(1948)
The Great Game	(1959)
Crusade	(1965)

Coming Soon

Ride of the Valkyries	(1972)

CHAPTER ONE
OPERATIONAL REQUIREMENTS

Stonewall Jackson Elementary School, Hanleytown, South Carolina

The man was giggling as he held the schoolgirl up as a shield. Behind him, the rest of the children were sitting on the floor whimpering gently with fear. Not far away from them, Miss Clarke, the schoolteacher, was lying in a corner. She was dying and she knew it, bleeding out from the deep knife cuts in her arms and legs. She'd accepted her own death but she was mortally afraid for the children that had been in her care.

Ever since the man had burst into the schoolroom, shouting incoherently about the sin of teaching boys and girls in the same class, she'd known that there was little hope for any of them. When the little girl had started crying loudly, the man had grabbed her and was now using her as a shield while he shouted abuse and what appeared to be demands out of the window. He had been getting more excited every moment and now he was making wild gestures, waving the knife in his free hand over her head. That's when it happened.

For a moment, Miss Clarke didn't know whether she was really seeing it or whether loss of blood was causing her to hallucinate. The glass in front of the man's head shattered inwards and she saw, or thought she saw, his forehead flatten slightly as the bullet struck it. Then the sides of his head rippled with the shockwave before his skull exploded in a shower of blood and bone. A few seconds later? Or a few minutes? However long it was, the door burst open and the police emergency response team entered the schoolroom. First in was Hanleytown's only black policewoman, who dropped her shield and made straight for the little girl on the floor. She swept her up in her arms.

"It's over honey, it's all over, the bad man won't hurt you any more, the bad man won't hurt anybody again." She looked down at the body with a shattered head lying on the floor. "Lord have mercy on us, is that ever the truth."

Meanwhile, the medical team was getting Miss Clarke onto a gurney and rigging an emergency blood transfusion. The wounds themselves weren't fatal but she'd lost so much blood her skin had gone gray-white. But, with a medical team, and a good supply of blood, well, it looked bad but with luck, she'd make it.

Outside, the Hanleytown Chief of Police was waiting. He'd been rehearsing what to say ever since the sound of the shot, this was something he wanted to get right. The maniac in the schoolroom had picked his target well. The school had been in the middle of open ground with more than two hundred yards to any cover. He had made it clear if he saw any police approaching the building, he would kill all the children, but he'd miscalculated very badly. There was good cover for a sniper, six hundred yards or more away and visiting Hanleytown was a sniper who could make the shot.

A couple was approaching him, a middle-aged American man with the bearing a Marine never quite lost no matter how long he'd been retired and a younger Russian woman with the imperturbable solidity that Russian women seemed to acquire almost at birth. She was carrying a Moisin-Nagant rifle with a powerful PMU telescopic sight. Captain Novak came sharply to attention and threw the best salute he could manage. "Gospodin Klavdia Kalugina, the community of Hanleytown is deeply in your debt. On behalf of all our citizens, I wish to express our heartfelt gratitude for how you have saved our children with your skill."

"Thank you Chief, but your thanks are not necessary. Any man who would threaten children in such a way is evil and it is the duty of us all to confront evil at every opportunity." Her voice was completely flat, without any intonation. Tony Evans glanced at his wife; her gray eyes still had the cold lifelessness that marked her as being in a place it was better not to ask about. Then, even as he watched, the animation flicked back in and her eyes once more had the dancing humor that made them so beautiful. "Anyway, it was not such a hard shot."

"Gospodin Klavdia," Novak was careful to use the very respectful 'Gospodin' rather than the more casual 'Grazhdanin,' "it was a better shot than any of my men could have made, and some of them have been hunting deer since before they could walk. If you have the time, could I further impose on you to give a couple of my best shots some help in improving their skills?"

"Of course Chief Novak. What rifle do your men use?"

"M1 Garands, Gospodin Klavdia."

"Then I suggest you start by getting rid of them. It is impossible to make good shots with semi-automatic rifles. The movement of the action throws off the aim. I recommend you replace them with '03 Springfield rifles and the best telescopic sights you can find. Now, if you will excuse me, I would like to secure my rifle and wash."

The two men watched her head for their car, one of the new Mustang convertibles. "Tony, I'm sorry if this mess has ruined your evening but Klavdia's presence was an advantage we couldn't neglect. She's probably saved a lot of lives tonight. I'd offer her a reward or something, but it might offend her. Any suggestions?"

"Don't worry about the evening, we were going to see Judy Garland and Jane Russell in Anna Karenina but tomorrow will do. If you want to make Klavdia really happy, see if you can find her an Ikon, a real one. They're rare in Russia, the communists burned most of them and the Germans destroyed most of those left. The Russians take their religion really seriously now.

But, Captain, what the hell happened here? I grew up here and I don't remember anything like this ever happening before."

"Nor me Tony, and I've been living here a lot longer than you. On the surface, well, my head is telling me its just some nut-case out to make a statement, but my gut disagrees and says it's a lot worse than that. I got a feel there is something here we don't understand yet, can't tell you how I know that, but I do."

Captain Novak lay broke off for a minute and took a message from a state trooper. "You know The Manor?" Evans nodded; it was reputed to be the best restaurant in South Carolina, "The owner has asked you and Klavdia to be his guests there for dinner. Any time you like and as often as you like. His kid was in that room."

Town Square, Yaffo, Palestine.

The square was filled with howls and the weird ululating noises the local women made at such events. The hysteria in the crowd was building constantly, even though the glare of the noonday sun was painful as it reflected off the white-washed buildings and glass windows. Dispersed throughout the crowd were the agitators, who made sure that the fever of the crowd was constantly being stoked. The crowd itself had long since ceased to be made up of individuals and now had a life of its own, a life that blotted out the minds and feelings of its constituent parts. The agitators, though, had another function. Anybody who didn't show the required frenzy would be singled out for investigation. Next week, the crowd could be gathering for them.

Then, the doors of the court building were opened and the condemned were thrown out. They were a family, or so the posted verdicts had said, but they had been so badly beaten that it was impossible to determine whether they were young or old, male or female. Had anybody in the crowd been detached enough, they could probably have guessed at the victim's ages by relative size but if anybody was capable of doing so they hid it well. The condemned wore only torn rags so somebody who retained the ability to see clearly might have been able to pick out the women but any who could do so hid that as well. It didn't matter anyway,

8

the condemned were all dead no matter what their age or sex. They just hadn't stopped breathing yet.

The guards dragged the victims through the crowd, taking their time about it so those nearest the path could throw stones at or spit on the condemned family. If they had been so minded, if the dynamics of crowd behavior had been less overwhelming, the more perceptive members of the crowd might have spotted some very strange things about those guards. They spoke to each other in a strange, guttural language, one that completely lacked the lilting melody that made Arabic a pleasure to hear. Some of them had blue eyes and fair hair, most had skin that was reddened from the sun rather than bronzed. All of them were large, powerful men who handled their victims with the brutal efficiency of long practice.

Once through the screaming crowd, the victims were hauled to stakes in the middle of the square and shackled to them. Brushwood and kindling was already waiting and it only took moments to stack it around them. That was another strange aspect about the scene for those with the wits to see it; execution by fire was a European practice, not a Middle Eastern one. Who would burn valuable wood just for executions? Had any members of the crowd retained the ability to analyze the events taking place in front of them they might have wondered just what was going here. This was a ritual execution, shouldn't stoning be the method used? But, questions were irrelevant and asking them was dangerous.

The strange men, the 'Guardians of the Faith,' lit the fires. The chanting and howling in the square reached a new pitch of excitement, drowning out the screams inside the fires. The black smoke drifted across the square and into the sky. 80,000 feet higher, an aircraft with absurdly long wings turned again, its gyro-stabilized cameras recording the scene below. Nobody in Yaffo Town Square knew they were being filmed, and none of them would have cared if they had known.

Main Conference Room, National Security Council Building, Washington D.C.

The film projector shut off with a series of clicks that echoed around the silent room. "That must be the most horrible thing I have ever seen." President Lyndon Baines Johnson's voice was shaking "I never believed I would see human beings being publicly barbecued in the twentieth century. Who were those poor people? And, how did we get this film?"

"Mister President, answering your last question first, for twenty years it has been Strategic Aerospace Command policy – and the policy of the United States of America – that SAC aircraft go where they wish and do what they want. We call this policy "Open Skies," by which we mean, of course, that other people's skies are open to us. Now, other nations are used to that policy, most accept it, some resent it but more welcome the sight of our bombers overhead.

"We make a point of taking film and giving copies to the governments in question. This means they can make accurate maps of their countries, something we take for granted but many countries have never seen before. We can spot water resources and other national assets. In fact, some countries find our aerial photography so valuable they actually ask us to over-fly them and pay us for the products. In this case, though, the imagery you have seen was taken by a U-2 reconnaissance aircraft. Its flight was not welcomed, but those underneath could do nothing about it.

"The victims of this dreadful event were a Moslem Imam and his entire family. He'd been running an escape route for Jews hiding out in Palestine, up the coast through Lebanon and into Turkey. Whether somebody informed on him or the authorities found out some other way, we'll probably never know. I must admit I thought that the Jewish population of Palestine had already been exterminated when the Jewish settlements in the area were overrun but it appears that a significant number went into hiding. We have now learned that the Moslem population has organized a substantial underground movement dedicated to helping them escape. Obviously the ruling authorities regard the existence of that movement as a serious threat to their rule so they have gone to great lengths to stamp it out.

"Those performing the executions are part of an organization called 'The Guardians of the Faith'. There are some highly anomalous features of these murders. For example, they bear far more resemblance to the legends of the Spanish

Inquisition or the European witch trials than any part of Islamic culture. This is because the 'Guardians of the Faith' are Europeans. We know them better as Einsatzkommando. When Model and the survivors of his army escaped from southern Russia a few years back, the SS Einsatzkommado escaped with him. They found refuge in what is now the Caliphate, Model's troops have become a sort of Praetorian Guard for the Caliphate leaders. The Einsatzkommando became the 'Guardians of the Faith' and, as we can see, are carrying on the same old way."

The Seer thought for a moment. "In fact, there is quite a culture clash here. It's pretty obvious that Model's people don't really understand the people they are living with and their hosts don't understand them. This execution by fire we've been watching is a good example of that phenomenon. It's so bizarre as to be almost inexplicable in local terms and it highlights just how alien these 'Guardians of the Faith' really are and that's going to cause a lot of tension in the medium term. Be that as it may, it would appear that this atrocity was intended as a public example of what anybody who helps the 'ungodly' escape the 'Guardians of the Faith' can expect. Not just them, but their entire families. The Jewish family in question here were simply executed, beheaded as we understand, along with a number of Druze from the Lebanon and a few others.

"At the time of Operation Jungle Hammer, the Russians captured a mass of evidence that pointed to the birth of the Caliphate and shared it with everybody who would be affected. As a result, the Caliphate plans were knocked a little askew; the birth and growth of the new state was in public, it did not spring on the world as a fully-developed entity. That was fortunate for us and for the rest of the world. The three countries that formed the original core of the Caliphate in 1961 were Afghanistan, Iran and Iraq.

"It's not a coincidence that all three were occupied by us during the Second World War and we treated them with a certain degree of disdain. We needed to build supply lines through them and we needed their oil, so we built the lines and took the oil. Across the borders, the Germans were treating the Moslem populations of areas they occupied with much more than disdain. They ruled it the way they ruled everything else, with maximum

11

brutality.   That radicalized the populations in question and, combined with resentment at our conduct, we have this.   In one sense, its our baby, we created it and now we have to live with the consequences.

"Anyway, that's the past, and its long gone. Our problem today is that inner core was joined in 1962 by Saudi Arabia and, in 1963 by Syria, Jordan and Palestine. Last year, the Lebanon and Kuwait fell to what were allegedly coups but were in fact thinly disguised invasions by Caliphate forces. Those gains are much less impressive than they sound, the countries taken over were chronically weak, chronically unstable and the convoluted events that took place there during the war pretty much destroyed any legitimacy the existing rulers had. The British used to keep that area in order, now they've left, it was a power vacuum that got filled.

"In every case, a country joining the Caliphate has been 'cleansed,' that is, non-Moslem inhabitants have been exterminated. In Caliphate eyes, any who do not support that concept are either apostates or non-Moslem. It is important to note that, for non-Moslems, leaving is not an option. The choices they face are convert or die. It appears that an attempt to incorporate Turkey into the Caliphate was made but it has, so far, failed. However, the Turks are facing endemic terrorism as a result. There are also signs that Caliphate terrorism and subversion are spreading north, into the southern Russian provinces. You may recollect that there was recently serious fighting in Chechnya as a result. The Russians had a hard time putting down what amounted to a rebellion there."

"It was a barbaric display. How can we call such people our allies?" Secretary of Defense McNorman looked defiantly at the other occupants of the room. He'd taken on the post of Defense Secretary with much talk of how he was going to re-organize the department and bring in modern managerial practices. Then, he'd found out his post was largely ceremonial and consisted primarily of opening airbases and launching ships. He was a powerless figurehead and everybody in the room knew it. Most of them were staring back at him with barely disguised contempt.

"Robert, I don't think we could ask for better allies than the Russians at this time. And they are the ones who had to deal with that problem, not us." President Johnson's voice was kindly but the real message was an unmistakable 'shut up.'

"That is indeed the case, Mister President. The Chechnya situation was a hard one for anybody to crack. The Caliphate rebels were mixed in with the civilian population and used them as cover. The Russian troops had no way of knowing who was hostile and who were civilians caught in the crossfire. The Russian troops, of course, did what they had to in order to protect themselves. Fortunately, the casualties on their side were light, but Russia cannot afford even small losses in manpower.

"The good news is that staunch resistance in both Turkey and Russia seems to have stalled Caliphate advances there. Instead, the Caliphate has turned its attention westwards towards Egypt and the Sudan. It appears those two countries have been earmarked as the next stage in the expansion of Caliphate control. From there, our guess is that they intend to advance their control along the entire North African littoral of the Mediterranean.

"There is one final aspect to this situation that is perturbing. There is a growing incidence of terrorist attacks around the world. Mostly they have been in Europe and the Triple Alliance but we have had a few here as well. There was that sniper incident in Maryland and a school hostage situation in South Carolina last night. I understand, the latter was resolved by the Russian wife of an American citizen who now lives in Russia. There have been a couple of other attacks on civilians here, a bus attacked, few other things. None serious, if necessary towns can call out their militia but we're a long way from that at the moment."

"Your precious bombers can't help us now, can they?" McNorman sneered "My financial models show that if we'd gone for missiles instead and scrapped the bombers, then abandoned the bloated fighter and missile defense systems, we could save enough money to afford a proper army."

"This would be the same mathematical model that produced the Edsel?" For the first time in the meeting President Johnson's voice was amused.

"There was nothing wrong with the Edsel, Mister President, Ford just did not promote it properly. Look what they're producing in its place, the Mustang. Who would want to buy a car like that?"

The Seer looked as if he was going to say something then shook his head. There was no need to dignify the man by arguing with him. The missiles versus bombers argument had been fought and won years ago. "Mister President, at the moment the primary military threat to the United States still comes from Chipan. Over the last four years, they have made great strides towards creating a leaner and more efficient military force structure, one that is a substantially greater threat to us. They have equipped their long-range bombers with air-launched missiles that are much faster and longer ranged than before. They even have submarine-based ballistic missiles stationed off our west coast.

"Fortunately, that's nothing we can't handle and our defenses are able to protect the west coast against attack. However, for all its military power – which we should not and must not underestimate - the Chipanese are rational players on the world scene. We can negotiate and make deals and generally come to accommodations with them.

"The problem with the Caliphate is that they are not rational and we cannot deal with them. As a simple example. It is their state policy that women should not receive any sort of education. It is their desired aim that women should become an illiterate class. Effectively they are eliminating half their total workforce in the name of the strictest possible interpretation of some very ambiguous claims. It may well be significant that the man who attacked the South Carolina school seemed primarily concerned with the fact that girls and boys received the same education in the same room.

"Their educational system is theocratic and largely dependent on repeating long passages of religious teachings. Any scientific data that contradicts their religious dogma is discarded.

In doing so, they have eliminated whole stretches of physics, biology, geology, oh, more ologies than I can name. But they're gone. In a couple of generations time, they won't have the scientific base to run a modern country. Which suits them just fine I might add. Their idea of a functioning state comes straight out of the seventh century."

Viceregal Palace, New Delhi, India.

Sir Martyn Sharpe woke up bolt upright. It was the nightmare again, the one he'd been having now and then, ever since he'd seen that painting in the Thai National Museum. It always started the same way, there were a group of people playing cards in a room. The Ambassador, The Seer, a man in a Navy petty officer's uniform, a grizzled army sergeant, others as well. He couldn't understand the rules of the game so he'd looked closer and realized that he was one of the cards being dealt, so was his country and so was everybody he knew. Then he understood he wasn't just a card, he was part of the stakes as well. And that's when he woke up.

His chest was hurting, a vicious cramping pain that seemed to spread down his left arm. He tried to relax and breathed deeply, feeling the pain ebb as he did so. He'd have to see a doctor about the pain; it was getting more frequent these days. The first few times he'd written it off as cramp or indigestion but it seemed more than that.

It wasn't as if he hadn't enough problems. The long-running insurgency in northern India and Kashmir had turned very ugly after the Caliphate had become a reality. What had been a traditional insurgency now had evolved into outright terrorism. Hindu temples had been blown up or burned down, a few nights ago a crowded cinema had been set on fire – after somebody had chained all the exits shut. More than 300 dead. It hadn't taken long before the Hindu population had started striking back. Mosques had been attacked and there had been communal rioting. The North was on the verge of civil war and he couldn't see any way of stopping it.

The Philippines was being hit as well. Mindanao had always been a lawless area but the never-ending banditry down in that part of the world had taken on an ugly religious overtone. There too, it was the symbols of the religious majority that were singled out for attack. A couple of cathedrals had been destroyed and car bombs detonated in religious processions. The Philippine government had tried to negotiate with the bandits but the response had been chilling. "Convert to Islam, adopt Shariah, prohibit all other religions and then we'll negotiate your surrender." So, the Philippine Government had activated the military clauses of the ASEAN agreement and ASEAN had done the same with the Triple Alliance treaty. Now, Thai and Australian troops were helping put the Mindanao insurrection down.

Idly, Sir Martyn wondered if the Ambassador was down there. He hadn't seen her for a couple of years now, but he somehow doubted she'd changed very much. And the mess in Mindanao was the sort of situation she was likely to give her personal attention. Sir Martyn smiled; he'd have to read the local newspapers and see if anybody had died under mysterious circumstances. He poured a glass of water from the carafe and drank it down, the pain in his chest had gone now, just leaving a dull ache. Now, if only the other problems could go away that easily.

Cockpit, RB-58C "Marisol", Bunker Hill Air Force Base.

"I'm bored. We never do anything wild any more. I thought we were going to have a fun time together."

Marisol's voice was petulant. Major Kozlowski could sympathize, After a lively first year that had put markers for four destroyed enemy aircraft and three radar sets under her cockpit, he and *Marisol* had spent their time on routine training, enlivened only by the annual Red Sun exercises and the occasional "Open Skies" demonstration flights. Mind you, Red Sun had become interesting of late, especially since the SAC F-108 Rapiers had joined the battles. That had annoyed *Marisol* as well, she wasn't the fastest, highest-flying aircraft on the block any more. In a year or so, the NORAD F-112B Blackbirds would be around as well; that raised the spectacle of triple-sonic dogfights. It looked like the Air Force was going to have to buy even more of Nevada to keep the range big enough.

Kozlowski felt the thump as *Marisol's* main wheels touched the ground. The nose reared high and he brought it down gently onto the runway. Then, he popped the drogue chute and lifted the nose again for aerodynamic braking. Slowly *Marisol* came to a halt on the runway. Kozlowski taxied her slowly into the parking area. With almost 1,200 RB-58s and PB5Ys in service, the aircraft had ceased to become a temperamental hot-dog and was now a routine part of SAC operations, but taxiing the aircraft still took care or the tires would blow.

A few minutes later, he was standing on the runway beside *Marisol's* nosewheel when General Declan arrived.

"Good flight Mike. Now tell me, do you like spaghetti?"

Helicopter Deck, USS Austin LPD-4, Eastern Mediterranean

"A little bird with a yellow bill
Came upon my window sill
I coaxed him with a piece of bread
Then I crushed his tiny head"

"SOUND OFF"

"ONE! TWO!"

"SOUND OFF"

"THREE! FOUR!"

"SOUND OFF"

"ONE! TWO! THREE! FOUR! THE CORPS!"

Gunnery Sergeant Esteban Tomas looked at the platoon drawn up in perfectly-aligned attention on the helicopter deck with an expression of undiluted misery and disbelief.

"How could the Corps have come to this?" His voice was almost - but not quite - shaking with grief. "A routine morning work-out and you're sprawled on the deck, sobbing your guts out with exhaustion. With a bunch of squids watching as well. What

17

has the Corps come to? When I enlisted we had to run from the barracks to the mess hall and back. For every meal, it was five miles and uphill both ways." There was a snort of laughter from behind him. Tomas whirled around and unerringly descended on the guilty party.

"You think that a ten mile run for each meal is funny Marine?"

"No sir."

The Marines on either side edged back, the wind cringed, the sky darkened and the ever-present seagulls circling the amphib fled in sheer undiluted terror. "No... WHAT?"

"No Gunny."

"So if the idea of the run isn't funny perhaps you think I am? Do you think I am funny, Marine?"

"No Gunny."

"Perhaps you need some time to decide what is funny. You know what the distance around this flight deck is?"

"No Gunny."

"It's 524 feet. That means ten circuits of the flight deck are equal to a mile. So Marine, you can run 50 times around the flight deck, about face then run another fifty times. Now."

The Marine set off on his long, lonely run around the flight deck. Despite it's name, the helicopter deck's prime purpose wasn't to operate helicopters but to give the embarked Marines a large flat area they could use as a parade and exercise ground. Like all her fellow LPDs, *Austin* was primarily designed to keep her Marines fit and in good condition during the long active deployment. It showed in strange ways, the flight deck was just one. Her hatches were sized so a Marine in full combat gear could move through them quickly and easily, the traffic areas were designed so the Marines could get to their landing craft unhindered. Fully loaded, *Austin* carried a battalion of Marines and could keep them fit for action.

Plowing along beside them was another amphibious warfare ship, USS *Alamo*, LSD-33. Superficially, she looked the same as the LPD but inside there was a critical difference. LPDs were personnel transports, designed to look after Marines, keep them safe and well and deliver them to the beach-head. LSDs were designed to do the same for their vehicles. The *Alamo* carried the unit's tanks and self-propelled artillery. As a result, her docking bay was bigger, housing tank landing craft, LCTs, rather than the tracked carriers of the infantry.

In front of them was another type of amphibious warfare ship, the helicopter landing ship or LPH. This was intended to do the same job as the LPD but she delivered her marines by helicopter rather than amphibious armored personnel carriers.

Finally, bringing up the rear was the fourth member of the team, the LKA supply ship. She carried the stockpiles of food, ammunition, fuel and everything else the group needed.

The four ships made a balanced combat group, capable of putting a battalion landing team anywhere it was ordered. For bigger jobs, four such groups would come together and a command group would join them to land an entire regimental combat team. If the situation really demanded it, all sixteen amphibious warfare groups and five command groups in the Atlantic fleet could concentrate on a target and put an entire division of Marines ashore.

Surrounding the amphibs, shielding them from potential attack were a group of destroyers, missile-armed with a mix of explosive and nuclear warheads in their magazines. Their nuclear-tipped Terrier missiles could devastate a target but Gunnery Sergeant Esteban Tomas knew that only his Marines could go ashore and take possession of the area. That was their job, and it was his job to see they were fit and well-trained. So...

"Right girls. We'll run through the program again. And this time, try not to humiliate the Corps in front of the squids."

"How is Chief Williams?"

"Not good sir. The surgeons on *Westover* saved his leg but he's going to be out for a more time that I care to think about."

Chief Williams had been working on a maintenance failure on the docking well when one of the LVPTs had shifted in the heavy swell, trapping his leg between its tracks and the steel deck. Another reminder that any seaman's real enemy was the sea itself. Chief Williams was lucky, the hospital ship *Westover* was close at hand and he'd been helicoptered over within a few minutes and on the operating table in less than twenty. But, with the bones crushed, it would be a long time, if ever, before he went to sea again.

Another tick in a ledger that was already measureless. A ledger that grew every day, sometimes slowly, sometimes with terrifying speed. Even in peace, training accidents, human error, equipment failure just plain inexplicable bad luck took lives every day. Sometimes, Captain Pickering wondered if civilians understood that or if they just assumed being in the military was another job, just one that had better-looking uniforms and more expensive toys. What was it that British author Kipling had said "If blood be the price of admiralty, Lord God, we ha' paid in full?"

And there was no way around it. The supposedly learned commentators back home were fond of saying how SAC had destroyed Germany at a cost of less than 200 men, yet they were careful not to mention the hundreds of thousands of American soldiers who had died in Russia setting the stage for The Big One. Nor did they mention the tens of thousands of Navy pilots who'd died over France.

On Pickering's first ship, the *Shiloh*, over a thousand had died even while the atomic bombs were falling on Germany. America was free because of them all, and the butcher's bill would continue. There was a new *Shiloh* now, in fact she wasn't so far away. Nuclear-powered, bigger with an airgroup whose capability the old *Shiloh* could only have imagined. Would she die the way the old *Shiloh* had died, gutted by fires?

"We're in luck sir. I talked with BuPers and managed to get us a new Senior Chief. A good man, one of the very best according to my man in the Bureau. Seems to have served on every ship in the fleet and been everywhere a US warship has dropped anchor. They say he was Senior Chief on Old Ironsides herself and whipped John Paul Jones into shape."

Captain Pickering was beginning to get a terrible sense of impending doom.

"In fact, Sir, he's an old shipmate of yours. You served together on the old *Shiloh.*"

Pickering felt the sense of impending doom thicken into a solid fog of certainty. With almost supernaturally perfectly timing, a well-remembered voice echoed around the superstructure.

"YOU, you there with the paintbrush. You some sort of DEMOCRAT or something? The people in their benighted stupidity may have put a damnable DEMOCRAT into the White House but the Navy is still the Navy. Its up to us to keep things running until sanity returns. CHIP before you paint. Chip that rust off, wire brush the area to bare metal then red lead prime and paint. You put paint on top of rust and it'll be off faster than a DEMOCRAT chasing a bribe."

The door opened and the figure Pickering had last seen when they were plucked off the burning wreck of *Shiloh* entered. "Permission to enter the Bridge Sir. Reporting for Duty, Senior Chief P.... Captain Pickering Sir. Its good to see you again Sir."

Physically, Captain Pickering was standing in the middle of his Bridge, returning the textbook salute with one of his own. Mentally, he was hiding behind the Pelorus. "Senior Chief, welcome on board. I see you have mellowed with the passing years."

Woomera Test Range, Australia

Hangar Alpha was sealed and guarded. Two long limousines were already parked outside and a third was pulling alongside. Sir Martyn Sharpe went to meet the new arrival with barely suppressed delight. The escort opened the back door and a familiar figure slipped smoothly out.

"Madam, it is, once more, a very great pleasure to see you."

"Sir Martyn, thank you. It has been too long since I last enjoyed the pleasure of your company. I am sad to say that the problems in the Philippines are proving most intractable. The tactics we have employed successfully elsewhere are not effective in the face of the enemy and the operational environment we have in Mindanao. But, let us not speak of such things. Today is a day of achievement, a day for pride and rejoicing."

The dignitaries entered Hangar Alpha. Inside, there was a shrouded shap, obviously an aircraft but its details hidden. The VIPs took their seats and the lights dimmed. Smoke started to rise in front of the shrouded shape, colored by spotlights playing upon it. Wagner's "Ride of the Valkyrie" started playing. Then, the Program Manager's voice came over the loudspeaker system.

"My Lords, Ladies and Gentlemen, Honored Guests. Ten years ago, Great Britain started a new program, one intended to return the country to the forefront of aviation technology. Alas, this program was doomed to failure. Less that three years after its inception, that program was canceled by the British Defense Minister Mr. Duncan Sandys, who recognized that the cost of its development was far beyond Britain's means.

"Indeed maintaining a military aircraft industry at all was too much for the country and, except for a few minor programs it was wound up in favor of the civilian aviation sector. The British engineers and designers went abroad, to Canada and to here. With them, they brought knowledge of the planned British aircraft. We purchased the details that we needed and, in 1960, we restarted the program as a Triple Alliance joint venture. My friends, this was a program managers' dream. Australian brains, Indian workers and Thai money."

Sir Martyn smiled, he knew the second half of the joke. A program managers' hell; Indian brains, Thai workers and

Australian money. It was true too. Indian industry lacked advanced technology skills but its people were renowned for their ability to get jobs done by sheer hard work. On the other hand, the Australians had acquired a reservoir of high-technology, not least from Europeans who wanted to emigrate somewhere with better prospects. The problem was that their financial resources were very limited, Australia had spent most of the 1950s in a deep economic depression and was only just coming out of it. The Thais had all the money now, their banking and investment position saw to that, but their workers were notorious for seeing hard labor as something to be studiously avoided. Put together in the right way, the results could be astounding. As they'd been this time. The program manager had stopped speaking, the music swelled to its crescendo and then.

" I present to you.....The Alliance Aviation TSR-2"

The shroud was rolled back, exposing the gleaming white aircraft. A long fuselage, short, high mounted wings that bent down at the tips, two seats, a small nose. A dedicated, long-range low altitude supersonic strike bomber. There was a collective gasp and then a swelling round of applause. Under it, the Ambassador turned to one of her friends, "Sir Eric, what was TSR-1?"

"The Fairey Swordfish, Ma'am, an old biplane torpedo bomber used by the Royal Navy." The Ambassador smiled her thanks. She'd had to bang heads together to get this program running. The Thai Air Force needed the aircraft and their experiences trying to keep their American-built F-104s and F-105s flying had convinced them of the need to build aircraft locally.

The Indians needed the aircraft even more to replace their ancient F-80s and F-84s. Then, the people who'd done the initial negotiations had wandered into a morass of calculations over purchase orders, workshare and a thousand other bits of administrivia. She had cut that Gordion Knot easily. None of the three members of The Triple Alliance could build this aircraft alone, they all needed it equally badly. So she'd forced through an agreement that saw the formation of Alliance Aviation as an equally-shared venture by the three governments. The workshare issue would be sorted out by open bidding on the subsystems and components; the best bid won the contract no matter who it came from. That wiped out the workshare issue and the program had gone ahead from there.

There was more to come; The Triple Alliance had found out that Canada was about to follow Britain's example and drop out of the military aviation business. In doing so they were canceling a new and very promising long-range interceptor called the Arrow. Alliance Aviation was negotiating with the Canadian Government to buy the prototypes and production line, design art and everything else needed to build the aircraft here. It wasn't sealed down yet but the negotiations looked promising. If that went through, The Triple Alliance would be building world-class aircraft, the only better ones would be those in SAC's terrifying arsenal.

Faluja, Iraq Satrapy, The Caliphate

Janissaries, that's what they'd become. Janissaries. Walther Model, once a Field Marshal of the Wehrmacht, once the Fuhrer's Fireman, once the Baron of New Schwabia, was now the leader of a corps of Janissaries. Oh, it was a privileged position enough on paper. His community was the private and personal guard - and the striking force - of the Caliphate itself. Or, to be more precise, the Satraps who made up the ruling council of the Caliphate.

Model's people had also provided the expertise and support manpower for the Council's spy and covert services to keep the Satraps in line. Model had vehemently refused to provide the operational manpower for the new Caliphate secret service since it bore far too many resemblances to the infamous Hashishans for comfort. The original organization had terrorized the mid-east in the Middle Ages and their new equivalent looked set to do the same. Any of the Satraps were likely to think twice about defying the Ruling Council if suicidal, drug-crazed fanatics, convinced they were going to paradise, could be sent after them on whim. Effective yes, but Model wanted no part of it. He had too few of his people left to send the survivors on suicide missions.

Model was under no illusions about the people he was working for. They were a clique of dogmatic opportunists who had taken advantage of the chaos in the Middle East to carve themselves out an empire. Well, calling it an empire was putting it all too strongly. They had taken religious dogmatism, rhetoric and a level of brutal ruthlessness and imposed their regime on a substantial area of the Middle East. Imposed their regime, yes, but only as one contending power faction amongst many. It was an interesting situation, their survival depended on them holding absolute power and not letting that power slip even for a second. For if they did, the wolves would close in on them.

That's where Model's force had come in. The Caliphate might look imposing on a map but it was nowhere near as homogenous or unified as it appeared. In fact, the only thing that held it together was that the various sects and schisms all hated the outside world a little more than they hated each other, not that there was much in it. The Caliphate was in a perpetual state of near-civil war, a crazed morass of little better than random violence, with each group trying to expand its power at the expense of the rest.

Even now, after only a few years of formal existence, the boundaries of the Satrapies of the Caliphate looked nothing like the largely arbitrary national boundaries that had existed before it had emerged from the shadows. They'd already changed to reflect ethnic and tribal loyalties, and the differences in economic structures had modified them still further. They were still changing and would continue to do so.

Model suspected that the ruling council were very well aware that it was only external pressure from the outside that was holding the whole thing together. That would explain their truculence and aggression towards the rest of the world. The more the Caliphate provoked its neighbors, the greater would be the pressure on it. The Caliphate needed to be hated and reviled if it was to survive. The constant outward pressure was another example of the same line of thought. All the Satraps wanted to expand their influence within the Caliphate, but doing so meant they were facing a zero-sum game. Every advance made by one was a loss for somebody else and that increased the chance of others combining against him.

But if a Satrap expanded to areas outside the Caliphate, it meant he was adding to his own power without reducing that of his rivals – a much safer proposition. Of course, the fact his attention was focused outside meant the position of the ruling council was all the more secure. Model knew that the rest of the world believed the Caliphate was expanding as a result of some carefully-calculated master plan but he knew that was far from the truth. There was no master plan, just the opportunistic efforts by the individual Satraps to expand their own power and influence. The ramshackle, chaotic nature of the Caliphate allowed for nothing more than that.

Of course, the problem was that the Ruling Council itself could easily fall foul of the perpetual struggles inside the Caliphate. They had seen that possibility and Model's troops had been the answer to their prayers. Tough, hardened soldiers who answered only to the ruling council and gave it a devastating military edge over any rivals. Soldiers who had nowhere else to go, nobody else to serve. The Caliphate had been very generous in its provisions for Model's community; they had established it as a hereditary, highly professional standing army. That army would supplement the existing Caliphate forces that were mostly composed of tribal warriors whose loyalty and morale could not always be trusted. They were modern Janissaries, an old tradition recreated because similar circumstances lead to similar answers.

The catch was that Model knew his history; the first janissary units formed by the Ottomans had been war captives and slaves. Later, Sultan Selim I filled their ranks with conscripted soldiers, non-Muslim, usually Christian. Mostly they were Albanians, Bosnians and Bulgarians. Like the Janissaries of old, Model's community was being, at least, encouraged to convert to Islam. Some already had, even so, the others still enjoyed high living standards and lived more or less as they wished. Model knew why and it had nothing to do with hospitality. The Caliphate looked after its Janissaries because of the poison gas and biological warfare factories that they were building.

The catch was that the Caliphate knew its history as well; back then, as soon the original Janissaries became aware of their own importance they had revolted demanding higher wages and more privileges. After 1451, every new sultan was obligated to pay each Janissary a reward and raise his pay rank. Soon they had such prestige and influence that they dominated the government.

They mutinied in order to dictate policy, changed sultans as they wished through palace coups. Eventually, they grew so powerful that their danger exceeded their value and the Sultans had destroyed them. That destruction was called The Auspicious Incident.

Model knew that his community here would survive only as long as his value exceeded the risk it posed. His people had been useful so far, they'd put down rebellions against the strict fundamentalism of the Caliphate. They'd put down Shi'ite rebellions against the Sunni Moslems, and Sunni rebellions against the Shi'ites. They'd crushed the infighting between various sub-divisions of both. That was another advantage his troops had, being part of neither sect, their actions were independent of either. It meant, of course, that they were hated by both. That didn't matter, not to the Ruling Council. As long as threats to their power were eliminated the effects on the tools they used went unnoticed. Then again, his Einsatzgruppen had been working with gusto 'cleansing' the territory of 'infidels' and 'apostasy'.

Thinking about it, it was strange how his army and civilians had taken brutal casualties escaping from Russia but the Einsatzgruppen had hardly lost a man. It had been the Einsatzgruppen that had been the first to convert when the suggestions had started. They'd built gas chambers to dispose of those useless as slave labor and factories where the slaves could be worked to death. Jews, Christians, Druze, Bahais, Kuwaitis, Bahreinis, Saudis, the camps were full. The Einsatzgruppen had done so well they'd been given their new name of 'Guardians of the Faith' and ostentatiously demonstrated their loyalty to their new masters. Those masters did not include Walter Model.

Model sighed. He'd been so proud of getting his people out of Russia, of beating the Russians one more time. But, all he had managed to do was to lead his people into yet another trap. Every time he pulled off a miracle, every time he had done the impossible, the only result was lead his people into another trap. Each time, the traps grew tighter, the number of survivors smaller, the chances of escaping again even slimmer.

Even if they could escape, there was no way home and, anyway, there was no home to go to. He had reports from what was left of Germany, there were people there but they were scattered across the countryside in small farming communities. The Ruhr Valley was a blasted and lethal ruin, the Rhine was a polluted mess, the lovely Black Forest, Germany's lungs, was blasted and burned. There was no home for his soldiers to return to.

He'd tried to build a new home but had seen it perish under a whirlwind of high explosives and steel as the Russian Army had crushed it. Instead, he'd become the commander of an army of slave-soldiers. An army under a suspended - but still very much present - death sentence. Now, he had to find another way out, another escape and hope this time it wouldn't lead to another trap.

CHAPTER TWO
MOVE TO CONTACT

Home of Admiral Soriva, Yokohama, Chipan

As he sprinted down the corridor in his home, Admiral Soriva could not help but reflect that paperwork especially bureaucratic paperwork and bungling, badly written, bureaucratic paperwork in particular was a lifesaver. It had saved his life anyway. His task for the evening had been reading a long dissertation from a Navy officer, written in excruciatingly jaw-breaking grammar, proposing that the decision to scrap the four Yamato class battleships should be reversed and the ships be returned to the active fleet. It was nonsense, of course, the ships had been decommissioned four years ago and had already been stripped ready for scrap.

By the end of the sixth page, frustration had overcome patience, making him screw the report up into a ball and throw it across the room. He'd almost immediately regretted the outburst of temper, the author meant well, he was doing what he thought was interests of the fleet - and was doing so in the proper, disciplined manner. Slightly ashamed Soriva had gone to retrieve the document. Walking past the window, he had noted the guard on his gate had gone. That had made him look harder, to see a body-sized shape crumpled under a tree and then a dark figure - perhaps more than one - slipping through the shadows.

The sight had made him go to his desk and take the American Colt automatic from the top drawer along with the half dozen loaded magazines he kept there. Then, he had stepped out of his office, just in time to see a figure entering the front door. A figure dressed in black from head to foot with a scarf covering the lower part of his face and a sword in his hands. A ninja, an honest-to-legend ninja. Straight out of bad novels and worse films, something this tasteless had to have Masanobu Tsuji's hand in it somewhere.

The ninja raised his sword up and Soriva shot him between the eyes. The intruder went down in a heap; Soriva had almost expected him to fly backwards like the movies, then he would have known this was a bad dream. He didn't and this wasn't. A second intruder was directly behind the first, Soriva shot him in the stomach then again in the head after he was down. The third intruder tripped over the bodies of the first two, falling flat on his face. That had never been in the movies either. Soriva shot him anyway.

It was as if the shots had been a signal, there was a ripping crash from the back of the house. More intruders, that was when he'd started his run to where his family were sleeping. Even as he reached the family rooms, he heard a scream from his eldest daughter's room. A scream that ended in a terribly final cut-off. He would have time to grieve later.

Three more intruders were coming towards him but he was between them and the rest of his family. He hosed off the remaining rounds in his pistol, dropped the magazine and slapped a new one home. All three intruders were down, one still moving. Soriva remembered the scream from his daughter's room and fired another shot, killing him. In front of him, his wife was standing in the entrance to their room, her eyes round with shock and her hand over her mouth. He grabbed her by the arm and half-pushed, half-dragged her back to the room used by the other two children. As they reached it, his son opened the sliding door and pulled Soriva's youngest daughter through.

"Father, I heard the noise so I got Hana ready to leave."

Another thing to remember later, time to be proud of a young son who not only kept his wits when his world was falling apart but remembered to look after his little sister as well. They had to get out of here, the six dead assassins wouldn't be the end of it. There had to be another plan in case their attack failed.

Admiral Soriva's car was parked behind their house, by all the laws of logic, the attackers should have disabled or booby-trapped it. But anybody who could send assassins dressed up as Ninjas might be so obsessed with historical mythology he'd forget there might be modern options. It wasn't as if they had much of a choice anyway. Soriva pushed his wife and children out and towards the car. Their driver was lying dead by its side, his head neatly removed. Soriva reflected that the swords weren't quite such an insane idea after all, they were silent and, if he hadn't had that few seconds of warning, the assassins would have been on him and his family before he could get to his gun. On the other hand, if they'd had grenades and sub-machineguns, he and his entire family would be dead by now.

Next question; was the car booby trapped? There was no time to do a careful check, he pressed the starter button and the engine roared into life. No fires, no explosions, so far anyway. Car into gear, (still no explosions, still no fire) but the car was rocking as his children got into the back and his wife climbed into the front seat with him. Then, he rammed the bamboo gate.

It burst open, scattering fragments of wood everywhere, the car pitching and lurching as Soriva swerved out of the driveway onto the road. As he'd guessed, there were four cars parked just around the corner from his house. Estimate four attackers per car, that left ten more. A group were still standing beside the cars, Soriva guessed the rest had gone into the house to find what had happened. His window was down, as he swept past, he emptied the magazine from his Colt into the group. In the mirror he saw at least two were hit and on the ground. Almost without thinking, he thumbed the magazine release, then steered with the hand holding the gun while he fished another magazine out and reloaded.

As the car swerved down the road, he saw his wife rocking backwards and forwards and whimpering. Behind him, the children were on the floor between the seats. He hit a corner too fast, almost lost control as the car started to spin, but he pulled the car out of it just in time, slamming a utility pole with the rear fender.

Just down the road was Admiral Iwate's home. It was burning and there was another group of cars outside. Poor Iwate. There was still time to give him a bodyguard on the way to the Yasukuni shrine where the souls of dead heroes rested. The men by the cars were scattering as Soriva's car roared up to them. One of them threw a sword at his car but it clattered and bounced off the hood, then the car swept past and Soriva emptied the magazine of his pistol again. "Sorry. Iwate, its the best I can do," he thought "we can't stay around to do more." He glanced in the mirror, it seemed three of the men by the cars were down.

There was an intersection ahead, blocked by some vehicles. Soriva swerved his vehicle onto the pavement, bounced off a wall and scraped through the gap on one side. He could hear a grinding noise on one side, a damaged bearing probably, and the car's controls didn't feel right any more but it was a straight run to the naval dockyard now. Only a couple of kilometers, the car would hold out until then. Rather to his surprise, Soriva noticed he'd reloaded his pistol again; he couldn't remember doing that. The Americans may be uncivilized barbarians but they made good handguns. If he'd had a Nambu, he'd still be struggling with the first magazine.

The dockyard gates were up ahead. Soriva started flashing the lights on his car - three short, three long, three short, SOS, over and over again. If the guards were really on edge, it wouldn't matter, they'd open up anyway. Come to that, he wasn't sure that the dockyard people weren't in on whatever it was that was happening. But, a Navy base was the only safe place he could think of. And, the gates were opening as he approached.

Once through, they closed behind him. There were armed Navy and Special Naval Landing Force troops all over the base. Those in the area were pointing their weapons at Soriva's car. Their commander saluted as Soriva got out of the beat-up wreck.

"Admiral Soriva sir, you're safe. Word was that you'd been killed. There are attacks going on all over the city. Its chaos nobody knows who is alive or who is doing the killing. What do we do?"

"Hold the line here. Get me to the dockyard office. The ships here are sitting ducks, we've got to get them to sea. Tell your men to hold the dockyard perimeter regardless of loss until we've got them out."

Prime Minister's Residence, Canberra, Australia

Sir Eric Haohoa rubbed sleep out of his eyes and tried to make sense of what was going on. He and Sir Martyn had been dragged out of bed early the previous morning when news of the events in Japan had started to come in. The Ambassador had been there when they arrived along with Prime Minister Joe Frye. They'd been in the emergency command center ever since. The whole Chipanese system was in turmoil, that much was clear but news of what had happened was spotty, erratic and of dubious reliability.

"Sir Eric, could you try and persuade Sir Martyn to get some rest? He does not look well and I fear for his health. I have to give a summary of what we know now, but after that, it will probably be many hours before the situation develops further. Please give him my word that I will call him personally if anything he needs to know breaks. Please tell him I seriously recommend that he take the chance to get some rest."

The Ambassador watched Sir Eric take her advice. Sir Martyn's face was greyish-white with fatigue and he was holding his left arm as if it was cramped or aching. Another problem to worry about.

She cleared her throat, catching the attention of everybody present. "Gentlemen, if I may have your attention? We have received some information over the last few hours that appears to put the developments in Chipan into better context. The trouble erupted about 2200 local time last night with a coordinated series of attacks on prominent military and political personnel. At first, it appeared that this a straightforward power-play between the Army and the Navy, such things are quite common and the number of killings was on a par with such events. Most of the early casualties were senior naval officers which gave some credibility to this interpretation of events.

"However, fighting has continued between elements of the Japanese armed forces throughout the day and into the evening. Notice that I said Japanese; the situation appears to be confined to the Japanese islands and surrounding seas, it has not spread to the Chinese mainland to any great extent. Indeed, much of the fighting appears to be confined to units that remain largely Japanese in establishment; units that are mostly Chinese have, with some significant exceptions, remained uninvolved. Our sources in the Vietnamese People's Liberation Army indicate that most units on the mainland are at a heightened state of alert but remain at their posts.

"During the night, a number of warships sortied from ports and naval bases around Japan. By dawn, these came under attack from aircraft of the Chipanese Army and - it is very important to note - Chipanese Navy. Aircraft of both armed services have been engaged in combat, but again, there have been Army and Navy aircraft on both sides. Land fighting appears to be in progress between elements of the armed forces but there is no clear distinction as to who is on which side. In short, this is not an Army against Navy dominance struggle, nor is it a Chinese versus Japanese civil war. Until a few hours ago we did not understand what we were seeing.

"Things began to make sense when the first lists of those killed in the initial wave of assassinations became public. It appears that the majority, by a very high margin, were those who have been associated with the recent attempts to reform the Chipanese military and political structure.

"Over the last four years, the Chipanese have made extensive efforts to rationalize their military forces and to reduce the burden military expenditure has inflicted on their economy. This has resulted in a severe reduction in the numbers of troops in the land forces, matched by the mechanization of the remainder, substituting mobility for on-the-ground numbers. We have seen old ships retained from World War Two, and even, in one remarkable case, from World War One, withdrawn from service and scrapped.

"The money saved has been invested in new ships that are of modern design. The same process has affected aircraft production; older types have been withdrawn and the Army and Navy attempted to standardize, as far as they could, on both aircraft types and equipment for those aircraft.

"It therefore appeared that the events in Chipan could best be explained by a conflict between the new-style military leadership, the Reformers if you like, and the representatives of the older-style military philosophy. We can refer to them as the Traditionalists if you wish. We applied this model to the news of fighting and it appeared to hold. The initial wave of assassinations appears to have been an attempt by the Traditionalists to decapitate the Reformer's command structure. This appears to have been largely successful and the fighting today represents a dislocated and sporadic effort by the Reformers to hold on to their position.

"A few minutes ago we received a copy of a message that is being circulated within the Chipanese Armed Forces. It describes the events of the last 36 hours as the 'Showa Restoration', an obvious reference to the Meiji Restoration of almost a century ago. It describes the reformers as having usurped the Emperor's authority and abused his trust. The Traditionalists claim to have returned rightful authority to the Emperor and to be acting on his behalf. The document is signed by the person claiming to be the leader of the traditionalist factions, Masanobu Tsuji.

"It goes without saying that this document would not have been issued if there was any doubt over the success of the Traditionalist operation. It would therefore appear that the events of the last 36 hours can only be described as a coup, albeit a bloody and poorly organized one. Our expert opinion on this suggests that the planning of the operation contained a certain level of personal vindictiveness against naval personnel who were part of the Operation A-Go fiasco five years ago. That, in its turn, points to Masanobu Tsuji being an active participant in this operation rather than just a figurehead."

There was a long silence in the room. Eventually, Sir Eric asked the questions that were in everybody's mind. "What happens now ma'am? What does this mean for us? Where do we go from here?"

The Ambassador stood silent, her eyes defocussed. In her mind she was visualizing the likely flow of future events, a cascading stream of colored lights that mingled, split and merged as possibilities, probabilities and outcomes jostled for significance.

"In the short term, the prospects for us are very dangerous. Chipan will revert to its former policies of expansionism and aggression. We can expect provocation and attempts to extort financial, political and territorial advantages from us. We can expect Chipan to greatly increase its expenditure on armaments and on its forces. That expenditure will be substantially uncontrolled. Because of its precarious economy, we can expect it to use those forces.

"In the longer term, the situation is much more hopeful for us. Chipan cannot stand a long period of such military expenditure, within a decade, two at the most, its economy will start to implode. The critical point will come when that process becomes irreversible. At that point, they will be faced with the temptation to use all their military arsenal before they lose it. In anticipation of that time, we must start the planning necessary to bring them in for a soft landing.

"There is one question that could be of critical importance here. Many of the reformers have escaped to sea on Japanese warships. What will they do? Where will they go?"

Cockpit F-108A Rapier "Wicked Stick," 103,000 feet over Nevada

Even the big fighter was running out of power up here. *Wicked Stick* was wallowing on the edge of her zoom climb performance envelope, the air around her so thin it hardly existed. The sky had long ceased to be blue and had taken on the blackness of space. The fighter was so high that Brigadier-General Charles Larry could see the curvature of the earth below him. Almost 20 miles up, well on the way to space itself but the F-108 wasn't going to make it any further. The difference between maximum speed and stalling speed was now so thin it could barely be measured and the J-93s were gulping the few molecules of air still around in an attempt to keep the great white fighter airborne.

In the back seat, Larry's Bear, his electronic systems operator, was trying desperately to get a radar lock on the satellite before the plane stalled out. They'd been under ground control the whole way, the satellite had been tracked by a ground-based radar and *Wicked Stick* had made her zoom climb under strict orders. Now she was where the ground control intercept had put her but the satellite hadn't appeared.

"Got it" The voice from the back was triumphant. "We have lock on the target. Wait One - Fox-November."

There was no bump, no lurch. If this had been a real launch, there would have been a whirring noise as the rotary launcher moved a GAR-9 into firing position then a thump as the 1,000 pound missile was launched. Here, in this simulation, there was nothing. Nothing that could be felt anyway, but something had changed. Stalling speed now exceeded maximum speed, the thrust from the J-93s wasn't enough any more and *Wicked Stick* departed controlled flight.

The stall was vicious. Neither the F-108 nor its huge cousin, the YB-70A were known as pilot's aircraft. The nose slammed down, a wing dropped, and the aircraft simply tumbled out of the sky. One advantage of being up here was that they had more space to recover than any aircraft had ever had before them, and they would need it. Stick centered and forward, dive the aircraft out of its spin. Slowly the big fighter stabilized, the horizon stopped rotating and the F-108 was back under control.

"Control, this is *Wicked Stick*. Things got exciting for a moment there. Did we hit?"

There was a long pause from ground control as the range instrumentation measured speeds, trajectories, guidance arcs and lethal radii. The reply when it came was flat.

"Negative, *Wicked Stick*, your shot missed. Went behind the target satellite and was outside lethal radius. Nice recovery from the stall though."

"Thank you Ground Control. Better luck next time. *Wicked Stick* is returning to base. Fuel situation normal."

Larry set his F-108 on its course back to Nellis AFB. The combination of a fighter capable of flying at unprecedented high altitudes and a long-range nuclear-tipped missile had raised the question of whether the system was capable of taking down satellites. It was a good idea but so far it hadn't worked. The F-108A/GAR-9 combination was right on the edge of its performance envelope for anti-satellite shots and so far, nobody could make it work. This had been their third attempt. Larry knew it wasn't going to work. Good as the F-108 was, it wasn't quite good enough. That didn't matter though. Between the stand-down of the F-85 groups and the formation of the first F-108 unit, he'd been involved in the Air Force X-plane program and that had shown him where the future lay. Satellites were only the start, the Air Force was already planning a Manned Orbiting Laboratory that would put men in space for whole tours of duty.

The real jewel was another program, the X-20 Dyna-Soar, a manned, winged vehicle. The first prototype, Dyna-Soar I was already flying, dropped from a B-52 mother ship. The next stage would be rocket-launched near-orbital booster flights by the end of the year. Dyna-Soar II would be a manned hypersonic reconnaissance vehicle, flying at over 200,000 feet to a range of more than 6,500 miles. The prototype Dyna-Soar II was already under construction, if all went well it would fly by the end of 1967. Another version of Dyna-Soar II was going to be a nuclear-armed anti-satellite fighter. Even further down the line was Dyna-Soar III, a full-fledged manned, hypersonic, global, strategic bombardment and reconnaissance system. SAC was going into space and taking its bombers with it.

Aviano Italian Air Force Base, Italy

It was a dress uniform, no-flourishes-spared occasion. An official reception to mark the first visit by SAC aircraft to an Italian air base since The Big One had ended World War Two. A much more significant event than just a courtesy visit by four aircraft that normally showed no reluctance to flying over Italian air space any time their flight plan demanded.

The visit was taking place at a time when the political situation in Southern Europe was in a greater state of flux that usual. Both Franco and Mussolini had survived the destruction of Germany. Certainly, they'd been German allies but they hadn't quite been good enough allies to merit destruction. Then, the situation in Europe after The Big One had been so confused that nobody had wanted to add to the mess by removing two functioning, if tainted, regimes.

When The Great Famine of 1948 - 1950 had struck Northern Europe, Spain and Italy, or, to be more precise, Franco and Mussolini, had bought their survival by shipping free food into the stricken countries. The supplies of Spanish rice and Italian pasta had probably been the margin that prevented the famine from killing hundreds of thousands of northern Europeans by starvation. Even now, with the Baltic and North Sea too polluted for fishing, most of Europe's fish supplies came from the Mediterranean.

They'd won survival, not acceptance. Throughout the 1950s, Spain and Italy had been pariah states. The standard description of southern European politics in those days had been "Mussolini speaks only to Franco and Franco speaks only to God". Almost inevitably, the two pariah nations had gravitated together, at first informally, then in an ever-growing network of trade and tariff treaties. Eventually, they'd been formalized in an alliance known as the Mediterranean Confederation.

It wasn't as close as it sounded. Appearance had always counted for more than reality in both Spain and Italy, but it was still a group to be reckoned with. In fact, with Spanish control at the Atlantic gateway by way of its fortresses at Gibraltar and Ceuta and Italian control in the middle by way of Sicily, Malta and Libya, the Mediterranean Confederation had a potential stranglehold on trade across the whole area. There was an American fleet in the Mediterranean, and one of the reasons they were there was to make sure that potential did not become reality.

But, all of that was appearances, not reality. In reality, the Mediterranean Confederation was a weak structure on shaky foundations. Despite its name, it was an alliance, not a discrete political entity and its members had differing aims and objectives. They were also very different countries.

Spain was still a dictatorship, ruled with the absolute authority of General Franco. Certainly, his relationship with Hitler had allowed him to seize Gibraltar when the British had started their slow collapse under Lord Halifax but that was all. It had taken decades for Spain to recover from the depredations of the Civil War and its isolation hadn't helped. Spanish rule in its North African provinces was weak and ineffectual, they only retained authority because there had been no credible challenger to that appearance.

Now, that was changing. Once the situation on the African Littoral started to deteriorate, they had nothing to fall back on. The Spanish Air Force still flew German piston-engined fighters and bombers from World War Two. Their Navy was mostly port-bound relics of the same era and their Army hadn't changed since its victory in 1939. Spain was a grim, bleak place these days

Italy, now that was a different matter. Mussolini, dismissed pre-war as a pseudo-Hitlerian buffoon, had turned out to be a cannier politician than anybody had credited. He'd pulled out of Greece, withdrawn forces from the Egyptian border and made peace with his enemies, internal and external. In the late 1940s and early 1950s, Italy had been faced with a virtual civil war between Mussolini's Legati, the Monarchists and the residue of the communists. He'd managed to avert that, allegedly inspired by a shot of a Roman legionary standard and its inscription SPQR in a film about the Roman Empire. Critics had said that the compromise he'd come up with was one only an Italian could think of and only Italians could make work.

Even Mussolini's worst critics had to admit that the scheme had worked. The Italian Constitution provided for a Parliament with two chambers. The senior of the two was the Senate whose members were supposed to represent the institutions of state, the Church, the Judiciary and the provinces. The other chamber was the Legate which was supposed to represent the people and was directly elected by popular vote. The hereditary Speaker of the Senate was the King, the hereditary head of the Legate was Mussolini and his heirs. The two were supposed to balance each other and, because their positions were hereditary, take a long-term view that the elected members of the houses would lack.

Mussolini had also shed the bombast and posturing that had made him a laughing stock during the 1930s. Perhaps the total destruction of Germany had given him a dreadful foresight of where such behavior would lead. Perhaps he was smart enough to understand that the time for such performances was over. Nobody knew for sure, but for the last decade of his life, his behavior had been as circumspect as earlier it had been boisterous. When his wife had died he'd married his long-time mistress Clara Petacci and lived quietly in Rome. He'd died eight years ago and his official position had been inherited by his son Romano Mussolini.

It was Romano Mussolini who was approaching in the line of limousines. A talented painter and jazz musician, he was a very different man from his father. On taking power, he had announced that his objective was to create a second renaissance for Italy, a rebirth of culture and style in an era that sorely needed it. He'd taken Cosimo Medici as his model and become a patron of arts and humanities, a builder of monuments and wonders. Most rulers with such plans created megalomaniac atrocities but Romano Mussolini had simply made money available and looked for the best architects and artists he could find. Then left them to do their jobs.

Under his rule, Italy had been reborn as a country of gaiety and vivacity; one where good food, good wine, music and laughter were not just considered the desirable norm but an indispensable part of life. The country made a brilliant contrast to the austere and stark dictatorship in Spain. With the renaissance had come prosperity. Italy now had the cultural authority that France had once held, Italian goods were sought worldwide for their style and a visit to the country was considered essential for any self-respecting tourist. Italy, Kozlowski thought, could have done far, far worse than Romano Mussolini.

Two men, two women and a young child got out of the middle limousine. One of the men was Romano Mussolini, the other the American Ambassador to Italy. "Colonel Hazen, Major Kozlowski, I have the honor to present the Speaker of the Legate, Signor Romano Mussolini."

The two pilots snapped out textbook parade ground salutes. Mussolini looked faintly embarrassed, as if he knew he should return the salutes but didn't know how. Which was true.

"Gentlemen, forgive me for not returning your salutes but I am embarrassingly bad at such things." Mussolini gave a disarming smile "My father was much better at military courtesies. I hope it is enough that I say how delighted I am to see you. I am most grateful that you have come to visit our country and brought these beautiful aircraft with you. May I present my wife, Anna Maria, my daughter Alessandra and my sister-in-law Sophia."

Kozlowski followed Colonel Hazen down the guest line. Mussolini beamed proudly when he introduced his family and had an engaging friendliness that both pilots found instantly likable. His wife had the slightly flustered charm of most young mothers at a formal affair with a young child to care for. At the end of the line Mussolini's sister-in-law was purely, undeniably, drop-dead gorgeous. Colonel Hazen was already taking Mussolini and his family over to his RB-58 *Spider Woman*. Heaven be praised, that left Kozlowski to look after the sister-in-law.

"May I show you over *Marisol* Signora?"

"Please call me Sophia, Major, I have too much formality in my life. But I would very much like to see the legendary *Marisol* who lead the raid on Myitkyina."

"I'm Mike, Sophia. Please be careful on the steps, its easy to slip. This is my crew station here, the pilot's cockpit. Aft of me is the Bear's Den where Eddie Korrina works and right aft is the Electronics Pit. That's Xav Dravar's seat. I'm just the bus driver, I fly the aircraft. Eddie is our offensive systems operator, he operates our air-to-air and air-to-surface missiles while Xav looks after the defensive systems, the jammers, decoys, threat location systems and the rest."

"May I sit in your seat Mike? I've never sat in the pilot's seat of a real aircraft. My brother-in-law Bruno was a test pilot you know but one of his tests killed him. I never really knew him."

"Certainly Sophia, I'll have to ask you to take your shoes off though, we've put some padding down here in case you wanted to get in. Here, I'll help you in. Just swing in, put one foot on the seat and sort of slide in. That's right."

"Thank you. This is so small, how do you and your crew stay in here? Did you fly over in one stage or land in the middle? And what have you seen of Italy so far?"

"*Marisol* is cramped. When we go for training we are all measured and weighed, then only the smallest SAC pilots fly the RB-58s. We came over in one stage but we refueled from tankers based in the Azores. We could make it in one flight, just, but we would be running on fumes by the time we got in so why take the chance?

"We haven't had a chance to really look around yet, that's something we're all promising ourselves. The thing about Italy we love already is your food. In America, all we really know of Italian cooking is pizza and spaghetti. We'd never guessed there was such a fantastic variety of food and wine here. I'm not sure we'll fit in the cockpits when it comes time to go home."

Sophia laughed and ran her hand over her body "Do not underestimate spaghetti Mike. Everything I have, I owe to spaghetti. But tell me something. I have heard that in SAC you pilots talk to your aircraft and sometimes you believe your aircraft talk back. Is this true?"

Mike glanced at his crewmates. They nodded slightly. "Sophia, its more than belief. All three of us talk to *Marisol* and she speaks back to us." His guest gave him the "boys and their toys" look that women have used since Caveman Ug proudly showed Cavewoman Nug the latest addition to his collection of stone axes. "Honestly Sophia, she really does talk with us."

Sophia gave him a famous dazzling smile. "Mike, I have been asked to take part in a film about the Siege of Myitkyina. I'm supposed to be the wife of one of the bomber pilots. If we have dinner together tonight, could you give me some help with the correct language and way of speaking? Tell me the sort of things that the wife of a SAC pilot would be concerned about. And also tell me more about the relations you have with your aircraft? I would like to know more about you and your *Marisol*, she is very beautiful indeed."

"Why, thank you Miss Loren." *Marisol's* voice came out of the intercom speakers either side of the seat.

Sophia Loren's eyes went wide and danced with incredulous delight. Kozlowski and his crew raised eyebrows - for *Marisol* to speak to somebody outside their tight little circle was unique, unheard of. Bombers only spoke to their crews and then only when a special rapport existed between aircraft and humans. Even then it was never quite certain whether the aircraft really spoke to them or their crews just imagined that they did. Then something else registered and the impact stunned him. Unless his ears were deceiving him, Kozlowski realized he had just been invited to spend an evening with the fabulous Sophia Loren.

North American Aviation Facility Palmdale, California

Her first two sisters were aerodynamic prototypes, barely more than empty shells. They didn't even have the proper crews, being restricted to a pilot and co-pilot. They'd done their job now, they'd be retired to test and research work. Their great white shapes waited outside for the roll-out of the youngest member of the family, the first YB-70A. She was very different, a fully-equipped bomber with a crew of four; a bomber-navigator and a defensive systems operator sitting behind the pilots. Her appearance was strangely different from the original two prototypes. Her shape looked the same although there were subtle differences. It was her color that really marked her out, instead of prototype white, she'd been painted a peculiar translucent creamy-silver.

She'd be faster than her older sisters as well. They'd topped out at Mach 3.2 at 72,000 feet. The prototype test flights had taught the designers a lot though; the YB-70A was expected to reach Mach 3.3, perhaps Mach 3.4. Sometimes, quietly, the engineers spoke of getting to Mach 3.5. They also spoke of flying her at 80,000 feet and over ranges of almost 8,000 miles. If her test program went well, the first of the 250 production B-70As would be joining SAC in less than a couple of years. They'd be replacing the B-52s. The replacement was not before its time. The Gray Lady was a formidable foe, one that even the triple sonic interceptors never took for granted, but her speed and altitude put her within the intercept envelope of ground defenses. That wouldn't be the case with the B-70; there was nothing known that could stop her reaching her targets.

Taking shape in the Palmdale lofts was a design for something that was, in its way, even more remarkable. An airliner that looked like a B-70 but could carry 76 passengers. Pan American had already put in an order for them as the Star Clippers, that meant TWA would be following soon. Flying on the Star Clippers would be expensive compared with the large Convair, Boeing and Douglas airliners but they could get from coast to coast in around 90 minutes. That mean it would be possible to make daily commutes from California to New York and back. The social implications of that were intriguing to put it mildly.

Also in the background was another airliner, one a long way in the future but the reason why representatives from Boeing were here today. North American and Boeing were collaborating on a Mach 3 airliner that would carry more than 200 passengers. That would be truly revolutionary, it would make supersonic air travel something that ordinary people could reach, just as the Convair 990 and the Boeing 707s had made flying a routine activity that the passengers never really thought about.

Today, though was the day of the YB-70A. Her roll-out, the day she would be revealed to the world. The dignitaries and guests were already gathering, waiting for the ceremony to start. North American Aviation had laid on a magnificent buffet lunch for the guests; a copious supply of champagne was chilled and available. The walls of the hangar were covered with briefing panels showing the aircraft, what she could do and how she would perform. In one corner there was even a simulator of the flight deck so people could get in and pretend to be flying America's latest bomber.

Then, there was a hush as a government limousine pulled up. Secretary of Defense Robert McNorman got out and walked up to the aircraft parked in the hangar. The President and CEO of North American Aviation went out to greet him, hand outstretched, but McNorman walked straight past him without saying a word. He pushed the waitress with the tray of champagne to one side, then walked once around the YB-70A. Then, still without saying a word to anybody, he got back into his car and was driven off. Behind him, there was a buzz sweeping through the rollout guests. On the VIP stand, The Seer leaned over to his personal assistant and whispered "Lillith honey, I think he's just declared war."

CHAPTER THREE
ENGAGEMENT

Chang-Sha, China-Tibet Border

Smoke was still drifting across the base, buildings were still wrecked and bodies still had to be removed. The order from the Showa Restoration Council in Tokyo to remove the General from command and replace him had been obeyed, but only at the cost of some bitter fighting. The General and a battalion's worth of loyal troops had dug in and fought hard. They'd been defeated in the end, of course, but it had taken longer and cost more than the plans had anticipated.

Now it was time to move on to the next part of the plan. The whole logic behind Showa Restoration was that the reformists over the last five years had abandoned the path of conquest and turned their backs on their destiny. If the Council was to have a legitimate claim to power it had to produce a conquest fast, a visible, undeniable demonstration that Japan and China were on the move again.

Colonel Hu Kai-Lee had command of the division now. Or what was left of it. He had to recruit - a more accurate word might be kidnap - replacements for his casualties and get them trained to some rudimentary level of capability. He didn't have forever; two or three weeks at most. Then, the assault on Tibet would start.

It had been carefully planned. A revolutionary government was already waiting to issue its claim to power, the divisions along the border were already waiting to go. As soon as they were over the frontier, they'd become the "loyalist" faction of the Tibetan Army, driving the forces of the "revolutionary" priests out. By the time the mess was straightened out, the new government would be in Lhasa and it would all be over.

There was a plan within the plan of course, there always was. A close look at this division would tell people that. Technically, it was a division of the Japanese Imperial Army but the number of Japanese in it got smaller every day. Whenever the Japanese wanted a job done, they used one of the divisions they felt they could rely on, that is, one where the majority of the troops were Japanese. But, of course, that meant the casualties fell on the Japanese, not the Chinese. Now, there were very few units left where the Japanese were a majority. In some "Japanese Divisions," there were only Chinese personnel left.

Colonel Hu laughed, the Japanese really thought they could rule China with their paltry millions when there were over a billion Chinese? Had they never read history? They could have their 'Emperor' and prattle on about their Bushido, but with every year that passed, the joint country was becoming more Chinese and less Japanese. One day soon, the Japanese would be gone, absorbed into the infinite number of Chinese.

"Sir, we have dug a pit for the enemy rebel dead. The men are putting their bodies in now. What shall we do with the wounded rebels?"

Hu thought for a moment. The deposed general was Japanese and his defenders had been mostly Japanese troops. Hu's family had come from a place called Nanking and he still had nightmares over what had happened to them there. His revered father had been beheaded by a Japanese Lieutenant, Mukai Toshiaki, simply to win a bet with another Lieutenant as to who could cut the heads from 100 Chinese the fastest. It turned out Mukai Toshiaki had miscounted, he'd actually killed 106 Chinese in the race. For all that, Father had been the luckiest of his family.

"Go through the wounded rebels, separate the Japanese from the Chinese. If the Chinese repent and wish to rejoin us, let them. We need as many trained soldiers as we can get. Bury the Japanese wounded along with their dead."

Oh yes, thought Hu, China is absorbing Japan, step by step, but that will just be the start. One day soon there will be no Japan left at all. And one day, one day he would find Mukai Toshiaki and then Colonel Hu would avenge his family. The Japanese might believe otherwise but nobody in China had forgotten Nanking. The invasion of Tibet was a step along that road as well.

Bridge INS Mysore, At Sea, South of Taiwan

"My God, she's a mess."

She was - or had been - one of the new Chipanese Kawachi class missile cruisers. The design ancestry was vaguely apparent; the Tone class cruisers had been the starting point. The Kawachi class were much larger; 20,000 tons at least, probably more. Japan may now be Chipan in the eyes of the world, even if the Japanese themselves refused the name, but old habits of understating official displacement figures died hard.

The long sweeping foredeck was still there, but the guns had gone. In their place were ranks of inclined launch tubes for missiles: four ranks of four. A total of 16 long-range, nuclear tipped anti-ship missiles. The aviation facilities were aft; now they handled helicopters fitted out with surface search radars for target acquisition. Amidships were the anti-aircraft missile batteries. Point defense only of course; the Japanese still hadn't got around the problems of trying to handle crossing targets in an area defense mode. Nor, for that matter, had anybody else. Even the Americans were reported to be in trouble there.

According to the recognition diagrams and the photographs in *Mysore's* CBs, the midships section should have four funnels in two pairs, angled outwards and two heavy tower masts that carried an array of radar and electronic warfare antennas. All of that had gone: instead, the midships was a charred tangle of burned-out wreckage. The cruiser was down by the bows, to the point where her foredeck was awash, and she was listing. The visible damage wouldn't allow for that, she must have been hit underwater.

"Sparker, make 'Indian Warship C12 to Chipanese cruiser. Do you require assistance?'". There was a long pause then a signals lamp started to flash from the crippled ship.

"*Mysore* this is Admiral Soriva on **Imperial Japanese Navy** warship *Kawachi*. We have many badly injured. Medical assistance urgently needed." The emphasis on the 'Imperial Japanese Navy' had been very strong, repeated twice in the signal.

"Soriva" Admiral Kanali Dahm looked thoughtful. "He was one of those listed as being killed in the Showa Restoration Coup. So he made it out. Only just by the look of it. It must be bad over there if they're asking for assistance. Sparker, make back to *Kawachi* 'Am sending medical teams immediately. Stand by to receive helicopters.' Number One, alert the Ship's Poisoner and tell him he'd got clients to experiment on. Take whoever he needs to assist. Then make to *Godavari* and *Gondwana*, advise them of the situation and tell them to get medical teams over also. If the butcher's bill over there is as bad as that ship looks, they'll need all the help they can get. Once Comms is clear, get on the long-range radio troposcatter link to New Delhi and advise D-Ops of what's happening. Jim Ladone needs to know what's going on out here ASAP. Oh, and order *Gondwana* to lock her missiles onto that wreck. Just in case."

Mysore and her two destroyers swung parallel to *Kawachi* while the helicopters started to shuttle medical personnel over. Dahm was pacing the bridge, waiting for his people to radio a report. He needed to know what was happening. Eventually, it came.

"Captain, Sir. Its a bloody mess over here. Ship's been torn up, casualties are worse than anything I've ever seen. Women and children too, a lot of the crew had their families on board. I'm going to set up a first aid station here then shuttle the worst wounded back to *Mysore*. They need our medical facilities, we can't do the job here. And Sir, Admiral Soriva wishes to speak to you in person. Requests permission to come over."

"Affirmative Doc. Women and children first. Put the Admiral on the first available helicopter seat." Dahm sat down, remembering the carnage on the quarter-deck of *Hood* five years ago. It was still something he saw on the nights when sleep wasn't a refuge. It was widely accepted that Masanobu Tsuji had been behind that atrocity. That it had been a failed attempt to pull Australia and India apart.

A few minutes later two Marines escorted Admiral Soriva onto the bridge. He was tired, desperately so, his face worn and haggard with the strain of the last few days. He still wore the tight-collared uniform of a Chipanese officer though. It was an article of faith in the Triple Alliance that if Chipan gave its officers more comfortable uniforms, they wouldn't be so truculent.

"Thank you for seeing me, Admiral Dahm. As you can see, our condition is desperate. We've lost our pumping capacity and we're trying to prevent further flooding using manual bucket chains." Soriva rubbed his eyes. "We've taken two torpedoes, one forward and one amidships. It happened when we broke out of Yokohama with our sistership *Settsu*. A sub got us both on the way out. *Settsu* was going down, we got the women and children off her then aircraft arrived. We couldn't stay Admiral." There was a haunted look in his eyes and the pain in Soriva's voice was obvious. "We had to get clear. The last thing we saw was *Settsu* sinking and the aircraft strafing the survivors. Then they came after us. We took three more hits from missiles, all amidships. If it hadn't been for a rainstorm that blocked out their radar, they'd have finished us too."

Soriva's expression wandered for a few seconds. "Admiral Dahm. We are on our way to Kaohsiung in Formosa. We will be joining forces there that have refused to acknowledge the Showa Restoration Council. But we have our families on board and the women and children from *Settsu*. Admiral, I beg you, please take our women and children, give them sanctuary."

Dahm nodded. A true sailorman could do no less when another was in distress. "We'll do that, Admiral. Have your people get them ready for transfer and we'll bring them over by helicopter. How many do we speak of?"

Admiral Soriva was looking at his shattered ship, the tormented look in his eyes again. Dahm repeated the question to his Number One and got an answer via the medical teams. About a hundred and seventy, many wounded. After a while, they started to arrive as the helicopters landed on the deck. Many had crudely bandaged wounds, all were shocked and exhausted. Admiral Soriva was watching them arrive on the closed-circuit television that showed the bridge crew what was happening on the flight deck aft. Suddenly his gray and prematurely elderly face rallied as a woman and two children got off the helicopter.

"Your family, Admiral?" Soriva nodded. "Look, my cuddy is just aft of the bridge. If you want to have some time alone with them, you can stay there." Dahm ran a quick mental check, everything that was classified or confidential was locked away. "Frankly Admiral, you need some time to rest. We'll get some portable pumps over to your ship."

Behind him, his Sparker cleared his throat. "Return message from D-Ops Sir. Signed by Admiral Ladone himself."

Dahm took it "Render all possible assistance. If *Kawachi* sinks, place survivors under your protection and transport to Manila. If *Kawachi* remains under way, offer medical and damage control support." Dahm sighed with relief; Admiral Ladone had guessed what would be happening here and given orders to cover Dahm's rear. Dahm would have to send a much longer report soon. If Taiwan was breaking away from Chipan, the Triple Alliance authorities needed to know straight away. That bit about the new Chipanese air-to-ship missiles not working in the rain was worth passing on as well.

Longland Jungle Training School, Atherton, Queensland, Australia

"Very good men. Before we start our training cycle I have some good news for you. The battalion is giving up Old Smelly at long last and we will now receive the Self Loading Rifle Number One Mark One Star. You will hand in your old rifles and receive your new weapon. Battalion Sergeant Major Shane, if you would lead please."

BSM Shane walked up to the armorers table and put a Bren gun down.

"What happened to your Rifle Number Five, Sergeant Major?"

"Lost in Combat sir"

"Well, where did you get this from?"

"Battlefield salvage, sir."

"Very good, Sergeant Major." Shane moved to the next table where an SLR No.1 Mk.1* was signed out to him. Meanwhile the next soldier had approached the table and put down a Chipanese Arisaka Type 12. Before the ordnance officer could speak the owner anticipated the question "Lost in Combat sir. Battlefield salvage sir. All ammunition is MF headcode sir we chucked the MFC stuff. That goes for all the boys"

"Very good, Sergeant. Next."

Another Arisaka Type 12 "Lost in Combat sir. Battlefield salvage sir."

A 7.62mm Capsten sub-machine gun. That, at least, was an authorized-issue weapon. "Lost in Combat sir, battlefield salvage sir."

An AK-47. "Lost in Combat sir, battlefield salvage sir."

Another Arisaka Type 12 "Lost in Combat sir, battlefield salvage sir."

Another Capsten submachine gun. "Rifle No.5 lost in Combat sir, battlefield salvage sir."

Another AK-47. "Lost in Combat sir, battlefield salvage sir."

The piles of assorted weapons grew steadily. The ordnance personnel started segregating the "battlefield salvage" into piles. The old SMLEs were very conspicuous by their absence. The men who'd received their new weapons were standing around inspecting the rifles. They'd been anxiously awaited, the rumors were that the new rifle was something quite special. The authorized Bren gunners were getting a version of their old weapon, chambered for the new 7 mm round. There were a lot of good things said about that as well.

Suddenly the OIC heard an intake of breath from one of the reception tables. On it was a new weapon, something that looked like an AK-47 on steroids, with a telescopic sight, a long barrel and a bipod. "What the devil is that?"

There was a touch of awe in the Ordnance Sergeant's voice. "Its a SVK Sir, the Designated Marksman version of the AK-47. Chambered for the old Russian 7.62 rimmed. Its supposed to give infantry units a bit more reach than the AK-47. The Teas only started taking delivery of these a couple of months ago. Give one of them per squad. How did you get this soldier?"

"Battlefield salvage sir." The Ordnance Sergeant looked as if he wanted to say something then decided otherwise. Then turned to the officer in charge. "Sir, I suggest we keep this one, we haven't seen one of these yet and the tech guys here would like to play with it."

Slightly numbed by the variety of weapons being handed in, the OIC nodded. The SVK was carefully carried away and stowed somewhere discreet. Relationships between the Australian infantry, more commonly known as 'Diggers' and their Thai equivalents, equally commonly known as 'Teas' were close, but sometimes interests did diverge. And they stole equipment from each other with worrying enthusiasm Privately the OIC would have laid heavy odds that a Tea designated marksman had done much KP for losing that rifle. Unless he'd managed to steal an Australian Bren as a replacement.

By the time the exchange had been completed, there were indeed a few SMLEs handed in, from new recruits who had only just joined the battalion. They'd be sold on the export market, going to dealers who would feed America's apparently inexhaustible appetite for firearms. The AK-47s would be returned to the Teas with a few good-natured gibes about their soldiers needing to look after their kit better. The Arisakas would be going to Thailand as well, to be handed over to the Vietnamese People's Liberation Army. The rest would be going to the training school arsenal, there was always a need for a variety of odd weapons when jobs that couldn't be described had to be done.

The ammunition was being sorted as well. The .303 would go back to store, the 7.62 x 39 would go back to Thailand. The 6.5 Arisaka, that was different. The ammunition would have to be carefully checked out. The instructions issued had been quite clear, 6.5 mm Arisaka head-coded MFC was a heavy load intended for use in machine guns and should never, ever be used in the Type 12 Arisaka rifle. The real reason why the MFC coded rounds had to be dumped was quite different and much, much nastier. The propellant had been replaced and anybody who used it would find their rifle blowing up in their face. Only, the people who'd thought of that trick hadn't allowed for the possibility that Australian troops would be picking the stuff up and using it.

Lieutenant Colonel Golconda looked at his men. They were hardly recognizable as the same army that had gone to Burma five years earlier. In retrospect, looking back on that Army he was embarrassed by their ingenuousness. Then, the Australian Army had been a colonial version of the old British Army, even down to the soup-plate helmet and old-fashioned khaki uniforms. Now the uniforms were jungle green and the helmets were the American pattern, though not that many of the boys wore them. Most preferred the floppy camouflaged bush hat known irreverently as the battle bonnet. They handled their weapons with casual ease and competence. They had become an army their enemies feared.

The Australian Army had found its new self in the Burmese jungle. Building on the foundations laid down at Gallipoli decades ago, it had been hardened by the sun and toughened by the wind. The Tea Long Range Recon Patrols had taught them to make friends with the jungle, to treat it with respect and to accept the gifts it offered.

After five years, the Australians looked on the jungle as home. Most of the troops half-believed the Tea stories about spirits who lived in the woods and lakes and who could be friendly or hostile according to how they were treated. Most of the troops half-jokingly, half seriously, left presents for the jungle spirits now and then, and a surprising number believed that doing so brought good luck. It wasn't true of course, the units were doing what good units always did, they were making their own luck.

The Australian Army had found more than itself, Golconda though, it had found its place. The numerical backbone of the Triple Alliance armies came from India, sheer numbers dictated that. The Indian regiments included the stately Sikhs whose bearing was the very epitome of military dignity and the cheerfully homicidal Ghurkas as well as dozens of others. The Teas had good kit and their troops were disconcertingly capable once they got off their lazy backsides and did something. The rest of the ASEAN troops, well, they needed a lot of work. The tiny Singapore detachment was OK, the Philippine troops were good material but they had so much to learn. Just like us, five years ago, whispered a little voice in Golconda's head. As for the rest? Better not to say anything.

The Australian Army had found its niche in special operations. They were good at it and were getting better all the time. At first there had been a few irregular forces, Popski's Private Army was one, the Darwin Light Horse had been another. They'd attracted the hard cases, the ones that were not the sort to thrive under normal regimental discipline. Good men all, very good men in some cases, and the PPA and DLH had given them the room they needed to develop.

The criticism was the usual one, that the special forces were bleeding off the men who would provide the vital leadership cadres for the regular units. That might have been true but it also became apparent that most of the Australian troopers were the sort who didn't thrive under normal regimental discipline. More and more of them "Ran off to join the Circus" as the Australian officers called it. Those that came back brought their experience and attitudes with them and they'd remade the regiments in their own image - and the regiments were much better for it. The Australian Army had become an Army of special forces units.

In Burma it had worked fine. The Indians had provided the main force units, the Teas had done the counter-insurgency work in the villages and towns and the growing number of Australian special forces groups had looked after the deep penetration, long-range patrolling and the covert offensive operations. If ever the Australian Army had to fight a regular war against a conventional opponent, they'd be in trouble but, as poor old Locock had known, if it ever got that far, Australia had lost anyway.

The new Australian Army was just what the country needed to keep its enemies at arm's length. And that's what they would be doing again, very soon. The word was already spreading around the Army that they had new places to go, new jungles to patrol. This time there would be a difference.

The Teas vaunted expertise in counter-insurgency had shown to be less than effective in the latest flare-up. Bringing the local population onto your side was all very well where they were sane but when they irreversibly hated you because you didn't worship their god their way, it was a non-starter. What was left was hunting down the terrorists and killing them all. Then, the local nutters might still hate you but they'd been defanged.

"Battalion Sergeant Major. A word please."

BSM Shane had been sitting with a group of the men helping them orientate themselves to their new rifles. Now, he leapt to his feet with alacrity. In private, things were much more relaxed, every officer at each level knew his senior NCO was a partner, not a subordinate, but here, in front of the men, formality was the watchword. Especially with newbies in the unit.

"Sergeant Major, we have about three months to get the men qualified on their new weapons and get the newbies indoctrinated into the way we do things. Then we're going back out again."

"Burma Sir?"

"No Sergeant Major, that's winding down, at least for the while. Unless the new government in Chipan really heat things up. We have a new jungle to play with. We're going to Mindanao in the Philippines."

Kirkuk, The Caliphate

They were called kessel. The whole town was being cut up into those small sections, armor seizing the streets and dominating the area by fire, preventing movement from one kessel to the next. Then, once each kessel was isolated, it was brought under assault. The infantry would close up, pinning down the occupants while the engineers got into position. Then, they'd finish the defenders off with blowtorch and screwdriver. That was what they called the combination of flamethrowers and satchel charges they would use to wipe out everybody inside the buildings. Then, when everybody was dead, they'd start on the next section.

It wasn't quite that easy of course. There were underground tunnels connecting the buildings so the engineers pumped those full of thickened Soman. The nerve gas would cling to the walls, turning the tunnels into a poisonous deathtrap that would last for years. Or they'd pump gasoline into the underground shelters then toss down a thermite grenade. Sometimes the explosions were quite spectacular and every so often there were a series of secondaries from fuel and munitions stored down there. But, step by step, building by building, the town and its inhabitants were being destroyed.

That was the idea. The town had been the headquarters of some group or other opposed to the Caliphate. Model had been told their name but didn't remember it. Pathists or Bathers, something like that. They'd been a socialist group that had tried to stage a coup about the time the Caliphate itself had seized power in Iraq. They'd gone underground, tried to fight a guerrilla war against Caliphate forces and, at first, had been quite successful.

The Caliphate's local forces were hardly more than tribal militias and they'd played by the old rules of tribal warfare. Despite its amorphous, contradictory and always mutually hostile nature, the generally ill-organized Caliphate could raise quite impressive numbers of tribal levies. The problem was they were ill-armed, ill-disciplined and capable of little more than the night-time raiding of undefended camps. Faced with even marginally-competent troops, they were ineffective.

So, the Caliphate had called on Model's Janissaries to put down the revolt. They'd had enough experience in Russia fighting partisans and they knew the rules of partisan warfare as well as the Arabs had known those of tribal warfare. Lidice Rules.

First Rule. There are no rules. Here ends the Lidice Rules.

Kirkuk was the third town they'd destroyed. Behind Model's infantry were the Guardians of the Faith, once the Einsatzgruppen, who would kill off any inhabitants of the town that had survived of the infantry assault. That had lead to a minor, rather good-humored, dispute between the Guardians and the representatives of the Caliphate. The Guardians had wanted to burn the prisoners at the stake in the good old inquisition style; the mullahs sent by the Caliphate wanted them stoned in accordance with their traditions. They'd compromised, of course; the men had been burned, the women stoned. The only survivors had been babies less than a year old. They'd been sent back to Model's colony to be brought up as the next generation of Janissaries. After everybody was dead, the ruins of the town would be leveled and plowed under.

Kirkuk would probably be the last, in this campaign anyway. The back of the resistance up here was broken. That wouldn't end his usefulness, Model thought, there was plenty more work to be done. His troops were the trump card of the Caliphate. Any competent Western army could cut the Caliphate's levies to pieces and his troops were far more than just competent. So, when there was resistance to Caliphate rule, he could put it down, fast and bloody. In a very real sense, he had the only really effective military force in the Caliphate.

That was deliberate policy of course. Each of the once-independent countries that was now part of the Caliphate was a province ruled by a Satrap and the districts forming the country were ruled by lesser officials appointed by the Satrap. Officially, ruling a province entitled the ruler to be part of the Ruling

Council. In fact, it worked the other way, only members of the Ruling Council were entitled also to become a Satrap of one of the provinces. The whole structure of the Caliphate Council actively encouraged the Satraps to intrigue against each other and changes in Satrapy boundaries achieved by such intrigues made the map of the Caliphate a fluid and changing thing.

It was not uncommon for Satraps to gain control of territories not actually in their Satrapy. Of course, the Satraps required official approval once such changes had been made. The more capable and effective the Satrap, the greater his influence on the Caliphate Council - which meant the gains of the Satraps were more likely to be approved. But, if one of the members of the Caliphate Council gained too much power, the rest could combine and order Model's Janissaries to cut him down to size. Obedience to the verdict of the Caliphate wasn't optional, and there was a point when the wise backed down. Because the other option would be facing Model's troops or an assassin. It was a brutally Darwinian system and Model approved of it as it stood. What it would become still remained the problem of the future.

It wasn't as if religious or ethnic differences were the only ones that impacted the constant shifts in power and influence that made up the Caliphate's political geography. Anybody could have anticipated that. Nor was the Ruling Council the only center of power no matter how much they liked to pretend otherwise.

The Caliphate's central dogma might be provided by the theocrats in the Ruling Council, but the country was actually run by the surviving economists and technocrats. They had their heads down at this time, restricting their involvement with the interplay of politics and the intrigues between the Satraps to a minimum but they were there. One day, their time would come, one day the constant intrigues and outward pressure would result in a blunder that would fatally reduce reduced the ruling council's power and influence. Then, they would fall or be reduced to impotence, and that would also bring down Model's Janissaries. No matter which way Model looked, his options were running out.

So where would his men be sent next? Saudi Arabia was a possibility. The old king, Ibn Saud, had sired a huge number of children in his lifetime. Not surprising, he had over 900 wives and concubines. Model thought about that for a second and mentally raised a glass of schnapps to the old goat. Despite the best efforts of the Caliphate, it had proved impossible to wipe out the Royal Family, the country was covered with wandering princes with a claim to the throne who had shown they could rally traditional support in the tribes. Saudi Arabia was a turmoil of low-grade civil war between the tribes now, with the effort against the Caliphate taking a second place.

The Caliphate wasn't that worried, for every tribe fighting against the Caliphate government, there was another that saw the opportunity to pay off some old grudge or other, and regardless of their opinions on the Caliphate, thus allied with it to help get their revenge. Divide and rule worked well in the endless tribal conflicts simmering under the region but the danger was that Saudi oil production would be affected. Oil was the Caliphate's life blood. If oil production stopped, then disaster beckoned. So, Model thought, that might be his next job. Secure and protect the oil fields, then the rest of the Saudi population could continue slaughtering each other - and good riddance to them all.

There was a respectful knock on the door of his command caravan. Model gave permission to enter and one of his guard stepped in. Before he could speak, a black-turbaned mullah pushed past him with a message scroll in his hands. That was one of the affectations of the Caliphate; they wrote their messages and records on scrolls, not pages. The fastidiously clean Model wrinkled his nose, the mullah had the 'odor of piety' around him. If one of Model's soldiers had smelt that badly, his squad mates would have scrubbed him clean with sand and floor-brushes. The messenger thrust the scroll at Model and left, without saying a word.

"An accident waiting to happen, that one." Model said absently. His guard grinned and nodded before leaving. Model guessed that if he listened hard enough, he'd hear the "accident" before too long.

The scroll contained Model's orders from the Caliphate. Once the cleansing of Northern Iraq was completed, he was to take his entire force, families included, to Gaza in Palestine. That would be his new base of operations for the future. Model thought about that. Palestine had been thoroughly cleansed already so his troops weren't required for that. No, it was more likely that the Caliphate was about to expand again. Egypt was the obvious target and Model's troops would be on hand to eliminate any resistance once the expansion took place. After all, if Egypt became part of The Caliphate, Sudan would fall soon after and then the whole of the North African Littoral would be opened up.

Conference Room, The White House, Washington DC

"Mister President, the House/Senate Budget Conference has completed its deliberations, reconciling the differences between the House and Senate versions of the FY66/67 Defense Budget and has sent the reconciled version to you for signature. If we leave out the points on which House and Senate were in agreement with your original budget proposal we are left with the following.

"Dealing with the Navy first. The House authorized the construction of two new aircraft carriers, CVN-69 and CVN-70. The Senate authorized only CVN-69. The Conference has authorized the construction of CVN-69 and the procurement of long-lead items for CVN-70 with full funding for this ship and CVN-71 to follow in FY67/68. In addition, Conference notes that, with the scrapping of the last battleships in 1965, state names are no longer the source for a specific class of warship. They therefore mandate that all aircraft carriers from CVN-67 shall bear state names. Subject to Navy approval, the propose that the four carriers building or authorized should bear the following names. CVN-67 USS *Texas,* CVN-68 USS *Oregon,* CVN-69 USS *Maine* and CVN-70 USS *Massachusetts.* Conference also proposes USS *Ohio* for CVN-71.

"Conference agreed upon the construction of six CGN-166 improved Long Beach class missile cruisers with the first pair to be ordered this year along with long-lead items for the rest. A Senate proposal to build two enlarged versions of this class with enhanced aviation facilities aft was deferred until next year. The CGN-166s will replace the CA-139 Des Moines class cruisers, that will mean the last heavy gun ships will have gone from the Navy.

"The House proposed the construction of six new large missile destroyers to replace the CG-106 Fargo class conversions, the Senate transferred that funding to research and development pending the completion of a new air warfare system for those ships. The Senate version was agreed since the air defense system is insufficiently mature for deployment at this time. Finally, the House called for the construction of six nuclear-powered attack submarines, the Senate for four. Conference compromised on the construction of eight SSNs but mandated the removal of *Nautilus* and *Seawolf* from front-line service.

"Moving on to the Army, the House presented the Secretary of Defense demand for the reorganization of the six Pentomic Divisions to a new standard, the Re-Organized Army Division. This would effectively convert them into heavy armor divisions. The House also presented the Secretary of Defense's proposal to bring the two reserve Pentomic Divisions to active status and to form six new ROAD divisions using manpower from the Army portions of NORAD. This would provide an Army force structure of fourteen active divisions. Conference evaluated these proposals and rejected them.

"In its place, Conference accepted a Senate proposal that will see continued production of the M60A3 for the National Guard and the formation of four new National Guard brigades, one armor, one artillery, two mechanized infantry. Conference notes that the National Guard is actually over-subscribed with applicants at this time. Conference does not fund any substantive changes to the Regular or Reserve Army.

"In the Air Force, Congress presented the Secretary of Defense's demand that funding for the B-70, F-108 and F-112 be terminated and the resources directed into Army and ballistic missile procurement. Conference soundly rejected this proposal and has authorized production of 96 F-108s, 90 F-112 and 100 B-70A aircraft, the last subject to successful testing of the YB-70 pre-production aircraft.

"In addition, the Budget Conference supported continuing development of the XB-74 Dominator for a planned entry to service in FY70. A House proposal for a 50 percent reduction in the interceptor and missile units forming NORAD was rejected by

Conference as was a proposal to restart ballistic missile development. In Tactical Aviation, the proposal to terminate further F-105 procurement and transfer funding to the F-110 was agreed. Finally, funding for the first batch of RB-58F aircraft was included as proposed by both House and Senate. However, the senate also added funds for the remanufacture of RB-58C and RB-58D aircraft to RB-58F standard and this was approved by Conference.

"Mr President, Conference presents the FY66/67 budget for your signature."

President Johnson signed the document. "If there are no further..."

"A point of order Mister President." Secretary of Defense McNorman was standing. "Under the terms of the 1958 Department of Defense Enabling Act, the Secretary of Defense may refuse to release appropriated funds and reallocate them if a national emergency so demands. It is my judgment that the weakness of our army and our lack of missile development constitutes a grave national emergency and I am therefore refusing to release the funds appropriated for the F-108, F-112, B-70 and B-74 programs and re-allocating the money to the planned reorganization and enlargement of the United States Army."

McNorman sat down with a conceited grin on his face. President Johnson shot a furious look in his direction, this was the sort of thing Presidents pulled on their Secretaries, not the other way around. Then he turned to his National Security Advisor. "Can he do that?"

"In a manner of speaking, Mister President. The power to which the Secretary of Defense referred does exist. It was included in the act as a safety provision in case a grave national emergency required a very sudden change in our defense posture. It was never intended as a means by which the Secretary could circumvent the standard budget process. However, fortunately, the possibility that it may be misused was foreseen and a safety catch was installed."

The Seer leaned forward and pressed a button on the intercom. "Lillith, honey, will you bring in Volume Seven of our contract with the United States Government? Marked to Article 666, sub-section four."

Lillith came into the room, the volume open in her hands. Taking it, the Seer surreptitiously ran a finger to check the ink was dry, a gesture that got him Lillith's best "what do you take me for, an amateur?" look.

"Mister President, this section of our contract with the US Government provides that when a disagreement over funding between Conference and the Secretary of Defense causes the latter to withhold funding allocated by the former, the dispute shall be referred to the Contractors, that's us, for arbitration and resolution.

"As the representative of the contractors, I must say that I feel bound to support the elected representatives of the people over an appointed official," Lillith started making little choking noises at that, "and advise that you, as President, over-rule Secretary McNorman's opinions. The Conference appropriations and allocations should be allowed to stand. The final decision is, of course, yours sir."

Johnson relaxed slightly. "I agree. Thank you Seer. Secretary McNorman, your initiative is overruled, the Conference Report funding allocation stands. You will execute them according to the provisions made by Conference. This meeting is adjourned. Seer, if I may speak with you for a moment?"

"Mister President. I must pro..."

"I said this meeting is adjourned, Robert. Now."

After the room emptied, Johnson looked at his notes. "Seer, does Article 666 sub-section four really contain that provision?"

"It'll be there when Secretary McNorman looks for it, sir."

Johnson nodded. "The goddamn bastard though he could railroad me. Ramsey Chalk put him up to it. That legalism has the Attorney General's smell all over it. You know he told me we were all war criminals for what we did to Nazi Germany? Tried to tell me there was no difference between us and them. Even said our bomber crews and everybody involved should be hauled before a war crimes court. You know his latest idea? Some assembly of all the nations where international disputes can be referred for solution. One nation, one vote. Majority rules. Calls it The United Nations. Where'd you put a thing like that Seer?"

"Ground Zero, Mister President?"

Johnson snorted with laughter. "That'll do. I run this country, I make the decisions and there's no way I'm going to turn that over to a bunch of deadbeat jawboners. You know what really gets me? That proposal Robert tried to force through, it would kill our aviation industry dead. Texas lives on its aviation industry, I'm not going down in history as the President who pauperized his own state. That scheme of his would destroy me. He did have one point though; our regular army is terribly weak."

"Deliberately so sir. America has a long history of intolerance for the maintenance of a large standing army. Navies are a different matter, they don't live on home soil and Air Forces are seen as a version of the Navy. We have a small standing army its true, but we do have a large and powerful reserve we can mobilize if we need it. All history teaches us that countries that have large standing armies get tempted to use them. Eventually they start getting used for things that are not in the national interest. They get committed to actions that are far from any areas than are of primary national concern. Eventually, the nation gets tired of taking casualties and we end up unable to sustain force commitments when they are a vital national interest.

"That's why our national policy is not to fight our enemies but to destroy them. If an issue is important enough for us to get involved, its important enough to destroy our enemy. If it isn't that important, we shouldn't be involved. That's a primary reason why our strategic forces are based around bombers, not missiles. We can send our bombers out, our enemy can see we mean business and, assuming he sees sense, we can call them back. Once missiles are launched it's all over, they can't be called back or their attacks aborted. Depending on missiles is a suicide pact. Its like two cowboys fighting a duel on mainstreet at high noon - at one pace range and armed with sawn-off-shotguns.

Johnson nodded. A political operator without equal in Washington, he hated the idea of making a decision he could not later reverse, modify or compromise. At the Conference table, Lillith was collecting up the documents for secure storage, brushing her heavy black hair back when she bent over the table to collect a pad that had migrated to the table center.

"That assistant of yours, I wish I had a dozen like her. Where did you find her?"

"She had a dispute with her previous employer over positions, so we hired her sir."

"You lucked out. She's an angel."

"No, Mister President, she isn't."

The King Tut Club, Cairo, Egypt

The music was provided by a reasonably good imitation of an American swing band. Perhaps a little old-fashioned by modern standards but suited to the clientele. Mostly rich tourists from America and the Mediterranean Confederation with some from the Triple Alliance and a few from Northern Europe. And then, of course, were the local luminaries who wanted to show off their "modernity" by going the places the tourists went and doing what the tourists did. There was a floor show as well, one that was allegedly Egyptian but was really straight Wilson, Keppel and Betty with no Wilson, no Keppel and a lot more Betties.

What made the King Tut different from the other nightclubs that serviced the tourist trade in Egypt was its food. Despite the dated music and tacky floorshow, the King Tut was actually a first-class restaurant. Even more remarkably, it was the British who were responsible.

The British armistice with Germany in 1940 had left Egypt in a state of confusion. Just over a week earlier, Italy had declared war on Britain and France, The British position in North Africa seemed hopelessly outmatched. British Army General Percival Wavell commanded 40,000 Dominion soldiers caught between 200,000 Italian troops in Libya and 250,000 to the south in Ethiopia and Somaliland. Wavell's immediate response to the Italian declaration had been a bold gamble. He'd thrown a small force into Libya, seizing a few border positions and, essentially, doing little more than show the flag. The Armistice, just nine days later, had left the overwhelmingly outnumbered Wavell in the almost incredible position of having won a victory, albeit a purely symbolic one, that his enemy had been left with no means of reversing.

In doing so, and although he had no means of knowing it, Wavell had struck a blow that was to have profound long term consequences. During his negotiations with Germany, Lord Halifax made it quite clear that maintaining the Suez Canal under British control was a vital and non-negotiable interest. The problem was that it was by no means clear whether Wavell and the forces he commanded actually considered themselves bound by any British government decisions. Most of the rest of the Empire had already given a very clear negative to that question but Wavell had kept quiet. Mussolini hadn't, he wanted the British out of Libya and he wanted the Italians in Egypt. In the end, the negotiations came down to one thing, the Suez Canal was considered as being vital by the British; it was not vital to the Germans. The German government agreed to a status quo in North Africa and its surrounding areas and told Mussolini if he didn't like it, he would be on his own.

Mussolini's reply came on August 17, 1940, two months after the UK/German armistice and two weeks after the peace agreement. The Italian Army under Marshal d'Armata Rodolfo Graziani invaded and occupied British Somaliland, threatening merchant transit through the Red Sea and cutting of the British from India. The attack went relatively well on land, the capital of Berbera was evacuated on the 14th and the garrison was withdraw by sea to Aden.

For the Italians, though, the sea war was a disaster. The Italians had a small fleet in their Red Sea, base at Massawa, seven destroyers, eight submarines and two torpedo boats. Within five days, three of the submarines had been sunk and one captured intact. One of the submarines managed to sink an Indian sloop before being destroyed. As a result, Australia, Canada, India, New

Zealand and South Africa, all now acting as independent countries, declared war on Italy. Over the next few weeks, the rest of the Italian Red Sea fleet was methodically hunted down and sunk.

Four weeks after the assault on British Somaliland, Graziani reluctantly invaded Egypt under pressure from Mussolini. Under his command, the Italian Tenth Army recovered the captured border posts, then crossed the border into Egypt. The sheer momentum of the Italian assault carried them all the way to Sidi Barrani, 65 miles inside Egyptian border before the attack came to a halt. At that time, there were barely 30,000 British troops standing between 250,000 Italian soldiers and Cairo. However, Graziani didn't know that and chose to stockpile fuel and ammunition while fortifying Sidi Barrani as his main operational base. Aware of the overwhelming force that Graziani could deploy once that base was completed, Wavell sent his best field commander, General O'Connor to raid the Sidi Barrani base and destroy its supply stockpiles.

The raid was expected to be difficult and the British anticipated heavy casualties. Instead, the Sidi Barrani defenses collapsed almost without a fight and O'Connor seized the moment. He turned his raid into a full-scale assault, drove the Italian Army out of Egypt and then launched a full-scale invasion of Libya. Within a month, he had advanced in Cyrenaica and taken almost 130,000 prisoners. Simultaneously, the assault to drive the Italians from East Africa started. Eritrea in the north was invaded from the Sudan by largely Indian forces, while East African and South African troops attacked Italian Somaliland from Kenya to the south.

With one army rampaging through his North African provinces and another sweeping through Italian possessions in the Horn of Africa, Mussolini was in despair. In February 1941, he appealed to his German allies for assistance, only to be told "You have made your bed. Now go whore in it."

The Germans were already gearing up for the invasion of the USSR and unimportant sideshows against already-neutralized countries were anathema to them. Hitler swore that not a man nor a round of ammunition would go to aid the Italians in North

Africa. Eighteen months later, Mussolini would have his revenge when an overstretched Germany demanded troops for service in Russia. Vichy France and Halifax Britain refused and were occupied as a result. Mussolini supplied just enough Italian troops to avoid that fate but the Italian force in Russia was small and never fit for more than rear area duties. Quite without realizing it, Wavell had been responsible for bringing about a decisive split in the German-Italian Axis.

However, that still lay in the future. Before then, Mussolini had to face the fact that he was being defeated. The capital of Italian Somaliland, Mogadishu, fell on the 25th of February, after which Wavell's British-Australian forces advanced northwest into Ethiopia. British Somaliland was recovered by early March 1941, with all Italian resistance ending in the horn of Africa by the end of the month. It was rumored that Mussolini had had a stroke or nervous breakdown on hearing the news.

Certainly, when he re-appeared he was a changed man. The bombastic self-confidence had gone and he negotiated a cease-fire that recognized the status of Egypt and the Horn of Africa in exchange for a withdrawal from Libya. Significantly, the deal was negotiated with Wavell and the authorities in Cairo; the London government under Lord Halifax was never even consulted. By April 1941, a delicate, tenuous, but lasting peace had been established.

For the rest of the war, Cairo's ambiguous status, undefined sovereignty and geographical position made it a hotbed of espionage, subversion, treachery, double-dealing and international chicanery that was to become legendary. The atmosphere of the city in those days was best caught by the immortal Humphrey Bogart/Ingrid Bergman film "Cairo." People who pretended to be insiders insisted that the "Rick's Bar" featured in the film was modeled on the King Tut Club. Real insiders knew that "Rick's Bar" was actually inspired by The American Club a few doors down from the King Tut.

The King Tut itself had been founded by the pursers and stewards from a P&O liner that had been trapped in Egypt when everything started to fall apart. It had quickly gained a reputation for excellent food and wine, to the point where the German,

Italian, French, various British and American intelligence organizations had an informal agreement to keep the King Tut as neutral ground. For five years, secret agents who had been industriously trying to kill each other a few minutes earlier, would dine on adjacent tables in uninterrupted, if strained, peace.

Post-war, when Egypt became a truly independent country, the King Tut management had sold out to local interests but the reputation and standards of the club had been maintained. It had benefited from the upsurge in tourism that had started when air travel had become commonplace with the huge American Cloudliners. Now, it was crowded.

Looking out over the floor, Achmed Faowzi was a happy man. Still early in the evening, the clientele had settled down for the long haul. Another prosperous night meant happy owners and a substantial commission for Faowzi. He earned it and he knew it. For how long, that was another matter. There was an edgy, uncertain air in Egypt now, as if the country was living on the edge of a volcano. For that was exactly what it was doing. The green fundamentalist stain on the map that had started in Afghanistan and Iran had spread across the map of the Middle East and had now reached the Egyptian border.

There was a young couple entering the club and Faowzi sized them up quickly. Both were Arabic but the man was in a western-style tuxedo and the woman in a fashionable evening gown. Probably a couple of the young business owners who were turning Egypt slowly into a modern country. As Faowzi watched, the man fussed around the woman a little too much. A wife or mistress? Faowzi watched, interested by them. Then he saw the woman's waist was slightly thickened, she was pregnant. That explained it. A young man and his pregnant wife, their first baby probably, and he was overdoing his care for her. Understandable, and touching. Faowzi had five children and he'd got over such things long before.

As the couple reached the body of the club the wife leaned over and whispered in her husband's ear. He smiled at her and she set off for the lady's rest-room on the other side of the floor, joining the group of women who were gossiping by the door. Her husband joined a crowd of men at the bar, almost exactly opposite her. Then, Faowzi saw the wife wave at her husband.

Faowzi couldn't see properly. The interlocking blasts from the two human bombs at opposing sides of the room devastated the King Tut Club, and also had done something to his eyes so that all he could see was blurs. Then he realized it wasn't just his eyes, the smoke and dust in the room was a fog nobody could penetrate. There was nothing left of the women waiting by the rest room or the men at the bar, just smears and stains. The girls in the floor show had caught the worst of the blast wave, the rags of their gaudy costumes and sequined outfits were mixed up with ghastly lumps of unrecognizable flesh. Perhaps they were the lucky ones. Many of the guests were still alive but had been hideously mutilated by blast and debris. Arms, legs blown off, bodies ripped open, faces mutilated beyond recognition.

Screams, whimpers and weeping started to penetrate through the wool that seemed to surround Faowzi's ears. Even as he watched, a blurred unrecognizable figure on the debris-ridden ground moved, its intestines snared on the ground underneath it. The figure collapsed again, and was still.

Faowzhi felt somebody take his arms and lead him out of the catastrophe. A rescue worker, an ambulance man. As he looked back on the devastation he realized the King Tut Club wasn't neutral ground any more.

Sheikh 'Ijlin Mosque, Cairo, Egypt

"Allah drowned Pharaoh and those who were with him. Allah drowns the Pharaohs of every generation. Allah will drown the little Pharaoh, the dwarf, the Pharaoh of all times, of our time, in our land. Oh, people of Egypt, the Egypt of Islam and Arabism, the Egypt of civilization and history. I am amazed at some of the clerics of the nation who cooperate with their treachery. I am amazed that they are trying to keep the nation away from Jihad and they issue Fatwas according to which we should not rise to defend Islam, against calf worshippers or fire worshippers. Aren't they Muslims? Why Egypt, Oh Muslims? Wake up. You're being attacked because of your religion. Islam is being attacked for a number of reasons: there are economic and security reasons. There are reasons stemming from personal vendetta, there are historical reasons, and there are religious reasons. Hence we have no choice but to start a war. The only way to remove the shame is to topple down the Egyptian regime. Just as Egypt is sacred so is also the lands of Islam, because the Prophet said so. All the lands of Islam will be united in the Caliphate and the Middle East will become a cemetery for oppressors."

The crowd had poured out onto the streets and rampaged towards the business center of the city. That was where the agents of the Great Satan, the businessmen and idolators who polluted the pure land with their filth, plotted their evil schemes. Only the night before, two heroic martyrs had struck at them where they fornicated and destroyed them in the midst of their debauchery. As they surged down the streets towards the offices and banks of the business district, they found their first victims. A cab containing a young man in a western business suit was stopped, turned over and set on fire though not before the passenger had been dragged out and kicked, beaten and slashed until all that was left was a mass of unrecognizable rags. Not far away, in a doorway a young woman lay screaming and holding her face. Probably a secretary sent out on an errand, she had been in the wrong place at the wrong time. Many of the rioters carried bottles of acid to pour over the faces of women who were not decently shrouded in their burkas.

By the time the police riot squad had arrived on the scene, the crowds had merged into a single, raging mob, streaming down the roads in an apparently unstoppable fury. The riot squad had been ordered to contain the surging mass within the sections of the city it had come from, but that was easier said than done. In truth, the police came from backgrounds not so very different from the rioters and they had heard the sermons also. They went through the motions of containing the crowd, but their hearts weren't in it and they fell back before the mob, slowly handing control of the streets over to them. As they gave ground, the howling mob pursued them, catching the sluggish and turning them into the same unrecognizable scraps as their other victims.

There was another alternative to the police riot squad. As the Government lost control of the streets, it was that other riot control force that took over, one that was run by the Egyptian Nationalist Party, not by the local authorities. Intended primarily as an anti-coup force, the Gendarmerie were far better armed and equipped than the local police. They arrived in armored busses and their first order of business was to stop the slow retreat of the police.

The first indication the original riot squad had that the rules of the battle had changed was the sound of pistol shots immediately to their rear. Those of their number that had tried to fade away from their duty were lying in the roadway, shot in the back of the head. Now, it was certain death to go back, and certain death not to stop the advance of the cacophonous swarm it front. With the Gendarmes behind, forcing the police to hold ground, the advance of riot stopped.

That didn't end it. Containing the riot was one thing, dispersing it was another. The mob was contained, certainly, but it still existed. There was an answer to that as well, one contained in two large bus-like vehicles that pulled up behind the lines of beleaguered riot police. Safe behind the now-steady control line, their engines revved up and white jets shot over the police line, plowing into the rioters. Water cannon.

The operators were good, some kept the jets high, hitting the rioters in the face and chest, the power of the jets sweeping the rioters off their feet, hurling them back into each other. Others kept the jets low, knocking the rioters legs out from under them. Legs and arms broke, jaws were crushed and people drowned as the remorseless water jets drove the mob back. As they fell slowly back, the water cannon started to split the mob into smaller groups. Sometime, there would come a point where the groups would be too small for the mob to maintain its group identity and it would dissolve into a mass of terrified civilians. Then it would be over.

Only those who had organized the riot had expected the water cannon. As the mob had pushed forward, they'd moved onto the roof tops with Molotov Cocktails, glass bottles filled with gasoline and fitted with a crude fuse. The bottles arced down, flaring in the line of riot police and hitting the water cannon trucks. Now, the gendarmes and their pistols were the lesser of the threats facing the riot police and they started to edge back again.

The water cannon backed up also, their jets hosing the ground, washing the burning gasoline towards the mob.

Even that might not have been enough; but the Gendarme commander had expected the Molotov Cocktails and had a lesson for those who used them. Unnoticed by the mob and its organizers were a series of small trucks, scarcely bigger than taxis. Only they were blue, armored and had a turret. With a long-barreled gun.

As the mob surged forward in the wake of the volley of Molotov Cocktails, a roar and plague of fireflies filled the street. The armored cars were equipped with 14.5 millimeter machine-guns and they were firing armor-piercing incendiary - tracer ammunition. They didn't make the mistake of firing over the heads of the crowd, reinforcing its sense of invulnerability, instead they fired directly into it, the high-velocity API-Ts tearing through three, four or five bodies before the heavy bullets finally came to a halt.

Up above, helicopters cruised over the rooftops, their door gunners spraying the Molotov cocktail throwers from above. Normally, in military work every fourth or fifth round was a tracer but this time was different. Every round left its streak of fire behind, demonstrating the sheer volume of fire that was being poured into the rioting mob.

The crowd couldn't take the deadly machine-guns. Those at the front broke and ran, trying to get away, somewhere, anywhere away from the swarms of fireflies that were tearing them apart. Those at the back of the mob continued to press forward, and in the middle, the two surges collided, fighting to get through each other.

As the armored cars lashed the mob with their heavy machine-guns, piles of bodies started to mass at each intersection. The opposing crowds were getting in each others way, and effectively the mass of people formed into a single large, static target. Eventually, even the organizers couldn't hold the crowd and it broke into a mass of individuals frantically trying to find shelter from the armored cars and the helicopters overhead. As they ran, the survivors heard the staccato crackle of pistol fire as the Gendarmes finished off the wounded.

Eventually, it was over. The streets were empty except for the emergency crews clearing the bodies that carpeted the main streets of the slum. As night drew down, they took the corpses away for burial. The shaken riot police buried their dead and quietly asked themselves what had come to their city. The gendarmes cleaned their weapons, reloaded their vehicles and waited for the next time. In the slums, the black-turbaned Mullahs once again started their sermons, inciting the people to go out again the next day and attack the security forces that had martyred so many of their friends and relatives.

CHAPTER FOUR
SKIRMISH

El Khalq, Cairo, Egypt

The city of Cairo was dying. Port Said Road had become the front line, between the administrative heart of the city and the mosque districts of El Khalq, El Dhab and El Kamaliya. It was a battle of wills and of endurance. Could the Mullahs pour people into the streets faster than the gendarmerie could pour bullets into the people? Would the people run out of the will to die before the Government ran out of the will to kill?

All over the city people looked to the pall of smoke that darkened the sun and wondered at the madness that was taking place. Not all the people of the city however, over the last few days posters showing the acid-mutilated faces of women who had dared to appear in public unveiled had started to surface all over the cities. The potential victims were taking no chances and the sight of women in enveloping burkas was turning what had once been a vibrant cosmopolitan city into something else entirely.

The casualty rates were running enormously in favor of the security forces, dozens, perhaps hundreds, of rioters killed for every security man lost. Not that the police and Gendarmerie casualties had been light After the first day, there had been improvised mines laid in advance of the riots. The rioters themselves had been supported by rifle fire, most of it wildly inaccurate and hopelessly ineffective yet every so often single shots would pick off key members of the security force teams. The mob itself was killing few security personnel but the explosions and snipers were racking up an increasing score.

Yet the problem was that the essential need to contain the situation in the capital was pulling in the police and gendarmerie from the countryside and there, too, the situation was deteriorating. Government-built secular schools were being burned down and their teachers killed. Coptic Christian churches were meeting the same fate, the buildings burned, the priests killed, the congregations scattered and hunted down. The police had been either killed by mobs or had decided discretion was the better part of valor and had left to safer regions. Buses had been ambushed on the roads and their occupants killed, rail lines had been blown up at key points. The ability of the population to move freely had gone and with it the ability to support a functioning society. It wasn't just the city of Cairo that was dying, Egypt itself, as a modern state, was on life support and losing the battle to stay breathing.

Cairo remained the key. The day there started the way all the earlier ones had, the hysterical ranting tirades from the Mullahs and the screaming mob pouring into the streets to attack anything that wasn't part of their creed. They'd driven the riot police back but then the Gendarmerie had arrived to stiffen them and their heavy machine-guns had driven the rioters back. Now, the Port Said Road was a no-mans land, carpeted with the bodies of the rioting mob that had tried to cross it into the Abdin, the area of the city occupied by the Ministries and financial houses.

On the east side of Port Said Road, the rooftops were occupied by the groups armed with Molotov cocktails, attempting to throw their firebombs across the road at the police and Gendarmerie who held the west side of the road. It was just that bit too far though, and all their actions achieved was to attract the attention of a Gendarmerie helicopter that swept parallel with the road, spraying the east-side roofs with machine-gun fire.

As the helicopter passed, two men scrambled from cover, one carrying a longish tube with a complex looking box mounted on top. The gunner waited until the helicopter was moving away from them, its engine exhaust silhouetted against a cool part of the sky. The box on top of the launcher warbled then gave a continuous growl as the seeker locked on. A squeeze of the trigger, a blast from the tube, and a brown-gray spiral of smoke shot up from the launcher, heading straight for the Gendarmerie helicopter.

The pilot saw the approaching threat and made a fast climbing turn to get away but the missile followed him, homing in on the heated exhaust of the engine. The warhead explosion wasn't great, the missile was too small for that, but it was enough to cripple the tail rotor. The helicopter spun out of control, stalled out and crashed in the middle of Port Said Road.

"Sehr Gut." The gunner's assistant clapped him on the back then started to reload the launcher. It was the work of a minute to slide another round into the tube, plug in the connector and ready the second missile for firing. Two slaps on the gunner's shoulder and another lethal surprise was waiting for the next Gendarmerie helicopter to show its face.

Further along the line of buildings, more two-man crews left their cover. With the threat of the helicopter gone, they could do something about the armored cars with their deadly heavy machine-guns. The crews were armed with Type 19s, a Chipanese copy of the Russian RPG-2 anti-tank rocket. Not a particularly accurate weapon but the range wasn't that great. The warhead didn't have that much penetration either but the armor on the Gendarmerie vehicles was intended to stop rifle fire at the most.

The rockets streaked out from the rooftops, heading for the Gendarmerie positions on the west side of the Port Said Road. A boiling cloud of black and orange marked the spot where one of the armored cars had been hit and penetrated. More salvos shot out, more of the little armored cars were hit. Then, the mob boiled out from the east side of Port Said Road and howled its way across. This time, with the concentrated machine-gun fire broken, they made it and started to spread through the maze of small sidestreets and alleys.

The gendarmerie had no choice, they had to pull back. The mob was already bypassing their positions, threading through the streets and threatening to isolate the armored cars and riot control troops. As the blue vehicles fell back, the local population saw what was happening and hysteria ran rampant. They also streamed for the west and the illusory safety of the river.

The mob had broken through opposite the El Ezbekiya part of the city, the area largely inhabited by Coptic Christians. Those that dropped everything and ran for their lives would make it to the river. Those that stopped for anything, for a vital document, a possession or a member of the family did not. The mob ran them down and tore them to shreds. It was start of a massacre that would go on for days.

In the northern part of the El Ezbekiya, the great Coptic Cathedral was already in flames. Some of the Christian inhabitants had sought sanctuary within its walls, now they died there as the cathedral was burned with them inside. Further to the west another part of the mob burst into the Egyptian Museum and started the destruction of its contents. As thousands of years of Egyptian history, from priceless relics of the earliest Pharaohs to a portrait of King Farouk, were smashed, burned, and shredded, the Curator begged one of the black-turbaned Mullahs to stop the devastation. "We need nothing other than Islam" was the only reply he got before the mob tore the Curator and his family apart. Even before he died, the entire museum complex was already ablaze.

For it was fire that marked the passage of the rebel horde through El Ezbekiya. The front line of their advance could be traced by fire, burning buildings, overturned vehicles and the funeral pyres of people unfortunate enough to have been caught in the street. From above, it would have looked like a burning map, with the brown, charring edge of the paper preceding the flames being the people desperately running for shelter. The whole mass of refugees from the El Ezbekiya were funneling in on two bridges that lead to one of the islands in the center of the Nile. Those who faltered or hesitated were crushed under the stampeding humanity. There was no way that the bridges could carry the mass of people trying to escape over them. It was only the small groups of Gendarmerie still desperately trying to hold back the swarming rioters that allowed as many to escape as they did.

The other thing that saved some of the refugees was that they were running west while the mob was swinging south, towards the Abdin. There, the occupants had warning from the fate of the occupants of El Ezbekiya and had started their flight early. Also, the roads out were better, wider and there were three bridges, not two. Adding in the greater number of Gendarmerie and the lack of narrow alleyways for the mob to infiltrate past their positions, things were in the Abdin's favor.

Most of the government, bank and insurance company people there managed to escape, first to the Geziret island, then to the west bank of the Nile. Nevertheless, by evening all of Cairo on the East Bank of the Nile was in the hands of the Mullahs and their mob. The Egyptian National radio station was also in their hands and, from it, their leader made his broadcast. Claiming to be a representative of the pious Egyptian people who had risen up against the idolaters and blasphemers who had subverted the country, he begged all good Islamic countries to send the Egyptian people help in their effort to bring their country back to the true faith. As it happened, he was an Iranian who had arrived in Egypt for the first time three days before, but surrounded by the burning city and the screams of the massacre, that seemed an unimportant detail.

The Oval Office, The White House, Washington

"Dean, what the hell are we going to do about this? Perhaps State can give me an straight answer. All I've had from the Attorney General is a lecture on human rights and the infamy of the Egyptian government and the Secretary of Defense keeps telling me if we'd done things his way, this would never have happened. The National Security Advisor keeps telling me 'on the one hand this, on the other hand that' and outlining options. Will somebody give me a straight damned answer to a simple question?"

"Mister President, in defense of the National Security Advisor, we pay The Business to study problems and outline the available options and their probable consequences. Then we, as the Cabinet, select the options we think are best. The Business doesn't set policy sir. We do that.

"In this case, our options are pretty limited. The Egyptian Government is collapsing and has lost control of most of the country. An hour ago we received word that the Sudanese Government has applied to join the Caliphate. Already, Sudanese "volunteers" are crossing the border in large numbers to assist their "brothers" in Egypt. We anticipate Somalia will follow very soon.

"If we're going to intervene, we are going to have to do so in force and do so very quickly or there won't be anybody to intervene on behalf of. I understand we have a Marine brigade in the Eastern Mediterranean that we could land in Egypt but that's hardly enough to make any difference. If this was a regular war, we could flatten the entire Caliphate in hours but that isn't the case. To straighten Egypt out at this point, we'd need a massive and infinite-duration deployment and we just don't have the troops. To get the troops, we'd have to gut our strategic offensive and defensive forces and that would harm our position all over the world.

"Anyway its really questionable if we could do it. It's that industrial thing again, sir, we were out of power for twenty years and we're only now getting a handle on what the situation really is. The machine tool shortage is the problem and its hitting us all over. We came into office with plans and priorities and everywhere we've gone we've found that damned industrial bottleneck is strangling us.

"It is the opinion of the Department of State that, despite Secretary McNorman's assertions, we lack the capability to intervene in this situation. What we're seeing from Egypt, Mister President, is a done deal. Its the culmination of a long process. Most devastating of all from out point of view, the existing Egyptian Government had lost its assumption of authority. Sir, when you go out, your driver stays on the right hand side of the road and stops when the lights are red. He never thinks about it. That's a government's assumption of authority. People obey because it is the Government. The Egyptian Government has lost that. So if we send troops to restore the situation, we're supporting a lame duck, a lost cause.

"At the same time Mister President, we can't just leave this. We've made that mistake once already and its haunting us to this day. Back in 1951, a guy called Mohammed Mossadegh seized power from the then-ruler, some glorified warlord who called himself The Shah, and got himself elected as Prime Minister. By 1953, he virtually controlled the country, he was quite popular by the way, and was taking the country off down his own path. Now, back then there was a CIA plan to remove him from power but President Patton had a virulent dislike of covert operations of that type and he vetoed the whole thing. Mossadegh stayed in power, the Shah left for exile and that was that.

"The problem was anticipatable to anybody who's studied history. Mossadegh had started a revolution but he wasn't radical enough for the radicals, wasn't religious enough for the religious, wasn't corrupt enough for the corrupt and wasn't conservative enough for the conservatives. He ended up just like the Shah before him, representative of a small clique who told him what he wanted to hear. The problem was that he didn't actually represent any major strand in Iranian opinion. He was an average, you know, he appealed to just enough people to just the extent necessary to gain superficial popularity.

"In Iran back then, there were two threads of belief that people subscribed to. One was the glory of Persian history and tradition, that was represented by the Shah, and the other was religion, represented by Khomeini and his cohorts. When Mossadegh deposed the Shah and forced him into exile, he sacrificed the respect and reverence that conservative parts of society had accorded to the Shah. That eliminated any chance of him getting any real support from anybody in that faction no matter what he did. Mossadegh lacked support from the traditionalists, thus the religious elements could gain power almost unopposed. That was how the Caliphate came into the world.

"I think the Mossadegh lesson is quite clear Mister President. This situation cannot be allowed to stand but, also, we have to be extremely careful what we commit ourselves to. Mister President, in a sense we rule the world, we can destroy any enemy we wish and those enemies can do nothing to save themselves. Our power, lies on that perception and we cannot do anything to endanger it. In a very real sense, our power relies on an aura of invincibility which is credible because it has never been discredited. And, it's never been discredited because we've been careful never to get into a position where it can be discredited. When we do something, we do it via proxies. Usually, the Russians or the Triple Alliance. At the moment, we're not involved in the problems of Egypt and there is no immediately obvious reason why we should get involved. Sending our own troops into Egypt would be a disaster, I thank God we haven't got the forces needed to do that so the option isn't open to us.

"Also, Sir, Egypt isn't the problem. Its a symptom of a much larger problem. the Caliphate is growing fast but its growing because its picking off the low-hanging fruit. If we look at what they've actually achieved, they've simply consolidated what was more or less in their power anyway. Every time they've tried to move outside that area, they've been hammered. Turkey, the Southern Russian provinces, attempts to extend Caliphate influence there were total failures.

"By the way Mister President, its interesting to note the Caliphate calls its current expansion "The Third Great Jihad". Jihad means Holy War. The First Great Jihad was the original Arab expansion after Islam was founded, the Second was the Turkish outthrust. This is the Third. The question arises, what is going to happen when there is no more low-hanging fruit?"

"Dean. You've told me what we can't do. Now tell me what we can."

"Mister President. We have to learn. We have to watch the Caliphate and understand how it works. The Russians described the Caliphate as an organization that hangs together because its individual members hate the rest of the world a little more than they hate each other. A very good description that implies there are more internal divisions in the Caliphate than are apparent at this time. The obvious one is the religious divide between the Sunni and Shi'ite sects but there are others as well. Those divisions are something we can play upon in the future.

"So, the Caliphate has weaknesses that we can exploit, it has limitations we can pursue. Soon, it'll be hitting the natural boundaries of its growth and we have to make sure that it is contained when it reaches those boundaries. Some, we don't have to worry about, others we do. We helped the Triple Alliance a little when it suited us, now we must help countries that are in the front line against the Caliphate. That means mostly southern Europe and Sub-Saharan Africa. For example, with Somalia dropping into the Caliphate's orbit, that means Kenya is in the front line.

"The North African littoral is a write-off. The Italian and French hold there is tenuous at best and a good sneeze will boot them out. The French won't listen, but the Italians will. Tell Mussolini to cut their losses and arrange to get out with as much dignity and as little fuss as possible. We'll make good any losses they suffer. Since Libya and the rest will fall into Caliphate hands anyway, its better it happens quietly and causes as little damage as possible.

"That's another good reason why we shouldn't have troops in Egypt by the way. There'll come a time to do something about Egypt but it isn't yet. We should be concentrating on getting ahead of the curve and anticipating what the Caliphate will do. If we charge into Egypt now, we'll be getting behind the curve, seen as reacting to others, not dictating to them. That'll be more damaging to our worldwide position than anything else I can imagine.

"One other thing, Mister President. The Caliphate has an eastern edge as well as a western one. Its expanding, or attempting to expand, into territory held by the Triple Alliance as well as the Middle East. That's another situation we're going to have to watch, but there, we have a much better hand to play. The odds are the Triple Alliance can hurt the Caliphate a lot worse out there than we can at this time.

"We're facing a worldwide war Mister President, the first since The Big One ended World War Two. The one thing we must avoid is becoming so focused on one particular part of that war that we neglect the others. May I counsel you Sir, as emphatically as I can, to meet with the Triple Alliance as soon as possible. Especially the Ambassador-Plenipotentiary from Thailand, I am advised that her understanding of insurgency problems and irregular warfare is unmatched."

LBJ nodded thoughtfully. "The Attorney General has described the Ambassador as an international assassin who should be brought to trial before an international court. He's even swallowed the old Chipanese conspiracy theory that she assassinated Gandhi. The problem with Ramsey is that he has a little mind, the only way he can cope with people who's achievements exceed his own is to denigrate them at every opportunity. I want to meet with the Ambassador but not here in Washington. A Presidential visit to the Triple Alliance perhaps? A summit conference on world affairs would do nicely. Dean, find an auspicious event in Thai history for late this year or early next, preferably the hundredth anniversary of something or other, and set up a Summit Conference, held in Bangkok to honor that event."

"Very good Mister President. I'll set the wheels in motion."

The President leaned back in his seat as Dean Rusk left the Oval Office. A summit conference would be a good way of discussing the problem The Caliphate posed worldwide. Before it took place, they'd have to arrange a series of agreements, trade, representation, cultural exchanges and so on, to be announced after the meeting. Only fools left the results of negotiations to the negotiations themselves.

That left the problem of the Attorney General. He talked too much and couldn't accept that his statements had consequences. Consequences that were of immense use to America's enemies. Furthermore, he was trampling across the boundaries that separated the responsibilities of varying departments. His absurd posturing was interfering with the smooth running of State, Defense, the Treasury, everybody. Yet, he couldn't be booted into the outer darkness, he was a favorite of the Kennedy clan and they ran the Democrat Party.

LBJ was well aware that the Kennedy clan considered him a placeholder, keeping the Presidential seat warm for John F Kennedy's brother, Robert. They'd made it an open secret they planned to run Robert Kennedy as the Democrat candidate in the 1968 election. They didn't have much choice, with John F dead, and Edward with the death of his brother and the resulting reckless endangerment conviction hanging over him, Robert was the only real option left. The prospect of a Kennedy in the White House filled LBJ with foreboding.

Conference Suite, Hyatt-Regency Hotel, Woodley Park, Washington

Ploesti Night. The night when Strategic Aerospace Command gathered to honor its own. There would be smaller gatherings at all the SAC primary operating bases and even smaller ones where SAC units were stationed on temporary duty. This one, though, was the centerpiece. There were 50 tables in the suite, 20 people per table. The room was sorted by rank, the exalted ranks of Generals sitting at the tables on the right, the lowly Airmen sitting at those on the left. Yet, the tables, the settings and the meals were the same. Just as they were for the top table, even though, this Ploesti Night, the President himself was attending. Ploesti night had two functions, the award ceremony reminded people of what happened when things were done right. The fact it was Ploesti Night, the anniversary of the raid where every single B-29 involved had been shot down reminded people of what would happen if things went wrong.

President Johnson looked at the array of Air Force Blue in front of him. Normally, the Secretary of Defense attended Ploesti Night but McNorman's performance over the last few months had made his appearance here politically unwise. The last thing LBJ wanted was for a senior member of his administration to get hissed "off the stage" by a room full of America's heroes. The effects of the insult on McNorman's ego would be too dire to contemplate; he'd probably try to cut funding for the entire Air Force. So he'd come himself, avoiding the problem, getting some good publicity for his Presidency and honoring the men who defended it.

Even the Targeteers were here tonight, sitting quietly in the shadows. It was odd, Johnson thought, wherever they were, they always seemed to be in the shadows. He'd suggested their senior personnel ought to be on the Top Table but he'd been politely yet firmly declined. They were just the hired help, the Seer's assistant had said, the honors belonged to those who acted, not those who moved paper.

The meal had finished and the coffee and brandy had been served. Now, the main business of the evening was under way. The series of presentations, awards for a wide variety of professional achievements. The big ones came first. The LeMay Trophy for highest level of operational readiness, to the 100th Bomb Group with their B-52Hs, The Dedmon Trophy for overall bombing accuracy during Red Sun. The Angel Eyes Shield for best performance by a Strategic Recon Crew, an RB-58C called *Marisol* had won that three years running but this year they were in Italy on TDY so an RB-58D *Lady Hawk* from the 45th had taken the prize. Then a new one, the Yeager Cup, for best performance by a Strategic Fighter Group, won by the F-108s of the 357th.

Prizes for groups, prizes for individual aircraft. Prizes for performance, prizes for safety, prizes for professional achievement. As LBJ presented the award to each winner, his photographer took a picture of the event so each would have a memento of his meeting with the President. Another private grin, if McNorman tried that, they crews would be sticking pins in his picture within 24 hours. Prizes for officers, prizes for enlisted personnel. They were running through those now. Getting to the end of the awards at last. Thank God this wasn't a Hollywood style ceremony with artificial tension, faked surprise and forced theatricals. Every award winner here had been given at least 24 hours notice of their prize and they'd had time to write a thoughtful two-minute speech of thanks. It hadn't been required for the winners to have their speech approved by higher authority but the wise ones – and that was all of them – had done so.

The Master of Ceremonies took a drink of water and returned to his list. "And now, for the Association of Old Crows Shield awarded to the electronic warfare engineering cadet who has shown the highest level of professional advancement in their first year of service, I am proud to call on Airwoman Selma Hitchins."

LBJ raised his eyebrows slightly. A young black woman was walking across the open space towards the top table. The Master of Ceremonies passed him the small shield with the black crow embossed on the front and he shook the young woman's hand. "Congratulations, Airwoman Hitchins, a fine start to what I hope will be a long and distinguished career. There's always success waiting for a fine American who's prepared to work hard and do what it takes." Then he dropped his voice so the conversation was private. "Turn a little, hold the shield so the cameraman can see it clearly. That's right. I'll have some extra copies sent to you so you can send them home."

"Thank You Mister President". Hitchins stepped onto the podium, made the usual introduction and then started her speech proper. "I must admit I had an unfair advantage in winning this award. You see Crows are black too."

A roll of laughter went around the room. LBJ nodded, smart girl. She'd got rid of the race issue in the first line by making people laugh about it. Although LBJ had noted that, while southerners had laughed immediately and freely, northerners had hesitated a fraction, wondering if it was acceptable to laugh about race. Hitchins was quickly thanking her instructors, her parents and teachers and a police officer whose glowing character testimonial had eased her acceptance into the Air Force. She made a quick comment on how important electronic warfare was likely to be in the future and the impact of the new generation of computers then, after two minutes to the second, she'd finished and was on her way back to her seat, clutching her award.

LBJ watched her sit down and accept congratulations from the rest of her table. Something worried him about the episode. That girl had won an award against competition from the whole of the rest of the Air Force cadet intake. To do that she had to be very, very good, even to get nominated, let alone approved. So why should her first words have to be an effort to defuse a potential awkwardness over her color? Damn it, she shouldn't have to do that, her achievement spoke for itself. Why did she think she had to defuse an issue in order to be accepted? Then LBJ put his professional politician's smile. Another award winner, this one for excellence in first year flight medical training. Another little speech, more photographs.

By 0100 the event was over, the Air Force busses were taking the attendees back to their accommodation. LBJ saw the

Seer's assistant checking off things on a clipboard and sent one of his Secret Service Agents to bring her over.

"I would like to go to the kitchens and service areas please. Can that be arranged?" The woman smiled and nodded, her mane of dense black hair shifting in a wave.

"If you would come with me Mister President". She lead him through the serving doors at the rear of the hall, into the food preparation area. The staff there looked at their visitor and every motion in the room froze as they realized the President was with them. LBJ picked out the head chef and addressed him.

"Chef, I wanted to thank you and all your staff here for the efforts you've made on our behalf tonight. I know you all have families to go to and you have already worked longer and harder than we had any right to expect but I would like to thank you all in person. Chef, could you introduce me to your staff please?"

The Chef lead LBJ around the kitchen staff, introducing each one in turn. LBJ gave each one a quick handshake and a small White House medallion from a box carried by one of the Secret Service Agents. Less than ten minutes later, he was out and walking back down the service corridor.

"Won't you also have a family to go to.... Lillian isn't it?"

"Lillith, Mister President. No, I don't have a family as such. The Business is my family now."

"No husband or boyfriend Lillith?"

"No Mister President." Lillith looked at LBJ strangely. The man had a reputation for being course-mouthed and boorish but there had been no sign of that tonight. He'd been polite and gentlemanly then and was being so now.

"I was married once but it didn't work out." She paused for a second, somehow, for some reason she couldn't define, she wanted to confide in the President. "My husband was a control freak, everything had to be done exactly how he wanted it just so. Exactly this exactly that. Every little thing, he wanted to rule every aspect of my life. When I got pregnant I realized I couldn't bring children up in that sort of environment so I ran away."

LBJ looked at her and got hit by a feeling of ancient sorrow so deep that it seemed to have physical force. "He sent three of his thug friends after me. To bring me back. To 'persuade' me to return to him. Their means of 'persuasion' was hurting me." Then the feeling of sorrow was briefly, just for a split second, replaced by rage and for that brief LBJ got weird sensation that her eyes had turned red. It was just imagination of course, and a trick of light reflection from the red emergency exit signs. Before it could register properly, it was gone and her voice went back to normal. "When hurting me didn't work and I still refused to go back, they killed my children."

LBJ's mind reeled under the simple statement. What sort of man could punish his wife by killing their children? In fact, he had an uneasy feeling he may have heard the story somewhere. Perhaps in an old newspaper.

"Lillith, it sounds hopelessly inadequate to say this but I am dreadfully sorry. As an American I am appalled such things could happen in my country, and as a Texan I want to lynch the people responsible. As President, I can do something about this. I will instruct Director Hoover to give this matter his personal attention so that those who did this to you can be punished."

Lillith smiled. "Mister President that was a long time ago and very far from here. Far from America. But I am very grateful for your concern. Thank you Mister President."

Presidential Limousine, Du Pont Circle, Washington DC.

Sitting in the back of his limousine as it swept through the night on the way back to the White House, Lyndon Baines Johnson was a profoundly troubled man. What had started as a minor engagement intended to spare his administration a relatively trivial embarrassment had ended up by worrying him deeply. Two woman had managed it, that black airwoman and Lillith. They'd opened his eyes to something of which he hadn't been unaware, but also had never realized the full implications and meaning of before.

It was just plain flat out wrong that a skilled and intelligent woman who'd beaten out everybody else in her class should have to worry about the color of her skin. To almost apologize for it when making an acceptance speech for an honor she'd won fair and square. It shouldn't happen, not in America, this was the country where people were supposed to be judged on what they achieved not who their families were or the position some ancestor had held.

On top of that, the horror story Lillith had told him still filled him with rage. He didn't believe, not for one moment, that her ex-husband was outside America. If he had been, he would have been under a mushroom cloud by now. LBJ was sure about it. The words "they killed my children" still echoed in his mind and made rage boil up inside him again. Anyway, he was sure he had read that story somewhere. It disgusted him to think that a husband in America could even think of doing such a thing. In the rational part of his mind, he knew it wasn't unique or even unusual. In fact, he had a terrible suspicion that if he asked for statistics on such events, he would find more than he cared to know about. That didn't change the situation though. In a great society like America, such things shouldn't happen.

A Great Society. Now there was a name to play with. Other people should have their eyes opened, just as his had been opened. It was impossible to legislate how people thought, but one could use the law to set examples and provide guidelines. To make people think twice about casual prejudice or accepting obscene brutality. One couldn't do that of course without changing some of the environment people lived in as well. That's what was needed, an effort to build a great society, to build a place where the meaning of man's life matched the marvels of man's labor.

That would have to be the basis of a new program for Congress, to create a society where people could be free to develop their talents as far as they could go. A program to give aid to education so that people could compete on equal terms, to attack disease and the decaying heart of the big cities as part of an effort to prevent of crime and delinquency. One that would beautify the countryside, and conserve the monuments from the past. Most of all, to develop the depressed regions of the country as part of a wide-scale fight against poverty. Damn it, there were millions of elderly people who couldn't get needed medical attention, that would have to be corrected through an amendment to the Social Security Act.

It was a lot of legislation to be pushed through. Somebody would have to see it through, to watch over its progress and ease it through the inevitable dogfights. Ramsey Chalk, thought the President, that would be an ideal solution. It's the sort of thing that the pretentious charlatan would relish. And, pushing through a legislative program that big would take up all of his time. He wouldn't have the energy left to interfere with international politics. That would be a very good thing.

Chalk's forays onto the international scene were a constant embarrassment and were getting worse by the week. This insane idea he'd had for the United Nations had just been the start, his latest fad was for an international criminal court where war crimes could be tried. Ramsey being Ramsey of course, the first people in the dock would be Americans. But, it wouldn't happen. LBJ was firmly determined on that. If he gave Ramsey the job of shepherding The Great Society through, then that would keep his mind off such stupidities.

Unfortunately, Ramsey would try and do the job all too well. He'd spend the entire country's GNP and then some. And still want more. So he'd have to have a check and a balance. LBJ nodded to himself. The Targeteers. They'd be given a study contract to validate and cost out Ramsey Chalk's proposals and produce a working plan to execute them within a strict budget limit. LBJ had no illusions about welfare plans, left to their own devices, they grew like a cancer. So there would have to be boundaries and limits firmly established.

Of course, that brought another issue to mind. Of the Departments of the US Government, the Department of State, the Department of Defense, the National Security Council and the Directorate of Central Intelligence were all run under contract by The Targeteers. The Democrat Party had come to power quietly determined to change all that. Some wanted to do so because they honestly felt it was wrong for major parts of the US Government to be in the hands of private companies. Others resented the loss of patronage and the power to award plum, well-paid government jobs to favored cronies.

LBJ himself had entered the Presidency determined to return to the old ways of doing things. Now, he'd changed his mind. Compared with the other parts of the US Government, the parts run by The Targeteers were models of smooth efficiency. The reason, of course, was simple, if they didn't run smoothly people got fired until they did. The Business, as the Targeteers called themselves, recruited and trained their staff and provided the Department as a functioning package. The Executive appointed the Secretaries to head the Department. Three of the four were working smoothly and the Secretaries in charge had been converts to the system. Only Robert and the Department of Defense were in constant conflict.

LBJ sighed. He knew what the problem was. Over in State, the Secretary of State, Dean Rusk had established perfect co-operation with The Business people running his Department. He told them what his policy was, where he wanted his Department to go and together, they'd explored all the consequences of the new policies. Then, once Dean had made the decisions, The Business had followed through and made sure they were carried out. Smoothly and efficiently.

In contrast, McNorman had treated his staff the same he treated everybody – like dirt. He'd given abrupt, preemptory orders without considering the consequences of what he was doing. The Business people running the DoD had worked hard to limit the damage his attitude was causing, but they couldn't intercept all of it. LBJ thought grimly that McNorman would have to go. The problem was he was a favorite of the Kennedy family and they still ran the Democrat Party.

And that was yet another problem. When planning for a Democrat-run Government, it had been assumed that American industry dominated the world the same way American military power did. In the run-up to 1960, and then in 1964, they'd imagined American businessmen going around the world, doing what they wished, where they wished, in the same way SACs bombers flew where they wanted. Only it wasn't that way at all. While not precisely in crisis, American industry was facing problems all of its own. The Democrat economic planners had made a certain series of economic assumptions and based their tax and development plans on those. Unfortunately, those basic assumptions had been wrong.

The basic problem was simple and had literally stared everybody in the face, only none of them had seen it. They'd looked at a map of Europe with the big black smoking hole where Germany used to be and not realized that the same big, black, smoking hole was where most of the world's precision machine tools had been made. Before the Second World War, German industry had been the world's major source for top end high precision machine tools. The total destruction of German industry had left a gaping hole in that market, one that was proving very hard to fill.

There were some bright spots, Swedish machine tools were almost as good as German and the Germans themselves had re-equipped Polish and Czech factories to make the tooling. That hadn't been altruistic of course, the German plan had been all final assembly was done in Germany. Nevertheless, Poland and Czechoslovakia were becoming suppliers of good-quality machine tools. The catch was that they just didn't have the production capacity to make up for the incinerated German factories. So, the supply of high-quality, advanced machine tools was a sellers market with high prices and long delivery times.

This had some curious effects. One of them was that a whole industry had grown up, modernizing, reconditioning and rebuilding pre-war German machine tools. Another was that the machine tool issue had a direct bearing on how SAC operated. One of the reasons why SAC's bombers were so aggressively deployed and so prominent in international affairs was to give the impression that they represented an industry that was at the cutting edge of technology and free of the constraints that were crippling other industries. That wasn't true, the United States was as badly affected by the machine tool shortage as everybody else.

McNorman wouldn't accept it but that was yet another reason why his demands to shift from bombers to missiles wasn't possible – missiles required much more precise machining than aircraft and the tooling to do it in the numbers required just wasn't there. The same applied to tanks; it was all very well to demand the construction of huge numbers of tanks but how were the turret rings to be made?

It wasn't just the military sector that reflected the machine tool bottleneck. American cars were derided because of their big, lazy and inefficient engines. The Europeans with their smaller and more economical engines were held up as being the way of the future. The catch was that those small, efficient engines required much more high-grade machining than the bigger American motors. If Detroit went to European-style designs, they'd have to re-equip with the scarce advanced machine tools and that would impact directly on the rest of US industry competing for the same equipment.

It was a worldwide problem. American sources inside the new Triple Alliance aviation program had revealed that both the Arrow and TSR-2 programs were dropping behind schedule due to the shortage of high-end machine tools. Apparently, there were only four slide-way grinders (essential for making big machine tools) in Australia and the biggest grinder in the Southern Hemisphere was a 1930s German import. The Russians were being hit as well, even though they'd captured some equipment when they'd re-occupied the western parts of the country. The shortage of machine tooling was crippling their recovery from the Second World War and Treasury estimates were that it would be the end of the century before that problem was overcome.

It was also a simple problem, German machine tools were undoubtedly the best but they weren't around any more. The easy answer that 'America would take up the slack' just wouldn't cut it. The American industrial genius was in production methods and machines, not the basic tools of engineering. Engineers would take a rebuilt 1930s German tool over a new-built Polish, Czech or Swedish machine any day and they'd take any of those three over an American one equivalent. The world may run on love, or so the kids said, but it spun on bearings and bearings were in short supply. A study done by The Business had suggested that The Big One's destruction of German industry had set the world back at least a decade in the key areas, and that was cascading through the whole industrial production system.

LBJ sighed. Running America had seemed so simple when the Democrats had been in political exile. They hadn't had a clue what the real problems were or how intractable they could be. Perhaps this was the lesson that they'd forgotten, that some problems don't have solutions, all you can do is work around them and find other routes to where one wanted to go. Yet everything linked into everything else, change on thing and it echoed through the systems and turned up in the most unexpected of places.

He caught himself in the car's driving mirror, he could see that the strain of the job was already aging him. The Presidency was a killer, Both President Dewey and President LeMay had been aged beyond their years by the strain of the job and it had, quite literally, killed President Patton. As his car swept through the White House gates, LBJ reflected that at least his "Great Society" plan wouldn't impact on the problems caused by the machine tool bottleneck. He'd thought the Presidency would deal with the great issues of the day and initiate sweeping changes in the Great Scheme of Things. He'd been right too, only he hadn't known that the great issue of day was the supply of machine tools and The Great Scheme of Things ran on bearings.

Aviano Italian Air Force Base, Italy

Eddie Korrina struck an exaggerated pose. "Mister Ford, Major Kozlowski is ready for his close-up now."

"You want to get banged out somewhere over Libya?" Kozlowski growled. "Nobody would miss you. Just have to report you as having become existentially divergent and that's that."

Ever since he'd become involved in the film industry, his leg was being pulled mercilessly. It wasn't fair, really it wasn't. He's spent his first evening with Sophia Loren and her husband answering questions about SAC and Operation Jungle Hammer, the Myitkyina operation. Then, after some diplomatic strings had been pulled behind the scenes, he'd been seconded for a week as a technical advisor to the film "Mission to Myitkyina." Then, he'd found out something that people who'd never been on a film set would find hard to believe. The first day had been fascinating, the second routine, the third and subsequent mind-crackingly boring.

The upside was he'd become firm friends with Carlo Ponti and his family.

Kozlowski had earned his keep as technical advisor though. The first thing he'd been shown was the set that was used for filming scenes in a B-58. The prop makers had done an excellent job, the nose had been built so it split in three sections so the pilot's cockpit, the Bear's Den and the Electronics Pit could be filmed from varying angles but somebody had done them a bad turn. The pictures they'd been given to work from were the wrong aircraft, a Navy PB5Y, not a SAC RB-58. It had circular dial instruments, not the tape gauges that SAC had adopted and the radar screens in Eddie's Bear's Den were completely wrong, just the single screen for the ASQ-42. He'd got them some pictures of Marisol's instrument panels and the set had been changed overnight. They'd also missed the bulge under the nose for the ASQ-42 surface attack radar; the PB5Y carried that in the nose where the RB-58 carried its ASG-18. Still, at least they hadn't painted it dark blue.

He'd also been amused to discover the misconceptions that Italians had about how Americans. It had taken some time to persuade Sophia that American wives didn't spend all day wearing cocktail dresses and swilling martinis. American daytime television had a lot to answer for. Also, that bringing children up, getting them to school and doing all the other things parents did were the same the world over, even when one of the parents did fly a nuclear-armed bomber. He'd also had to give the actor playing the RB-58 pilot, an American called Eastwood who worked in Italy, a quick few lessons in how SAC officers behaved on and off duty. Well, how SAC would like the public to believe its officers behaved on and off duty anyway.

Still, his time in the wonderful world of cinema was over at last and he was back to doing what he was supposed to. Flying.

"Right guys, we're back in the real world at last. Mission orders. The television news showed you Egypt has fallen apart, the Sudan and Somalia have joined the Caliphate and all is most certainly not well with the world. There are refugees streaming out of Egypt, by air as well as by sea and over the land frontier. Our hosts are doing their best to collect them and give them some form of refuge. I guess a refugee camp is better than what's going on over there now. The problem is, they can't find them all so they've asked us for help.

"We're to fly recon missions over the area, land and sea, find the refugees trying to escape and steer Italian rescue teams in to get them. In case you think this is a milk run, let me tell you something. The Caliphate people are trying to find the refugees as well, and when they find them, they kill them. So we've got to find them first and its up to us to protect them until they can be picked up. We're pretty confident that if we get in the way of the Caliphate, they won't take too kindly to our appearance on the scene. Mind you, they don't take too kindly to us when we are off the scene.

"We'll be carrying four GAR-12 Sparrows and four GAR-8 Sidewinders for self defense. Plus eight GAR-9s, four air-to-air and four for anti-surface work. We probably won't need them, our run is over the sea this time, looking for small craft and anything else that can carry people trying to escape. But *Spider Woman* is doing the run along the Egyptian border and *Tiger Lily* will be running along the Egyptian coast towards Palestine, trying to map out any military movements along there. the Caliphate may well try something with them. If they do, then we'll come to their support. So this whole business could get very ugly, very quickly. In the future, we'll be overflying the territory the Caliphate is in process of seizing, partly to find out what is going on, partly to show that we can. That is also likely to get ugly.

"We also have a secondary mission. Some refugees are flying out in Egyptian aircraft and the Italians are staging an airlift of their own from an airbase on the coast. They've got a lot of the gendarmerie and police people plus their families out that way, how long before they have to shut down, that's anybody's guess. Until they do, if the Caliphate threatens those aircraft, we have orders to remove that threat.

"One more thing people. The Italian military are the butt of a lot of jokes, especially after what the Brits did to them back in 1940. They don't have many people and, compared with the kit we operate, their equipment is crap. But, they are good people who are trying hard to do the right thing here. Let's not let them down, right?"

Kaohsiung, Taiwan, Chipan?

Kawachi had almost made it. Almost, but not quite, Even with Indian help, the pumps had lost the battle to hold the flooding perimeter about an hour out from the port. Admiral Soriva's last action had been to take her out of the shipping lane and into the reefs where he'd beached her. In honesty, even that was a bit of an overstatement, it was an open question whether he'd beached her or whether she'd sunk far enough to hit a reef. Still, she'd settled with her main deck above water.

Soriva thought that if he was a German he'd claim she was only damaged. What was that old joke he'd heard years before? "If a German captain yells 'scuttle her' before his ship sinks, the Germans claim a strategic victory. If he yells 'scuttle her' after she's sunk and he's swimming, they claim an operational victory. If one of his descendants yells 'scuttle her' at any time he's in the same ocean as the wreck, the Germans claim a tactical victory." Soriva reflected that, since he'd never given a scuttle order, he'd lost.

But in a real-world sense, he'd won. *Kawachi* had arrived with her nuclear-tipped missiles still on board and already they'd been stripped off the wreck and moved to batteries along the coast facing mainland China. With a range of over 500 kilometers, they were a healthy deterrent against an invasion. Naval engineers were going over the wreck of *Kawachi* while he watched, trying to determine if she could be refloated and repaired, if not, what else could be stripped from her wreck and salvaged for future use.

The question was, what would the new regime in Tokyo do? They had the power to wipe Taiwan as thoroughly from the map as the Americans had obliterated Germany. If they chose that path there was little that anybody in Taiwan could do to stop them. They could make Tokyo pay for it, that was certain, but they couldn't stop it. What was stopping Tsuji and his fellow conspirators from obliterating Taiwan was political, not military.

100

They'd seized power on the basis that the Reformers had deviated from the path of glorious destiny and turned their back on the possibility of further extending Imperial power. The reaction of the military to those claims had been mixed. A few hadn't accepted it at all and they were now trickling into Taiwan. A few, of course, had accepted the whole line. The balance, they were waiting on events, to see and hear what would happen, to judge the new regime on its deeds not its words.

So the new regime was committed to expansion and to the conquest of new territories. It would be a mortal blow to its credibility and to its moral authority if its first act was the nuclear incineration of one of its own provinces. In fact, the rebellion of that province was, on its own, bad enough. Almost any action taken in reprisal would make it worse. If nothing was done, if the situation was placed on the "to do' list, a problem to be addressed when the time was right, then it could be downplayed and presented as one of those local difficulties, a thing of no great import. Masterful inactivity was the most tempting, indeed almost inevitable, course of action. And, the longer action was delayed, the harder doing anything about it would become.

The great trick now was to avoid goading Tsuji and his conspirators into doing anything. There had been one row about that already, a group of hot-heads had tried to demand that Taiwan declare its independence and establish itself as a new country, standing on its own feet. They didn't seem to understand that if Taiwan stood on its own feet, it would be cut off at the knees. They had to remain, nominally at least, part of the Imperial Japanese Empire. That way, as a rebellious province, Tokyo would have to step carefully and find a way to a solution. In fact, under those circumstances, Tokyo may find the current status of Taiwan useful. If malcontents and dissenters found refuge on the Island, they wouldn't be causing trouble elsewhere in the Empire. However, declare independence and all that would be gone, Tokyo would be forced to do something.

From Tokyo's perspective, they wouldn't have too many options. Even now, an amphibious operation across the Formosa Strait would be a hazardous undertaking and every week that passed made it more so. There were enough military units here to put up a stout defense and they also were growing stronger as the local Taiwanese joined up. That was a well-kept secret, one the Chinese definitely did not like mentioned. They habitually claimed that Taiwan was Chinese and it wasn't.

Taiwan had originally been settled by the Dutch and Spanish and the local population were their descendants and those of the workers they had brought from elsewhere in the Pacific. Plus a few pirates of course. It had been almost a hundred years before the Chinese had invaded and occupied the islands and started to bring their own people over. Even then, the Chinese had never been more than a minority on the Island. When the Japanese had taken over in 1895, their administrators had been startled to find that, outside the small ruling elite, the islanders didn't even speak Chinese.

No, Soriva thought. Keep the situation cool, keep it quiet, keep everything low key. Don't draw too much attention to the problem. If a delicate balance could be struck, if the political cards were played properly, then Taiwan could get away with its rebellion for a good number of years. Perhaps enough to end up with Taiwan taking over the Empire.

Officer's Quarters, USS Austin LPD-4, Eastern Mediterranean

"Commander Thomas Sir. One of the Marines, Gunnery Sergeant Esteban Tomas, wishes to speak with you."

"Very good. Send him in."

The SEAL team had arrived on board the *Austin* a few hours before. Their specialized insertion craft were now housed in the well-deck aft and the SEALs themselves were settling into their quarters. It hadn't taken a genius to work out what was going on here. Egypt was collapsing and falling into the hands of the Caliphate, there were streams of refugees trying to get out before the borders slammed shut. Some of those people would have intelligence and insight invaluable to the United States. The SEALs were the acknowledged experts in getting into heavily-guarded places, finding people and escorting them safely out again without anybody interfering. Or, to be more precise, without anybody who attempted to interfere living to tell the tale. Thomas guessed his men would be finding the senior people in the refugees, government, military, whoever, and bringing them out.

He guessed why the Gunnery Sergeant wanted to speak with him. Probably wanted to transfer from the Marines to the SEALs. That couldn't be done, the SEALs recruited from the Navy and the Marines had their own covert operations group, Fleet Recon Force or FRF. Their job was a bit different from the SEALs; FRF had to get into heavily guarded places as well but once in, their job was to stay there, watch what was happening and report back. Good question which was harder, getting out with civilians in tow or staying put and reporting back.

"Sir, Commander Thomas Sir."

The Marine was standing in front of his desk, rigidly to attention. "Gunnery Sergeant Tomas?". Thomas frowned slightly, the man looked vaguely familiar. But then, most Marines did. The Corps did that to people.

"Sir, thank you for seeing me Sir."

"No problem Gunny. At ease. However, you do realize that we do not allow transfers from the Marines to the SEALs. If you want to get into our line of work, I can put you in touch with the Fleet Recon recruiter."

"Sir, I realize that Sir. But I saw your name on the arrivals list this morning and I wanted to thank you Sir. For this Sir." Tomas put a dog-eared and aged business card on Thomas's desk. One side had a cartoon of a seal balancing a ball on its nose, the other a laconic "He's OK" and the signature of a Lieutenant Commander Jeff Thomas. "You remember Sir, ten years ago. You and your people were rescuing a young American girl who'd fallen into," Tomas grinned "bad company down in Mexico. Sir, You gave me that card and suggested I see the US consul."

Suddenly it snapped into focus. Thomas had been assigned to rescue a young American girl, Ellen Case, who'd run off from a holiday tour and got in over her head. It had been a ridiculously easy job, just a matter of finding where her bus had been ambushed, following the trail and then extracting her. The highlight hadn't been the rescue itself, it had been throwing a fat, lazy, corrupt police chief out of a window. That, Thomas regarded as a treasured memory.

However, he remembered the leader of the bandits who'd attacked the bus. He had the brains to understand that hurting the American girl was a death sentence so he kept her safe. More, at the end, hopelessly outgunned and surrounded, he'd still managed to behave with dignity. Thomas had thought the man had potential and hinted he might like to try the Marines. Obviously he had taken the hint.

"Good God yes. I remember now. Sit down Gunny please. Gunny, you've changed a lot since then. You take the oath?"

"Sure did Sir. Did my five, got sworn in as a citizen in the morning, re-upped in the afternoon. Now doing life so to speak. You know Sir, shooting up that bus was the smartest thing I ever did.."

Thomas agreed but couldn't say so. "Can I offer you some ginger ale Gunny?" American warships were dry but "ginger ale" was a winked-upon subterfuge for special occasions. And this was certainly that. The two men clinked glasses.

"You know Sir, I've learned a lot since then Don't think you could sneak up that close to my boys now. Not in daylight anyhow."

"Want to try some day, Gunny?" Thomas's face was positively wolfish. His SEALs had left a trail of Marine units wondering what had hit them and learning from the experience. "Be a good exercise for us both. You set up and defend a target and we'll infiltrate. Sort of training exercise we do all the time. We're going to be here for a while, until this Egyptian thing cools down and possibly longer than that. Give me a couple of days to get my people settled in and I'll speak to the command and arrange for a schedule."

"Sir, You're on Sir. But do you know whatever happened to that girl you rescued? She was cute."

"Still is Gunny. We took her back to the States and returned her to her parents. Who were mightily displeased with her behavior and even more pleased to get her back alive. A bit later, she moved to Tennessee for a while then to Virginia where she got a job with Newport News. That's where we bumped into each other again, I was with the Teams at Little Creek. One thing lead to another and she's Mrs. Thomas now."

"Sir, congratulations Sir. You got kids?"

"One at school, one on the way. How about you Gunny? Hooked yet?"

"You bet Sir and I got you beat. Wife at home, three kids in school. Met my lady when I was training in California. Been back down south a couple of times as well. Try to catch the kids there before they go bad. You know Sir, the people down there still talk about that Police Chief you threw through his window."

The 'ginger ale' glasses clinked again. "Gunny, when this mess is over, come down to Little Creek and I'll show you round the training facilities we have. Maybe there's some stuff that might help your people out. You got the new rifles yet?"

"The 'fourteens? Sure Sir. We dumped the old Garands before this cruise. Guys are taking time to get used to it though. Hard job to persuade them the twenty seven - fifty nine can do the job when they're used to firing the old thirty oh six."

"You think you got a problem Gunny? Somebody tried to convince us to switch over to a point-twenty-two for God's sake. Had the company bringing the rifle around. Looked good but a twenty-two varmint cartridge? And the rifle was made of plastic would you believe? Rattled like crazy.

"For now, we've still got the old greaseguns. We're looking for a new point forty five submachine gun. Trouble is its got to take a silencer and that's a pain. Means the bullets got to be subsonic so we're stuck with the old point forty five." Thomas got his wolfish look again. "After all, we don't want everybody to know where we are."

Major Kozlowski viewed the piece of fish on his plate with the gravest suspicion. Aviano was filling up quickly and becoming a regular SAC base. What had started as a week-long courtesy visit had stretched to a month and then turned into a full-scale temporary deployment. The rest of 1/305th had arrived so there were now 24 RB-58s on the base and a full group of F-108 Rapiers, the 357th, was filtering in.

That was the bad news. After all, when there had been four SAC aircraft and their crews here, they'd eaten at the Italian officer's mess where the food was beyond exquisite and the wine was better. Those happy days were gone for now, with almost 100 aircraft on the base, they had their own mess and their own cooks. The American cooks had realized they were up against serious opposition from their Italian rivals almost immediately and they'd organized a series of "American Regional Specialty" days. Today was Friday, the specialty was Cajun and, therefore, with impeccable logic, the evening meal was blackened fish. It looked, well, suspicious somehow.

"Hey Frenchy, you're Cajun, what did your momma call this when you were growing up?"

Pierre "Frenchy" Thibodeaux poked the blackened fish despondently. "A mistake?" he offered a bit hesitantly. There was no actual guarantee the fish was either dead or a fish and he didn't want it coming back to life on him. He thought carefully and decided not to chance it. The cramped Bear's Den of an RB-58 wasn't the place to come down with salmonella. Opposite him, Kozlowski had come to the same decision. Anyway, in his case, he was joining Carlo and Sophia tomorrow for a day in their country home and they'd feed him properly. "Mike, what happened today? Anything you can pass on."

RB-58C "Marisol" Eastern Mediterranean, 6 hours earlier

It was amazing, from up here the Eastern Mediterranean really did look the way it was supposed to. The coastline was shaped the way the maps showed and the sea was the right color. In the Bear's Den, the radar picture was showing much the same thing except it had paints the eye couldn't see. One of them, a big one, was to the west of them. The USS *Shiloh* and her battle group. Others were much, much smaller. The two nearest were *Farfalla* and *Minerva*, 700 ton Italian coastguard ships.

They were patrolling the waters, looking for refugees fleeing from Egypt ahead of the Caliphate takeover. Technically, *Marisol* and her crew were just idling around on a training exercise, in reality, they were helping the Italians by vectoring them in on the refugees, the Boat People as the press was calling them. They were also covering the Italians against attack. The Caliphate was grimly determined to kill as many of the refugees as they could and they'd do the same to anybody who got in their way.

They could do it too. The Caliphate naval crews were operating a new naval weapon in these waters. Small patrol craft, fast attack craft the naval people called them, armed with a pair of heavy anti-ship missiles. They lurked in port and only came out when they wanted to kill something. A week or so earlier, there had been a small tug, crowded with refugees, trying to cross the Mediterranean from Egypt to Greece. One of the Caliphate's FACs had attacked and hit it with one of its anti-ship missiles. The big missile had been designed to take down destroyers and it had made short work of the tug. There hadn't been any survivors and the wreckage looked like matchwood. The Caliphate had answered diplomatic protests by stating that anybody who tried to leave the Caliphate without permission was an apostate and apostasy was punishable by death.

So *Marisol* was providing cover for the Italian ship and also protecting any refugees in the area. They were on the radarscope as well but faint flecks, so small and indistinct that they were hardly visible. Still, it was possible and it was a job worth doing. In the Bear's Den, Eddie Korrina suddenly looked down at the scope. The situation had suddenly become complicated.

"Boss, we've got problems. I think there's some refugees down there, must be a raft or something, it barely shows. Whatever it is, *Minerva* must have it as well, she's picking up speed and moving to investigate. The bad news is, there's some bogies out there also. Two at least. They're on a collision course also and they're hauling ass. My guess is hostile FACs."

"Roger that Eddie. Xav, keep a watch on emissions. I'm going to order up some squid." Kozlowski changed channels on the radio. "*Shiloh* this is *Marisol* we have a problem developing here. Italian corvette picking up refugees possibly threatened by unidentified surface craft. Need some back-up here guys."

"Launching ready flight. Two Leatherneck Phantoms coming your way. They'll orbit out of sight. Communication is Romeo-Quebec. Verification as per book. Good luck *Marisol*

Kozlowski started a gentle descent. Speed and altitude were life but in this situation he could drop to 30,000 without too much risk and it would give Eddie and Xav much better coverage. Below them, the Italian corvette closed on the contact, an extemporized raft built of oil drums and timber with at least a dozen people on it. How they'd sailed it as far as they had was anybody's guess. Off to the east, the two Caliphate FAC were closing on them.

"Vampires, vampires!" It was Xav in the Electronic's Pit. "Enemy fire control radars, identification Square Tie. That confirms it, Mike, Djinn-class FAC-M. They must be warming up to fire. Designating them now as Bandit-One and Bandit-Two. They're reaching for us too, but their Pot Head radars don't stand a chance. I'm jamming them anyway."

"Eddie, shift to air mode, paint those targets. Get a pair of the Sparrows on line. If those Djinns fire, I want the missiles hit as soon as they leave the tube. Get ready to do anti-radar shots as well." Kozlowski flipped channels. "Romeo-Quebec this is *Marisol* twenty eight."

"*Marisol* this is Romeo-Quebec. Twelve. We're closing fast on you. We have contacts to the east and ESM detection from that bearing. Are we hot to trot?"

Kozlowski checked the book. 28 plus 12 was forty. OK. Everybody was who they said they were. "Hold please Romeo-

Quebec. We just have threatening radar emissions at this time. They tried to lock on us though and that is a terminal mistake."

He wasn't joking. It was one of SAC's guiding principles, threaten a SAC aircraft and it would eliminate the threat, If that meant taking out the country the threat came from, so be it. The result was predictable, nobody sane threatened SAC aircraft.

"Boss, they've fired. One vampire airborne, targeted on Minerva" Korrina had already fired off a pair of Sparrow IIIs, they was streaking down towards the anti-ship missile heading for the corvette. From the pilot's seat, Kozlowski saw the gray-white trails heading down towards the black streak of the anti-ship missile. One explosion was a white ball on the sea surface, a miss. The other turned the black streak into an orange fireball. "OK Eddie confirm that, one Vampire down. We have missile fire Romeo Quebec. They're all yours."

Cockpit F4H-3 Phantom II "Tisiphone"

Colonel Scott Brim firewalled the throttles and the dark blue Phantom leapt across the water. Ahead he could see the black and orange fireball where the anti-ship missile had been shot down. There was a certain poetic justice about it he thought, an attempted act of murder being struck down by a bolt from above. The two hostile Djinns would be just behind that blast. The catch was he had to get in fast while the crews were still working out what had happened and getting another missile warmed up. If he timed it right, that missile would never get out of the tube. The Square Tie tracking radar only had a very limited arc, the bows on the Djinn had to be pointing almost directly at the target. If he could force them to turn they couldn't fire. Of course if he was really lucky, they'd open fire on him.

He could see them now, two glorified speedboats with the big, clumsy missile hangars perched on the stern. Behind him, the concussion wave from his passage was throwing up a wall of spray, there was no doubt that they'd seen him. Please, please let them open fire on me. Brim was actually praying.

As if in answer he saw a line of red blobs floating out from the bow of the lead Djinn, quickly followed by a second stream from the craft behind. The Djinn only carried a single gun mount, a triple 25 millimeter forward. 'Thank you God,' Brim thought, then poured in the reheat and swept *Tisiphone* up in a steep climbing turn. Obediently, the two streams of tracer followed him, just lagging behind that little bit.

Before the gunners could correct, *Alecto* was making her run. The gunfire drawn away, she could make this pass good and solid. Suddenly she seemed to erupt in flame, brilliant orange fire spreading along her wings and under her belly. Then, she also was making a climbing turn, leaving the massive salvo of unguided rockets to do its work.

The two Phantoms had the same load, 38-round packs of 2.75 inch rockets. Three packs under the belly, three on each inner wing station, two on each outer. A total of 494 rockets. The analysts had worked out that at a given range, there was only a limited area that a FAC could occupy in the time the rockets took to get to their target. So, the packs were designed to fill that area with rockets. In effect, *Alecto* had fired a giant shotgun at the lead Djinn. It really wasn't fair.

Brim watched as the sea erupted in a boiling elliptical mass of white, green and orange-brown as the salvo swamped Bandit-One. Even as he did a wingover and curved down, it was subsiding and beneath it, there was .... nothing. Just a few oil stains and fragments of shattered debris. To the east, Djinn-Two had turned and was running for the coast. Brim let her go, the primary job was to protect the Italian corvette and the refugees. There was no guarantee a second pair of Djinns were not out there, already lining up for an attack. Anyway, *Marisol* was overhead and she could make Bandit-2 vanish in a very emphatic manner.

Alecto formed up again on *Tisiphone's* wing and Brim lead them back over the Italian corvette. She was stopped now, alongside some crazy looking contraption crowded with people. As the two Marine Phantoms swept over, Brim thought the raft looked like the things he and his childhood friends had put together on summer afternoons by the lake. Those people down there hadn't taken the contraption out to splash around in a local lake, they'd sailed it hundreds of miles across the open sea. What in the name of God could be happening that drove people to take such desperate risks?

The Italian corvette crew had nets over the side of their ship and were going into the water to pick up the refugees. Brim wished them well and took *Tisiphone* up to where she could watch over them

Aviano Italian Air Force Base, Italy

"And that was more or less it. We stayed up top watching over the situation until *Tiger Lily* relieved us and we came back. Advice? Make sure you have support ready and waiting, when the situation blows, it blows fast. *Shiloh* has birds waiting on the catapults to go, take advantage of them.

"I'm not so sure it was a good idea for us to come down, it improved radar coverage in terms of what we could pick up but it shrank our horizon and put us into an area where we could be intercepted.

"The Djinns are pretty much helpless against us, they have that triple 25 forward but its only useful against things that fly low, slow and close. I'd guess they have those shoulder-fired missiles as well but intel says they don't work against anything more than 8,000 feet up.

"The Caliphate people can't be dumb enough to keep sending them out unscreened though, after they've lost a few, they'll start trying to act smart. Fighter cover will be the first thing they try. I don't think the Caliphate has any real warships otherwise they might try operating FACs with proper ships.

"One other thing Pete. Buy those Italian Navy crewmen a drink when you get a chance. What they're doing takes real big brass ones. Its not just that they're out there with those poor old corvettes but we watched them go into the water to help the refugees. You've heard of the human bombs the Caliphate loves so much. How long d'ya think its going to be before they start putting them in 'refugee boats?' And how much of a mess they'll make of the rescue ships?"

"Dean, what's just happened in the Mediterranean? And why?"

"Mister President. One of our aircraft was flying a routine mission over the Eastern Mediterranean when it observed an Italian corvette rescuing a group of Egyptian refugees. They saw two Caliphate warships fire a missile at the Italian rescue ship so they shot down that missile and called in assistance from the *Shiloh*. Two Marine F4Hs arrived, did a run to see what was going on and one of the Caliphate warships opened fire on them. The F4Hs returned fire, sinking one of the Caliphate ships and forcing the other to disengage. The Italian corvette completed its rescue work safely and returned to port. That's our story Mister President and we're sticking to it."

"Now what really happened?"

"We are providing air cover for the Italians doing their humanitarian rescue work. The Caliphate are killing every refugee they can get into their gun-sights. They blew a tug out of the water just a week ago. Usually just the presence of our aircraft is enough to keep things cool but this time it escalated. The public story is pretty much correct if you exclude the fact that we were covering the Italians.

"Anyway, we've had a diplomatic protest from the Caliphate. The warship sunk was a Djinn class fast attack aircraft, crew of nineteen. The Marines really did a number on her, no survivors. The Caliphate are accusing the crews of murder and demanding we hand them over for trial and execution. As your Foreign Secretary Mister President I recommend we tell them to go and initiate a maternally incestuous relationship."

"Ramsey, what is the legal position here?"

"Mister President, in my opinion the pilots in question are guilty of a war crime in that they sank a warship in international waters. I rule that we are obliged to comply with the Caliphate request and extradite them to Caliphate custody for trial. I understand a Strategic Air Command aircraft was also involved and was probably carrying nuclear weapons. That also is a war crime."

"Mister President, I must object in the strongest possible terms....."

"Please, Dean. I will answer this. Ramsey. You misunderstand a fundamental part of our relationship. You do not make rulings. You, along with the other members of my Cabinet, advise me. Then I issue rulings based on my decisions that may, or may not, include your recommendations as I see fit. It is clear to me that our aircraft were acting in self defense and to protect a neutral ship engaging in humanitarian rescue work. We will not just hand over our people in the manner you suggest. Is that clear Attorney-General?"

"Mister President, America has been acting in this high-handed and arrogant manner for far too long. It is time that we made clear to the world that we accept limits to our power. We must accept that we are answerable to the world community for our actions. We must make amends for the crimes that......."

"IS THAT CLEAR ATTORNEY GENERAL?" President Johnson's voice slashed across the Cabinet Room. Ramsey Chalk settled down in his seat, a small, sulky, reluctant nod conveying his acceptance. LBJ stared at him until he was happy that Chalk wasn't going to push the matter further.

"Ramsey, the reason why I wish you to drop this trivial matter is that I have something much more important that requires your full attention. This incident with the Caliphate is an unimportant matter, the sort of minor flare-up that will be forgotten in a week or a month. State and Defense can handle this incident. I need you to undertake a legislative program that will change the face of America in ways that will last for centuries."

LBJ started to explain his Great Society program, stressing the depth and extent of the changes that had to be made and the fundamental alterations in the financial and legal structures required. He stressed the importance of the legal issues involved, the complexity of which meant that the head of the Great Society effort would have to be Attorney General. By the end of his presentation, Chalk was leaning forward in his seat, his eyes shining in anticipation.

"Of course Ramsey, a program of this scale and magnitude requires a very high level of managerial expertise. Your own time will be fully consumed in supervising the program and coordinating between the varying departments. For this reason, we've approached the consultants who already run several Government departments under the direction of the appropriate Secretaries to provide you with a professional administrative staff. The contract has been accepted by them and they are recruiting the personnel while we speak."

"Mister President I don't see the need for such arrangements."

"I agree with Ramsey Mister President. These people from 'The Business' are greatly over-rated. Why in my department I have discovered enormous waste and duplication. For example, there are two aircraft, the Air Force F-110 and the Navy F4H that are almost identical in performance and characteristics. If we had ordered the same aircraft for both services, we could have saved vast sums. I have found another such example. The Air Force B-58 and the Navy PB5Y are also nearly identical, again a joint program would have saved the country much unnecessary expenditure." McNorman sat back in his seat, directing a smug smile at the National Security Advisor. The smile faded as Orville Freeman, the Secretary of Agriculture, burst out laughing.

"Robert, the F-110 and the F4H are the same aircraft, just different designations. Same for the B-58 and the PB5Y. Same aircraft, just the sort of joint program you're talking about."

"Secretary McNorman." The Seer leaned forward. "We've found using different designations for the same aircraft used by the Navy and the Air Force is useful because the different services have varying requirements. But, the missile system designations are confusing and we are introducing a joint services system for them. Attorney General, we've found an ideal candidate for your new executive assistant. Lillith, will you bring her in please?"

Lillith ushered in a woman with hair as gloriously red as Lillith's was midnight black. For a moment LBJ was envious until he saw her eyes. He'd been expecting the magnificent mane of hair to be matched with emerald green eyes, flashing with fire. Instead, they had the flat muddy green of pond slime and so lacked expression as to seem lifeless.

"Mister Attorney-General" Lillith said "I would like you to meet your new executive assistant, Naamah."

Rosario, Surigao del Sur Province, Mindanao, Philippines

Evening Mass was over and the traditional entertainment was starting. The Cathedral was in the town center where it belonged, looking out over the grassy square with its statue of Rizal. Families were already sitting down there, enjoying the coolness of the evening and exchanging family news with their neighbors. Not all of them though, the younger girls, the unmarried ones had already started their evening promenade through the town then up the hill that dominated it. It was a dirt track road, but a good, wide and well-used one. There were rumors that the road was to be resurfaced, given black-top in place of laterite. The rumors might even be true this time, there was a lot of construction work going on in the area around Rosario.

The hill top was an example. It had always been the local government area, Rosario was the local capital after all, but the buildings had been few and poorly-equipped. In the last year that had changed. The government had built a new administrative block up there. Nothing elaborate, that was certain, but functional and, above all, new. There was a sports stadium up there as well and the high school children could play basketball on a proper court now. There was another new building up here as well, and that had brought the citizens of Rosario great pride for they could now boast of having their own University.

Yes, the new construction and all the new buildings were a good excuse for people to make the walk up the hill to see what was going on. That was only an excuse though, the Sunday evening promenade had been going on long before the construction had started. It would even affect some of that new construction for down the middle of the road were a series of crude benches. If rebuilding the road removed those benches, there would be civil war.

Traditionally, by the time the young women had reached the top of the hill and started down, the young men would be starting up. And that was the whole point of the exercise, as the groups of young men and women passed, glances would be exchanged. Sometimes a boy's interest in one of the girls would be met with giggles or ignored but sometimes the girl would return the glance with one of her own. Then two sets of parents would notice and, if they approved, there would be a quiet meeting between them during the week. Then, the next week, the kids would exchange glances and leave their groups to sit on a bench together, decently separated of course, and carefully chaperoned, to talk and get to know each other. And the older women watching would smile knowingly and start to anticipate Rosario's next wedding.

What nobody in the evening walk had noticed was a subtle change in the buildings. The boys were interested in the girls and the girls were interested in the boys and their parents were making sure that everything that took place did so in ways that placed nobody's reputation in danger. Quite understandably, none of them thought to count the antennas on the roof of the government building. For, every week there would be one or two more added to the growing array.

Ortega farm, Rosario, Surigao del Sur

A few miles away from Rosario, in the hills that overlooked the town, Graciella Ortega was gathering vegetables from the farm. It was one of three her family owned, this one was for growing vegetables, some for sale and the rest for her family. There was a second farm down by the shore, that one grew pineapples and coconuts and other fruit. Finally, there was the main one, inland where it was sheltered from the storms that blew in. There the family bred water buffalo and chickens and other livestock. The Ortega family wasn't rich but they ate well.

The vegetable farm was Graciella's favorite, it was a two hour walk to get there, no mean trip for a woman who was already over sixty years old, but it had a wonderful view overlooking the town and its small harbor. Out to sea she could see the small islands that punctuated the coral reef, some were inhabited by a few families, others were not and the only visitors were fishermen sheltering from a storm. One was so infested by poisonous snakes, nobody dared go there. Still they were all beautiful, dark green ringed by white surf against the deep blue sea.

While she worked on the farm, weeding the field and gathering the food she needed, she could look at the view and it would make her feel good. Normally there were two people who worked the vegetable farm, looked after it and made sure that nobody took any of the produce. They weren't there though, perhaps, Graciella thought, they'd gone down to the town for Mass or to meet friends. No matter. She continued to collect her basket of vegetables, her daughter's fiancee was coming for dinner and this was an important event, deserving of a special effort.

She never heard the men come behind her, the first hint she had of their existence was when a cloth was flipped over her eyes and she was dragged backwards. A knee ground into the small of her back but the pull on the cloth continued so her body was bent backwards like a bow. She could feel the aging bones and disks in her spine screaming against the brutal treatment. Terror at the sudden attack combined with outrage and filled her with anger at the ill-treatment.

"Ortega your children work abroad, your daughter is married to a foreigner. They send you much money. You will give it to us. You will give us fifty thousand pesos each month or we will kill you understand?"

"It's not true." Graciella was trying to keep control of her voice but she could hear it shaking and was ashamed of her fear. "Two of my sons work abroad it is so but they have families of their own to support. I only have on daughter who is married and her husband is a sergeant in the army. It is we who send money to her for the army does not pay enough to support them."

"You lie." The voice was furious and loaded with spite. "We know the truth do not try to deceive us."

"It is true, we are not a rich family. We do not have the money you ask."

"Then we have no use for you." Graciella felt a blinding pain in her stomach as a knife slashed across it. She felt herself falling down, her eyes still covered, then another, duller, pain as a boot crunched into her ribs.

Road from Morales to Rosario

Angel Hernandez was a very happy man. An Australian construction crew was building a bridge across the river between Morales and Rosario and their engineers were working hard during the week. It was a wide river, not deep, but enough to make building a bridge a major project. Once the bridge was finished, the road could be black-topped all the way. At the moment, the trip between the two towns was a major enterprise that lasted all day; when the bridge and road were finished, it would be an hour's drive at most.

That wasn't why he was happy though. He had heard that the Australians were well-paid so he'd picked out five of his best girls and taken them down in his truck to the Australian work camp. He guessed, after a week of hard work, they would be ready for a party. He'd been right, the girls had worked hard all evening and all the stories were true. The Australians were indeed paid well and seemed to have no idea of the exchange rate, something the girls all knew to four decimal places.

They'd earned more money in an evening than they normally would in a month and, even after they'd given half to Hernandez, they still had enough to see their families lived well. And, Hernandez thought, half was fair. He was the one who looked after them protected them when a customer got rough or tried to refuse to pay for their services. He was the one who thought up things like taking the girls to the Australians and spent his evening driving them over and then back to their homes. Half was fair.

"Jesus save us!" For a moment Hernandez had thought there was a dog at the side of the road, half-seen in his headlights, then he realized it was a person, crawling by the roadside. He

118

swerved the truck to a halt and ran back to see what was happening. His Best Girl, the most senior of the women who worked for him and the one who represented their interests and dealt with their problems, had been riding in the cab with him. She had seen the person as well and was at his heels. The other four women were in the back of the truck, it took them a little longer to get down.

It was an old lady, crawling along the roadside, leaving a trickle of blood in the dust behind her. Hernandez knelt beside her, she seemed hardly aware of his presence at first, then whimpered slightly. And tried to turn away from them as if to hide.

"Its all right mother. We're here to help you. We'll look after you now." Hernandez turned to his Best Girl. "Do you know who she is?"

The girl shook her head. She had her arms around the old lady and lifted her slightly. The movement exposed the savage knife wound across the woman's stomach and the bruising to her ribs. Whoever she was, she'd taken her dress off and wadded the material into the knife slash. It had slowed the blood loss and allowed her to get this far but she didn't have much longer. Hernandez didn't make a decision, in his eyes there was none to be made.

"You four, lift her gently get her into the back of the truck. Do what you can for her. We'll take her to the hospital in Rosario. You hold on, mother, you'll be in the hospital soon."

Saint Iago Hospital, Rosario

"She is a very lucky lady Senor Hernandez. If you and your who....... girls........ hadn't come along, she would have died. Another few minutes at most. The knife wound in her stomach is deep but she was lucky there also, it did not penetrate the stomach wall. And the kicking did not fracture her ribs, at her age fractured bones would have been as dangerous as the knife."

The doctor was furious at whoever had done this to an old woman and was trying hard to keep his voice impersonal and matter-of-fact. He wasn't managing it very well.

"Who is she Doctor?"

The town priest, Father Faulcon, answered. He'd come the moment he had heard one of his flock had been hurt and was in critical condition.

"She is Graciella Ortega, Mister Hernandez. We have sent somebody to tell her family, they live in the south of the town. They will be here soon. But what can they do?" The Priest's distress was obvious. Hernandez looked confused.

"What the Father means is that the lady has very serious injuries that will require much care and attention. She has lost much blood that we will have to replace by transfusion. Her wound is deep and will require careful treatment if it is to heal properly. Also, it is certainly badly infected and will require some expensive medication. The family are not poor but this amount of treatment is far beyond their resources. And without it, well, its not good."

Hernandez looked at the doctor and thought it through. Ah well, perhaps his successful evening had been part of a greater plan, and anyway, there was always next week. He dug into his pocket for his share of the money his girls had earned that evening and gave it to the Doctor. "Will that cover the treatment necessary?"

The Doctor took the money and raised his eyebrows. It wouldn't but it was a very substantial part of it. Across the room Hernandez's girls had been trying to make themselves inconspicuous. It was a hard job, their heavy makeup and alluring clothes had made their profession obvious and they'd been the subject of quite a few hostile looks. Hernandez's Best Girl had spoken to them quietly and they'd been digging in their bags.

Now she came over with another roll of money, smaller than Hernandez's gift, the girls had to live after all, but enough to make up the difference. "Father, can you make up a story about this money. I do not think the family will accept it from people like us, even for their mother."

Father Faulcon mentally agreed. The family would throw the money down the drain rather than accept help from the town pimp and five of his whores. But, Graciella needed the medical treatment the money would buy and the offer was sincere no matter who it came from. There was also a parable about a good Samaritan to keep in mind.

"Mister Hernandez, I believe the Knights of Columbus have established a fund to help provide treatment for those who have been the victims of vicious crimes like this. Or, they have, just this moment established such a fund, and I intend to see that they will support it generously. Mister Hernandez, ladies, the Ortega family will not know what you did tonight but remember God knows and God does not forget such things."

Magasay Palace, Manila, Philippines

"The question is, just how closely is Abu Sayaaf linked to the Caliphate? Is it linked at all? Or is it a rival?" Prime Minister Joe Frye leaned back in his seat. With increasing numbers of Australian troops arriving in Mindanao, he needed to understand exactly what he was committing his troops to. And for how long.

"Prime Minister, the answer to all your questions is 'Perhaps'." Frye grimaced and The Ambassador smiled sympathetically. "That isn't very helpful I know so let me explain further. Abu Sayaaf is just the local branch of a larger organization, Jamyaat Islamiyah. This is a fundamentalist organization that shares much in common with the Caliphate. Both look back to the days, centuries ago, when Islam dominated the area and its warriors swept all before them. The Caliphate seeks to revive the great days of an Islamic empire based on Baghdad, Jamyaat Islamiyah also seeks to revive those days but the state they wish to resuscitate is the Empire based on Malacca. That one was destroyed by Dutch traders and the troops of the Siamese Empire.

"So Prime Minister, in the short term, both the Caliphate and Jamyaat Islamiyah have the same aim and the same enemies. Their aim is to rebuild the ancient power they once held and to attack those who stand in their way. Even in the medium term, their aims, their methods and their objectives are the same. But in the long term, they are opposed. The Caliphate sees its Fundamentalist Islamic State being primarily a Middle Eastern one, owing its final allegiance to Baghdad, Jamyaat Islamiyah sees its state as a South Eastern Asian one, owing its final allegiance to Djakarta.

"There is one fundamental difference between the Caliphate and Jamyaat Islamiyah. The Caliphate is rich, it has oil revenues that bankroll its every move. Jamyaat Islamiyah does not. It is poor, it has few resources of its own and even the ones it can access are erratic and difficult to manage. Because, in the short and medium term, the Caliphate and Jamyaat Islamiyah share so much, the Caliphate is financing their operations. That won't last, in the end the two groups will come into conflict, exactly when depends on how successful they both are. The more their success, the sooner war between them will occur.

"For that reason, Jamyaat Islamiyah has to establish its own financial independence. Without access to resources or to legal trading, they have resorted to criminal actions. They are behind the outbreak of piracy that has taken place in these waters, they are behind kidnapping and robberies here and in Malaya, they are behind bank fraud back home and in Singapore. In Mindanao itself we are seeing the start of a widespread and deeply rooted extortion racket, preying on families who have members working or living abroad. These criminal enterprises are Jamyaat Islamiyah's future. Without them, they have no long term prospects."

Sir Martyn Sharpe leaned forward. His left arm was aching unbearably and he had cramp in his back again. It as time to retire, more than time. If he could just see this crisis out, he could do so. Sadly, he thought, he'd said that about the previous crisis and the one before that. "Madam Ambassador" the formality felt strange talking to somebody who had become a firm friend over the years but he didn't feel comfortable with any other form of address.

"If I understand you correctly, what we are treating as a single conflict is, in reality, two linked but quite distinct wars. The conflict we face along our north west frontier is ideologically and religiously linked to that we face in South East Asia but, defeating one of these threats will not implicitly mean the defeat of the other. We have to address both if we are to achieve long-term success."

"That is perfectly correct Sir Martyn. We cannot afford to ignore or neglect either situation. The recent takeover of Egypt by the Caliphate has focused attention on their part of this conflict but we cannot allow it to absorb all our attention. If I may make a medical analogy, we have a patient suffering from appendicitis and cancer. We must treat the appendicitis now or the patient will die, but if we ignore the cancer the effort spent of treating the appendicitis will be wasted.

"It is my recommendation that we give priority to securing and containing the situation along the north west frontier. That is largely a military matter, we can push and push hard there. We have superiority in technology if not numbers and that runs for us. Here in the Philippines and at sea, we strike at the criminal enterprises of Jamyaat Islamiyah and cut them off from their source of non-Caliphate funding. Prime Minister Frye, I urge the Australian troops now arriving in Mindanao to treat the Jamyaat Islamiyah terrorists as gangs of criminal bandits and hunt them down accordingly.

"We have made a bad mistake in Mindanao and one for which I am responsible. We have treated the conflict down there as an insurgency and applied our counter-insurgency strategies to it. We failed to see they were inappropriate to what was happening and continued with those inappropriate strategies too long. We sought to win over those who could not be won over and attempted to conciliate the irreconcilable.

"Instead, we should hunt down and kill the bandits. Muslim commandments dictate that an observant Muslim must support other Muslims who are in conflict with unbelievers, even if the Muslim is in the wrong. That means we cannot separate the local population from the terrorists; their religious requirements make such policies futile. We have to eliminate the terrorist groups so that the requirement to support them is no longer of any consequence. The religious demand is to *support* fellow-Muslims. This can have a variety of meanings, ranging from joining in their efforts to simply not aiding their enemies. The more effectively we can eliminate the terrorist groups, the more likely it is that we can persuade people to adopt the least hostile of the possible interpretations. Of course, representing them as bandits and criminals who prey on everybody regardless of religion will not be a bad thing.

Joe Frye nodded. "So I can tell my commanders to let the troops off the leash then. Permanent hunting season, no bag limit. They'll like that. The boys in the jungle down there have seen some pretty bad things and they're aching for a chance to do something about it."

The Ambassador gave a feral grin. "Indeed so. Our troops will hold the Christian towns and villages and teach them to defend themselves. Yours can start chasing the bad guys. And, Sir Martyn, we must all help you push hard against the terrorists operating across your borders."

The feral grin grew more savage. "We've been pushed far enough. Its time for a Crusade."

CHAPTER FIVE
MELEE

Motor Fishing Vessel "Karma", South China Sea

The *Karma* appeared no different from hundreds, perhaps thousands, of Motor Fishing Vessels, the MFVs that plied the rich fishing ground of the South China Sea. The reefs and atolls were a fertile breeding area for enough different types of fish to keep an astounding large number of people alive and the most discerning gourmets satisfied.

Karma had a black hull, a large white eye painted each side so the ship could see her way and a green superstructure aft. The bows reared high, the seas might be rich but they could also be treacherous. To make money fishing meant getting the catch home and that meant weathering storms. In the old days, *Karma* would have been a sailing ship and her hull design still had that legacy but she was a modern ship powered by a diesel. *Karma* was indeed almost identical to the MFVs, only she wasn't one of them. She and her crew were pirates.

It had started over a year before, when *Karma* was still a relatively honest fisherman. It had been a bad cruise, the fish hadn't been running and her hold was empty. Her captain had seen another fishing boat, on her way home, heavy in the water with a rich catch. Nobody could remember how they'd decided to do it but they'd boarded the other ship, thrown the crew over the side and watched them drown. Then they'd trans-shipped the cargo and opened the sea-cocks on their victim. She'd gone down quickly, just another casualty of the sea. They'd got a good price for the cargo as well, and it was a lot less work to take another ship's cargo than catch their own. Soon, the *Karma's* crew had almost forgotten how to fish.

Then, they'd been contacted by somebody who represented somebody else who then represented somebody else even further away. It was suggested that a mutually beneficial arrangement could be made. It suited somebody back along the chain to support the piracy and that support could make the career of a pirate much more profitable. They'd talked and the deal had been struck. The others gave the *Karma* guns to fight with and ammunition and a cheap navigation radar to spot their prey. In exchange, the *Karma* gave half her take to the people. Sometimes, they kept their victim afloat when the others wanted a ship and for that extra risk the rewards were generous. But, more than money, the *Karma's* crew was now fighting for Islam as well and if they died, they would get the rewards of a holy warrior.

The radar had been showing a contact for some hours, probably not a fishing boat, its course and behavior was wrong. Very small though, perhaps a small craft in transit with a cargo between coastal villages. There was another possibility, one that made Captain Ismail lick his lips. It could be a pleasure yacht loaded with luxury goods. Even if they killed the occupants and sank the ship, the pickings would be good. There was another, thing that made the small contact an even more enticing prey, if it was a pleasure yacht, there could be women on board.

There she was. Small and white, almost certainly a yacht. He focused his binoculars on the craft. Prominent bridge forward, open area on top. Raked goalpost mast with a small radar on top at the rear of the bridge, still well forward. Chrome railings at the bow, catching and reflecting the sun. Long open area aft of the bridge with high sides and what appeared to be a seat aft and another set of chrome rails. There was a very faint trace of smoke, bluish, from that area. It was probably a barbecue and the occupants of the yacht were cooking a meal.

A luxury sports fishing vessel then, perhaps from Sydney or Melbourne or Darwin. And ripe for the plucking. Then a movement back on the bows caught his eye. Yes! There was a woman stretched out on the bows, sunbathing. That proved it, even without the blonde hair that had caught his eye. Asian women didn't sunbathe, to have a suntan was the mark of the lower class, somebody who had to work in the hot sun instead of paying others to do it. They had to be Australian, ripe for the plucking indeed. Ismail signaled his helmsman to push the throttles on *Karma* forward, it was time to close in for the kill.

"Come on baby, come to momma." Captain Vichai was watching the MFV pick up speed and close on him. His patrol craft had a lot better radar than she appeared to have and he'd been watching the MFV shadow them for some hours now. At first she'd looked like an honest MFV, but an honest MFV went with the fish, not with surface radar contacts. "Come on baby, Momma's waiting." Vichai had trained at the US Coast Guard Academy and he thought in American as often as Thai these days. Helped when working with Australians of course.

The MFV was less than a hundred meters away when she swung broadside to the pleasure craft. There was a crackle of rifle fire and a series of splashes in the water ahead of the yacht. The MFV wasn't so very much bigger than the yacht, in fact the two craft were probably about the same length, but the rifle fire had been designed to give the intimidation power *Karma* lacked in size. Vichai glanced forward, up on the bows, Lillee had rolled off her couch and was now huddled behind the armor plate for protection. "GO" he yelled. On the gun-deck aft, his chief kicked a retaining latch and the sides of the yacht flew open. Flew was the right word, they were spring-loaded and it would take four strong men to return them to the "conceal" position.

What they revealed was a pirate's worst nightmare, a 35 millimeter BOER. Made by Bharat Ordnance under license from the Swiss Oerlikon company. It was a single mount, self-contained and powered by a diesel generator. The yacht, or to use her proper name PCQ-83, had been specially reinforced to carry the gun and now she justified the investment. In theory, the BOER hurled 900 rounds a minute, in reality her 112 round magazines limited that to a much lower sustained figure.

It didn't matter because the effect of the seven-second burst on *Karma* was catastrophic. The magazine was loaded with alternating rounds, one high explosive, the next armor-piercing incendiary and they tore the ship's heart out. The gunner had started on the engine room, the armor-piercing shells ripping into the machinery and shattering the cylinder block of the big diesel. The explosive shells tore apart the fuel feed system spraying raw diesel into the air. Diesel doesn't burn easily, but sprayed in a fine mist into the air and then lashed with incendiary ammunition, it catches fire well enough. Within a second the engine room was an inferno.

The deadly burst marched forward along *Karma's* waterline, ripping it open in a frenzy of explosion, fire and fragmentation. The deafening roar of the BOER cannon stunned everybody but the crew of PCQ-83 had this down to well-honed routine. Up on the bows, Lillee, her blonde wig now discarded on the deck was kneeling behind the armor plate while aiming an RPG at the blazing pirate ship. The rocket seemed silent as it streaked across the sea surface, but its explosion ripped at the bow, tearing a huge hole in the wooden structure. *Karma* was already listing hard, her whole portside in flames and her shattered bow rearing at the sky like a dying shark. Her crew were trying to abandon ship but they had to do so in the face of fire from two machine guns mounted on PCQ-83's bridge. They didn't make it. The converging streams of bullets cut them down on the deck, tossing their bodies around like rag dolls.

By the time the ready-use magazine on the BOER was empty, it was all over. If anybody had been timing, it was less than ten seconds from the time the pirate ship had opened fire. Now she was sinking fast and PCQ-83 closed in on the wreck, taking pictures of her death. After the crashing roar of the BOER, the silence was almost uncanny, the sailors could hear the water lapping at the hull of PCQ-83 and the crackling as *Karma's* wooden hull burned. Then, Captain Vichai saw movement in the water. There was a survivor swimming in the oil-filled waste that was staining PCQ-83's pristine white hull. "Hey Khun Lillee. We have a survivor, would you like to do the honors?" The girl waved and trotted aft, pulling a T-shirt over her swimsuit as she went.

In the water, Ismail saw the figure leaning over the side and throwing him a rope. He was still stunned by the suddenness and enormity of the disaster. One second he had been looking forward to an evening of looting and rape, then all hell had broken loose and he had been blown into the sea by a deafening, overwhelming blast of gunfire. His beautiful *Karma* was a blazing wreck, already slipping below the sea. He had just enough presence of mind to catch the rope and felt himself being pulled towards the patrol ship. A girl reached down, stretching out her hand to him. He reached out but, instead of pulling him on board, she slapped a handcuff around his wrist. The other end was attached to a 10-kilogram lump of pig-iron.

"Pirate. You think you are a holy warrior? Well, if a holy warrior is killed by a woman, he goes to hell for all eternity. Enjoy eternity, pirate." The girl blew him a kiss then pushed the lump of iron over the side. As it dragged the pirate to the bottom of the sea, Captain Ismail wished he'd had the sense to listen to his mother. She'd always told him to stay away from infidel women.

Hindustan Aviation Gnat F.2, Vishnu-1, 10,000 feet over the North West Frontier, India

The Gnat was a pilot's aeroplane. Unlike the monster American fighters that hurtled around the sky so wrapped in speed and electronics that the pilot might as well be driving a train. Unlike the Alliance Aviation Arrow that was no better. The Gnat was the minimum possible airframe that could be wrapped around a pilot, an engine, and two 30 millimeter cannon. It was so small that, standing beside it, Squadron Leader Kintha could hardly believe he would fit in it. But fit he could. Just. He didn't even need steps to get in, he could swing a leg into the cockpit the same way he could swing over the door of his sports car.

For all its diminutive size, the Gnat was a formidable little aircraft. Its two fast-firing 30 mms, semi-copies of the German MG-213C designed by Mauser in Switzerland and license-built in India, gave it respectable air-to-air and air-to-surface firepower. Under its short, stubby wings, the Gnat had four hardpoints. Today, the outer ones carried fuel tanks, the inner ones a pack of six five-inch rockets on each side.

The Gnat had other advantages, not obvious ones, but important. It was rock-steady, making it a perfect gun- and rocket platform. It was agile and had a blinding roll rate, in a dogfight it could reverse its turns so fast that an enemy would be dazzled into bewilderment. In mock dogfights it had wiped the floor with the old F-80s and F-84s.

Above all it was cheap, easy to build and easy to maintain. Hindustan Aviation boasted that they could supply an entire wing of Gnats for the cost of one of the American's fabulous F-108s. It was true, too, and a lot of countries had appreciated the fact. Hindustan Aviation had an order backlog for Gnats that stretched for years and the Indian Air Force were in two minds on that. It was good that the company was making so much money on their export orders because they subsidized the Indian's own production. The bad news was that deliveries to export customers meant that the Indian Air Force was getting fewer Gnats than it would have liked.

Still, his wing had them now. Three squadrons, each with 16 Gnat F.2s. a section of four Gnat R.3s and another of the two-seat T.4 conversion trainers. It was about time too. The rules had been changed along the north west frontier and this flight was being made to announce the fact. Until now, the terrorists crossing the border had had sanctuaries in Afghanistan and Iran but no more. Under international law, the victims of cross-border raids had a right of hot pursuit and now, India was going to take advantage of it. The previous night, a patrol from Skinner's Light Horse had detected a group of terrorists crossing the border. They'd set up an ambush, caught the terrorists and bloodied them badly. Now the terrorists were retreating for what they believed was their sanctuary. It wouldn't be of course, not this time.

Early that morning, one of the Gnat R.3s had done a sweep along the border. Its cameras had picked up another ambush, one the Caliphate was laying for the SLH. They'd fire across the border and rip up the Indian unit, then retreat into the trackless wastes their side of the border. So they thought, anyway. Kintha looked down at the map marked with the enemy positions. They were just about there. This was going to take some timing.

"All Vishnu Elements. Time to go." He pulled the Gnat's nose up and did a perfect wingover, translating his forward motion into a 30 degree dive at 90 degrees to his original course. The Gnat was supersonic in a dive and its little airframe went through the sound barrier with hardly a shudder. Behind him, the remaining three Gnats of his section were following his move, turning their finger four formation into a diagonal line diving on the Caliphate position.

Discipline always had been a Caliphate problem; their troops were tribal levies and did more or less as they wished. This time, they fired on the Gnats with their rifles and machine guns. That made what the Gnats were about to do legal, although the consideration made very little difference. It also gave away the Caliphate positions and that made a very big difference.

Kintha adjusted his dive slightly and waited to the position grew to fill his sight. Then, a gentle squeeze on the firing switch and the rockets flashed out from under his wings. He started to pull back, seeing as he did, the explosions roll across the target area. He was watching for the corkscrew stream of smoke that would mark one of the shoulder-fired anti-aircraft missiles coming his way but there was none. That was good, but those missiles had taken so much of the fun out of a day's work. The days when fighter-bombers could go on a low-level rampage through the enemy defenses were going fast. As he climbed clear, Kintha saw the second section of Gnats dive on the target area, releasing napalm tanks.

"This is Pegasus-four-three hee-ah." The voice on the radio had the upper-class English nasal drawl that Indian cavalry officers affected. It was said in the Triple Alliance that the Gods, in their wisdom, had decided Englishmen were necessary and since the English weren't really English any more, Indians were taking their place. Pegasus four-three was the Skinners Light Horse unit they were supporting. "Thank you my faithful flying fiends. We'll take it from here."

"Pegasus four-three, this is Vishnu-one. We have two more sections of Gnats with rockets and napalm waiting up here and lots of 30-mike-mike. We can't stay too long but we're here if you need us."

"Thank you Vishnu-one. Hot day's work, what?"

HMAS Tobruk, entering Rosario Harbor, Surigao del Sur, Mindanao

"I see the locals have come out to welcome us."

"I think they're actually watching to see if we'll run aground Number One. Bump a pebble on the way in and they'll have a line on us and be claiming salvage you mark my words."

The heavy lift ship nudged into the tiny harbor. It was a hard approach, the channel was deep but sloped sharply either side, there would be little warning if they strayed out of the proper line. And, to make matters worse there was a 90 degree bend in the channel and a river running in from one side. The pilot bringing them in seemed to have forgotten about it and *Tobruk* was heading for the other side of the channel with dismaying speed. It seemed as if *Tobruk*, her crew and the battalion combat team on board her were steaming at six knots to catastrophe. They were already passing the mouth of the river when the pilot suddenly extended his hand and *Tobruk* wheeled neatly into the final approach. The pilot took the turn off before the Navigating Officer had expected and ordered starboard wheel. *Tobruk* was perfectly lined up on the unloading ramp with ten degrees of starboard wheel on.

The Navigating Officer let out the breath he'd been holding. The Philippine pilot grinned at him "The river current really messes things up when the tide's ebbing. Quite strong here."

Tobruk nudged up to the dock and let down her bow ramp. The harbor was quite well equipped by local standards, there was a quay they could unload cargo onto by crane and a slipway for the heavy vehicles. First ashore were the artillery, a battery of six Nulla self-propelled guns, their long barrels waving as they crested the ramp and moved into the shore. Based on the Monash tank chassis, they had a modified 3.7 inch anti-aircraft gun as their prime armament. It wasn't used as an AA weapon of course, instead it was been modified into a medium artillery piece. The Monash had been too small for a 155, a shortcoming that had

132

turned out to be serendipitous. The 3.7 fired a small shell, one short on destructive power, but it fired the shell a long, long way. The American 155 had a range of 14,000 yards, the Russians were proud of their 130 that could reach out to 24,000. But the Nulla could reach a stupendous 32,000 yards, more with supercharges. It wasn't just reach, the gun was accurate, even to such unthinkable range.

The battery positions were already prepared, pits dug, ammunition dumps in place, all the standard fittings. Rosario was a Christian town, one that had been carefully chosen as one of the starting points of the campaign. It would be a fine base for operations. The Nullas here could reach far inland, so the infantry patrols hunting the terrorists could call on fire support. As they drove deeper into the mountains and jungles of Mindanao, more firebases would be established, more Nullas would be moved up so that the whole province would be covered in an interlocking network of artillery fire. The Australian troops would drive out, their deep penetration patrols pushing forward to find, fix and destroy the terrorists.

"Mister Shane. A few words please."

"Sir?"

"Once the battalion has unloaded, I would like you to accompany me to meet the town authorities and take a trip to the hospital. There is an old lady there, a Graciella Ortega, we need to speak with. She may have information that can help us get started. Where's my interpreter?"

"Here Mister Golconda Sir." The young man almost tripped over his own feet in the hurry. The cause of the urgency was obvious, a police officer had come down to the unloading area. A very senior police officer and in the Philippines very senior police officers were not to be trifled with or kept waiting.

"Please tell this distinguished officer that I am Lieutenant Colonel Golconda, in charge of the Australian forces here. I am very pleased to meet him and look forward to working with him."

The interpreter spoke in Tagalog and the officer smiled in a confused sort of way. Seconds stretched to minutes and it was obvious nobody understood anybody. Then, a man in a business suit emerged from the onlookers and joined the group. "Perhaps I can help sir? I am Mister Acaragua, manager of the Philippine National Bank branch here."

"Thank you Mister Acaragua. I was just introducing myself but we seem to have a problem, my interpreter can't make himself understood."

The bank manager started speaking and suddenly everybody started laughing. The police officer seized Golconda's hand and pumped it vigorously. Mister Acaragua wiped his eyes. "Colonel Golconda sir, your interpreter speaks English and Tagalog, indeed he speaks both very well. But this is Mindanao and here we speak Visayan not Tagalog. Until you speak our language, you will need an English-Visayan interpreter. I have a cousin who can help perhaps."

Golconda looked at the group and chuckled. Trust the army to send the wrong interpreter. Well, it was a better start than the Burma Campaign had.

Forward Messdeck, USS Austin LPD-4, Eastern Mediterranean

Even at sea, training never ended. The younger seamen, the ones on their first deployment were green, knowing even less than they thought they did about the world they had just joined. It was the Chiefs who were giving their professional education its final polish. Of all the Chiefs, the Senior Chief was renowned as the best and most competent tutor of them all. Later in their careers, seamen discovered that their notebooks of his lectures were more detailed and complete, not to mention easier to read, than the official textbooks issued by the specialist departments.

Even officers attended his sessions, officially to supervise training, in reality to pick up insights into practical skills gained from a lifetime in the Navy and also to enjoy the anecdotes that summoned up the spirit of a battleship Navy that had died in the 1940s. It was those anecdotes that gave the new seamen a glimpse into their future and the information they needed to make a success of their lives. It was information not written down anywhere, but vital nonetheless. The correct facial expression to wear while waiting for an officer to make a difficult decision, the appropriate words of condolence for a shipmate who had lost a relative or been passed over for promotion and the deadly dangers that lay in wait for those who mixed the malt and the grape. The Senior Chief gave freely of his own experience, gained bitterly by trial and error.

"When you see a light at sea, the first thing you do is take a bearing on it. Don't worry if its *Shiloh* on a collision course or a drunken seagull. Get that bearing before you do anything else. Then you take action, inform the officer of the deck, whatever is appropriate. You there, the dopey looking one. Yes, you, not the one you hope is behind you. What do you do when you spot a light?"

"Err, take a bearing Senior Chief?"

"Right. Now for the different types of light. Navigational lights can be red, white or green. No other colors are allowed. If you see a ship showing yellow, purple or blue lights it's probably the Staten Island Ferry or some demented DEMOCRAT. Now, look at these slides, they show a whole series of examples of lights. As we run through them we can see that they are quite logical. You, over there, they are logical aren't they?"

"Yes Senior Chief."

"So you see a 150 foot vessel aground on a reef at night having just been streaming minesweeping parvanes to port and acting as plane guard for Big E with a DEMOCRAT as Captain. What will she be showing?"

"Two black balls, Senior Chief."

"You bet, two black balls, indicating a ship in distress, would be a good decision for a ship suffering the desperate misfortune of having a DEMOCRAT as her Captain. But there would hardly be much point in hoisting them at night would there? Especially since we've spent the last half hour talking about using navigation lights at night. So, double around the helicopter deck repeating slowly and reverently 'I will only have two black balls when I am out of control in daytime' until I tell you to stop.

"Now, where were we. You hoist black balls in daytime when your ship is out of control, for example, the steering gear breaks down or the Navigating Officer gets rabies."

"How about when you are refueling at sea, Senior Chief?"

"Good point, a very good example. The ship would not be under control and would be attached to the oiler by hose or line so, yes, hoisting black balls would be appropriate. Also when we've got our docking bay open, and are launching our landing craft, then we're really not responsible for our actions. We should hoist them then as well. Now, back to lights at night."

Helicopter Deck, USS Austin LPD-4, Eastern Mediterranean

Captain Pickering saw the lonely figure doubling around the helicopter deck. As the man passed the Captain, he saluted, "Sir, I will only have two black balls when I am out of control in daytime" and carried on his solitary tour. Captain Pickering turned to his Exec.

"I wonder what he did to annoy our Senior Chief?" he said pensively. The Senior Chief was giving one of the training lessons and this sailor had probably made an idiot of himself. Pickering shook his head, he knew now what he hadn't when he'd been an Ensign, that he had an irreplaceable chance to learn. It was the Senior Chief who'd taught him how to run the accounts of the Officer's Mess at a profit without being court-martialed for fraud and he was very sure that lesson wasn't written down anywhere

"I thought he was a Marine at first, Sir, they're usually the ones doubling around this deck. They certainly train hard sir."

"Yes Exec." Pickering's voice was doubtful. He was worried about the Marines, oh not the ones on this amphibious group, they were as fine a force as a man could wish for. His worries went deeper, about the whole amphibious force itself. Perhaps it was time to talk. "Our Marines train as hard as they can and they're as good as they get. What worries me is that for all the training and for all the quality, the whole doctrine we use for amphibious warfare is untested and unused. Its all theory, all put together from the book. We've never tested it out under fire.

"You know the history as well as I do. We formed the Marines and the Fleet Amphibious Force for a landing in Europe in the event The Big One failed. As it all worked out, it didn't and we never made those landings. Damn it, the only assault landings we ever made were the ones in the Azores and the Portuguese had agreed to be attacked and ordered their garrison to surrender without firing a shot before we ever put the first man ashore. If their position in Iberia hadn't been so precarious, they'd have been in on our side before that. We *bought* the Azores from Portugal for Heaven's sake.

"We've got all this doctrine, all this equipment, all these men and ships, and we really don't know if any of it works. All we've done is a few in-and-out rescue missions, a few groups of citizens rescued from assorted riots, insurrections and various other examples of civilian nausea. The SEALS have done more actual operations than our Marines and they operate on the squad level. One day, we're going to have to go into a hot beach in force and we have no real idea whether what we will do is going to work or not. That day might be a lot sooner than we think."

"Trouble Sir?"

"You heard about the Caliphate taking over in Egypt and points south. The refugees are all over the sea around here, trying to get clear. A couple of Caliphate gunboats tried to take out an Italian corvette helping them and SAC blew them out of the water. Or so the story goes. Nobody in their right mind threatens SAC so the Caliphate's going to try something else to get even. And we happen to be the closest American units to their coast."

The Ruling Council Conference Room, Jerusalem, The Caliphate.

Once, many years before, when the most junior of cadets, Model had learned to go to sleep with his eyes open and sitting erect. He wasn't quite asleep now, but he had tuned out most of what was going on around him. He'd finished the transportation of his people to Gaza, and he'd found himself in the middle of a major Caliphate base.

Gaza Harbor was the base for a whole fleet of the modern FAC-Ms, there were 18 already based there and more due to arrive. There were a pair of anti-ship missile bases with a battalion each of the long-range supersonic missiles that were arriving from Chipan. There were three anti-aircraft missile bases as well, and the missiles there were also new. So new, nobody quite understood how they worked yet. They had Chipanese experts manning them and those experts, living manuals Model called them, were training Model's troops. And right in the middle of the complex was Model's community. His troops, their families, everybody. There was better news. The Einsatzgruppen, sorry, the Guardians of the Faith, were elsewhere, working in Egypt to "cleanse" the country. That was what had made Model turn off.

In the middle of a major expansion with the deadly danger of facing the Americans looming, what was the Caliphate leadership discussing? Geostrategic imperatives? Operational requirements? Tactical lessons? Future concepts? Plans for consolidation or expansion? No. They'd spent two hours complimenting themselves on blowing up the Sphinx. As if blowing up a piece of rock a few thousand years old was any great achievement. Then they'd discussed more plans to blow up the tombs along the Valley of Kings. And then they'd talked about how to blow up the great Pyramids. Model wasn't even sure it was possible to blow them up, he honestly doubted if even the American Hellburners could do the job. Well, perhaps, if one was put inside.

That didn't make any difference to the Council of course. They'd discussed the destruction with expressions of almost orgiastic delight, with the same sort of glee that Model had seen on the faces of his men when setting off for a brothel. There was a moral there, something a psychiatrist would be able to explain. Was the sexual repression that dominated the Caliphate the root cause of their insatiable urge for destruction? Good question.

Model stirred and turned his ears on. The discussion had shifted to the recent events in the Mediterranean. There were long, gloating reports of the numbers of refugees who had been

138

intercepted at sea and killed. That was mad too, why not just let them go? They weren't wanted in the Caliphate and looking after them would drain the economic resources of whichever country took them in. But no, the Caliphate wanted them dead. As usual, the discussion made no sense at all. Each person would make grandiose claims, strike theatrical poses and issue bloodcurdling threats. Then one of them would quote something from the Koran he claimed supported his position and that settled it.

That wasn't the problem, the trouble was that they'd done the impermissible. They'd had a confrontation with the Americans. Listening to the story, it seemed that a pair of their fast attack craft had engaged an Infidel ship that was helping refugees. They'd sunk it but a vast fleet of American aircraft had arrived and attacked the FACs. The Caliphate's ships had shot the unbelievers down in their dozens of course but one of them had sunk an FAC. So revenge was needed and quickly.

Model had to work hard to stop himself laughing. If they really had shot down dozens of American aircraft, the Caliphate would be a radioactive wasteland by now. Just like Germany, Model reminded himself. The Americans did not make war upon their enemies, they destroyed them. And there was no word of any American ships being sunk, or anybody else's for that matter. No, the whole story was fiction, except for the loss of the FAC. That was true enough. Once again, Model reminded himself, believe nothing these people say. They will say and do anything rather than admit defeat or failure.

Still, the Council was now discussing how to take its revenge. Dear God, Model thought, let them keep talking until they grew tired and something else took their attention. He wanted out of this meeting, wanted to get back to his people in Gaza and get back to trying to find a way out of the trap they were in. And, please God, don't let these fools come up with a plan to attack the Americans again.

Gartokh, Eastern Tibet Border

It was time to move. By sheer chance, the Caliphate's move in Egypt had focused the world's attention on the Middle East and the "change of government" in Tibet had gone virtually

139

unnoticed. To those that had seen the news, buried at the bottom of the page or at the end of the news bulletins, it was a good thing. Another religious government, another theocracy, had been cut off short, before it too could become a threat to its neighbors. The new government had said all the right things, made all the right actions. They'd declared an end to religious rule, driven the Dalai Lama out of the country and asked the rest of the world to help them build a new, democratic freedom-loving, society. Only the first people to respond had been the Imperial Empire of Japan and China and they'd slammed the door behind them.

Colonel Hu Kai-Lee was moving his division south east, to the border with India. He was up to strength, nominally at least although his trainees had barely reached a rudimentary level of capability. But, he had a division in numbers, probably a regiment in capability.

His first job was going to be to secure the communications lines and the population centers, such as they were. At least, there wasn't going to be any resistance to worry about. The Tibetans weren't like the Vietnamese who had created a virtual living hell for the Japanese in Indo-China. There, it was impossible for a unit of less than platoon size to move without vanishing into the jungle as if it had never been. There were stories circulating that whole companies and battalions had marched into the jungle, never to be seen again. No, the Tibetans weren't the Vietnamese. More the pity.

The column of trucks stopped. The roads in Tibet were hardly world-class, this one was barely more than a stretch of cleared ground between two cliffs. They'd crossed the headwaters of the Indus a day earlier and the so-called roads had become consistently worse since then. Colonel Hu seriously considered ditching his motor transport, in terrain like this his soldiers could move faster on foot than in vehicles. The trouble was, that would leave them cut off from resupply. He lurched forward, the convoy had come to a halt again, another rockslide. Just a few boulders, he could see where thawing snow had split them away and tumbled them down.

At first he'd been suspicious of the falls but they were commonplace here. The Tibetans ignored them because their donkeys could thread around the obstruction when a truck couldn't. The first few times he'd been stopped, he'd sent out a security guard and cover details while the engineers cleared the rocks. That had succeeded only in wasting time. He'd stopped doing that two days ago, and picked up progress markedly as a result.

One of Hu's officers had already taken a work detail out to clear the rocks and had been waving his sword to urge his men on. Now Hu saw him suddenly collapse. Instinctively Hu started to count. Thousand-and-one thousand-and-two, thousand an.... The shot echoed around the cliffs, rolling like a clap of thunder. The shooter was much more than half a mile away, the shot had to be 900 meters at least. And now his officer lay dead, shot through the head. Now, they would have to go back to sending out patrols and securing an area before clearing rockfalls. An old poem Hu had read once, written by an Englishman he'd heard, echoed through his mind "ten thousand pounds of education shot down by a ten rupee jezail". It looked like the Tibetans weren't quite the ineffective sheep he'd assumed, they were going to fight after all. And that opened up all sorts of entrancing possibilities.

High in the cliffs, overlooking the road, the sniper team had already disengaged. They'd chosen their position well, there were secure, covered escape routes for both the sniper and his spotter, their gray robes blended in with the background perfectly. Even the sun was in the right place to make searching for them hard. It wasn't surprising though, they'd been fighting skirmishes along the frontier every week for the last eighty years. Even since the Chipanese army had started moving, the Chitral Scouts had been exploring this terrain, meeting up with local tribal leaders and preparing to make the lives of the Chipanese units in Tibet very unpleasant. Now, that process was starting.

South of Lhasa, Tibet

The wreckage was strewn over a wide area, the Mitsubishi Ki-46 had been under partial control at least before the pilot had lost it and crashed. The Ki-46 was an old aircraft, it had once the finest recon aircraft in the world but that time was a quarter of a century in the past. Its piston engines marked it as being a survivor of a departed era, by all rights it should be in a museum.

Yet, oddly, for the role it now fulfilled, the Ki-46 was as good as anything else available and better than most. It flew high enough to get it above rifle and machine-gun fire, it was fast enough to get to an area quickly yet slow enough to look carefully and thoroughly for hostile forces. It was unarmed but it was large enough to carry the radio equipment necessary for calling in airstrikes. Over Indo-China, the Ki-46 had proved an invaluable aircraft looking for the guerrillas that plagued the forces trying to secure the area. They'd hoped it would do the same thing here in Tibet. Yet, they'd been in the country less than a week and already the first one was down.

The Kempeitai man in charge of investigating the shoot-down was speaking. "Definitely hostile. There is evidence of an explosion near the port engine. I think the pilot was trying to bring her in on the starboard engine and almost made it. It looks like the port wing failed at the explosion point and he spun in at the last second."

"I didn't think the Tibetans had anti-aircraft guns."

"They don't. But this wasn't a gun. From the metal around the explosion site and its position near the exhaust, I am certain this was a missile, one of the small, shoulder-fired ones. A heat-seeker.'

"You mean this aircraft was shot down by our own forces?"

"Possibly. It could also be an American Redeye or a Triple Alliance Kris. They're virtually the same missile, the Tripehounds build it under license. I doubt it though, I've seen aircraft downed by these missiles during tests and this one looks to me like it was one of ours. We will be interrogating all the anti-aircraft crews in the area and accounting for their ammunition. We're going to take the wreckage back home and do a proper examination there. Its amazing what you can find when you look hard enough. We will find fragments of the missile, with luck we may even get enough to identify it and, if it is ours, find which batch it came from. With luck.

The man from the Kempei-Tai rubbed his face, he and his teams had long days of work in front of them, determining what had brought this aircraft down and accounting for all the missiles held by loyal troops in the area. Even that wouldn't answer all the questions though, he was uneasily aware that the Empire had sold very large numbers of these shoulder-fired missiles to the Caliphate and those religious maniacs had passed them on to who-knows-who. If it turned out this aircraft had been brought down by one of those missiles, there would be hell to pay.

Town Hall, Rosario, Surigao del Sur Province, Mindanao

He was a repulsive, reptilian man, Lieutenant Colonel Golconda thought with distaste. Greasy hair, greasy skin and even as he sat in his chair, he seemed to be constantly fighting a strong underwater current. He'd asked for an appointment on a business matter and that's what he had been given. That didn't mean Golconda had to like it or him.

"Honored Colonel, I believe we have a matter of mutual interest. You have a battalion of your troops here, more, a battalion combat team in fact, with a battery of artillery and a company of your Monash tanks. That is more than a thousand soldiers. Those soldiers will be going on leave in this small town and, not to mince words honored Colonel, they will want to enjoy the company of ladies. But this is a town of good devout Catholics who honor the virtue of their women.

"If your men start to approach the ladies here, it will cause much offense and bad feeling, there will be fighting, perhaps some of your men will be hurt, perhaps some of the men here. If there is much trouble it may even cause outraged menfolk to consider helping the bandits. That would be a very sad thing. Even if your men do not offend in this way, if they try to find their own amusements, they may fall into bad company, perhaps women who will give them foul diseases or who will rob and even kill them. Even worse, the women may be working for the bandits and will extract information from your men that will damage your work here. So much room for problems.

"But, honored Colonel, I can offer a solution. Working for me are a number of ladies who enjoy the company of men. They are good girls, they take care of their health, they are honest and they do not steal. If they can talk your men into giving them gifts, well that is the way of the world yes? But they will not steal. You ask any of the young men in the town, the girls who work for Angel Hernandez are clean and honest. I do not suggest we have a formal agreement between us, but if your NCOs make sure the men in your command only go to the cafes where my girls work, I will guarantee those men will not be harmed or cheated. And if your doctors help my girls look after their health by giving them regular checks and if your military police keep an eye on the cafes so that those who have had a little to much to drink are quietly and discreetly assisted back to their barracks unharmed, well, this benefits us both yes?"

The damnable thing was, the repulsive man was right. Facilities for soldiers on evening passes were always a problem and this was as good a solution as any. If this man could be trusted, it would be a good solution indeed. And, as he'd pointed out, fraternization between the soldiers and local women was going to happen anyway. Better it should be controlled.

Like it or not, Rosario was going to be a garrison town now and the problems of garrison towns were as old as soldiering itself. Disease would hit his ready-for-duty strength and, sooner or later, he would start to lose men, stabbed in back alleys or poisoned. The arrangement being oh-so-tactfully suggested was indeed a good one. Golconda nodded almost imperceptibly to his senior sergeant-major who returned the gesture. The pimp would be met on the way out and the arrangements made. But the poisonous character was talking again. He'd caught the exchange of nods and interpreted them correctly.

"I am very pleased that we are able to establish friendly relations, honored Colonel. To have unwanted advances made to respectable women always causes trouble. Take the girl who works at the PNB in the square, Miss Narisa. She is a very attractive lady, very well educated, she had a degree in accountancy from Santa Theresa College. She handles all the foreign exchange dealings of the PNB, the money sent in from our foreign workers in India and Australia, the money sent back from our ladies who have married foreigners. Miss Narisa does all the paperwork for those transfers and helps the families get their money. Every time money arrives, Miss Narisa knows of it.

"A fine catch for a husband you might think. But she is a devout Muslim girl whose faith has deepened much in the last year or so and she will see nobody outside her own faith." Hernandez sighed deeply "Such a pretty girl, but she spends all her time off work with the most pious of her fellow Muslims. It would cause much trouble if your men spoke to her."

Good heavens, Golconda thought, *He didn't come here to discuss his business, he came here to discuss mine.* And the bit of information he has just given me is a piece of the puzzle that helps everything else drop into place. Other pieces dropped into place as well. If this place became bandit country, Hernandez had realized it wouldn't just ruin his business, he and his girls would die ugly. That meant the unspoken agreement he offered was indeed important to them both, especially the doubly unspoken part. His girls would pass back any information they picked up in the course of "business". They might also pass back identities of any of his men who spoke too much about things they shouldn't speak at all.

Golconda mentally apologized to the man, he was still a disgusting pimp but Golconda had allowed that to blind him to the very real value of the services he offered. He appreciated the ambiguity of the man's last remark, he'd left it open as to exactly who would be caused much trouble if his men spoke to the girl in question. Then an anvil dropped. There was a much better way of handling that situation, one that could pay enormous dividends.

"Mister Hernandez, I would like to thank you for coming here and giving me your insight into local customs. Before you leave, would you join me in a drink? To celebrate the new friendship of our peoples?"

Market Street, Rosario, Surigao del Sur Province, Mindanao

Dahlia Tuntoya fingered her rosary and said a small prayer to herself. They would be coming soon and the thought terrified her. She'd agreed to the plan to avenge the injury done to her cousin Graciella who even now lay in hospital in grave pain from her wounds but that didn't mean the she wasn't terrified of the risk she was running. She was on her own, her house was quiet, her husband was away in Bacolod, her children, all but the youngest were away also, working or in college. She and her husband were proud of the fact that they'd managed to put every one of their children through school, even though they'd had to sell some of their land to do it. After all, the only better investment than land was an education.

Her eldest son was working in Australia, an engineer, he was gaining the practical experience he needed to match his school work. Then, as promised by the big Australian Colonel, a letter had arrived. Her son had completed a job far under budget and ahead of schedule so the company had promoted him and given him a big, big bonus. A draft check was enclosed with the letter and Dahlia had taken it to Miss Narisa to be cashed. When the conversion had been done, Miss Narisa had given her no less than a 100,000 pesos, enough to buy back the land they'd sold. A fortune indeed. Or, looked at another way, bait.

The doorbell rang. Dahlia kissed her rosary again, said another quiet prayer and opened the door. As she slipped the latch, the men outside hurled the door open into her face.

Across the road, the watchers grimaced as the three men forced their way into the Tuntoya house. They heard a gasping scream, cut sharply off and then nothing. Shane looked at the specialist who was monitoring the listening equipment in the house. He was white with anger and the skin had tightened over his cheekbones until they seemed ready to cut through the skin. The rage was unmistakable even through the whisper.

"They're working the old girl over. Didn't even give her a chance, just knocked her down and started in on her. .... They want the money, all of it. She's crying in there, begging them not to hurt her any more."

"Take it easy, we knew this would happen and so did she. I don't like this any more than you do but you know very well what's going on. Half the reason why they're doing it is to find out if the situation is a set-up, they're assuming that what they're doing will make us come charging in to rescue her. We've got a fisting party ready, if it looks like they're going to finish her off, we'll go in, but otherwise we stay put."

The specialist continued listening, promising himself that, one day, he would teach those thugs why men fear the dark. "OK, she's given them the money, they're counting it. One of them's telling the old girl that she fell down the steps. If she goes to the police, they'll come back and kill her. Describing how they'll kill her. They're leaving now, the bastards. That bitch in the bank, she fingers the victims. She picks out the middle-aged and older ladies, probably gets them talking and finds out when they'll be alone in the house. Then she passes the information to her friends, lets them know when the women are on their own, unprotected. A man might come to the door with a gun and start shooting so they wait until their victims are by themselves. It's times like this I start to think the Teas might be right. They keep telling us we can have a disarmed society or we can have a free society but we can't have both."

The three bandits left the Tuntoya house, slipping away into the darkness. What they didn't see were the trackers following them. That wasn't surprising, the trackers were Maoris from New Zealand. When the Maori scout team had arrived, the Australians had dismissed most of the stories about their tracking skills as legend or gross exaggeration. After seeing them work at first hand, the consensus was that they could follow a fart in a thunderstorm. That was still not doing them justice.

The watchers relaxed. After a while, a local boy came down the street, a pot in his hand. His mother, Dahlia's sister, had borrowed the cooking pot from Dahlia earlier that day and now he had been sent to return it. He went to the house and saw the door was open. Cautiously, he went in - and the watchers didn't need listening equipment to hear his scream. He ran out into the street, crying and screaming for help. A couple of neighbors ran out to see what was happening. The boy took a few minutes to make himself understood but then the adults went to the Tuntoya house. They also came out in a hurry. Wives were called to comfort the victim and a servant was sent off to get help from the hospital. An ambulance arrived and Dahlia Tuntoya was brought out on a stretcher.

As she was being loaded into the back of the vehicle, the doctor took his stethoscope from around his neck and folded it away in a pocket. Shane and the surveillance team relaxed a little, that was the agreed signal that Dahlia hadn't been seriously injured. People were crowding around the ambulance, curious to see what had befallen their neighbor. In the noise and confusion of the street, another bandit slipped away. He'd stayed behind after the robbery, to see what happened and make sure nobody followed his fellow bandits. He'd never seen the trackers, and he never saw the pair that were following him.

Aviano Italian Air Force Base, Italy

It didn't sound convincing, perhaps sincerity would help. Sophia had told him that, in show business, sincerity was everything, if you could fake that, whatever else you had to do was easy. So, try again with sincerity Major Kozlowski thought.

"Look guys, it really is a very simple system and it will save us all a lot of heartache."

Eddie Korrina looked mutinous. "The old system worked fine. Why did the ying-yangs in Washington go and have to change everything? Means we're going to have to learn the whole lot now. We've got better things to do."

Kozlowski realized that the "better things" included Eddie's Italian girlfriend. He didn't have a chance to cut in, Xav Dravar was a lot more than just mutinous. "I heard that prize dead-head McNorman got the system changed because he screwed up in a Cabinet meeting and assumed a lot of things with different designations were really different bits of kit. Why should we have to bail him out?"

Time to seize the initiative Kozlowski thought. "Look GUYS. Its a simple system. We'll be using it, the Navy will be using it, the Army will as well. All the missiles are in a single number series. The prefix describes the type of missile it is. First letter is the launch platform. A for an aircraft, U for a submarine, M for the ground and R for a ship."

"Why didn't they make it S for a ship? Damned ying-yangs."

"Don't know. Its R. Second letter tells you where it goes. I is an air target. it stands for Intercept. G is a ground target. G for ground, told you it was logical. Then the third one tells us whether its guided or not, M for guided, R for unguided. Missile and Rocket. So, what used to be our GAR-8 has changed to Air-launched Intercept Missile number nine or AIM-9. Our GAR-9s are now the AIM-47. The GAR-12s are now AIM-7. Don't ask me how they got in this order, the Falcon NORAD uses is the AIM-4. The air-to-surface version of the GAR-9 has become the AGM-76. Our nuclear Bullpups are now AGM-12D, the ones with conventional warheads are AGM-12C. Clear?"

His crewmen nodded reluctantly. Kozlowski breathed a sigh of relief, that question about R for ships had been too close. What he knew, but wasn't supposed to, was that S was indeed included in the system. S meant Space-launched. An SGM, a space-to-ground missile, and a SIM, a space-to-air missile, were already being developed. Time to get the guys thinking about something else. "The G mission code also covers our anti-radar missiles. So they are now the AGM-45. A Tiger Team will be coming out soon to change the displays in the aircraft over, it'll only take an hour or so. So we've got to get used to the new names fast.

Missile Base Aldabaran, North of Gaza, Palestine Satrapy, The Caliphate

The trucks were huge, six wheels each side, two under the cab for steering, four spaced out under the large cylinder that seemed to be precariously perched on the back of the truck. The convoy had been offloaded from a Chipanese merchant ship at Al Zubayr in Iraq Province, then driven overland all the way to Gaza. There were six of the big cylinder trucks, followed by a whole line of other vehicles. Command trucks, radio trucks, engineer trucks, reload trucks, the infantry guard units. The commander from the Caliphate curled his lips at those, they were men from Model's force. Janissaries, they were nothing more then Janissaries. The problem was they were orders of magnitude more capable than any other troops the Caliphate had.

149

The battery positions had already been dug out. Six positions for the cylinder trucks, the missile launchers. Each had a single missile in its launcher. They were new, and it was claimed, deadly. They were launched by a short catapult built into the cylinder and by rocket boosters. Then, the turbojet would take over and boost them to just over supersonic speed. They could reach out to over 300 kilometers and had their own radar homing system.

These missiles, the ones the Caliphate had bought, had 2,000 kilogram explosive warheads, a shaped charge behind the main fuel tank of the missile. When it hit its target the warhead would blast a hole deep into the enemy ship and fill that crater with blazing rocket fuel.

Long-range anti-ship missiles were hardly new but the problem was targeting. Over the horizon, there was no way to know precisely where an enemy ship formation was. The new missiles were partly a solution to that. Each missile had its own search radar but also sent a copy of the radar picture it could see back to the battery command post. The missiles would be launched in a fan, covering a wide arc. Once one missile spotted the enemy, the others could be sent course corrections that would take it to its target. There was another advantage to that plan, the missiles would approach their target over a wide arc, complicating the defenses job of shooting them all down.

The other part of the solution was a very special radar, a low frequency set that used a strange phenomena called 'surface adhesion'. At certain frequencies, radar pulses would actually stick to the surface of the sea and travel far over the horizon. The information they got back wasn't accurate but combined with the radars in the missiles, it gave an over-the-horizon capability nobody had achieved before.

Somewhere out there was an American task group. A few days earlier, they'd sunk a Caliphate missile craft with 19 men on board. Wiping out that task group would be a fair exchange. And if these six missiles couldn't do it, there were six more in a battery further south that would help.

USS "Thomas Jefferson" CC-3, Command Flagship, US Mediterranean Fleet

She was the oddest-looking warship in the world, looking as if an aircraft carrier had raped a passenger liner late one night and the offspring had been so frightened that her hair was standing straight up from her scalp. She had the multiple decks and cabins of a passenger liner but the flat top deck and offset island of an aircraft carrier.

Only what looked like a flight deck had never known the beat of wings and there was no hangar inside the strange-looking hull. The deck was to provide optimum positioning for the big radio and radar antennas. Instead of a hangar there were conference rooms, combat information centers and a worldwide data display system, truly the most elaborate and secure communications equipment money could buy. *Thomas Jefferson* could download information from satellites, from SACs reconnaissance aircraft, from anywhere the command staff chose.

There were only three other ships like the *Thomas Jefferson, George Washington*, CC-1 was with the Atlantic Fleet, CC-2 *Abraham Lincoln* was in the Pacific and *Ulysses Grant*, CC-4, was in the Indian Ocean. Two more were being built to cover times when one or more of the others were in dock.

Thomas Jefferson had been built at enormous expense so that one man could have the finest command facilities in the world. Here, now, that man was Admiral Mahan, Commander of the Mediterranean Fleet.

"Admiral Sir, there is some sort of major activity going on along the coast of the Sinai peninsula and Palestine. We have a mass of radio traffic, reports of heavy movements, all consistent with a major build-up. There is a massive base area under construction around Gaza. We're picking up surface-to-air and surface-to-surface missile sites being built, airfields are going up and air units moving in. There are extensive reports of troop movements into that area. In all, Sir, it appears that the Gaza Area is becoming the primary base for Caliphate forces in the eastern Mediterranean. "

151

Admiral Mahan looked out across the sea. One of *Thomas Jefferson's* escorts was visible, the USS *Fargo*. She was barely recognizable as the same ship he'd commanded so many year before, her guns had gone, replaced by surface-to-air missile launchers, Talos fore and aft, Tartar on each beam. Times had changed, technology was unrecognizable but somehow it all seemed the same. One thing was certain, he wasn't going to make the same mistakes that had broken Admiral Spruance and Captain Madrick.

"Sinking that FAC stirred them up, but there's much more to this than that. Put the fleet on ready alert, Tell *Shiloh* and *Enterprise* to put up Hawkeyes for airborne command and control and link us through to them. I want to see their radar picture. CAP is to be up at all times, a mix of Missileers and Super-Crusaders. That takes priority over everything. And make sure both carriers have strikes ready to go if needed.

"Then, get through to Aviano and patch me through to the commander of the 357th, I want Chuck Larry's F-108 drivers fully briefed as well. Finally, get through to Washington. We need to do a recon run along that coast, find out just what is going on over there. A U-2 would be nice, or an RB-58."

Mahan looked out to sea again. He had one thing that Spruance and Madrick hadn't, the deadliest naval weapon ever devised. A lethal piece of equipment that *Thomas Jefferson* had been built to exploit. The Naval Tactical Data System, otherwise known as NTDS.

CHAPTER SIX
CASUALTIES

Office of the Secretary of Defense, Washington DC

It was an outrage. He was the Secretary of Defense and he was being treated like a doormat. Nobody was giving him the respect and deference he deserved. Nobody would listen to him or pay any attention to his ideas. Today's cabinet meeting had been an example. The matter of reconnaissance flights along the coast of Palestine had arisen. There was some sort of military build-up in the area and Commander Sixth Fleet had demanded more information. McNorman despised the senior military officers, all they cared about was buying the latest, most expensive toys to play with. Even worse, they were set in the past, they ignored the prospects that only those who understood the new wave of the future could appreciate. The hidebound fool didn't want information anyway, he was hoping for an incident so he could shoot his shiny guns at things.

The President had approved the U-2 and RB-58 flights without even consulting him. McNorman seethed at the memory. He'd tried to re-establish his authority by laying down course and coverage orders for the aircraft. After he'd finished, LBJ had just looked at him and said "Yes Robert" in the same tone of voice he'd have used to a small child who had claimed to have seen fairies in the back yard. And his input had been completely ignored.

The door opened and Ramsey Chalk walked in. Unannounced and without the courtesy of a knock. That was another thing that infuriated McNorman, The Attorney General had been assigned one of the legendary Executive Assistants supplied by the contractors yet McNorman hadn't. Dean Rusk had asked for one and they'd recruited his assistant within a few hours, a young woman called Inanna. Rusk never stopped singing her praises. When he wanted something, it was organized for him, when he went somewhere, the itinerary was timed and arranged to perfection. Yet, he, Robert McNorman still had a secretary rather than an Executive Assistant. It was an insult, McNorman thought, a deliberate insult.

"Robert, I have been considering the implication of today's decision to fly reconnaissance flights over the Palestine coast. It is my ruling as Attorney General that the planned flights constitute a breach of International Law and by carrying them out, the United States will be committing a war crime. Since it is your department that will be responsible for these illegal flights, you also will be committing a crime.'

McNorman stared at Chalk with disbelief. He knew that the man had developed a habit of going well beyond his departmental remit in his search to place the United States under the control of international legal systems and organizations but this was going too far. The President himself had cleared the flights and, anyway, everybody knew SAC flew where it wanted, when it wanted, and woe betide anybody who tried to interfere.

"Robert, it is my decision to establish a series of rulings that will mitigate the severity of our criminal activities. I call them Rules of Engagement." SAC already had those, McNorman reflected, as a rule, if somebody engaged SAC, they ceased to exist shortly afterwards. "I have written these out as a series of instructions for your crews. Distribute them before the flights tomorrow."

McNorman looked at the list "Restricting the flights to subsonic speeds?"

"Going to supersonic speeds causes a bang that damages private property on the ground. Therefore it is illegal. You will make sure these rules of engagement go out tonight."

Chalk strode out of the office, leaving McNorman seething behind him. Then, the SecDef started to read the document outlining the 'Rules of Engagement'. As he did so, a slow smile spread over his face. Quite unwittingly, the Attorney General had given him the precise tool he needed. The 'Rules of Engagement' were a godsend, a gift from providence. If they turned the mission into a disaster, Chalk would shoulder all the blame and suffer the penalties. But, the disaster would prove McNorman's own point about the vulnerability of the bombers and the need to replace them with missiles. He'd get his way and somebody else would take the penalty.

But, if the 'Rules of Engagement' did not bring about a disaster, it would be proof that the high speed and high altitude performance of the next-generation bombers was unnecessary. He would have the justification he needed to cancel production of every one of them - and Ramsey Chalk would think that McNorman was his ally. No matter what the effect of the 'Rules of Engagement' proposal, he, McNorman would get what he wanted, the fundamental reconstruction of the entire US Department of Defense. At last, all those who stood in his way would have to admit that he had been right after all.

McNorman picked up the message with the 'Rules of Engagement' and read it again. It was truly the key he had been waiting for. It had to go out to Aviano straight away, before anybody could countermand it.

Aviano Italian Air Force Base, Italy

The four RB-58s were in a line on the taxiway, surrounded by their ground support equipment, waiting to go. *Marisol* was in the lead, she had the longest mission, up to Beirut and then down the coast to Gaza. After that she would follow the Sinai coast and then come back home. *Tiger Lily* would be following her, she was carrying an electronic intelligence pod under her belly. Her job would be to record the electronic signals from any systems that attempted to track *Marisol*. Behind them,

Spider Woman and *Queen Bee* were waiting to follow up, they'd probe any unexpected areas of activity that emerged. It was a routine mission for the RB-58C, the only thing that wasn't routine was that an Air Police pick-up truck was heading straight for them. It swerved to a halt in front of *Marisol* and Colonel Hazen jumped out, his face a mask of fury.

"Mike, the rest of you, you had better read this and read it now. It just came in. It's a piece of trash called 'Rules of Engagement', it comes right from the top. From McNorman himself. I can't believe it."

Kozlowski took the message and went white. "Subsonic only? Altitude not to exceed 40,000 feet? Do not fire unless fired upon? Do not fire unless enemy weapons have actually been launched? Do not engage other nation's fighter aircraft unless they fire upon us? Get visual identification of targets before firing? Don't fire on ground targets that are within ten miles of civilian population areas regardless of circumstances? Are these maniacs trying to get us all killed?"

"Mike, these 'Rules of Engagement' are absurd. If you want to abort this mission while I get this confirmed, I'll back you all the way. These orders make any penetration mission virtual suicide. According to McNorman's covering orders, these are the legal determinations made by the Attorney General. I can't believe the targeteers know about this. These orders will be reversed, I'm sure of it. If you want to refuse this mission, nobody will blame you. All of you, you want to scrub it?"

The four RB-58 crews looked at each other and shook their heads. SAC did not turn back. Kozlowski turned to Hazen "Sorry Allen, can't do that. My old man would throw a fit. Anyway, the Navy needs the information we'll be getting. We'll take this one real careful and if the bad guys start shooting, then to hell with these, these 'Rules of Engagement', we'll do what we always do."

Hazen nodded, it was what he'd expected. He had a card to play though. "Mike, you carrying nuclear-armed AIM-47s and AGM-76s?'

"Of course." The reply was irritable and impatient, Hazen couldn't blame him.

"Well, under these 'Rules of Engagement' even carrying, let alone using, nuclear weapons is prohibited. So we'll have to pull *Marisol* and *Spider Lady* from the flight line and reload them. We've got conventionally-tipped Bullpups for air-to-surface and we'll borrow some conventionally-armed AIM-47s from the 357th for air-to-air. That'll take at least an hour, buys some time to get this cancelled at least."

Kozlowski nodded. "OK boys, mount up, we have a job to do."

Hazen watched the crews board the bombers, then got back into his pickup truck. In addition to the hour needed to swap out loads, it would be a couple more before the aircraft were in a danger zone, the question now was whether he could get through to Washington, get these damned 'Rules of Engagement' countermanded and then get the word to the crews in time. Then, he had a brainwave. There was a direct link to the USS *Thomas Jefferson* the Mediterranean Fleet Flag, she had a direct link to Washington as well. He could try and get a message through her also.

Anyway, it may not be all bad. Nobody in their right minds opened fire on a SAC aircraft and those who did got nuked. No if, buts or maybes. Everybody knew that and held their fire as a result. So even if these orders increased the vulnerability of the bombers, then the difference might not be critical. It all depended on how rational the enemy air defenses were and if they knew about these insane 'Rules of Engagement'.

Outside Restaurant "Pizza-Dacha", Zentral-Prospekt, Moscow, Russia

One thing that had always amazed Tony Evans was that Moscow could be baking hot in summer. He'd always had a picture of the city being perpetually wrapped in snow but today, the sun was beating down and people were taking the opportunity to enjoy it. They'd been walking the Prospekt window-shopping and were now waiting for his restaurant to open so they could have pizza. Evans had parked his Mustang by the building, he owned the Moscow and Petrograd dealerships for Mustangs now and they were selling well.

In fact, the Mustang was doing for Russia what the Model T Ford had done for America. It was cheap enough to sell widely, robust enough to be reliable, simple enough for people to maintain, sporty enough to appeal to youngsters and practical enough to appeal to their parents. When people bought cars, they wanted roads to drive them on, so the Mustang was slowly driving a road construction program in Russia.

"Tony, why is that man wearing a leather coat?" Klavdia's voice was puzzled. Evans looked at his wife. She was wearing one of the boldly-floral print dresses that Russian women favored, a thin, summer-weight one. Evans was in shirt-sleeves as dictated by the weather. So were the passers-by. The militiaman, one of Moscow's police, admiring the Mustang was in shirt-sleeves also. So why was that man wearing a long, heavy leather coat? The militiaman nodded. This deserved investigation.

"Hey You. Stop there. I wish to see your papers." Russia was a free country now, by the standards of its past anyway, but people were still expected to carry state identification papers and show them on demand. But the militiaman's shout set the man in the incongruous leather coat running, straight at a group of people gathered the other side of the Prospekt.

The militiaman cursed and there were a couple of light cracks as he drew his Makarov pistol on the runner. Evans cursed and went for the M1911 he kept in the Mustang's glove compartment. Then, there was a dull crash and he realized he needn't have bothered. Klavdia might be wearing a light summer dress instead of Frontniki khaki but her rifle was never far away from her. This time, it had been on the back seat of the 'Stang and she fired almost by reflex.

The man in the leather coat was stretched out in the middle of the Prospekt, his head distorted almost beyond recognition. Klavdia's 7.62 x 54 hollow-point had done its usual number and stopped him dead. The traffic was gently steering around the body, slowing down to see what was happening. Russia, Evans reflected, was getting more like America every day.

The militiaman went over to the body very cautiously and looked. Then he waved Evans over. Hanging from the man's jacket was a simple plunger switch, the type seen on lamps in every home. The man's coat had folded back and they could see the vest underneath, loaded with sticks of explosive. Construction dynamite by the look of it. People were beginning to edge closer to look and the militiaman ordered them back sharply. Then, one of the onlookers recognized Klavdia and "its Kalugina" was whispered through the crowd. Being married to a national war-hero had its problems Evans thought.

"There is a telephone in the restaurant, militiaman. Please feel free to use it. The Federal Security Service will wish to investigate this. And enjoy your free slice." It was a rule Evans had laid down for all his Pizza-Dacha restaurants. Any militiaman who came in wearing uniform was entitled to a free slice. It was a very low-cost way of ensuring that the militia would be on hand to deal with any trouble that arose. Yes, Russia was becoming more like America every day.

RB-58C "Marisol", over the Palestine coast, just south of Gaza.

They were on the last, and most important, leg of the flight now. They'd made their landfall just north of Beirut and run south from there. The first real information they'd picked up was around Yaffo, there were a lot of emitters that had tracked them but no hostile fire control radars had lit up. Still, Yaffo had been a lot busier than anybody had expected, Kozlowski had a hunch a second big base complex was going to be built there. Now they were running past the existing complex at Gaza. At 511 knots and 40,000 feet up, both Kozlowski and *Marisol* were uncomfortable, Kozlowski because the low speed and altitude put them at much greater risk, *Marisol* because her engines were optimized for the colder, thinner air higher up.

"More search radar emissions, Mike." Xav Dravar was reporting from the Electronics Pit aft. "All are long-range search emissions, no target acquisition or fire control radars yet. There are a lot of search radars here though, including a couple we haven't seen before. The Caffs have at least three new toys down there. I'm recording the signals for the brainiacs back home."

"Mike, why in hell are we down here, we can do this job better from 60,000?"

"According to the 'Rules of Engagement' we are only allowed a single pass so we have to get as much information as possible in that pass. So the authors specified we fly low. Oh, by the way, we can't change routes between missions, each recon flight had to follow the same path. Don't say it, you can't say anything I haven't already thought. This whole situation is crazy."

Marisol continued cruising south, soon she would make her turn and start to run along the Sinai coast before going home.

Missile Base Sirius, South of Gaza, Palestine Province, The Caliphate

Oberleutnant Hans Engstrom watched the aircraft approaching on his search radar scan. It had been tracked south ever since it had crossed The Caliphate coast in Lebanon Province. Now it was passing over Gaza. The initial identification had been an American recon aircraft but the flight path was all wrong. About 13,000 meters up and about 900 kilometers per hour. Too low and slow for one of the Americans. Or maybe not, it could be one of the old B-60s, the speed and altitude were about right for that. Just possibly a B-52. A few years ago it could have been a Navy A3D but they'd all gone now, they'd been replaced by the sleek Vigilantes. Perhaps it was time to have a look.

The battery was equipped with the latest version of the Chipanese-designed Hiryu surface-to-air missile. The missile itself was good enough but its guidance system was all too vulnerable to electronic countermeasures. The Chipanese had come up with a solution for that. Their Navy had always been advanced in its production and use of optical equipment, rangefinders, telescopes, binoculars. That background had been used to create an optical system that could track a target without using the fire control radar. The optics were coupled to television cameras so that the image they obtained was displayed on screen in the command van.

It was far from being a perfect system. It couldn't be used at night, it couldn't be used against very fast or high-flying targets and it wasn't that accurate but this target was within its capabilities. Engstrom switched the system on, after a second or two it warmed up and an image appeared on the screen. Empty sky. The field of vision of the tracking head was very narrow and actually framing an aircraft in it first time was virtually impossible.

Nobody said life had to be easy. The optical tracking head was controlled by a stick, just like the control column on an aircraft. Engstrom panned around a bit then caught something and focused in on it. He'd been lucky, normally the optical head couldn't scan fast enough to track one of the American aircraft but this one was moving slowly. Then he caught his breath. Delta wings, four engines. It was one of the American's vaunted SAC RB-58s. Why in hell was it moving so slowly? He flipped another switch in the control console. Now the fire control radar was aligned with the optical tracking head, he had a radar fix even without turning the set on.

"Fire a missile. Shoot the Satan down." The Mullah in the control center had the petulant expression of a sulking child. A very dangerous, sulking child. Engstrom thought as he looked at the display. It was a SAC bomber, from the people who had burned his country off the map. Engstrom's family had come from Gutersloh, one of the cities the Americans had annihilated. There was nothing substantial left of Gutersloh or the people in it. The city itself was just ruins and a cobalt-blue circular lake. And the people? There were less than a dozen survivors of Gutersloh, none of them known to Engstrom. It wasn't unusual of course, there were 200 other cities in Germany that looked exactly the same way. SAC had destroyed Germany so thoroughly, some people even tried to erase the name. The French never used it, they called Germany Nafoco. The Nameless Former Country. And it was SAC that was responsible.

"Wait, wait, they are still on the edge of our engagement zone, if we fire now they can evade us easily. If they carry on their present course, they'll be in our no-escape zone very soon. So have patience."

The Mullah stamped away, pacing the command post with his frustration. SAC's bombers were an offense against divine will, they were the tools of Satan, they needed to be destroyed at every opportunity.

At the missile control console, Engstrom manipulated the control of his optical head very carefully. He had the system on maximum magnification now and the field of vision was very, very narrow. If he sneezed or twitched or breathed wrongly, he'd lose the picture and he wouldn't be able to get it back. As it was, he had the silver bomber framed in the picture and the radar fire control system was slaved to it. Any second now, his finger went out to the switches that fired the missile. One armed the weapon, that had already been activated. It just needed one squeeze to fire.

RB-58C "Marisol", over the Palestine coast, just south of Gaza.

"Still no target acquisition or fire control signatures Mike. A lot of general surveillance radars though. Two more lit up just a minute or so ago. There's a whole scramble down in the port, our ESM system isn't precise enough to split them apart. Probably the ships in the harbor, maybe even navigation radars for the harbor itself."

"Any hostile air activity?"

"Negative Mike, we picked up a few airborne bogies far inland but they're keeping well away from us."

"Sensible people."

"Yeah, didn't think the Caffs had it.... RED, RED we have a missile launch. Surface-to-air, coming our way ... coming up on us fast. Its definitely targeted on us"

"Xav jam the son-of-a-bitch's guidance system. Ed, locate the guidance radar and take it out. Screw the 'Rules of Engagement'." Kozlowski slammed *Marisol's* throttles forward and felt the familiar thump in his spine as the reheat cut in and the engines surged to full power. He pulled the nose back and swept the aircraft into a climbing turn. As *Marisol* swung at 90 degrees to the original course, he did an abrupt wingover, pulling the nose

162

in and under so *Marisol* virtually reversed course in mid-air. At that instant, Dravar punched the release and a cloud of chaff spread from its launchers in the wings. The missile that had been on his forward port quarter was now port and aft and there was a spreading chaff cloud between *Marisol* and the inbound missile.

"Mike, I can't find a tracking signal to jam. There's nothing there. But that thing is coming for us, it followed our turn perfectly. I'm hitting flares, it may be coming in on infra-red."

Missile Base Sirius, South of Gaza, Palestine Province, The Caliphate

The crew were good, Engstrom noted. They'd picked up the launch almost immediately and the violent turn and wingover had almost caused him to lose their picture. He'd just held it though and he'd seen the cloud of chaff spreading around the aircraft. The sunlight reflecting off it had almost - almost - made him lose the target again but he'd held her. Now the aircraft was surrounded by white smoke and brilliant orange-white lights. Decoy flares, they were assuming the missile had a heat-seeking backup system. Nearly right but near wasn't good enough.

A few second to impact now. Engstrom flipped another switch on his console. This activated the fire control radar on the ground that illuminated the target for the radar guidance system in the missile. The electro-optical system wasn't accurate enough for the final intercept but the target wouldn't have time to jam its signals in the fraction of a second it would be on.

RB-58C "Marisol", over the Palestine coast, just south of Gaza.

Speed was life. Kozlowski put *Marisol's* nose down in an attempt to pick up as much forward speed as possible. He felt her punch through the sound barrier, if he could get her up to maximum and pick up enough altitude to get where the air was thin and she could run the way she was designed to, then they could duck this thing coming at them then take out the people who had launched it. And damn the 'Rules of Engagement'.

"Radar, we have fire control radar tracking signal. Jamming now..."

It was too late. The Hiryu missile had three warheads, spaced equally down the airframe of the missile. The design was intended to put up a wall of fragments through which the target had to fly. That assumed the missile exploded in front of the target. However, *Marisol's* evasive action had put the missile behind her, now it exploded directly underneath and about 150 feet below her. The wall of fragments slashed along her belly like a buzz-saw.

The crew heard *Marisol's* scream of agony as the displays in all three cockpits erupted into a sea of red warning signals. The screens in the Bear's Den blacked out with a terrible finality, in the cockpit Kozlowski felt the controls freeze solid in his hands. Around him the sky was starting to rotate. He fought the frozen joystick trying to bring the aircraft back under control but there was no movement, none at all..

"Get out Mike, get out now. While you can." *Marisol's* voice was weak but insistent.

"We told you, we don't bail on you. We'll get out of this. There's a divert airfield in Libya the Italians said we can use."

"Too late, I'm all smashed up inside. Get out now, its all over."

"I told you we won't b.."

"Get out, GET OUT *GET OUT*." At *Marisol's* last scream, Kozlowski felt the ejection capsule fold around him and the rocket of the escape system throw him clear of the cockpit. Eddie or Xav must have banged all three of them out, he thought. The three ejection capsules were in a tight group, falling together, with luck that meant they wouldn't have to waste time finding each other on the ground.

As the ejection screen fell away, Kozlowski saw *Marisol*. Her belly had been ripped open by the missile, the under-fuselage pod smashed and disintegrating. Both inboard engines were on fire, leaving two parallel streaks of black smoke across the sky. Between them a sheet of white, streaming from *Marisol's*

164

shattered fuselage filled the air. She was in a flat spin, dropping from the sky like a stone. Her last words had been right, if her crew had waited a second longer, the G-forces would have stopped them escaping.

Even as he watched *Marisol* started to break up. The port wing went first, fracturing at the inboard engine mount, the detached portion fluttering clear. Then the tail broke off just aft of the wing trailing edge, there was a known weak point there, where the fuselage had been extended from the original B-58A design. Suddenly, *Marisol* was simply falling out of the sky, tumbling end-over-end, shedding wreckage as she went. A split second before impact, she jerked her nose up. Then, her head still held high, she hit the desert and exploded.

White House Cabinet Office. Washington D.C.

Veteran Washington hands do not rely on press statements or contacts inside the Pentagon for advance notice of international crises. Instead, they cultivate the managers of fast food joints around the Pentagon and the White House for the first sign of international disaster is a sudden spate of delivery orders from those buildings. Now, in McDonalds, Dominos and a dozen others, the cooks were working overtime. Which wasn't surprising, emergency cabinet meetings were rare and deadly serious.

"Security Advisor, can you brief us on what has happened."

"Mister President, less than an hour ago, one of our RB-58Cs, *Marisol* crashed. Almost certainly she was shot down by forces belonging to the Caliphate. Information from *Tiger Lily* indicates *Marisol* was hit by a surface-to-air missile. There are a lot of things about the incident that we do not yet fully understand and we urgently need explanations."

Inanna entered the room and gave a note to Secretary Rusk. He read it quickly. "I am sorry to interrupt Seer. Mister President, the Italian Government has just issued a statement that their radar tracking station in Libya saw the incident. Their statement says the lost aircraft was flying much lower and slower

165

than usual and their initial assumption is that it was suffering severe technical problems. There is a classified note from Senor Mussolini attached Mister President, he says his government will act as independent witnesses to confirm whatever it is that we decide is the truth."

"Nice of him. What does he want? More importantly what happened can wait. I want to know what happened to the crew. Are they alive? Have they been captured? What are we doing to get them out. Seer?"

"Mister President, it is our understanding that all three crew members ejected safely and are currently somewhere in the Sinai desert. The good news is that they are certainly quite close to the coast and we have one of our best SEAL teams on the scene. Standard practice is, they'll go in, find the crew and bring them out. The crew have emergency beacons they can use. The SEALs are very, very good at this sort of work."

"Mister President. As Attorney General it is my ruling that any such rescue effort will contravene the territorial integrity of a sovereign nation and, as such, will be an offense against international law. I have issued orders that forbid any such rescue attempt."

Admiral Theodore crashed his fist down on the table. "I will not be a party to issuing any such order. The Navy will not let the Air Force down."

"Chief of Naval Operations." LBJs voice cracked out. "Three things. Firstly, I am the only person in this office who is allowed to crash his fist on the table."

"Yes Mister President. My apologies Sir."

"Accepted. Secondly," LBJ crashed his fist on the table. "I will not be a party to any member of my government issuing such an order. The Navy will not let the Air Force down." His tone and cadence matched Admiral Theodore's perfectly. "Thirdly, if any such orders have been issued, get them countermanded immediately. I want a rescue effort mounted as early as possible and with whatever forces it takes to do the job is that clear?"

"Sir, Yes Sir."

"Then Admiral, you are excused the rest of this meeting. Get that rescue authorized and organized. Ramsey, you and I have discussed your habit of exceeding your authority. I had thought I had made your position quite clear. Obviously I have failed. Your remit does not extend to giving orders to me or to the other members of my Government. What part of that do you fail to understand?"

"Mister President, it is my duty as the senior legal authority in the United States to interpret international law and to see that the United States complies with those interpretations. That is why I formulated rules of engagement and required the department of defense to comply with them."

"What the hell are 'Rules of Engagement?" LBJ glared around the room. The Seer shot a "what the hell are they?" glance at Lillith who returned a "beats me" gesture. McNorman was fumbling in a briefcase. He produced a paper.

"Perhaps I can explain Mister President. Last night, the Attorney General saw me and gave me these so-called "Rules of Engagement". He told me that they were compulsory for all US forces operating abroad. I assumed, Sir, that he had your authority for these orders and, reluctantly, issued them."

He passed the paper to LBJ who started to read it, stared sharply at Chalk, then read the rest. When he spoke his voice was quiet and measured.

"Mister Attorney General. In fifty years of public service I have never seen a document that was more crowded with infamous falsehoods and distortions. Falsehoods and distortions on a scale so vast in their implications that I can imagine no responsible gentleman on the face of this earth issuing them. Your resignation as Attorney-General and as a member of this government is accepted. Leave."

"Mister President, I..."

LBJ put his forehead in his hand. "Go. Just Go." Ramsey Chalk hesitated for a moment, causing Naamah to bump into him and push him slightly towards the door. He left, Naamah following closely behind him.

"Mister President." LBJ looked up at McNorman wearily. "Although I cannot condone the Ramsey's actions, I must say that they have demonstrated the truth of what I have been saying for many months now. The destruction of this RB-58 shows our force of manned bombers is obsolete and vulnerable. We should immediately initiate a major program for its replacement with land-based ballistic missiles."

"Robert, it should be obvious to you that this disaster has only happened because the aircraft in question was forced to fly at speeds and altitudes that allowed the enemy to fire upon it. Had it been operating normally, we would not be having this meeting. What this demonstrates to me is that the need for our new fleet of very fast, very high-flying bombers is more urgent than we realized. Henry, please get Treasury to prepare a budget supplemental to accelerate production of both the B-70 and B-71 as much as is practical. Now Robert."

"Yes Mister President?"

"I believe that the Bureau of Indian Affairs is urgently in need of your talents. You will take over as its head with immediate effect. Of course, if you prefer that we should stage an investigation into the extent of your involvement in this "Rules of Engagement" affair..."

McNorman shook his head and left. LBJ sighed and looked around the conference room. "Dean, Defense needs a capable and effective Secretary. One who can make the system work for our armed forces, not against them. I would like you to leave State and take over Defense. I realize I am asking a lot of you but the country needs your services there."

Dean Rusk thought for a moment. "Mister President I would be honored. May I ask if I can take Inanna with me?"

"That's a matter for the Contractors, she is employed by them not us." The Seer nodded approval.

"Very well then. Dean, your first job is to get this mess straightened out."

Dean Rusk and Inanna started leaving. As Inanna passed the Security Advisor he stopped her "Inanna, honey, State to Defense is a promotion, see me later about the appropriate salary increase."

Office of the Attorney General Washington D.C.

Ramsey Chalk was throwing papers into his briefcase. Around him, Naamah was carefully packing his personal possessions in boxes for transport. "It's an outrage, just who does he think he is?"

"I know Sir, its terrible what he has done. He had no right to dismiss you like that." Naamah's voice was oozing sympathy and affection.

"It is about time the people of this country understand they are answerable to the international community. The way America has trampled over the rights of the rest of the world is unconscionable."

"That's so true Sir, we only have to look at the nuclear bombing of Germany to see that."

"Exactly. We deliberately slaughtered tens of millions of ordinary German civilians. That is a war crime of unimaginable proportions. Oh, I know they have always claimed that they were bombing military and industrial targets but I know they really were trying to kill as many Germans as possible. There's no proof of that though, if there was I could create enough of a scandal to make this country see how criminal its behavior has been."

"But there is proof, Sir, didn't you know?"

"What do you mean Naamah?"

"In the basement of the National Security Building are all the documents concerning the planning of The Big One. They show quite clearly that the real target of the bombing was the German civilian population. Its all documented, how they planned the attack to kill as many Germans as possible. I worked on the papers when I was a research assistant. If you come with me Sir, I'll take you to them."

"Why would you want to help me?"

"Because I am your Executive Assistant and because I know what truly lies in your heart." Naamah smiled gently "You might say it's a talent of mine. Wait a moment Sir."

She disappeared into a back room of the office complex for a few minutes and came back with a large thermos flask. "We'll be working down there all night Sir, So I fixed coffee to keep us going. Now, shall we go?"

Ramsey Chalk and Naamah took the brief drive to the National Security Building and she let them in. Chalk felt the chill as he entered, partly from a deliberate temperature setting, partly from the huge statue of death that dominated the entry lobby. Chalk felt the statue staring at him as he entered, then got a weird feeling that it had made a respectful nod to Naamah as she passed. Pure imagination of course, just stress, anger and the effects of the strange architecture of the deserted lobby. Chalk looked at Naamah affectionately, the woman was risking a lot to help him, obviously she was a fellow spirit, somebody who shared his beliefs and aims.

"Sir?" Naamah had gone to the lifts on the left hand side of the lobby and called one in. It was open and waiting. Ramsey

Chalk stepped in and felt the red-painted doors close behind him as Naamah took him into the basement of the National Security Building.

Bridge, USS Austin LPD-4, Eastern Mediterranean

"Gentlemen, we have a serious situation. I am afraid I have to confirm what you have almost certainly heard via the ship's bush telegraph. Just over an hour ago, an RB-58 belonging to Strategic Aerospace Command was shot down by Caliphate forces. As far as we are aware, the crew ejected safely and are somewhere in the Sinai desert, our best estimate is no more than ten or twelve miles inland."

"Right then." Commander Thomas stood up. "I'll roust out the boys and we'll be on our way. Its getting near dusk, we'll insert just after sundown, that's when people's eyes will still be adjusted to daylight and they won't be seeing right. Captain, please flood the docking bay and we'll be out of your hair."

"Commander Thomas, there are a couple of problems." Captain Pickering's mask slipped and the anger showed up from under. "I have received orders from the Attorney General not to undertake any rescue operations or to conduct any hostile actions against forces deployed by the Caliphate."

There was an explosion around the bridge. "Gentlemen, please. Firstly I doubt the legality of this order. I do not believe that the Attorney General has the authority to issue such an order. In the event, I am advising you as Captain of this vessel that this order is null and void. I have conferred with the commander of this amphibious warfare group and the Captains of the other ships and we are of one mind. Commander Thomas, I am ordering you to prepare and execute a rescue plan as per your standing operational procedures. If there is any fall-out from that order, it will begin and end with the Admiral and the Captains.

"That brings me to the second point. We are close in to a major Caliphate base area, Gaza. We don't know what they have there, that's what the aircraft SAC lost was trying to find out. One thing we do know, they have something new and nasty in stock. We haven't lost a bomber in combat since The Big One almost twenty years ago. SAC has never claimed its bombers are invulnerable, merely that trying to shoot one down is incredibly foolish. The Caliphate has been incredibly foolish and the problem is, we don't know how they did it. Whatever is in there brought down a B-58 so its dangerous. As another result, we don't know what SAC have in mind for retaliation, we may have to pull you out fast, regardless of whether you've found the missing crew."

"Captain Pickering Sir, standing orders are, when aircrew down are in enemy territory, we have to go in and get them. They say nothing about us having to come out."

"Understood Commander, but you will be very close to a major enemy base. The opposition is likely to be very severe. I do not criticize the quality of your SEALS but you are twelve men, you could be facing a regiment or a division or more."

"So we'll have them outnumbered. " Thomas grinned. "Captain, if we get into a shooting match, we've failed anyway. Do this right, the Caffs will never even know we were there."

"Don't underestimate the opposition Commander. Its not just the Caffs we have to worry about. Model's Janissaries are in Gaza and they are the toughest survivors of a very tough bunch. They know we'll extract by sea, so they'll try to block the beaches. Getting in might not be a problem but getting out will be."

"Not if we hold the beach first Sir." Lieutenant Colonel Soren cut in. "We've got a battalion landing team here, infantry, tanks, artillery. After Jeff's taken his hooligans in, we'll seize a beach-head and hold it. That way, he'll have a secure base to fall back on. And the more of us who take part in this, the less likely we are to all get court-martialed."

A ripple of laughter spread around the bridge. "Good, Colonel, make it so. You are in command of the landing force so make up a plan and I'll forward it to the Admiral. We haven't got much time so we're going to have to work this one out this on the run as it were. Damn, I wish we had some air support we could rely on. Until we find out what brought down that RB-58, we can't put helicopters too close to Gaza. Wait one."

A signalman came onto the bridge from the radio room. Captain Pickering read the flimsy and relaxed slightly. Sanity was returning to the world.

"People, change in situation. This is a message from the CNO, Admiral Theodore, via Commander Mediterranean Fleet, Admiral Mahan. By Presidential directive the orders forbidding a rescue attempt are countermanded and canceled. For our information, Ramsey Chalk and Robert McNorman have both been relieved of their offices. President Johnson has ordered that the missing aircrew be rescued by whatever means necessary. Admiral Mahan has delegated command of the rescue operation to this amphibious group. For our information, the *Shiloh* and *Enterprise* battlegroups are merging and closing on our position to cover us. The *Bull Run* and *Seven Pines* battlegroups are entering the Mediterranean at flank speed to reinforce us. When they arrive, there will be ten carriers in the Eastern Mediterranean. That leaves the Atlantic bare but that's no great worry.

"Gentlemen. We're cleared to do what we were going to do anyway. A final note from Admiral Mahan. He reminds us that if we fail to rescue these men, there are postings enough in Alaska for us all. Good luck, and God Speed."

Magasay Palace, Manila, Philippines

"Damn, I knew it was going to happen. Its been hanging over us for five years now."

Sir Eric Haohoa looked at the Ambassador. She'd let her guard down and her voice had contained a mixture of annoyance, amusement and relief.

"How so Ma'am?"

"The Americans. We owe them much for the help they gave us during the start of the Burma Campaign. Now they are calling in the debt. One of their bombers has been shot down."

"Good God! Which country has ceased to exist?"

"They are all still with us. For the moment anyway. The Americans are concerned, they are not sure how their bomber was brought down. They know it was a missile of some sort, almost certainly one supplied by Chipan, but they do not know the details of how it made the intercept. So they want us to find out for them."

"How can we do that ma'am? Our intelligence on Chipan is mostly political, very good political, but political none the less.

173

Our sources on military systems are much less comprehensive. Most of our well-placed informants were killed during the Showa Restoration Coup. As for technical capability, we are at least a decade behind the Americans if not more. We still import all our most advanced military technology from them. How do they expect us to get information that they cannot even guess at? I think their demand is unreasonable."

"Perhaps. Let us put that to one side for a moment. Now let us proceed to a quite unrelated matter. We have received another communication from Admiral Soriva in Taiwan. He is quite desperate to find a source of supply for military equipment, especially aircraft and armored vehicles. He is keen to buy Gnats from India plus Monash II tanks and Nulla long-range artillery from Australia. Previously we have ignored such requests."

A light bulb went on in Sir Eric's head. "The Americans want us to agree to the sale of military equipment provided Admiral Soriva gives us the technical information they need! He'll never agree to that, he may be in a state of rebellion against the Tokyo government but he's a loyal Japanese officer, he won't hand over classified information. Anyway, how can Taiwan afford equipment on the scale he's speaking about?"

"I wouldn't be certain of Admiral Soriva's final loyalties. He is a loyal Japanese officer certainly, but he sees the Tokyo Government as the disloyal betrayers. Remember also it is common knowledge in the Chipanese armed forces that the Government has been supplying shoulder-fired anti-aircraft missiles to the Caliphate who immediately gave them to the Tibetans to use against Chipanese forces in Tibet."

"Um, Ma'am, we supplied those missiles to Tibet, from stocks we've captured in Indo-China, Mindanao, Burma and the Northwest Frontier."

"Details Sir Eric, don't be so concerned with mere details. I think Admiral Soriva will be persuadable on this issue. As for money, don't underestimate Taiwan. They have a significant industrial structure already and the potential to build more. Chipanese industrial weakness has always been a matter of mismanagement rather than actual lack of strength. Managed properly, Taiwan could become quite a prosperous little country, if it gets the chance. A worthy member of the Triple Alliance in fact. But, that is for the future. In the short term, the Americans are prepared to make short-term financing available for the deal on very generous terms. And, of course, we are in a position to charge premium prices for our products."

"So, in effect, we are the cut-out in a deal between America and Taiwan?"

"Precisely Sir Eric. The Americans have a C-144 supersonic transport waiting for us at Clark Field. By the way, Sir Eric, please try to persuade Sir Martyn to remain here and, preferably, take a rest. I am deeply concerned for his health. Every time we meet, he appears to be suffering from a more serious illness than before.

Parliament Building Taipei, Taiwan

If he listened very carefully, he could hear the thunder of artillery. The Imperial forces on the other side of the Formosa Strait were pounding Quemoy and Matsu islands again. They'd been doing so daily, ever since the administration here on Taiwan had established itself as a rival government for the Imperial Empire of Japan and China. Not a serious rival of course, in fact Taiwan's pretensions to representing the Empire as a whole were little short of a joke. Yet, it was a very important joke, for as long as Taiwan claimed to be the rightful rulers of the Empire, they were stating that the Empire was a unified whole. Thus, their actions could be - and were being - presented as a dispute between members of the ruling class, not a rebellion against that class. It was a power-play game, not a revolution.

And, like most games, this one had rules. Taiwan didn't claim independence, Tokyo didn't erase Taiwan from the face of the earth. Tokyo restricted its attacks to offshore islands, Taiwan didn't attack the mainland. Taiwan kept its contacts with the outside world muted, Tokyo made only formal objections to essential trade. There had been no meetings, no conferences, no written agreements. Everything had been done through third- and fourth parties, by inference and suggestions.

When Taiwan had mentioned it wished to buy replacement military equipment, Tokyo had objected ferociously but buried within the protests was a subtle distinction. Certain items of equipment were the subject of bile-filled warnings of grim consequences if the plans went through but others received only a pro-forma rebuke. The message was obvious, Japan would accept some Taiwanese defense purchases provided they were limited in nature and did not provide a strategic capability. Tokyo had threatened nuclear attack if Taiwan purchased Australian aircraft such as the TSR-2 and the Arrow but studiously not mentioned the purchase of Indian Gnats. They'd fulminated against the purchase of the heavy Indian Centurion tanks but only objected to the purchase of the lighter Australian Monash II.

At first, the Taiwanese approaches for trade links had been ignored, but now they had a response. A message from the Triple Alliance indicating that they were prepared to sell Taiwan military equipment after all. A hundred Gnats, including twenty for immediate delivery from Indian Air Force stocks, two hundred Monash II tanks and forty Nulla self-propelled guns. Soriva grinned at that one, Tokyo had seen the caliber, less that 100 millimeters and only made formal noises. They hadn't looked at the range or accuracy figures. The game had rules but that didn't mean they couldn't be bent a little.

Even better, the Triple Alliance message contained the offer of a financing package on extraordinarily generous terms. Long payment periods, low interest rates, no cash down payment. That was both good and curious. Good because Taiwan had a financial shortfall that would take years to correct. Curious because the prices the Triple Alliance was charging for the equipment were outrageous. They were asking for five times the amount the Triple Alliance air forces were paying for their Gnats. Generous financial aid and usurious asking prices were an odd combination.

Still, even at these inflated prices, the tiny Gnats were worth the cost. They were so small they could be flown off roads and hidden in buildings when on the ground. The history books told how the German bomber group that had sunk the *Shiloh* had survived the carrier-based aircraft sweeps because its commander had spread the aircraft across the countryside, hiding them in barns and flying them from roads. Of course, the same history also told how the group had been wiped out when it flew its attack. One of the things Taiwan was planning was a new road network. Those roads could have straight sections for flying and hangars built into the bridges for the Gnats. Soriva had heard the Americans were doing the same thing with their LeMay Interstate Highway system. He paused for a second, contemplating Japan's reaction to Taiwan purchasing the new American bomber, the Valkyrie, shuddered and returned to the subject troubling him.

The kicker for the deal was in the tail. The message said that the Triple Alliance was interested in purchasing anti-aircraft missiles and requested details of the fire control systems on the land-based systems in Imperial use. Soriva snorted. That was transparent. Face-saving at most. News that one of the American's vaunted bombers had been shot down had ricocheted around the world and everybody was waiting for the rumble of explosions that would signal another country joining the select group of ex-Nations. The Americans were being clever though, they would rescue the crew of the shot-down aircraft first so they could find out what had happened and they wanted this data so they could work out what had happened. Then they would take their revenge.

Soriva paced his office. He was, for all his current position, a loyal Japanese officer. The idea of giving away what amounted to state secrets appalled him. But, on the other hand, had not the Tokyo authorities made an even worse betrayal? Giving away a few technical manuals was bad but they were supplying missiles to people who were using them to shoot down Japanese airmen. If Tokyo found out - and they would find out - about the leak of the manuals, they would be furious but Taiwan was already on their to-do list. Taiwan didn't need more enemies but giving away the data wouldn't make any, only confirm the position of an existing foe. What Taiwan did need was equipment and friends.

It was an agonizing decision to have to make. Soriva sat at his desk. The top draw was open a little and he could see his American .45 automatic, the gun that had saved his life and the lives of most of his family. In the decision he was making, the sight of that gun counted for no greater weight than that of a feather yet when scales are evenly balanced, a feather on one pan or the other will cause a decisive tilt. Soriva decided to give the Americans the information they wanted.

The decision made, his mind started to range. The delegation was arriving in an American C-144, the transport version of their Hustler bomber. Another sign of who was really behind this sudden offer. He guessed the moment the Triple Alliance got the information they needed, that aircraft would be off to Washington, on full reheat all the way. Or at least as far as its fuel tanks would take it. Hawaii perhaps?

Now logically, he should make the Triple Alliance negotiators sweat blood for the data but was that really such a good idea? If he gave them the information they asked, as earnest money so to speak, the Americans would get it faster and speed was of the essence. That would allow The Triple Alliance to score markers with the Americans and they would owe Taiwan for those markers.

If he looked at the short term, he could screw down the prices the Triple Alliance was demanding. He looked at the list again. The Australians wanted how much for a Monash II? He shuddered at the number. But the medium and long term suggested that giving the information would be the better deal. The revered Admiral Yamamoto had been a great poker player, Soriva thought. Time to follow his example and gamble. It never hurt to be an American friend, one only had to look at Russia to see that.

Soriva sighed and wrote out an order for his technical staff to prepare a package of documentation on the fire control system for the Hiryu long-range anti-aircraft missile, the Katana medium-range and the Tanto short-range missiles. He thought for less than an instant and specifically added instructions to include the operational details of the new electro-optical adjunct to the guidance system for each.

That matter concluded. Soriva moved to more traditional affairs. *Kawachi* had been refloated and towed into Kaohsiung harbor. She was repairable although the work would take years. Nevertheless it would be done. One day, she would be the flagship of the Taiwan fleet, and one day, somehow, somewhen, she would regain her place in the Imperial Navy. One day.

International was a joke. The airport was a single runway, a single building, a shambles of wrecked and semi-scrapped aircraft and a handful of decrepit but workable ones. The airport building was shabby, the paint peeling of its walls, the door not quite properly on its hinges. Amongst the decaying disorder, the sleek Superstream looked horrendously uncomfortable, rather like a gently-raised heiress who suddenly found herself living in a skid row hostel, which, if anybody had asked the aircraft, was exactly how she did feel.

The delegation from The Triple Alliance emerged from the cramped interior of the executive jet to the cavalcade of cars that awaited them. As they came down, a group of sailors started unloading packages of books from a van and taking them to the pod under the C-144 that served as its cargo bay. The Ambassador grimaced and gave Sir Eric a US hundred dollar bill. She'd gambled Soriva would make them sweat for the information and it wasn't often she lost a bet.

Once again she reminded herself not to underestimate the man, his inoffensive air as a genial if slightly naïve civil servant was belied by the fact that he had been the head of the Indian intelligence services for more than a decade and nobody held that position without being both skilled and ruthless. About the only mistake she knew he had made was his assumption that she'd had something to do with the death of John F Kennedy. She hadn't, his death really had been an accident, but Sir Eric had never quite believed that. It wasn't as if she hadn't considered the possibility but she had decided that the potential risks far outweighed the possible gains.

As the delegation drove off to start the tortuous negotiations, the C-144 turned around to take off again with its vital load of manuals and documentation. On one point, Admiral Soriva had been wrong. The aircraft would not fly on full reheat all the way back to Washington It couldn't, it didn't have the fuel. Instead it was heading back to Clark Field in the Philippines. There, the YB-70 was waiting for the cargo and it would make the flight back to Washington at full speed. The YB-70 could do something that the C-144 could only dream about, it could cruise at speeds well over Mach 3. It was a strange fact that the YB-70 consumed less fuel per mile at Mach 3 plus than it did at subsonic speeds. To all intents and purposes, the YB-70s cruising speed was its maximum speed. That meant it cruised almost a thousand miles per hour faster than the C-144. The result of that differential was that the flight from Clark Field to Washington would take less than six hours.

CHAPTER SEVEN
RECOVERY

Sinai Desert, south of Gaza.

"She's gone Mike, we can't change that. We've got to get out of here. That fire is a 'Come get us' sign for everybody in a hundred miles."

Eddie Korrina was right and Kozlowski knew it. The column of smoke over *Marisol's* wreckage was rising hundreds of feet into the air. The crew had made a beautiful eject, landing a couple of miles away from the crash site yet within visual distance of each other. Dravar and Korrina had walked over to where Kozlowski was sitting on the sand, watching the smoke rising over *Marisol's* grave. He was staring at the site, hardly aware of anything else. Then, he shook himself and stood up.

"I know, I know. Its just, you know. I just feel there should have been something we could have done, they shouldn't have taken us down like that. Not a bunch of Caffs."

"Mike, there wasn't anything we could do. We were way too low and way too slow and the Caffs hit us with something we'd never met before. There was nothing we could have done."

Kozlowski shook his head, he felt as if a part of his soul had been ripped out. "I know that as well. We've got to get back and tell the brainiacs what happened so they can work out why it happened. By the way I don't know which one of you banged us all out but it was a good call. The rate we were spinning, another split second and the G-force would have been too high for an eject."

The other two crewmen looked at each other, confused. "Mike, we thought you ejected us. I was still trying to identify the signal on that damned missile when the seat fired."

Kozlowski frowned, *Marisol's* last scream was still echoing in his ears. "Guys, its getting close to sunset. We'll head west until midnight then swing to the coast. The Caffs know the book as well as we do, they'll be expecting us to go straight for the sea. They'll have patrols out to intercept us. There are a lot of bad people out there who'd just love to get their hands on any SAC crew let alone one from an RB-58 outfit. So we'll head west then north. Standard beacon drill. Two minutes transmission every twenty minutes but we'll hold off for a couple of hours. Then I'll transmit on the hour, Eddie, twenty minutes past, Xav, 40 minutes past. The SEALs will be looking for us, if they aren't ashore by now they soon will be. Let's go guys."

The crew set off, walking towards the setting sun and being careful to avoid getting skylined as they crossed the dune lines. Being silhouetted against the setting sun might look dramatic but it was terminally unsmart. Ahead, the red disk was just touching the horizon, behind them, *Marisol's* funeral pyre still stretched into the darkening sky.

Sinai Coast, south of Gaza.

Most traffic accidents happen at dusk. When the sun sets, the weakening light isn't strong enough to activate one set of receptors in the eye but is too strong for the other. Evolution designed the human eye to work in daylight or at night and, given a chance, it works fairly well in both. But, dusk is the gap between and there, the eye doesn't work very well at all. It flickers between its two optimum settings, detail is washed out, depth perception is messed up. The eye makes shapes out of random patterns and makes random patterns out of shapes. It sees things that aren't there and fails to notice the things that are. Dusk was a very good time for the SEALs to do their thing.

In any case, invisibility was a state of mind more than anything else. Not being noticed was a skill, not a matter of technology. Science helped, the SEAL's uniforms were the result of years of research into how the eye worked. Here, for the desert where everything was curved, the pattern was a strange mixture of gentle curves that subtly, but irresistibly, lead the eye across them, away to something else. The muted colors blended and eddied in ways that were downright disturbing when taken out of their proper context. If the SEALs had been going into a built-up area, they would have used different uniforms, one's with straight lines and jagged contrasts. Against the angles and corners of man-made structures blasted into rubble, the soft billowing curves would have been inappropriate and unhelpful.

Their equipment had the same elusive quality. Popular films of the SEALs had them covered with special equipment and deadly weaponry, their faces covered with masks or balaclavas. Here, where it mattered, such pretensions weren't even considered. They would catch an observer's eye, jar his attention and that would be fatal. Everything about the SEALs was nondescript and impalpable, designed to do everything but draw attention.

But, it was still the state of mind that was important. The SEALs looked at the rocks, the sand, the straggling plants and thought of them with affection and respect. They mentally apologized for disturbing them and, as they moved, they tried to tried to inconvenience them as little as possible. They thought kindly of the things that surrounded them, admired them and thought how much they wanted to be just like them. Treating their surrounding with affection and respect, they became part of them. On some intangible, miasmic level they ceased to be there at all. They became voids, an extension of their surroundings. They could walk into crowded rooms and people would look at them without seeing them because they had blended into the background so effectively.

In the bars around Norfolk and the other SEAL bases, it was a standing joke that the big men with tattoos and loud voices who occupied the bar, boasting of their exploits as SEALs were wannabee frauds. The real SEALs were the quiet, mundane men sitting in a corner - only you couldn't quite see them.

And so it was on the beach that was part of the Sinai coast. As the sun slipped below the horizon, Commander Jeff Thomas's SEAL Team Two slipped ashore. Even if anybody had been watching, they wouldn't have seen anything. Or, to be more precise, they wouldn't have been aware they'd seen anything.

Sinai Coast, North of "Marisol" crash site.

The Marines weren't SEALs. Their skills were entirely different. When their lead element hit the beach, there was no doubt about it. They were in amphibious tractors, LVTs, ungainly vehicles that were neither landing craft nor armored personnel carriers but somewhere in between. They swam through the surf then crawled up the beach taking the lead platoon towards the rock fields inland. More swam ashore and headed to the flanks. By the time all the LVTs were ashore, the Marine Company had established a perimeter that protected the landing beach against direct fire. Behind them came a pair of landing craft, LCTs, that unloaded a platoon of five M60 tanks, a Marine company headquarters, the heavy weapons platoon and a detachment from the battalion support company. By the time the last element came ashore, more than 250 men were on the beach.

The landing site had been carefully chosen. It was straight, smooth, and small enough to be protected by a company-sized perimeter. It was surrounded by a ridge of jumbled rock that provided cover for the Marines on that perimeter yet allowed the mortars on the beach to give them supporting fire. In fact, it was such a perfect beach for a night landing that the planners had guessed it had been used by smugglers back to Biblical days. There was supporting evidence for that, the one thing the planners hadn't liked, an old track that lead through the rocks to the north.

That was why the tanks were on the beach, along with two 106 millimeter recoilless rifles. Together with the company's 60 millimeter mortars and a pair of 81s detached from the battalion heavy weapons company, the firepower covering the beach was enough to hold it solid - or so the planners hoped. The

Marine infantry were already nesting down into firing positions on the outer edge of the rock-pile, sheltered by the boulders but with a clear field of fire outwards. Now, it was just a question of waiting.

AC-133A "Buffy", Eastern Mediterranean.

When asked, *Buffy's* crew always explained that the name stood for Big Ugly Fat Fellow. Which was almost right, except the last F didn't stand for Fellow. The first production C-133 Cargomasters had been built without an unloading ramp in the rear, that feature had been introduced with the B-model. Only 24 C-133As had been built, and two of them had crashed. The rest of them had been retired with only a few dozen flying hours on them and sent to the boneyard.

One night, all 22 had mysteriously vanished. Their new owners were Special Operations Command, a tri-service organization that existed to provide the various special forces groups with the equipment they needed. They'd modified the C-133s in ways the original designers would never have credited, ways that were merely suggested by their modified designation.

From outside, the AC-133A Slayers didn't look that odd. There were some strange bumps and bulges, that was for sure, but a lot of transport aircraft had those. They were painted an odd color as well, a very dark bluish gray that camouflaged them at night much better than black would have done. It was only when visitors went on board and stood on the cargo deck they realized what the SOCOM had done. The cargo deck looked like something out of an eighteenth century ship of the line.

At the front was Battery A, three 20 millimeter M61 Vulcans, six-barreled Gatling guns that poured out 6,000 rounds per minute each. They were the guns tasked with area saturation, as the Slayer circled an area, those guns would pour shells into the target. Nothing survived a blast from Battery A unless it was under armor or in deep cover. The center of the aircraft was occupied by Battery B, three old Navy 40 millimeter Bofors guns. They'd been modified and were on trainable mounts that were keyed to unusually complex targeting systems. They also fired some very sophisticated ammunition that could slice through the thinner top armor of even a heavily-protected tank. But behind them was Battery C. At this point, every visitor, without exception, stopped dead and said the same thing "This is a joke right?" Because Battery C had three 105 millimeter howitzers. They'd been stripped of wheels of course and were on special mounts that absorbed most of their recoil. Even then, even an aircraft as big as an AC-133 couldn't fire all three at once, they were there so one could be firing while the other two were reloaded.

Most outsiders had pictures of all three batteries firing at once, the Slayer flying over a target with a cloud of smoke issuing from the nine guns firing out of her port side. In fact, all three batteries required different approaches and different flight paths, different altitudes and different turn rates, for maximum effectiveness. They were an either/or proposition. Despite her massive brute-force gun battery, the Slayer was a precision instrument and, like most precision instruments, she required extreme skill if she was to deliver results.

Buffy had been operating out of Cyprus. By a historical quirk, the British still had bases there and every so often the U.S. used one of them. Now, *Buffy* was circling off the Sinai coast, with one simple job. Listen for the beacon signals from the crew of *Marisol*, plot their position and steer the SEAL rescue team in to pick them up. Of course, that assumed the crew had survived the shoot-down, hadn't been taken prisoner or simply been killed by the first enemy troops to the area. If the latter had happened, it wouldn't be a job for the SEALs any more. SAC avenged its own.

"Got them!." One of the electronics technicians was manipulating his antennas, trying to get the finest possible directional cut. Meanwhile, the pilot had broken out of the circle and was flying parallel to the coast as fast as the aircraft could manage, six miles a minute. Doctrine was that the people on the ground would transmit for two minutes in twenty. The longer the baseline that could be achieved in those two minutes, the more precise the position. That two minutes seemed like twenty.

"OK Boss. Got a fix. Not brilliant but it puts them eight miles west of the crash site. Sensible guys, looks like they're heading parallel to the coast before trying to get to the sea. We'll patch through to SEAL Team Two and get them going the right way. Tell them we'll get a movement bearing with the next hit."

Sinai Desert, south of Gaza.

The sun had gone down hours before and the night was pitch black. Kozlowski and his crew had grown up in an America where electricity was plentiful and cheap, even far from large towns, there were street lights and neon signs. They polluted the sky, lightened the darkness and dimmed out the stars. Here, there was none of that, the sky was jet black, the stars shone with ferocious brilliance and the shadows on the ground were as dark as pitch.

The three airmen were resting, they'd been moving as fast as they could manage, trying to put as much ground between them and the crash site as possible. By their reckoning, they'd moved a good five miles, perhaps even six. But, trying to move fast in the soft sand was deadly tiring, their lungs felt red-raw and their legs seemed to have turned to rubber.

"Oh Damn." Kozlowski whispered as if the desert was listening. He tapped Korrina on the arm and pointed. In the distance, hardly visible but quite distinct nonetheless, there were lights behind one of the lines of dunes. Either vehicle headlights or men on foot with powerful torches. Either way, they were clearly following the tracks left by *Marisol's* crew.

"Up guys, we've got to move. They're after us. Keep heading west and hope they're trying casts. If we go far enough west, they may try north. And, whatever else you do, don't forget to keep the beacon going."

Sinai Coast, south of Gaza.

Captain Ivan Jaeger thought of his command as being the 23rd Panzer Armee. It pleased him to give the outrageously exaggerated designation to what was barely more than a company combat team. He had nine Walid armored personnel carriers, at first glance they looked like the old SdKfz-251 half-track but they had wheels at the back, not tracks. The Caliphate didn't have the industrial ability to produce the elaborately engineered interleaved suspension of the older vehicles so they'd given the Walid four wheels at the back and a transmission that powered all six. The carriers were for his infantry, two platoons of them.

In addition he had a platoon of Chi-Teh-Kai tanks. They weren't bad, they were fast, lightweight and heavily-gunned with a 100 mm cannon. For artillery he had a mortar section, a pair of 120 millimeters, also mounted in Walid carriers. Not a bad command for an officer. Mobile, it had lots of hitting power and his German veterans were more than a match for the tribal warriors they faced, most of the time anyway.

They'd had a report that there were large numbers of infidels in the bay ahead. The conclusion was obvious, they'd come to get the crew of the American bomber some damned fools had shot down earlier. As if they didn't have enough to worry about, picking a confrontation with the Americans was the last thing they needed. Still, it might be just a bunch of refugees or even some real smugglers. It was time to find out. Fortunately, they had just the right people to do it.

Attached to his little command was another Caliphate vehicle, a small Safra armored car, barely more than a jeep. It had an officer and three men as its crew. Perfect for the job. Jaeger greeted the Caliphate officer effusively.

"My dear friend, I have not yet had a chance to tell you how much I value your services to my unit. Truly you are a great warrior. As such, I am going to ask you to accept the honor of leading us tonight. Surely, with such as you at our head, we cannot fail in our duty."

The Caliphate officer jerked to attention with a crisp salute and his little Safra started off down the track towards the bay. In the shadows behind one of the tanks, a German Sergeant grinned nastily and ostentatiously put his fingers in his ears. Everybody else paused and waited silently, the air full of amused anticipation. They didn't have to wait long, there was a flash of light then, a few seconds later, a dull boom and a brief crackle of rifle fire.

"Well, it appears we do have hostiles over there after all." Jaeger eased up to the top of the tune and looked down the goat track. The little Safra was on its side and burning about fifty or sixty meters from where the track entered a jumble of rocks. If he looked hard he could see the bodies of the Caliphate officer and his men surrounding the destroyed vehicle. The explosion had been one of the American 3.5 inch rocket launchers, a big clumsy weapon. Jaeger couldn't understand why the Americans kept it when they could have the much smaller, lighter and more effective RPG for the asking.

The rifle fire, now that was curious. It had been short, flat cracks, not the yapping noise of the Arisaka or the rhythmic jackhammer of the AK-47. All of Model's Germans knew the sound of the AK well, not a few of them had nightmares featuring it. Jaeger was one of them. His second worst nightmare was waves of Russian infantry running at him, firing their AKs from the hip and screaming their 'Urrah! Urrah!'

He preferred that to his worst nightmare. In 1947 he'd left his fiancée, a Luftwaffe telegraphist, in Berlin, they'd planned to marry in six months, that's when he would have come back on his first leave from the front. But before that could happen, the Americans had dropped a dozen Hellburners on the city. And two hundred more on the rest of Germany. Ever so often, in his nightmares, he saw his fiancée holding her arms out to him for help as she melted in the fury of the American attack.

No, this rifle sound was new. It wasn't even the deep thud of the American's Garand. Well, it didn't matter, he and his men would solve the mystery soon. The Battle of the Goat Track was about to start.

Sinai Desert, south of Gaza.

They couldn't fool themselves any longer. The men with the lights were chasing them. For three hours they'd slowly but steadily closed the distance and now they were just the other side of the previous dune line. What had been a vague hint of lights was now a bright glare. It was over, there was no point in running any more. Kozlowski checked his inventory of weapons. Three .38 Small and Weak revolvers with 12 rounds each, three M-6 survival rifles with 20 rounds each - of .22 long rifle. They could put up a small fight, that was it.

"OK guys, this is it. We'll hold here, it may just be a couple of guys and we can finish them before they realize we've stopped."

That was nonsense, it wasn't a case of vehicles or men with flashlights, it was vehicles and men with flashlights. Then, a miracle happened, without a sound to explain it, the lights went out. The men chasing them must have decided to turn back.

"Thank God for that. How far are we from the coast?" Kozlowski whispered.

"About twelve miles. Don't worry about the guys chasing you. They're gone."

The voice came from his right, where nobody was supposed to be. Kozlowski jerked his head around. A figure was sprawled flat on the sand just a couple of feet from him.

"Major Mike Kozlowski?" Kozlowski nodded "Commander Jeff Thomas, United States Navy. We've come to take you home."

Viceregal Palace, New Delhi, India

Sir Eric Haohoa had never seen an official state limousine do a skid-turn stop before. The maneuver caused a cloud of dust to rise around the vehicle but the haze didn't hide an even more astonishing sight. The Ambassador herself was driving, something he'd never seen before. Before, she'd always been sitting decorously in the back while the car was handled by her official driver. For her to be driving herself was unprecedented. Mind you, he had heard about her driving skills, good but excessively fast would be the official summary. Some reports were more picturesque, they said the Ambassador's driving was the only thing that made America's National Security Advisor go white and pray.

She left the car and ran up the steps, scanning the crowd waiting there for somebody she could trust to give an accurate, concise answer. "Sir Eric. How is he?"

"Grave, I fear Ma'am, very, very grave. It was just after dinner, Sir Martyn got up for brandy and cigars and, just, fell over. The doctors are dreadfully concerned. Sir Martyn has been asking for you. If you would come with me?"

He laid the way through the corridors of the palace. Normally they were bustling with life, with servants, both civil and domestic, going about their business. Even at night, the work of government never stopped but it had stopped now. People were standing, waiting quietly, trying to gather news. Some of the women were crying quietly, others looking towards Sir Martyn's private apartments. In some, hope surged as they saw Sir Eric and The Ambassador. Perhaps it would be all right now. Surely, those two, together, could fix anything?

They went through the double doors into the private living spaces. Lady Rebecca Sharpe was sitting in the waiting room, crying quietly with two of her friends comforting her. As they came in, a Doctor came out of the bedroom. He quietly called Lady Rebecca, Sir Eric and the Ambassador over.

"It was a very severe heart attack indeed. I am sorry to say this but there is no hope. The damage to his heart is just too great. He is resting quietly now but sometime tonight there will be another attack and that will be the end. Madam Ambassador, Sir Martyn has asked to see you in private, alone for a few minutes."

The Ambassador caught a look of pure, undiluted, hatred from Lady Rebecca. She understood, it must be very hard for a wife whose husband was in his last hours to see another woman asked in for a private meeting. She followed the Doctor in. Sir Martyn was in bed, she was appalled at how weak and pale he looked. Mentally she flayed herself, she'd known he was sick and she hadn't done enough to save him. The, as was her practice, she hid her real emotions beneath a false face and sat beside the bed.

"Sir Martyn, how do you feel? Is there anything I can do for you?"

His voice was weak but remarkably steady. "It is all right Ma'am. There is a very real comfort in knowing that one's time has come. No more doubts or wondering what to do or where the rights and wrongs of things are. You've done the best you can and that's it. When your time comes, you'll know what I mean."

The Ambassador smiled, under the smile, she thought that was the problem. If her time came, she'd understand. Sir Martyn was still talking.

"But I must know, Ma'am, how did you deal with Gandhi?"

The Ambassador chuckled. Speaking very quietly so none would overhear, she whispered "It was quite easy really. We stole a car from the Embassy compound. One of the drivers liked to visit low-class women of ill-repute so we kidnapped him after one such visit. Used a rubber hose and funnel to pour whisky down his throat. Then, we put him in the driving seat of the car, one of my people sat in the passenger seat with a wooden pole to push the accelerator and brake. Gandhi stepped out in the road, my man just accelerated the car into him. The he used the stick to pound on the driver. Everybody had been looking at Gandhi so they assumed my man had simply been one of the first Indians to attack the car after the "accident". As soon as the riot was underway, he slipped off. I had a second man in the crowd to push Gandhi in front of the car but he wasn't needed."

Sir Martyn laughed, coughed then laughed some more. "You mean the Japanese have been telling the truth for all these years and still nobody believes them? That's wonderful."

He settled back on his pillow with a beam of tranquil delight on his face. The Ambassador quietly stood and called for Lady Rebecca. As she entered she saw the peace on Sir Martyn's face and smiled her thanks to The Ambassador, she couldn't hold any resentment against somebody who had brought so much grace to her husband's last hours. As Lady Rebecca sat by the bed, the Ambassador looked out the windows. The square beneath was filling with people, all quietly standing and waiting, looking up as if they could somehow send enough of their own strength to help

Sir Martyn through this illness. Even as she watched, more and more people joined the crowd below. Then she turned to leave.

"Please don't go Madam Ambassador. I know my husband would want you to stay with us. Please, sit with us."

The Ambassador took the remaining seat by the bed. Lady Rebecca was holding one of Sir Martyn's hands, she took the other. Sir Martyn was in a light sleep that deepened as the minutes ticked by. Then, one of his hands clenched hard and what little color was left in his face went. The Ambassador had seen more people die than she liked to count and recognized the death-shadow sweeping down over his face. Knowing that hearing was the last sense to go she leaned forward and whispered very softly "You are loved, Sir Martyn. And we will meet again."

Lady Rebecca was sobbing quietly. The Ambassador went back to the waiting room and told Sir Eric that the wait was over. He followed her back into the room to say farewell to his friend. Outside, word was already spreading through the crowd. The people gathered were crying openly, gently, to themselves. Individually, none were making any great noise but together they were creating a murmuring wave of grief that was far more impressive than any more ostentatious or choreographed displays could possibly have been.

Sir Eric had finished speaking to Lady Rebecca. Together he and the Ambassador left the room as others started filing in to pay their respects. "What will happen now Sir Eric? I assume a successor has been appointed?"

"Indeed so Ma'am. The President has made arrangements so that Lady Sharpe can live here as long as she wishes. It is the least India can do. Sir Martyn had trained several successors, some of whom show great promise. I think the measure of his achievement is how little change will result from his death."

The Ambassador nodded. "Sir Martyn told me once he had a dream of restoring India's greatness. I wonder if he knew how well the two of you have succeeded. India is a great power again, one of the leading powers in the world. I understand one of the dignitaries in London has the epitaph on his grave 'If you seek a monument, look around you.' That would do well for Sir Martyn I think. He has made the whole of modern India his monument."

Deep in the Jungle, somewhere in Mindanao

Manuel Onorosa, known to his followers and the press as "Commander Torpedo" was a troubled and unhappy man. After his extortion success in Rosario, he thought he had finally made his mark with the shadowy figures that ran the insurgency. He'd been instructed to meet up with another group and pass a portion of the liberated funds over to them. He'd done that but bad luck seemed to follow the money everywhere it went. They'd met up with the other group as planned, handed over the money as ordered. And, just after they'd split apart after the meeting, not more than an hour or two in time and a few kilometers in space, they'd heard the crackle of rifle fire, the dull thump of the mortars. By the time they'd got there, all the other unit, every man, every one, was dead.

He remembered their first victim, the old lady in the vegetable farm. She had cursed them when they'd stabbed and beaten her. His men had laughed it off at the time but now they spoke of it no more. And that was a bad sign. There were other rumors too, the godless Siamese, the ones who went to the villages and formed the Christian militias that were slowly but surely shutting the warriors of the True Belief out from food and information and recruits, they were spreading rumors that the spirits of the forests had been offended by the warriors and had taken sides against them. The old animist religion that had been in Mindanao long before either Christianity or Islam had influenced both religions more than either liked to admit. His men laughed at the idea of jungle spirits and sneered at those who still respected them. But, in their hearts they were terrified by the idea that the jungle itself had turned against them.

Yet, the curse hadn't followed them. The strange thing was it affected everybody but them. The first rendezvous had been the first disaster. Then they'd been instructed to meet up with a second unit to ambush a Philippine Army patrol. The patrol had never turned up, the Philippine troops had probably decided to sleep in that day so the two units had split again. Only, the others had been destroyed by artillery fire. Just a few hours after the split, the Australian long-range guns had dropped shells on them and there weren't even body parts left to bury. The jungle had taken those again. And so it had been ever after. Every unit that touched them had died, by ambush, by artillery fire, by mortars or just by vanishing into the greenery and never being seen again.

But it was the guns that were worst. The original reports had laughed at the Australian artillery, comparing its 94 millimeter guns with the 150s used by others. Only those Australian guns could throw shells to a distance nobody had dreamed of. They were creating a web of fire, an interlocking network of steel and explosive that was slowly pushing forward. Within range of the Australian guns, nobody was safe, the shells could arrive at any time. "Commander Torpedo" knew he was in range of those guns now, the shells could be on their way, now.

Yet they weren't the ones he feared most. The big, long-range guns were in fixed positions, where they could reach, where they could not, all could be calculated. The dead zones were known and could be exploited. No, the worst were the little mountain guns. They'd never been listed in the reports because nobody took them seriously. They did now. Those guns could appear anywhere, at any time. Even in the most impossible terrain. They'd appear, pour fire into an area everybody had assumed was safe, then vanish again. When the battery position was attacked, there was nothing but empty jungle. Once, just once, the Australians had left some papers behind. The man who'd found them had picked them up and Commander Torpedo still remembered the explosion as the booby trap had blown his arm off.

Even the command had heard of the curse on his unit, the way it had leprosy, infecting everything it touched. He'd been ordered to retreat to this remote area and stay put. "Don't call us, we'll call you" had been the order. Nobody came near them, nobody spoke to them, nobody delivered to them or took from them. Their food was running out and Jose had never been much of a cook at the best of time. Now his concoctions were barely edible.

Suddenly 'Commander Torpedo' started, the 'meal', such as it was, in his bowl had slopped into his lap. Had that idiot Jose lost his marbles to the point where the meat was still alive? Then he looked down and saw the Australian-made version of the British Mills grenade in his bowl, and in the split second that was left to him, he realized that he wouldn't have to complain about Jose's cooking ever again.

A few feet away, a few minutes later

It had been like taking candy from a baby. The guards, such as they were, had their throats cut first, soundlessly. The Australian unit had moved quietly into place, blocking all the possible escape routes for the unit that was to die. Once everything was set up, half a dozen grenades had been tossed into the camp.

Sergeant Major Shane was proud of his throw, he'd tossed the grenade right into some poor dumb cluck's dinner bowl. Worth of the Australian First Eleven that throw had been. He hadn't had time to pat himself on the back, there was work to be done and rifles to do it with. The men who had survived the grenades were trying to rise, some to return fire, although where they would return it to was beyond their knowledge. Others, less brave perhaps but significantly wiser, had tried to make a run for it. It didn't matter, whatever they did, the staccato crackle of rifle fire had picked off the remainder.

They couldn't have done it with Old Smelly. The SMLE, despite its smooth, fact-acting bolt, couldn't match the new semi-automatics for rate of fire. There had been a lot of jokes about that, about how the new rifle replaced Old Smelly's single shot that hit with a lot that missed. As experience had grown, the jokes had faded away. The new 7mm rounds hit as often as the old .303s had and did a lot more damage when they bit home. Even the die-hards, the ones who'd learned their marksmanship before joining the Army, were beginning to see the virtues of their new rifle. They'd sworn that no semi-automatic could match the accuracy of Old Smelly. Now, they were slowly admitting, perhaps just one, this one, could.

They'd decided to take the terrorist unit out earlier that day. For almost two weeks they'd been following it, seeing where it went and who it had met. Almost a hundred Caffs had been whacked as a result. Almost a hundred stepped on and counted.

Probably a lot more blown apart by artillery. Every unit these poor suckers had contacted had been fed into the grinder. Every dump they'd visited had been quietly "vanished" or kept under surveillance. Now, at least a dozen more units were being followed, their contacts identified and eliminated. So this unit had ceased to be useful and the order had come to finish it off. It was a fair guess the Caffs were having their doubts about it as well, they'd ordered the unit into what amounted to quarantine. That's what had really condemned it to death.

"Recognize these two?" One of the soldiers was holding a body by its hair. The man had been shot half a dozen times in the chest and there wasn't much holding him together. "He's one of the bastards who worked over Missus Tuntoya. Can we tell her we got him? Might cheer the old dear up a bit." Their officer held a hand out and waggled it palm down. There were a few things to be sorted out first.

Rosario, Surigao del Sur Province, Mindanao, Philippines

Narisa Nurmahmud locked the doors behind her. The Philippine National Bank had closed for the day and she had a rendezvous to keep. During the day she was Miss Narisa the foreign exchange clerk at the PNB. Narisa Valadola according to the official records. But, in the evening she took her new Islamic surname and became a warrior for the jihad to turn Mindanao into a true Islamic state. One day she could wear her hijab and take revenge on those whose beliefs had prevented her from doing so in the past. She had lurid fantasies about how she would take her revenge on them.

It would come soon, the struggle was under way, financed by those who sent money back from the godless places they worked. She had taken another step on that route just today, three more foreign exchange payments had come in, a total of almost sixty thousand pesos. This meeting would get word to Commander Torpedo and he could take it for the greater glory of the jihad.

She didn't expect to be grabbed from behind, she didn't expect to be thrown into the back of a vehicle and driven off. She'd been walking around the town most of her life and that sort of thing just didn't happen. She tried to lift her head up and a boot mashed down in the back of her skull, shoving her face into the floor. A blanket was thrown over her and that was the end of any hope of finding out where she was being taken.

Wherever it was, the drive wasn't far, the vehicle halted, somebody grabbed her feet and hauled her out. She hit the ground with a thud that drove the breath from her, then her head still covered, she was half-dragged, half-walked into some sort of building.

There were voices around her, speaking in languages she didn't know. They were arguing about something, in fact there were two or three arguments going on in different languages, One of them sounded like Arabic and she felt a deep sense of relief, despite the violence with which she'd been picked up, these were the people she'd been working for. Another couple were speaking in Tagalog, she couldn't quite hear what they were saying. Then the world changed. One of the voices spoke in Visayan. "Oh just kill the bitch."

"No!" She gasped, her voice mostly muffled by the blanket. "Please no. I am on your side. I am working with Commander Torpedo. My work is to tell him who has received foreign currency transfers."

Suddenly the blanket was pulled from her head. It didn't help much, bright lights were shining on her and the rest of the room was in darkness. "See!" the Visayan voice said. "She lies. She claims to be a believer yet she walks with her face bare. Kill her."

To Narisa's horror a glass containing a viscous yellow liquid was produced and put on the table. She couldn't see it properly but it was there and it reminded her of her fantasies. The threat was making her sick.

"Please no. I wanted to take hijab but Commander Torpedo told me my duty was to stay with the Bank. Please. Ask Commander Torpedo he will tell you."

That caused more discussion, more talk in the languages she couldn't understand. Then the Visayan man spoke again. "You

198

will write a letter to Commander Torpedo asking him to confirm your identity. If he does so then you can go free. If Commander Torpedo does not confirm your story then you will be killed."

"That won't do. It could be anybody writing that note. How will Commander Torpedo know its her?" Another voice, foreign, it sounded like one of the men who had been speaking in Arabic.

" I know a way. Listen, bitch. Put things in there that only the two of you will know. You better make it convincing. A hand picked up the glass and swirled the yellow liquid suggestively. Narisa whimpered and started writing. When she finished, she gave the letter to a man, hidden in the darkness. He read it quickly.

"That's great. A lot of good stuff we didn't know and confirmation of things we suspected." The lights flicked on. The room held three Philippine Army soldiers and two Australians along with a couple of civilians. One of the Philippine soldiers picked up the glass of yellow liquid. Narisa whimpered again and tried to turn her face away.

Then, the soldier drank from the glass and shuddered. "This is disgusting. Fosters you call it? Dreadful. Look, I'll get you some crates of San Miguel sent over. We're allies, we can't let you drink this muck. If this came from a buffalo, we'd declare the poor thing unfit for work."

Narisa made a despairing grab for the papers she'd written. The Australian holding them whisked them out of reach. "Now, now my dear. That's not nice."

"What are you going to do with me?"

"Nothing. We're going to drive you back to your home and drop you off there. All very nice and polite. You see, we have no more use for you. Commander Torpedo and his gang of extortionists were ambushed and killed this morning by one of our units. So there is nobody to whom you can pass the doctored information we've been sending your way. Of course your people know Torpedo was killed today and they'll see you being returned home by an Australian Army jeep. Of course, they may assume it's a coincidence. And if they don't?"

Suddenly the Australian voice turned hard and shook with anger. "There's at least two nice old ladies got torn up because of you. One of them nearly died and the other has more guts in her little finger than you and all your friends put together. There are lot more who live in fear now, afraid to be on their own, afraid to answer their own door. So I think you'll get what's coming to you."

From the Rosario Sun newspaper, next day

"The body of local woman, Narisa Valadola, was found on a garbage dump behind her home last night. The victim had been driven home by two Australian Army soldiers in a jeep, After they left, she was seen to enter her home, alone, at least an hour before the body was found. Cause of death was a single knife wound to the throat, cutting the neck to the spine. Three suspects, all members of the local Muslim community, have been detained and are assisting local police with their inquiries. Unofficial police sources tell the Sun that the victim and the three suspects had all been drinking heavily and are believed to have had a dispute over Miss Valadola's sexual favors and the division of the proceeds from an extortion racket."

CHAPTER NINE
PITCHED BATTLE

USS "Thomas Jefferson" CC-3, Command Flagship, US Mediterranean Fleet

Ten years ago, it wouldn't have been possible. Five years ago it was possible, but it didn't work. Now it was possible, it worked and the Navy had to find out how to use it. It didn't even have the same name. It was the Combat Information Center on smaller ships, here it was called the Combat Direction Center. The heart, the nervous system of the CDC, was NTDS. It was NTDS that took the tactical data from the sensors, fed it to the CDC that turned it into a tactical picture and returned that picture to the CICs in the smaller ships. Looking at the system, Admiral Mahan knew he was getting a glimpse into the future of warfare. What that future would be like, he couldn't imagine, what he did know was that it would contain a hideous and terrifying number of acronyms.

Still, what he had in front of him was impressive enough. Over the eastern Mediterranean, close to the Sinai coast, the SOCOM airborne command post, an AC-133A called *Buffy* was circling while she coordinated the rescue operation for *Marisol's* crew. The SEALs had met up with them at last and were bringing them back to the coast.

Buffy was also acting as a relay point for the Marines ashore just a bit to the north and east of the SEALs. They had seized a blocking position between the Caliphate base area around Gaza, partly to stop the troops there interfering with the SEALs, partly to act as a diversion. The Phibron was a bit further out to sea, close enough to support the Marines, far enough out to be over the horizon and away from immediate danger.

The air operations were a thing of beauty. The Phibron was being covered by aircraft operating from the *Shiloh*, the *Shiloh* was being covered by aircraft operating from *Enterprise*, the *Enterprise* was being covered by Chuck Larry's F-108 Rapiers from Aviano. Also from Aviano, the surviving 23 RB-58s of the 1/305th were bombed up and ready to go.

Mahan had heard the mood in the 305th was ugly, and not all the rage was directed at the Caliphate. The *Seven Pines* and her battle group would be transiting the Straits of Gibraltar in less than 12 hours, the *Bull Run* and her group were less than ten hours behind her. That would make ten carriers, almost 800 naval aircraft, swarming into the Eastern Mediterranean. The two carriers already on the scene had their Hawkeyes up and those airborne radar posts were also feeding data back to the *Thomas Jefferson*. Once again the terse statement of policy swam through Mahan's mind. The United States does not fight its enemies, it destroys them.

In some ways this whole massive effort, aimed at the safe recovery of just three men was an example of just that. It was a message that said different things to different recipients. To the American servicemen, it was reassurance that if they went down, there was nothing, literally nothing, the United States would allow to get in the way of their recovery. It was a message to anybody who thought of fighting Americans, do it and the world of hurt that engulfs you will be beyond your comprehension.

The massive military operation now unfolding had another purpose though, one that was buried deep. It was a desperate attempt to make the other side realize what it was they had started, make them understand the sheer, raw military power they had provoked. It was a desperate attempt to make them back down before they were destroyed. America kept the peace by threatening the nuclear destruction of anybody who broke the peace. It was a hard and a brutal policy and it was one that had won America few friends in the world. But it kept the peace and peace, however hard-won, was more valuable than being popular. The catch was, if the arsenal of nuclear warheads was used again, if another country was wiped off the map, the peace that cost so much to create would be worth far less.

Admiral Mahan looked at the huge displays that dominated his CDC. *Shiloh* had her F6D Missileers up, for what they were worth. The F6D was pretty much a failure, Douglas had only built a handful of them and it wouldn't be in service much longer. Grumman were already designing a new heavy fighter for the fleet, the XF13F-1 Tomcat. Its J-58s would give it the double-sonic cruise of the latest Air Force fighters combined with the battery of long-range nuclear-tipped air-to-air missiles from the F6D. When it arrived, if it arrived, it would be deadly. Until it did, fleet air defense really rested with Vought's F9U Super-Crusaders. They could dash out at almost 2,000 miles per hour to intercept a raid but, unlike Chuck Larry's super-fast but clumsy F-108s, they were vicious, agile dogfighters as well. Just the tool needed for the operation tonight.

Mahan sighed. For all the super technology that was being displayed tonight, in the final analysis, it would all come down to the Marines holding a beach and the SEALs doing, well, something unspeakable, as usual.

On the Goat-Track, Sinai Coast, south of Gaza.

"Where do you think they are Sergeant, and who are they?" Captain Ivan Jaeger trained his binoculars on the rock field that lay just beyond the burning Safra.

"Where Sir? That's easy. See those rock scrambles either side of the track? Just there, they'll be. Sucker bait those rocks are. Look very good for cover but they're too far forward and too obvious. Who are they? That's a hard one. That was a 3.5 inch bazooka sure enough and that says Americans. Only the rifles were something different. They weren't Garands. They could be Italians, their BM-49 is chambered for the same round as our Stg-44s. Or perhaps they're Egyptian gendarmerie trying to escape. If that's so sir, I say we let them go. They deserve better than what's been done to them. Maybe its both, Gendarmerie on the beach and Italians come to get them. That makes sense Sir. We know the Italians are helping refugees escape, its driving the raggies mad."

Jaeger thought then made his decision. "Whoever they are, we know they are hostile. We'll take them on, we have to. If they are Gendarmerie and Italians, and they give it up, we'll turn a blind eye to any who escape." He marked his map with the likely hostile positions then he and his Sergeant slid off the low dune and back to where the unit was waiting.

"Mortars. I want four rounds rapid each, these positions here and here. Take one position each, then drop four smoke rounds in front of the rock line. Infantry, as soon as the smoke is down, get those carriers forward. There's a wadi about two hundred meters short of the rockline. Stop and debus there. That's far enough out so the carriers will be out of range of the anti-tank stuff but their machine guns can cover the infantry as they move forward.

"I think there's a mix of Italian and Egyptian gendarmerie in there, they're probably using the American rescue effort as cover. Anyway, the Americans are well west of here. Panzers, move off to our left and get into position to provide covering fire . My guess is a few rounds of HE will drive the people in that rockpile back. Just look for the muzzle flashes and take them down. Go to your commands, we bounce off in five minutes soldiers."

In the Rock-Pile, Sinai Coast, south of Gaza.

"You think that's it Gunny?" Lieutenant Admire nestled down in the rocks. The flames from the burning armored car were dying down now and the bodies around it had stopped moving. It had been brief, just a split second or two. The bazooka crew had taken down the armored car and the riflemen had killed the crew as they'd bailed out. A beach patrol probably, had done this run a hundred times and forgotten there was a hundred and first. He'd reported the contact, got his acknowledgment and so, that was it.

"Sir, no Sir." Gunnery Sergeant Tomas was trying to make something out in the darkness. It was just something a little smaller, a little further away than he could see. But there was something out there. "I think there's more out there. I can feel them."

"Learning something from your SEAL friends Gunny?"

"Sir, don't knock it. When you've had a couple of men walk up to you in broad daylight and you just don't see them, something sticks."

"They that impressive on the exercise Gunny? We hear a lot about them but I'd always thought..."

"No, not that Sir. SEALs and I met up a long, long time ago. Back in Mex......Holy hell."

The explosions had come suddenly, without warning. Eight of them, big ones that made the rocks shake and the ears rattle. Each one following the one before it so fast they merged into a single continuous rumble.

"Corpsman, Corpsman. For God's Sake, get a Corpsman over here."

Admire stuck his head cautiously over the rock as there was another series of explosions. White smoke was billowing in front of the Marine position. Over to his left, what he could see made him sick. He'd thought the positions he'd chosen for his bazooka teams were perfect. Rocks to give good cover, far enough forward to give a good field of fire. Only the mortars had landed straight on top of them. The Marine screaming for a medic was in the far position, those in the nearer one were ominously silent.

Even before the situation had time to register properly, he heard a roar of engines. He had his binoculars, they weren't as good as the night vision equipment on the vehicles but they'd do. Through the drifting smoke he could see more armored cars, big ones, how many he couldn't tell. They were dancing around, dipping into the ground and approaching mightily fast. However many there were, there were too many.

"Radioman. Charlie-Two-Zero this is Charlie-Two-Three we are under attack. Artillery and armored vehicles. Need support."

Ahead of the marine position, the armored vehicles had dipped into a deep gully. Now they could hardly be seen, just a sliver of their tops. The position didn't hide what they were doing, the Marines could see their infantry debussing. "November-Zero. Armored vehicles are armored personnel carriers. They are unloading about 200 yards in front of us. Estimate at least company strength. Am engaging."

The enemy soldiers were already in position, spreading out along the gully. Suddenly there was a roar and more than three dozen flames seemed to jab out from the lip of the wadi and the vehicles hull-down in it. At the receiving end, the effect was rather like being caught in a cloudburst, the hail of fire torrenting off the rocks and ricocheting across the gaps. In the middle of the hail, Admire saw a group of the enemy leave the protection of the gully and run forward to a new position. It was too quick for anybody to do anything but wait for the next one.

That didn't take long, there was another torrent of fire and again, a group from the gully tried to run forward. This time the Marines were ready, the MMG lashed out a string of tracers and a couple of the men went down. More were hit by the rifle fire from the new M-14s.

The response was immediate, half a dozen of the enemy machineguns concentrated on the MMG position while others hosed down areas where muzzle flashes had been spotted. The Marines who survived learned a valuable lesson, fire a shot, get the hell out of Dodge.

Admire shook himself, his command was already taking a battering, he'd lost both his bazooka teams and one of his MMGs and the action was only a few seconds old. Out in front, the enemy were still edging forward, small groups of men dashing up, supported by the sleet of fire from the machineguns. As the enemy infantry were getting closer, their own fire was becoming more effective.

"Classic fire and maneuver. Its what we teach but I've never seen it done this well before. Just who the devil are those people?"

On the Goat-Track, Sinai Coast, south of Gaza.

"Just who the devil are those people?" Jaeger cursed. It wasn't supposed to happen this way. The rules were quite clear, you'd hit the bad guys with mortars, charge them, give them a good blast with machinegun fire start to advance on them. Then the raggies would run away and his men could shoot them as they ran. Only it wasn't happening. The men in the rocks were fighting hard. And well.

Already Jaeger was losing men to the enemy fire. He's expected to have a couple hit by a machinegun if the enemy had one but his people were going down to rifle fire. On his command car, the nose machinegun was being fired by the driver, one of those infernal riflemen had picked off the original gunner. He was beginning to run out of time as well, the devastating concentration of fire from the MG42s could only be sustained so long, barrels were overheating, ammunition was running short. As the volume of fire slackened, the enemy would be able to fight back more effectively and those damned riflemen could make each shot count.

"Don't know sir. They aren't raggies that's for sure. Fight more like Russians. Sir, if they had experience to match their skills we'd be deep in hurt by now."

Jaeger nodded. The enemy was inexperienced, that was clear, their positions were too obvious and too far forward and that had cost them badly. And their fire discipline had left a lot to be desired. But, the survivors would be learning fast. Which didn't answer the question. Just who the devil were they?

"Sir, Panzers!"

"I know sergeant, they are out on our left flank."

"No Sir, not ours, enemy coming out of the rockpile."

Enemy panzers? Jaeger began to get a sick feeling of apprehension He focused his binoculars on the spot where the goat track entered the rockpile. There they were, tanks for certain. Jaeger twisted the focus on his binoculars, already sure what he was going to see. Sleek, low hull, five roadwheels, big flatsided turret with an absurdly long gun. M60A3s. American. And there was only one organization that could put heavy tanks onto a hostile beach. They were fighting American Marines. Jaeger shuddered and looked up at the sky, already expecting to see it turn black with SACs bombers. The stars still shone down though, through a desert-clear sky.

"Sergeant, we are fighting American Marines. We've got to get this finished before their air support arrives. Get the Landsers moving forward fast. This is going to cost us."

M60A3 "Fox-Two-Five" In Front Of the Rockpile

The tactical problem was that the track through the rockpile was the only way vehicles could maneuver. The rocks were too broken and jagged to allow the tanks across, they had to stick to the goat track. So they would be debouching on a narrow front. Fortunately the enemy troops that had been giving Charlie Two-Three a hard time were all north of the track. So he could swing his tanks south, form up then roll up the enemy position, south to north.

According to the fragmentary reports from Two-Three, they were facing infantry backed up with mortars, no big deal, the tanks could take them. Then, Fox-Two-Five hit a runnel in the track and lurched forward. Lieutenant Dixon bounced off the rim of the cupola and cursed. *Once they were out of the rocks and off this apology for a path of course.* Ahead of him, the long 120 millimeter gun come close to grounding with the lurch. The new gun had been a controversial feature of the M60 series, a lot of people preferred the faster-firing and more manageable 90 millimeter installed on the old M48 series. Eventually, supporters of the big gun had their way, the 90 was at the end of its development potential and the 120 had a much more effective HE shell.

The five tanks burst out of the Rockpile in line ahead and swung south, forming into echelon left as they did. Almost immediately Dixon's thermal viewer picked up a shimmer above the dune line ahead of them.

"Uh-oh guys we have company. Vehicles ahead, I'm picking up their exhaust plume."

That was a complication, with another vehicle force to the south of them, they would have to take that out before engaging the force to the north. So Charlie-Two-Three would have to hold for a little longer. The five tanks formed into line abreast, accelerating as they closed on the position to the south. The sand was a lot smoother than the track had been but it was soft and the treads weren't operating to maximum efficiency. Even so, the M60 was a lot faster than the old M48 had been.

Peering through the commander's station, Dixon saw the angular shape of a tank turret peeping just over the ridge. From what he knew of Caliphate armor, it would be a Chimp tank. That meant fast, well-gunned but paper-thin armor. He tried to get a range using the infra-red optical target tracking system but either he was unlucky or the Chimp tank had an infrared detector. As soon as he illuminated it, the tank backed out of sight.

A few seconds later another tank appeared, obviously taking over the watch. Illuminated - and disappeared. After a couple more brief visitors, Dixon realized the Caff tank crew had made a mistake, each time they reappeared, they did so in the same place. "Slow down, take them as they come over the ridge next time." Dixon followed his own orders, slowed Fox-Two-Five down and trained the gun on the piece of ridge the Caff had used last.

At first he thought he'd fired, there was the same crashing noise and the same choking smoke. Only this time the smoke didn't clear and the fire alarm was whooping. They'd been hit, an armor piercing shot had smacked through the side of the turret and the whole tank was burning. "Everybody OUT OUT OUT." Standard rule, after the third OUT anybody who said "What?" was talking to themselves. His loader wouldn't care, he was gone, smeared over the inside of the turret basket. Direct hits from AP shot tended to do that to a man.

Dixon went out through the cupola and jumped clear rolling as he landed. His gunner did the same. Two. Then Dixon heard the hammering from the driver's compartment. When the tank hydraulics had caught fire, the 120 had pivoted downwards under its own weight and jammed the driver's hatch shut. Dixon ran forward and jumped onto the burning tank, wrenching at the drivers hatch with his hands. He got it an inch open, then a couple of inches more but it was jammed tight. He couldn't work out who was ringing bells, then saw it wasn't bells after all. Somebody was machine-gunning the tank and the bells were bullets bouncing off the armor. He wrenched again at the tank, feeling his skin splitting and crackling with the heat in the metal. Then, there was a hammer blow in his back and he slid off the tank.

Lying on the sand he saw Fox-Two Five brewing up. The ammunition went first, then the diesel fuel, a multi-colored fountain of smoke pouring out of every crack. As if in a dream he saw a blackened hand come out of the gap he'd opened with the driver's hatch, flex two or three times then collapse. His gunner was dragging him clear of the inferno, as Dixon was pulled through the sand he saw Fox-Two-Four was also burning. That's when he knew what had happened. It hadn't been three tanks on the dune line, it had been one, moving up and down to simulate three and luring him in. The other tanks, there probably were two, Dixon thought, had moved around and taken him from the flank.

They'd taken Two-Five and Two-Four out with their first shots, even as he watched Fox-Two-Three take two hits and start to burn. The long gun started to pivot down, but the driver had his hatch open and was rolling down the frontal armor before the gun completed its arc.

Suddenly, Dixon's eardrums met in the middle, Fox-Two-Two had fired and the decoy tank on the ridge flew apart. Fox-Two-One had spun around so it faced the flanking positions. As his vision dimmed, Dixon saw two hits bounce off its frontal armor, then its own 120 crashed. The shot must have only gone a few feet overhead because Dixon felt the wind of its passing. He looked around, there was boiling black smoke on the ridge behind them, and orange fire. Another Caff tank dead. That made it two for three. The day, or in this case the night, was not going well.

On the Goat-Track, Sinai Coast, south of Gaza.

"Well, they walked into that like a bunch of schoolgirls didn't they?"

Jaeger was speaking to his command group but he knew the word would spread to what was left of his unit faster than the conventional laws of physics would admit was possible. It was true as well, the American tankers had driven into an elementary ambush that wouldn't have fooled a German or Russian tanker for a moment. It confirmed his impression of the Americans, they were superbly equipped, had excellent training, and were woefully inexperienced. They had all the tactical skills, they just hadn't learned how to apply them when the other side were playing for keeps. Now to gild the lily a little.

"See boys, the Americans aren't so tough once we take away their bombers and hellburners. Fight them in the field like men and we have their measure and some to spare. So let's show them how real men fight. Remember what happened in New Schwabia!" General Model had circulated secret reports he had obtained from the Red Cross. Every German who had been left behind when Model had lead the breakout to the south had been killed. Every man, woman and child, they had been taken out into the lonely Russian forests and killed.

"Remember what these people did to Germany!" Model had circulated another secret Red Cross report about that. Germany was a blasted, radioactive wasteland where nothing could live for a thousand years. Some of the soldiers who had done a bit more than high school physics frowned at that, but if the Red Cross said so, and who knew what the Ami devils had come up with?

"Remember what happened to our comrades who were in the occupied territories.!" Everybody knew the answer to that one, they had been gathered into slave labor camps and worked to death. The same awaited any of them who were captured now.

211

Model's secret Red Cross report on that had been harrowing to read.

"So, boys, follow the example of our gallant Panzertruppen and show them how real men fight, how Germans fight."

Jaeger hoped nobody would notice that at least two thirds of the panzertruppen had died in less than a minute. By the cheers that went up when the word spread. His infantry line had been noisy anyway, men shouting and yelling at each other, encouragement, insults, filthy jokes that were as funny as they were old. Anything to remind the men their comrades were around them. A man on his own could fail in his duty and rationalize it to himself but no man would show himself to be less than his comrades.

Yet that was the weird thing. The Americans were silent up there in the rocks. It was as if they regarded themselves as having a job to do, they had to finish it and they were going to finish it and that was all they had to say about the matter. Even the sound of their firing was different. The Germans infantry were putting down a steady roar of fire from their machineguns and automatic rifles, in reply the American fire was a crackle, a stutter. It wasn't even a spray of fire, it was a stream of individually aimed shots.

And that was the real worry. Jaeger knew his unit was running out of steam. He'd started with two platoons of panzergrenadiers, now he had the equivalent of one. The machineguns on his personnel carriers had already fallen silent, their barrels burned out, the ammunition sacks empty. The infantry were relying on their squad guns now, far fewer and with a lower ammunition allowance. To make up the difference he had stopped his 120s dropping harassment and interdiction fire on the beach, they probably hadn't achieved much anyway. Now they were supporting the infantry, or would be as long as their ammunition lasted.

That was another problem, after a few minutes, the American mortars had started hitting back. They were much smaller that the German 120s, Jaeger guessed 60s, the fire patterns suggested three of them and a pair of slightly larger ones, probably

81s. What their shells lacked in hitting power, they made up in numbers and five explosions suppressed better than two. In the end though, it was the infantry who were slugging it out. For all the brave talk about volume of fire, it was the precision aimed fire of the Americans that was doing the damage. Jaeger sighed quietly to himself, for all his bold words, he knew the truth. The Americans were wiping the floor with him.

In the Rockpile, Sinai Coast, south of Gaza.

The tanks had been a disaster, three of them were burning where they'd been hit, the other two had pulled back into cover, one, its gun drooping helplessly. There was something wrong with the M60, something seriously wrong. His men, what was left of them, had been stunned by the casual ease with which the Germans had killed the tank platoon. Now they were waiting for the German tanks to come and help the enemy infantry forward.

It was hard to believe, almost twenty years after The Big One, Charlie-Two-Three was fighting a German unit. They'd heard what was left of Model's army had become a sort of King's Guard for the Caliphate's leadership and they must have brushed into it. The key had been the machineguns. That vicious, high-speed snarl could only be MG42s. Combined with skilled infantry and tankers who might have been born inside their panzers meant Germans. Nobody could come to any other reasonable conclusion.

They were good, better than Lieutenant Admire had ever seen and they were destroying his unit. Admire thought that if he ever got out of this, he was going to go to the Pentagon and pound on desks until people listened to him. He started with three squads and a supporting detachment spread along these rocks, 47 men of his own and 14 detached from the company heavy weapons platoon. On paper, he had two squads left but that included the walking wounded. He was commanding one, Gunny Tomas was commanding the other. They were split, one each side of the goat track. And they were both getting hammered.

It was volume of fire that was crucifying him. Aimed individual fire be damned, for every round his men squeezed off, they got a hundred fired back at them. That's how most of his men had died, they'd taken aim, fired their shots and been riddled by the barrage that came back. Their M14s were semi-automatic, the Germans were full-automatic. The M14s shot, the Germans hosed back.

In machineguns the situation was even worse. When the Marines had switched from the 30-06 M1 Garand to the .276 M14, they'd also dumped their trusted BARs and been issued the M15. Which was basically the same rifle as the M14 except it had a full automatic option, a bipod, a heavy barrel and a 8 x 50 telescopic sight. On semi it was supposed to be an accurate infantry support rifle, reaching out to a thousand yards, on full auto it was supposed to be a passable light machine gun. Which sounded great until the enemy fired twelve hundred round a minute back.

And then there were the mortars, the Germans had started dropping their big mortar rounds on them again. The Marines on the beach had shot back with their sixties and eighty-ones but what the hell use were those pip-squeak little things compared with the dustbins the Germans were dropping. That was another thing desks were going to get pounded over. When outgunned, outmanned, in an impossible tactical position there was only one thing an honorable man could do. Call for help and if that failed, attack somebody. Admire tapped his radioman on the shoulder. "Charlie-Zero, this is Charlie-Two-Three. The issue here is in doubt. I need support, immediately."

The issue is in doubt, Admire thought as more mortar rounds pounded the Rockpile. That is a nice way of telling the truth. For the truth was that the Germans were wiping the floor with him

On the Beach, Sinai Coast

The artillery had stopped, that was one good thing. For a while it had been tense with the German heavy mortars landing all over the assembly area but they'd stopped. Now they were back to pounding on the rockpile. Major Michaels thought for a second.

"Comms. Get me *Buffy*. We need to call in some help down here. Lieutenant Shaeffer, Take your Charlie-Two-Two, pull it out the rocks and swing it around behind Charlie-Two-Three. Be prepared to move through Two-three and assault the German position after our support arrives. Klinger, extend Charlie-Two-One so that its frontage covers the area previously occupied by Two-Two. Move guys or we'll have Germans joining us on the beach.

"*Buffy*, Sir."

"*Buffy*? This is Charlie-Zero-Actual. We need help down here fast. Can you patch through to *Shiloh* and get some fast movers over here? Like now? F4Hs or A3Js would be nice but we'll take F2Gs and Adies if that's all we can get."

"Uh Sorry, Charlie-Zero we can't do that. *Shiloh* is tied down covering the Phibron, all hell is about to break loose around them. Look, you're a part of a bigger picture now and this thing is spiraling out of control. There's nothing to send you."

"*Buffy*, we need help down here."

"Wait One Charlie-Zero." The radio went blank for a second. "Right, Charlie-Zero. The Boss says, this is going to cost you more beer than you can possibly imagine but we'll help you. We're twelve minutes out. Can you hold that long and can you get your stuff for the ground action together by then. We really don't want to hang around close to Gaza longer than we can help."

"Thank you *Buffy*. Confirm we will hold and we will be ready to go. What are your plans?"

The voice on the radio chuckled. "Lets just say things are going to get terribly Napoleonic in about twelve minutes time. *Buffy* Out."

In the Rockpile, Sinai Coast, south of Gaza.

Lieutenant Admire groaned and tightened one of the field dressings around his leg. One of the German mortar rounds had shattered the rock behind him and the fragments had lacerated his leg from thigh to knee. Outside, not inside or he'd have bled out by now. He'd been ordered to hold for twelve minutes and he had but it had cost them dearly. The Germans had edged nearer, they were about 75 yards out and their rifle fire was lethal. He'd lost more men. The good news was that Charlie-Two-Two had moved up through the rocks and infiltrated positions beside his own veterans. Admire laughed quietly to himself, dammit, he and his men were veterans now, weren't they. The men of Two-Two seemed different somehow, boyish almost. Admire guessed his men had looked the same way an hour earlier.

The firefight was becoming patchier now, the periods of silence longer. In one of them Admire heard a quiet drone overhead. A turboprop transport, a big one. Looking up he saw a ghostly grayish shape.

AC-133A "Buffy", Over the Goat Track.

Captain James Masters aka "The Boss" was sweating, literally and metaphorically. *Buffy* was swinging right around the perimeter of the prohibited zone around Gaza. In addition, he was disrupting his role as an airborne command post.

If this failed, he would be busted and sent to Alaska, it was rumored there was a duty reserved for special cases up there. Clearing runways of foreign objects in sixty mile an hour winds and sub-zero temperatures. Legend had it a SAC crew had been up there for five years.... no, it was too horrible to think about. But even if he succeeded, he would have a lot of fast talking to do.

"Gunnery here, Boss. We've got the terrain worked out and we've plotted our friendlies. There's been a hell of a firefight down there. At least five wrecks we can see." Masters looked at the map in the cockpit. On course, altitude right and ready to start the turn. This was the moment he'd waited for.

"Battery A. Battery C. Run out the guns."

Doors slid open in *Buffy's* side and the stubby barrels of three 20 millimeter gatling guns slid out. Further aft, the maws of the 105 millimeter howitzers slid into the ready position.

On the Goat-Track, Sinai Coast, south of Gaza.

Captain Ivan Jaeger heard the drone as well. His binoculars, good pre-war German stock were better than any the

216

Americans had and he recognized the aircraft instantly. High wing, long fuselage, four turboprops. A C-133 transport. But what was it doing here? Were the Americans going to drop paratroopers as reinforcements? Did the Americans still *have* paratroopers?

Then there was a series of clouds behind the aircraft and a clutch of brilliant flashes. That was logical, the transport was dropping chaff and flares in case missiles were on their way up. But it was also turning and one didn't drop paratroopers while turning. Did one?

Anyway, it suddenly struck Jaeger that the aspect of the aircraft was remaining constant, that meant that as it described a circle through the air, he had to be standing at the center of that circle. Suddenly that seemed terribly ominous.

In the Rock-Pile, Sinai Coast, south of Gaza.

Once, when he had been a youngster in Texas, his home had been right in the middle of Tornado Alley. One day, one of the worst twisters on record had come right past his home, well, actually right over his home. He and his family had been in the storm shelter and he remembered the ear-splitting roar, the demented wailing howl and the hideous, never-ending vibration as the twister had leveled everything in its path. Now the twister had come again, only this time it was a column of glowing light.

It had started without warning, one moment there had been the eerie silence that happens sometimes on a battlefield, interrupted only by the faint drone of the aircraft overhead, then the twister had started. It was coming from the aircraft, an incredibly beautiful cone of light that reached down through the darkness to gently kiss the ground underneath. The sound, the earthshaking sound, had started a split second later. Now, as the column of light moved across the desert, the ground underneath was shaking and heaving, fighting desperately to throw off the unwanted kiss of the luminous twister.

Admire watched, stupefied by the sound and the glare, for underneath that berserk sight were the infantry that had been attacking his position. Even as he watched the curve of the aircraft's flight path took the column of light back and it washed over the position of the armored cars that had brought the German infantry. Admire could see the explosions as their fuel tanks erupted but they seemed weak, feeble, inconsequential against the howling inferno that engulfed them. Then, as suddenly as it had started, the column of light was gone and silence returned to the battlefield. Only the faint drone of the climbing Slayer and the crackle of burning vehicles broke the soundlessness.

On the Goat-Track, Sinai Coast, south of Gaza.

He'd survived. Incredibly, unbelievably, he'd survived. His command group had been between the infantry up front and the armored vehicles parked in the wadi behind. The thing, the demon, the monster, Jaeger couldn't think of a term descriptive enough, had walked its nightmare of fire along his infantry, curved it over his sole remaining tank and walked it back over the armored cars. But, as he'd seen, he'd been in the center of the circle and the deluge of fire and death had walked around him, not over him.

He looked up at the aircraft, it was climbing but also it was turning. It was coming back. *Please, God, no*, Jaeger thought, *not again.*

AC-133A "Buffy" , Over the Goat Track.

Buffy's forward gundeck was chaos. For almost a minute, the three gatling guns had poured fire into the desert beneath. The weight of ammunition expended had been so great the flight deck crew had been forced to correct the aircraft's trim constantly. In theory the expended cases should have been collected in the ammunition chests but 300 rounds a second left a lot of room for error. A Battery gun deck was awash with hot cases and two of the gun deck crew were down with minor impact injuries and burns.

As the sea of brass surged around the gun captain's ankles, he felt Buffy turn into her second firing pass. The gun captain issued the famous old-time Navy Prayer "For what they are about to receive, I hope they will be truly grateful."

Then *Buffy* shuddered as Battery C commenced firing.

On the Goat-Track, Sinai Coast, south of Gaza.

Jaeger saw the streak of fire from the aircraft and recognized it as a field artillery gun firing. By now, he was tired, terribly tired and he watched almost without interest as the first shells exploded in his mortar battery. Mediums, he noted, probably 105s. The Americans had put an artillery battery on an aircraft. It didn't surprise him, if the C-133 had suddenly started ballet dancing in the sky with a purple dinosaur, it wouldn't have surprised him. The shell explosions walked towards him and that didn't surprise him either.

In the Rock-Pile, Sinai Coast, south of Gaza.

Charlie-Two-Two bounced off as the drone of the Slayer faded in the distance. They moved forward by sections, just as they'd been taught. Gunnery Sergeant Esteban Tomas watched them with pity. He'd seen it done right now and he had so much to pass on to the rest of the battalion. They'd done it by the book, and the book had been right. Only applying what the book said was a whole different world.

There was no opposition. Charlie-Two-Two had been warned there would certainly be unexploded shells in the ground and they took trouble to stay away from anything suspicious. Apart from that, there was nothing to give them trouble, where the German infantry had been looked like a freshly-plowed field. The armored cars were scrap. Then, one of the squads called out. They'd found a prisoner. Badly wounded, unconscious but alive. Identity tags said he was a Captain, one Ivan Jaeger.

Then the LVTs turned up, to take out the wounded and the dead. Lieutenant Admire looked at his Butcher's Bill. Of the 61 men under his command, 19 were dead and 32 wounded, all badly. Those who had minor wounds had fought on until they died or had more wounds serious enough to stop them. Of the twenty men in the tanks, six were dead, four wounded, all the wounded had burns that would require long stays in hospital. Engineers were already getting ready to blow up the wrecked tanks. Admire just wanted to sleep. Michaels walked over to him.

"I thought you might like to know Lieutenant, the SEALs got the SAC crew out safely. Mission accomplished Lieutenant. And I think your stand here will become part of Corps History." Admire nodded dully. History just didn't seem to matter very much.

At Sea, North of the Sinai Desert

The three small craft pulled alongside the dark blue flying boat. A hatch opened in the side and one of the Seamaster's crew threw down a rope ladder. Each small craft had four SEALs and a member of *Marisol's* crew on board.

The SEALs helped the airmen up the ladder, then followed them. Commander Jeff Thomas was last, he paused in the hatchway and fired a short burst into each small craft, sinking them instantly. Then, the hatch swung shut and the PB6M-4 took off for home.

Missile Base Aldabaran, North of Gaza, Palestine Province, The Caliphate

The message had come in earlier that night. The American Navy group offshore had moved in closer. That message had also gone to the fast attack craft squadrons in the port, they'd slipped quietly out to sea, getting into position for the attack. Then a little later, there had been the explanation for the American move. Their troops were ashore, looking for the crew of the bomber that had been shot down. That was good, it meant the amphibious ships wouldn't be moving far from the beachhead.

They even had a fix on the American ship's position, not precise but much better than the one the missile's designers had envisaged. They were just under 300 kilometers out, 12 minutes flying time for the big anti-ship missiles. If the fast attack craft went to full power, they could move 15 kilometers in that time. Their missiles had a 40 kilometer range. As it was, they were closing on the Americans and were just under 70 kilometers away from the estimated position of the ships.

The attack plan was simple. The shore-based anti-ship missiles would be fired first, as they were launched the word would go to the fast attack craft. They'd start running in on the enemy. They'd get the refined position of the target form the explosions as the big missiles hit the American ships, nobody was foolish enough to believe that all twelve would get through but enough would to create chaos and panic in the American ships. While the Americans ran around, trying to save their ships and their men, the fast attack craft would launch their missiles into them. With the defenses down, nearly all of the ships would be hit.

The radio in the command truck buzzed. The Battery Commander took down the details and coordinates and read the latter back to command. Command re-read them and confirmed. Then, the primary command truck contacted the secondary unit and, once again confirmed the target data. It all matched.

There was a groaning noise, a squealing, as the big cylinders on the back of the launch trucks started to elevate, compressing the suspension underneath them. Then, they reached the launch angle and stopped. There was silence for a second, then another squeal as the dish-like cover to the end of the tube popped open. Once again, a brief silence, then the unmistakable sound of a turbojet spooling up. It was quickly drowned by the roar of the boosters and then the missiles left their tubes, climbing steeply as the rockets threw them up and out.

The battery crew were cheering, waving their rifles and screaming abuse at the Americans as the boosters, their job completed, separated from the missiles, leaving them to make their way to the target.

W2F-1 Hawkeye "Angel-Three" Zero minutes after launch. Missiles 180 miles from target

"Vampires, vampires. We have vampire launch. North and south of Gaza. Raid count twelve missiles. Two groups of six. Target is Phibron Four, repeat target is Phibron Four. Eagle Flight, go for it." The radar operator on the W2F-1 saw a group of aircraft detaching from the mass waiting in a holding pattern out to sea. One group streaked away from the rest, accelerating and eating up the distance. "Boy, look at those Super-Crusaders go."

F9U-2 "Rosie", 30 seconds after launch. Missiles 172.5 miles from target.

The Super-Crusader wasn't quite the fastest fighter in the world, the F-108 had her by a small fraction of a Mach number but she was certainly the fastest accelerating fighter around. Lieutenant (jg) Paul Flower felt the kick in his spine as he accelerated then the awesome thump as the big engine in the back worked up some enthusiasm.

The F9U was blindingly fast but the truth was she couldn't hold the speed for very long. She was built out of conventional aviation materials, not the sophisticated new alloys used by the F-108 and its bigger cousin, the B-70, and heat-sink effect would force her back down to normal speeds before too long. But, for the job of putting distance between herself and the ships she was protecting, engaging the enemy as far out as possible, there was nothing better. They were 200 miles from Phibron Four, *Rosie* and the seven other Super-Crusaders of Eagle Flight would cover that distance in six minutes.

USS "Thomas Jefferson" CC-3, One minute after launch. Missiles 165 miles from target.

"Now that's a surprise" Admiral Mahan saw the plot suddenly record the appearance of the anti-ship missiles on his displays. There was already a delay in the system, the computers that drove the NTDS links couldn't keep up with the changes, but already the battle management system had done it's job. The displays flickered again, and now they showed the Combat Air Patrol *Shiloh* had deployed to protect the carriers moving forward to intercept.

"Message from Angel Three to *Shiloh*. The fast attack craft are moving in to the attack." That was expected, they'd been watching those Djinns ever since they'd left port earlier in the night. Angel-One had spotted them and tracked their movement. That was why *Shiloh* had an anti-shipping strike up as well as the fighters. On *Shiloh* now, the crews would be stripping ground support ordnance from the aircraft still on board and replacing it with anti-shipping weapons. Just in case a second strike was needed.

"They must be out of their minds. This is a full scale attack. Everybody knows what happens to people who try that on us." It was one of the seamen on the air control center speaking, almost to himself.

"Don't sweat it son. We haven't destroyed a country since Germany. Well, practice makes perfect." A chuckle went around the CDC. That was the nice thing about being an Admiral, Mahan thought. One's little jokes were always funny.

USS Austin LPD-4. Three minute after launch. Missiles 135 miles from target.

The air raid warning siren was whooping, the shipboard alert system trumpeting "Air raid air raid this is no drill Caliphate missiles inbound." To one side of the formation, the two guided missile destroyers were moving onto the threat axis, the first group of inbound fighters would be taking the southern formation of vampires, the destroyers would be taking the northern group with their Terriers.

All over USS *Austin,* the ship was coming to general quarters, hatches closing, fire prevention measures in force, damage control teams closed up and waiting. Captain Pickering stood on the bridge wings looking out along the threat axis. The radars were telling him the missiles were inbound but he couldn't see them. He devoutly hoped they'd never get close enough for him to see them.

F4H-3 Phantom II "Tisiphone" five minutes after launch. Missiles 105 miles from target.

Rhino Force thundered across the sky, twelve F4H-3s, falling steadily behind the racing Super-Crusaders. They were the swing force, they were loaded down with unguided rockets to take on the fast attack craft but they also had their four AIM-7 Sparrows in case any of the anti-ship missiles got through.

Colonel Scott Brim checked fuel status and distance, his aircraft were much slower than the F9Us, all the more so for being

223

loaded down. It would be marginal if he could get there quickly enough for the first wave. But for the FACs, that was different.

Behind him, but closing fast was Viper Force, 12 A3J-4 Vigilantes, loaded down with cluster-bombs. They carried their 12,000 pound load internally and they didn't have the speed penalty that was hitting Rhino Force. So they'd get to the FACs first. Right at the back, plugging along subsonic, grimly determined not to be left out were the light attack boys in the Skyhawks. They were the reserve, the last ditch defense. Oddly, Brim had never thought of it before, but they were the only aircraft in the group that carried guns.

F9U-2 "Rosie", seven minutes after launch. Missiles 75 miles from target.

The needles on the temperature gauges were edging towards the red as the eight Super-Crusaders swept over Phibron Four. Lieutenant Flower cut the speed back to 1200 miles per hour and watched the needle edge back a little. His radar was searching out ahead of him, looking for the formation of six missiles that should be directly ahead. All three of his AIM-7s were warmed up, the pair of AIM-9s were on standby. So just where were the targets?

USS "Charles F Adams", eight minutes after launch. Missiles 60 miles from target.

The missile launcher aft swung to horizontal, the pair of Terriers slid out of the magazine onto the rails, then the launcher elevated and trained. The missiles on the rails had conventional warheads, there were too many friendly assets, too close, to use the nuclear-tipped missiles. In the CIC, radar had tracked the Super-Crusaders streaking overhead, saw them peal off to take the missiles coming in from the south.

The northern group were assigned to the destroyers. Six missiles, each destroyer fired her Terriers in pairs. The launchers cycled four times in each minute. The destroyers would keep a stream of missiles heading to the targets until they were splashed or the magazines were empty. Then, the computers calculated the target solution, came up with a go and the first two pairs of Terriers flashed into the night.

F9U-2 "Rosie", eight minutes after launch. Missiles 60 miles from target.

Rosie had been diving to bring her within the firing envelope of her AIM-7s. Now, he could see the missiles on his radarscope, a loose gaggle of six converging on Phibron Four, now more than 20 miles behind them His radar was already tracking a target. *Rosie* was third from the left so he picked out the third missile from the left. Stroke the firing switch and two AIM-7s, the side ones, dropped away before setting after the vampires somebody had been idiot enough to fire on an American warship.

The second ticked by, then, in the distance he saw two explosions. What the? Eight fighters had fired sixteen missiles and got two hits? His remaining AIM-7 was locked onto one of the four survivors. He fired again, again there was a brief wait before a single explosion, much closer flared in the darkness. This was bad.

"All Eagle aircraft, missiles are now five miles in front of us estimated speed 900 knots. Swing behind them and use the infra-red track and AIM-9s.

USS "Charles F Adams", nine minutes after launch. Missiles 45 miles from target.

The destroyer had two missile guidance channels, each designating a single inbound missile as its target. Thus, the two destroyers had designated four of the six inbounds and directed one Terrier from each wave of missiles at that target. All four Terriers in the first wave missed completely.

They were having the same problem the Sparrows from the Super-Crusaders were suffering. The inbound missiles were much smaller than the aircraft Terrier was designed to take down. The simple computer that worked the proximity fuse interpreted small size as being too far away and, although the missiles actually passed within their lethal radius, they didn't explode. It was the square law at work, to get a signal return adequate to fire their fuses, they had to be four times closer to their targets than the designers had allowed. Deprived of their targets, the Terriers went ballistic and exploded at the end of their runs. That was the bad news. The good news was that Terrier was a very good missile. One from the third wave and one from the fifth got close enough to blow an inbound vampire out of the sky. That left four.

F9U-2 "Rosie", ten minutes after launch. Missiles 30 miles from target.

The infrared tracker had a limited scan and a small screen but the radar got it pointed the right way. The brilliant flare of the Vampire's exhaust appeared suddenly, Flower caught it and maneuvered to place it in the center of the screen. The annunciator on the AIM-9 growled then went to a monotone as the seeker locked on. Whatever had gone wrong with the Sparrows didn't affect the 'Winders. Flower watched his missile fly straight up the exhaust plume and into the engine of the Vampire in front of him. It flew apart with the explosion. Around him, the two remaining anti-ship missiles exploded as the Sidewinders took them down. The southern missile group had been defeated.

USS "Charles F Adams", eleven minutes after launch. Missiles 15 miles from target.

They were going down slowly. One by one, the Terriers were picking them off. One more had gone with the seventh wave and two had been nailed by the ninth. The two destroyers had fired a total of 40 Terriers and scored five hits. That left just one and it was heading for the USS *Austin*. And it was now inside minimum range.

USS Austin LPD-4. Twelve minutes after launch. Missiles 0 miles from target.

The Vampire used an active radar homing system. It emitted pulses that saw the USS *Austin* as a mass of corner reflectors, a complex return that formed a crude, elementary picture of the ship. The guidance system digested that picture and calculated the geometric center of the reflector mass. Then, it adjusted the nose of the missile so that it was pointing directly at that geometric center.

On board the *Austin* the electronic warfare system spotted the slight turn and calculated the new course of the missile. With electronic dispassion it noted that the projected end of the course coincided with its own position. This, it decided, was not good. It picked up the missile guidance pulse and adjusted it a little, then returned it a touch stronger than the original. The guidance system aboard the inbound missile accepted the modified pulse and changed the missile course accordingly.

There were now two lines on the display. The original projected course that terminated in the center of Austin and another that represented the actual course of the missile. Slowly, the two were diverging, the real course of the inbound deviating away so the missile would pass aft of the target. Then, there was the critical point where the guidance system of the inbound wouldn't be pointing at the ship at all.

There was an answer to that; aft of the bridge there was a series of thumps as a launcher coughed five inch rockets loaded with chaff into the air. They created a new target, one that looked to a radar set like an extension of the ship itself. The vampire flew through the chaff cloud, emerged the other side and saw - nothing. Without a target, it went ballistic and crashed about two hundred yards aft of the USS *Austin*. As the plume subsided, a dozen dark blue shapes flashed over the ships, followed a few seconds later by the crash of their supersonic passage.

A3J-4 Vigilante "Tom Horn"

It was a bomber pilot's dream. Stretched out in front of them were targets, helpless, unable to shoot back. They'd spotted the Vigilantes on radar and started to take evasive action. To be fair about it, it was quite impressive evasive action. It was also futile of course. There were three formations, of six boats each. The twelve Vigilantes had split, one section of four taking each group.

Why the evasive efforts were so futile was a strange piece of history. The Vigilante had originally been designed as a nuclear attack bomber. The designers had a bright idea; instead of a conventional bomb-bay, they'd given the aircraft a long, thin one

227

that exited aft between the two engines. A great idea, only the problem was that the bomb dropped into a stagnation area and followed the aircraft along. Not a good idea. It had taken the Navy years to give up on the idea, the A3J-1 to J-3 had all been different efforts to make it work. In the end, they'd given up and the A3J-4 version had been redesigned to have a conventional bay with snap-action doors. The aircraft worked at long last. However, since the aircraft was being redesigned, the opportunity had been taken to give the new version the latest bomb-navigation system. Now, all the pilot had to do was hold a line and a square projected in a screen in front of him on the target and the aircraft's computer would do the rest. That was one reason.

The other was the bombload itself. *Tom Horn* was carrying six two thousand pound cluster bombs, CBUs in ordnance-talk. When the square at the end of the stick was over the target, the pilot pressed the button, the doors snapped open and the bombs dropped clear. By the time the doors had snapped shut, the CBU was on its way down and the Vigilante was blasting clear of the area. 500 feet above the FACs, the CBU broke open, dispersing 670 armor-piercing/fragmentation bomblets over a 30,000 square foot oval. With six bombs dropped per aircraft and four aircraft per group, the area occupied by the FAC formations was drenched with more than 16,000 bomblets.

The rolling sea of explosions covered the fast attack craft. Their maneuvers had indeed been futile; no matter how tightly they twisted and turned, the basic laws of physics meant they had to be within a specific area, and that area was far less than the lethal footprint of a CBU.

The detonations of the bomblets covered the sea with a twinkling mass, a harmless, even a cheerful, festive sight. And, when they cleared, it looked as if they had been both festive and harmless. The FAC-Ms had come to a halt, that was true. But they seemed untouched and undamaged. Only a close inspection would have showed that they were riddled with thousands of tiny holes, the biggest no larger than a thumbnail, the smallest, pin-sized. A close inspection might have shown that the craft were filling and sinking.

Their condition, in truth, was hopeless. A single large hole can be stopped, flooding boundaries established, pumps started. When every deck, every bulkhead is riddled, none of those things can be done and the ship is doomed. Naval architects call it progressive flooding. The Vigilante pilots called it a kill.

F4H-3 Phantom II "Tisiphone"

Colonel Brim was furious. He was certain one of the Vigilante crews had given him the finger as they had streaked past his heavily-loaded Phantoms. If he'd been flying clean, he'd have had their measure. But, the F4H carried its load externally and that made the difference.

Suddenly he forgot his pique. Covering the sea in front of him was the remains of a fleet. The Caliphate FACs were dead in the water, still, almost motionless. A couple were starting to burn, fuel line probably severed, or something. It didn't matter, they were all settling. Even as he watched, one rolled over, its bows pointed up at the sky and it sank stern first. It was strange, eerie, a ghostly sight in the moonlight. The twelve F4Hs circled the scene, watching the slow extinction of the enemy force.

Out of the corner of his eye, Brim saw one craft start to move. Perhaps it had been on the extreme edge of one of the coverage patterns, perhaps it had been lucky that a freak shift in the random distribution of bomblets had let it live. Perhaps one of the CBUs had malfunctioned. From the radio reports, a lot of things this night hadn't worked very well.

Brim rolled *Tisiphone* over and angled down into a long dive towards the slow-moving FAC. The previous engagement, he'd been left out of the kill and it wasn't going to happen this time. He lined up his rocket sight and let fly. The FAC-M's luck hadn't lasted, it vanished under the barrage of rockets. Amidst the sea of explosions, Brim saw the craft explode in the hail of rockets and sink.

"Jeez" his RIO whispered at the graveyard beneath the circling aircraft. "Have you ever seen anything like it?"

Brim looked down again. Already, there were fewer boats left on the surface and the rest had little time to live. "Nope. But what sort of idiot tries to suggest an overgrown speedboat can be used as a warship? Damned fools. Don't these people ever think?"

USS "Thomas Jefferson" CC-3.

The threat board was empty. US Casualties. Nil. Enemy casualties: Everybody. Admiral Mahan sighed. The US Navy had just fought its first modern naval battle. It had found out that its prized new missiles, the surface-to-air ones on the ships and the air-to-air missiles on the aircraft, had proved far less effective than thought. Yet, despite everything that had gone wrong, it had won.

CHAPTER NINE
AFTERMATH

Cabinet Conference Room, The White House, Washington DC

His confirmation hearings in front of the senate were going well, with a little luck his appointment would be confirmed by the end of the day. Clark Clifford would be taking over from him at State, Dean Rusk wondered if Clark would be getting one of the marvelously efficient Executive Assistants the Contractors seemed so adept at finding. Speaking of Executive Assistants, why was Naamah sitting in the seat allocated to the Attorney-General?

"Thank you for coming Dean. Confirmation Hearing going well?"

"Yes thank you Mister President. The Chairman tells me the vote will be taken shortly and the appointment ratified by the end of business today."

LBJ nodded sagely. He'd had some key figures over for drinks the night before and gently reminded them that he really wanted this appointment to go through quickly. Between the drinks and the crude jokes, he'd intimated that he knew where the bodies were buried. Literally and metaphorically.

"That's great Dean. We have a problem though. Ramsey didn't submit his resignation so it looks like I am going to have to fire him. I'd hoped to avoid that. The problem is, he's vanished.

The Washington City Police Department and Secret Service are looking for him, he was last seen in his old office. I hope he hasn't been foolish. Anyway, since we don't seem to have an Attorney-General right now, I've asked Miss Naamah to sit in on this meeting to provide any information we need from the Attorney-General's office. She has no executive authority of course and will not participate in making decisions."

Rusk nodded and took the seat next to her. The seat reserved for the Secretary of Defense. As he did, he noticed a scent, different from the smell of sweat and cigarettes that usually tainted the air here. Light, floral, and with hint of... sulfur? "I hope you don't mind me saying so, Miss Naamah, but your perfume is a very pleasant change for this room.

"Why thank you, Mister Rusk, please call me Naamah, not Miss Naamah. I haven't missed much in my life. The perfume's Diabolique, by Yves St Laurent. The French may have their problems but they still make the finest perfumes in the world. Mister Rusk, have you got your sh....... got your stuff together about what happened last night?"

"Inanna was up all night collating it for me." Rusk shook his head. The one thing everybody in politics wanted most was to be given one of the highest offices of state. The one thing they wanted least was to get it in the middle of a major crisis.

The President tapped lightly on the table. "Gentlemen, now everybody is here, doubtless you have all been following the fighting that broke out in the Eastern Mediterranean last night. Secretary Rusk. If you would provide us with an accurate summary of events?"

"Mister President. Last night US forces in the Mediterranean launched a rescue effort aimed at bringing out the crew of the SAC bomber that was shot down over the Gaza area yesterday. I am pleased to advise you that the operation was successful, the aircrew were located and extracted and are now safely on their way to the United States for debriefing."

There was a patter around the conference room as the assembled Cabinet applauded.

"However, simultaneous with the successful rescue, Caliphate forces launched a coordinated sea and missile attack on our ships offshore. That attack was met by aircraft deployed from the aircraft carrier *Shiloh*. Again, I am pleased to advise you that the attack was repelled at no cost to us. A total of at least twelve long-range anti-ship missiles were shot down and at least twelve, possibly as many as eighteen, Djinn class fast attack craft sunk. Caliphate loss of life was heavy, we believe up to 300 of their sailors may have been killed. The action raised a number of issues over the performance of some of our weapons. I will detail those later.

"On a less happy note, we had inserted a small blocking force on the coast, between the Caliphate base area at Gaza. That force was attacked by a Caliphate unit, in battalion strength, and roughly handled. Although the Marines held their beach-head and repelled the attack, they suffered severely. Casualties are presently believed to be twenty five dead and thirty six wounded out of a total of 258 effectives. We have taken some prisoners during the action.

"Mister President they are Germans. We believe they are part of Model's forces, the ones that escaped from Russia five years ago. Our intelligence indicates that those forces have been constituted as a sort of elite guard controlled directly by The Caliphate ruling council. The fact that such forces appear to have been concentrated at Gaza should be deeply disturbing to us."

"If I may ask a question Mister President" LBJ nodded, Treasury Secretary Fowler continued. "Dean, was the attack on our ships and men a response to our rescue effort?"

"No, Henry, it was not. The Djinn fast attack craft had left port and were closing on the position of our ships several hours before the rescue mission was launched. The fact that it appeared a pre-planned attack on our ships and was launched from the same base area as the missiles that shot down our reconnaissance aircraft suggests to me that the attack on our ships was part of the same operation as the attack on our aircraft. Seer?"

"I agree. Mister President, the timing and sequencing of events suggests that The Secretary of Defense is entirely correct. The shooting down of *Marisol*, the coordinated attacks on our ships to appear to be part of a single operation, I believe the firefight between the Germans and our Marines does not fit into that pattern. I think it was a random clash between a blocking force and a coastal patrol.

"I think we must take due recognition of the possibility that the shoot-down and the subsequent naval engagement are part of a concerted plan to drive us out of the Eastern Mediterranean. We know that the Caliphate has been trying to eliminate the refugees crossing that area and we have been preventing that massacre. We also know they have ambitions towards extending their domination along the southern Mediterranean Littoral. There is a very real possibility that attempting to drive us out of the area is an integral part of that plan.

"On a brighter note Sir, we have solved the mystery of how the Caliphate managed to shoot down one of our B-58s. I have had a preliminary message from The Ambassador-Plenipotentiary of Thailand indicating that the Chipanese Hiryu anti-aircraft missile had an electro-optical guidance adjunct. The technical details are on their way back to us now, but the key factor is that it only works against targets flying relatively slowly and at relatively low altitude.

"Under normal circumstances, *Marisol* would have been flying far outside its engagement envelope, as we know, this time circumstances were not normal. It does appear though, that the Caliphate prepared for its latest expansion by acquiring the latest technology weapons Chipan was prepared to release. The EO Hiryus, the Djinn FAC-Ms and their new coastal defense missiles."

Rusk nodded. "There is another disturbing possibility we must also take into consideration. We have noted a substantial increase in the number of terrorist attacks around the world in recent weeks. We have examined these and we have discerned a pattern. Every time the Caliphate makes a move to expand its territory, it is accompanied by such a wave. This relationship had occurred to me when Secretary of State and it does so even more strongly at Defense.

"Mister President, I believe that the Caliphate orchestrates these attacks in order to divert attention from its moves. I would note that a number of these attacks take place here in the United States. Since protecting our citizens is our paramount vital interest, I believe that this situation merits even closer attention. Finally, I was struck by a strange coincidence. A few weeks ago, we had a school siege in South Carolina. The perpetrator broke into a classroom full of children, attacked and almost killed the schoolteacher, then held the children hostage. His demands amounted to the conversion of the state schools into Moslem religious classes. He had a long history of mental problems but still, the link is there.

"He was killed by a Russian woman, a retired Army sniper now married to an American. Yesterday, the same couple intercepted a suicide bomber about to attack a restaurant they run in Moscow, again the lady shot the bomber dead before he could do any harm."

"They breed tough women in Russia, Dean."

"So it would appear, Mister President. I believe we have to recognize the possibility that the second attack was an attempt at exacting revenge for her part in the failure of the first.

"That is assuming that the school incident was a part of the Caliphate's preparations for the seizure of Egypt and the subsequent expansion. And that would link the Caliphate directly to hostile operations carried out on the territory of the United States. Our response to such an attack has always been made very clear."

The conference room fell silent as the message was digested. It was broken by an aide who entered and gave a slip of paper to LBJ.

"I have some good news. Ramsey Chalk has been found. He was in Arlington National Cemetery in what this note describes as 'a comatose yet highly disturbed condition' and is now in the intensive care unit of Bethesda Naval Hospital. Dean, please consult with the Seer and the other targeteers coordinate with them in preparing a strategic attack plan for use against the Caliphate. A comprehensive strategic plan.

"Clifford. Make up a document that will, if the Caliphate comply with its terms, makes it clear they have groveled in the mud to avoid our wrath. We will convene again at 4 pm to review the results of your preparations. Thank you."

Sick Bay, USS "Austin" LPD-4, Eastern Mediterranean

The subconscious stirred, feeling itself gain a glimmer of awareness. Cautiously it sent out feelers, running along the nerves, gently, delicately, probing for the first sign of trouble. Probing for the first sign of pain so that it could flee back to the safety of oblivion. It found none and sent back its message to the conscious brain, it was safe to come back to life now. The nerves and muscles twitched, the brain came back to life and Captain Ivan Jaeger recovered consciousness. He looked around, white room, hospital white. And there was a priest sitting beside his bed.

"Have you come to give me the last rites?"

"And why would I wish to do that Captain? Allow me to introduce myself. I am Father Andras Schneider of the Society of Jesus. When the Americans alerted the Red Cross that they had captured some German soldiers, I was asked to come here and look after your interests. Here, by the way, is an American amphibious warfare ship and you are in its sick bay."

"Some soldiers? There are other survivors?"

"There are five, one of whom really has received the last rites and I do not think he will live out the day. But two of your men have relatively minor injuries. In fact, one of the American Marines on board is already in the brig because of them. The Marines have some beer hidden away on board and he was caught smuggling a couple of bottles to your men. But let us return to you. You are Captain Ivan Jaeger? From Berlin?"

"Yes Father. I was in the 14th Panzer Division."

"Ivan, that is a Russian name, your mother had a fondness for Russian novels obviously."

"No Father, nothing so literary. There was a song back then about a duel between a Turkish nobleman called Abdulla Bulbul Ameer and a Russian named Ivan Skavinsky Skazar. My mother loved the song and she named me Ivan. I always gave thanks she chose that one and not Abdulla although the way things worked out perhaps she did chose the wrong one."

Father Schneider looked at a file and nodded. "Perhaps Captain, perhaps not. That was not in your official file but we knew of it from other sources. We have had many cases of SS men claiming to be Wehrmacht in order to escape punishment for their crimes. In some cases they killed Wehrmacht soldiers in order to assume their identity. But now tell me why you think I should give you the last rites?"

"Father, it is well known that all German soldiers are executed on capture. Did you not hear what happened after New Schwabia fell. The Russians killed everybody, even our women and children."

"Who told you this? There were many executions yes. The Russians executed all members of the SS and the Gestapo and the Einsatzgruppen that fell into their hands. And it saddens me to say your women suffered great indignities at the hands of the Russian soldiers. But killed? No. The women and children and those soldiers that were innocent of grave crimes, their lives were spared. The Russians made many statements in anger it is true but when it came to make a decision, they chose mercy."

"Father, is this true?"

Father Schneider stared at Jaeger for a second, then took out a bible and his crucifix. "I swear by Almighty God that what I say to you here is the truth as I know it and nothing but the truth. So help me God." He kissed the cross and put it on the Bible again.

"My apologies, Father. But we were told that they had all been killed. Field Marshal Model even had a secret report from the Red Cross. He showed it to us all."

"The Red Cross does not make secret reports my son. If you saw something that claimed to be so, then it was false. The survivors from New Schwabia were sent home to Germany."

Jaeger felt the surge of hope die. "Then they died anyway. Nobody lives in Germany."

"Again, Captain, if you have been told that, then you have been told falsely. Germany was smashed, destroyed, yes. The Germany you knew no longer exists and will never exist again. Many millions of Germans died in the bombing and many millions more in the aftermath. Even now, only about eight million live in Germany. But everybody dying? No. The radiation has faded and there are few areas where people cannot go.

"Every year those who explore the countryside declare more areas safe and free for access. Even the cities are becoming safe now although few people wish to go to them. There is almost a superstitious fear of those cities as if going to them will bring back the bombers. But, in truth, the new Germany is becoming quite a beautiful place. There are few people and most live in small farming settlements. The countryside appears untouched and the scars of the bombing are long gone. It is almost like a park, or perhaps the way Europe used to be before factories and cities existed. There is a life for you there Captain, though not as a soldier. Germany will never have soldiers again."

"Father, please tell me that something else. Those of us who were in occupation forces outside Germany. We were told they were used as slave labor until they died. Please tell me this too was a lie?"

"It is. Let me tell you a story. I was one of those occupation soldiers. In England. The last night of the war, we were told that the Resistance had attacked a radio station, Soldatensender Nottingham. I took my platoon there and it was true. The Resistance had attacked the station and taken it off the air so that Winston Churchill and the English King could make a broadcast. That broadcast told us what had happened then offered us a home. They said we had come an conquerors but we could stay as guests. Instead of fighting the resistance unit, we made our own truce with them that night.

"Over the next few days, we learned the full extent of what had happened to Germany. Some of the men went back to see if their families had survived. Some of us knew there was no hope and stayed. It was not easy, there was much to be forgiven and forgotten and there are always those who will do neither. But for me, well, you can see the path I chose.

"Not all countries had the generosity of spirit of the British. Some put our men in PoW camps, others were not so kind. But death by slave labor? This did not happen. At worst they had to work until they could be sent home. We all suffered terribly of course. In Russia you missed the Great Famine. For more than two years there were no crops in Northern Europe and the livestock sickened and died. Calves were born dead, chickens laid few eggs and those that were, well, nobody could eat them. If it had not been for the Italians and the Spanish, the Australians and the Americans sending food, I think nobody would have survived. But we did."

There was silence for a few minutes, Schneider remembering the horror of the nuclear attack and its aftermath, Jaeger trying to absorb the enormity of the deception that had been played on him. Eventually the Jesuit spoke again. "Captain. Before I came here, I looked up the survivors of Berlin. There were very, very few, the Americans singled out the city for special punishment. They dropped twelve atomic bombs on it. There are no Jaegers on the list of survivors. Is there anybody else I can look up, anybody else you knew?"

"Just my fiancée. We were to be married on my first leave. She was with the Luftwaffe, her name was Brucke, Sunni Brucke."

Father Andras Schneider couldn't help himself, he burst out laughing. Jaeger looked at him puzzled. "Captain, believe me that is one name I do not need to look up. Let me tell you one more story. Your fiancée was in the main German air defense bunker under Potsdam, just outside Berlin. The bunker was deep and well supplied and all down there survived.

"Among them was Herman Goering. The people in that bunker effectively became the German Government and Goering organized the surrender of Germany. Postwar, he and Miss Brucke became friends. I think he saw her as the daughter he never had. When he fell ill, she looked after him at his home in Karinhall. There he had gathered every art treasure in Europe. The countries of course were all arguing over getting their treasures back but nobody would agree on who owned what. Goering was a very bad man, but he spent the last two years of his life trying to atone for his crimes.

"In his will he left Karinhall and its treasures as a legacy for all the people of Europe. A center of art and enlightenment and culture to remind them what they could achieve if they worked together, just as the devastation around it reminded them of what would happen if they worked against each other. The treasure he and his Nazi conspirators had hidden away in Switzerland, that would support the center.

"There was one codicil attached to that bequest. He left the private apartments of Karinhall to your fiancée for her to live in, the condition being that she become the manager of the museum. She is a famous lady now, the Director of the European Center for Culture at Karinhall. You are something very rare Captain Jaeger, you have somebody in Germany who waits for your return.

Intensive Care Unit, Bethesda Naval Hospital, Maryland

"Woo-woo, woo-woo. Woo-woo, woo-woo."

Ramsey Chalk was hunched up in a fetal curl, crouched whimpering in a corner of the room. His cries had been muted at first but suddenly they exploded into a howl of sheer, undiluted horror as he started threshing around, fighting off some ghastly nightmare known only to him. Wails of terror, pain, misery and despair filled his room, they would have echoed off the walls if they hadn't been so well padded. The doctor pulled the curtains closed. President Johnson looked at him in shock. "What happened to him, Doctor. Some sort of nervous breakdown?"

Doctor Gan shook his head. "I'm afraid it's not that simple Mister President. I assume Director Hoover has been briefing you about the increasing drug use amongst kids, especially college kids?"

LBJ frowned. "College kids? The Director has been advising me about the increasing flow of illegal drugs into this country, but I was under the impression the problem was mostly heroin being sold in the poorest areas of the inner cities. We've had that problem for decades, ever since prohibition ended."

"That's one side of the problem Sir. But the truth is we are facing what amounts to an epidemic of drug use amongst college kids. Not the hard stuff like heroin, morphine or cocaine, but what some like to call soft drugs, mostly marihuana. Some of the kids have started to mess around with other chemicals, one of them is lysergic acid diethylamide or LSD.

"The kids call it acid. Its pretty easy to get, the kids buy it on the street in tablets, capsules, and, occasionally, liquid form. It is odorless, colorless, and has a slightly bitter taste so the kids put it on a cube of sugar and take it by mouth. They get what they call a trip, typically they begin to clear after about 12 hours. LSD's been around since 1938 but its use has only become widespread quite recently. We really don't know much about its long-term effects or just how harmful it is.

"The Attorney-General...."

"Former Attorney-General."

"My apologies Mister President, the former Attorney-General, has a reputation for being extremely sympathetic to youth movements and politics, particularly the extreme pacifist end of those circles where drug use is most common. We believe that he decided to experiment with LSD last night. Something went terribly wrong though.

"If I may explain, if taken in a large enough dose, the drug produces delusions and visual hallucinations. The precise nature of these is determined by the patient's mind-set as he goes into the drug episode. From what we can piece together from the patient's, well, ravings would be the best description, he viewed you and the other people in government, you could almost say everybody who surrounded him, as devils, evil incarnate.

"What is worse, he had apparently been reading a report on the destruction of a town called Duren during The Big One. The report was written by a Major Johan Lup of the Wehrmacht who entered the town less than an hour after the nuclear event. Its a very vivid report filled with horrifying images, Major Lup died of radiation poisoning a few weeks after the bombing and, well, its a very uncompromising description of the effects of an atomic bomb.

"It also appears that the former Attorney-General received some very bad advice. LSD is not considered an addictive drug since it does not produce compulsive drug-seeking behavior as do cocaine, amphetamine, heroin, alcohol, and nicotine. However, like many of the addictive drugs, LSD produces tolerance, so some users who take the drug repeatedly must take progressively higher doses to achieve the state of intoxication that they had previously achieved.

"It appears that whoever advised the patient was accustomed to a very high dose level. In combination, the two factors appear to have caused what the drug users call a very bad trip indeed. From what we can understand he appears to be trapped in a delusion where he believes he is in hell, surrounded by nightmarish demons and frightful devils who are inflicting the torments of the damned on him, all based on the descriptions in Major Lup's report."

"Dear God. How long will he be like this? Twelve hours you say?"

"Normally yes, Mister President. But that is for a normal dose. Here, the patient took a massive overdose, we believe he sweetened some coffee with LSD-doped sugar and drank a lot of it. It's all that seems to be in his stomach, we think he put a first

LSD dose in his coffee cup then just kept drinking more and more of the LSD-laced coffee.

"The best way of describing what has happened is that he has fried his brain. Or perhaps hard-boiled it would be an even better description. Anyway, the pathways in his mind are frozen into their present pattern. As far as we can determine, he will be trapped in that delusion until the day he dies."

War Room, Underneath the White House. Washington DC.

"The actual attack will take less than two hours Mister President. By that time, the lead aircraft, the RB-58s and the F-108s will already be well on their way home. The B-52s will be finishing their attack runs and also turning for home. Basically, Sir, its a very simple operation, its just the attack plan we used on Germany enlarged and, of course, using many more much more powerful weapons. We like to think of this as The Super-Jumbo Family Size One.

"Even the weather is running for us, the fall-out from the bombing will be swept out south, out to sea." Behind General McKenzie, the map of the Caliphate showed an eruption of red blots, representing the initiation points of the attack. Some were the small pinpoints of the 25 and 30 kiloton airbursts used by the RB-58s to take down the enemy defenses, others the huge areas of the 17 and 25 megaton bursts used to destroy area targets.

"I'd never envisaged something so devastating."

"Mister President, we find that incinerating entire countries gives meaning to our lives and enhances our manliness."

"Tell me General, when Bambi's mother was shot by the hunters, did you feel sad?" Lillith paused, letting the tension build up. "Just a little bit?"

"I am sure she was nicely mounted on the wall of a good home Lillith." She smiled and made a quick gesture of acceptance at the riposte.

"Please. Can we have a little less of the gallows humor here. I have a very serious decision to make."

"Actually Mister President, you don't. Not now at any rate. Even if we give the launch order now, it will take the bombers at least eight hours to fly to their fail-safe points. From there, it takes two hours for them to reach their targets. The bombers going over the Pole will take longer of course, and they'll be landing in Russia to refuel. The Russians are getting ready to receive them and their MiGs will escort the B-52s staging through Russia at least part of the way to their targets.

"You can order the bombers to turn back at any time right up to the moment they release their weapons. You don't actually have to make a final decision for ten hours or more."

"General McKenzie is right Sir." The Seer paused for a second. "That's why we have bombers, not missiles. They give us time. Much more importantly, it gives the other side time, time to think, to make decisions of their own. It gives both of us time to try and put an end to this.

"We can send the ultimatum to the Caliphate right now, they'll have it in less than an hour. We'll make sure they know the bombers are taking off. They can take their decisions knowing that we mean business. Germany never had that option, the Caliphate will. If they back down now, they can live. Otherwise, they won't."

"Do you really expect them to accept that ultimatum?"

"I honestly don't know Mister President. Its designed to be humiliating, its designed to make them grovel in the mud in front of the entire world. We have absolutely got to make sure that the whole world knows what the consequences of attacking us will be. That's as much for everybody else's benefit as for ours. We keep the peace and this is how we do it.

"Look, Mister President, we don't rule the world. We don't even come close. We never have and we probably never will. We just keep the peace. That's it, that's all we want to do. We don't really care what other nations do as long as they keep

244

the peace and don't step on our vital interests. Just to make things fair, we've gone to great lengths to make it quite clear what our vital interests are. We want a peaceful world. That's pretty much it, but we do want that rather badly. And we will use force to make sure we get the peaceful world we want. We aren't unreasonable, if nations want to fight insurgencies or have border incidents or a little self-contained killing spree where nobody else gets hurt, that's fine with us. Just as long as the world stays more or less peaceful.

"If you like, we are the cop on the beat. The cop walks his beat and very rarely does he have to pull his baton, let alone his gun. That's not because everybody is terrified that he'll go berserk and destroy everything. Its because everybody knows if they take a swing at the cop on the beat, the police will come in strength and never stop until the guilty have been punished so severely that nobody will want to pull the same trick again. This is why our national policy is called Massive Retaliation.

"Yesterday and last night, The Caliphate took a shot at the cop on the beat. Now, its up to us to show them that doing that isn't very smart. In fact it's terminally dumb. Then, once its over, we can go back to walking our beat and keeping the peace. Mister President, its painted on the nose of our bombers. Peace is Our Profession. Somebody has to do it, we got the job. We're not loved for it, very few people really likes the local cop on the beat, but we have to do it anyway."

At that point an officer from the communications center entered. He had a message flimsy that he passed to the President who read it and handed it to the Seer. "What do you make of this?"

It was a long description of the interrogation of one of the German prisoners taken in the fighting the night before. The Seer read it and lifted an eyebrow. It wasn't quite what he had been expecting.

"Well, Mister President, that explains a lot. It also gives us a little bit more leverage I think. We'd better modify that ultimatum before we send it out. And also we're going to have to change the curtain-raiser a little."

245

LBJ nodded and took a deep breath.

"Make the changes and send the ultimatum. Then execute the operational plan described. Launch the bombers in two hours time, send them out but tell them to hold at their fail-safe points until I give the order to go."

Chapter Ten
Reprisals

South Main Street, Brandon, Maryland.

Officer Frank Delmar believed that, for this time of year, evening was about the best time there was. Dawn was pretty good as well, but in the evening, the remainder of the day's heat mixed with the dusk breeze to make things just about perfect. He'd stopped his patrol car on South Main and was leaning up against the hood, keeping an eye on the street and just being seen. That was the real core of his job, he thought, just being seen.

Over in the west, the sun was setting, the bottom edge of the great orange ball just kissing the horizon, when he heard a rumble. It was familiar, almost routine, the sound of one of the B-52s from the local airbase. Taking off. Only it wasn't, quite, it sounded different somehow. Delmar caught sight of it suddenly, it was angry crimson, the giant bomber's silver skin reflecting the light of the setting sun, the white paint on its belly giving a more gentle and peaceful red. But it was lower, much lower than usual and the smoke behind it was black, stained blood-red and ugly by the sunset. With a sinking feeling Delmar understood why the aircraft sounded different. Its eight engines were straining hard, fighting to lift a full load of bombs and fuel up into the stratosphere where the bomber would be safe.

The B-52 passed over, the vibration from its laboring engines causing his car to shake in its wake. The noise was enough to make the local people, out to enjoy the peace of the evening, look up. Behind the first bomber was another, its engines also striving to get their load up high and fast. The first bomber's passage was still shaking South Main when its companion passed over and the third was approaching fast. As each one passed, more people came out of their homes and left the shops to look up and the sky filling with the streams of smoke from the engines, the brilliant reflected shades of red from the bombers passing overhead.

They stood silently and watched the B-52s reaching into the sky as the roar of their passage filled the town. As each aircraft passed, it seemed to be a little redder, a little darker, the smoke cloud from its engines a little less obvious as the sun set. Then, just as the last of the stream of B-52s passed, its fuselage and smoke trail hardly visible in the gathering gloom, the last edge of the sun dipped below the horizon. 'And on a pale horse rode death,' Delmar thought as the last of the bombers vanished into the growing twilight.

"God Be With You, Boys."

Thomas Hardy owned the town drugstore. If he had been cast into a Hollywood Western, there would be no doubt as to the part he would play. The kindly town merchant. Now he was looking at the bombers fading into the dusk, the sound of their passage ebbing. Suddenly the evening had a chill to it and it wasn't only the coming of night. Up and down the east coast of America, along its northern border with Canada, other people in other small towns stood and watched their bombers head out to their targets in a country far away.

"Amen" said Officer Frank Delmar

Aviano Italian Air Force Base, Italy

"Gentlemen. We have a go. About thirty minutes ago, the strategic bomber and reconnaissance wings in CONUS started to take off. They will be crossing the Atlantic tonight ready to launch the planned series of attacks tomorrow morning. We have received word from the Russians that the airfields designated as SAC staging points are ready. In addition, a regiment of Russian long range bombers, Tu-22s, will be supporting our attack. That brings me to the first point. We have received a message from that regiment, the 35th Guards Long Range Aviation. Could I have the picture please?"

The lights dimmed and a picture came up, a large, ungainly-looking bomber with a small cockpit well forward and two large engines mounted on top of the fuselage by the tail.

"This is a Tu-22. If you see one of these, don't shoot at it, they're on our side. The Russians will be operating well to the North of us, their bombers haven't got much range so they'll not be going beyond northern Iran. One thing, second slide please."

The picture changed to the nose of one of the Russian Tupolevs, showing the name painted under the cockpit. The Cyrillic letters took a little deciphering but were clear enough. *For Marisol.*

"Second thing. Earlier this evening, we were briefed on the one attack that will take place before the main raid strikes. We have now received new instructions, instead of launching that attack on the base complex around Gaza, we will be hitting a smaller complex around Yaffo further to the north. There are three reasons for this. One is that the coastal defense batteries at Gaza have fired their missiles, they are no longer a threat and, because they are relatively mobile, they may already have moved away. The missiles at Yaffo are still in place. Another is that there is apparently a high value target of opportunity in Gaza that we do not wish to destroy unless we cannot avoid doing so. Last, but not least, President Johnson himself has a personal distaste for the inhabitants of Yaffo.

"There are two coastal defense, anti-ship missile batteries in the target area, four surface-to-air missile batteries and an airfield. We believe there to be at least 16 enemy fighters there, Irenes, Chipanese-built Kawanishi J12K4 Shindens. They are fast-climbing and can reach B-58 operational altitudes. The strike force dedicated to taking down the Jaffo base complex consists of four

RB-58s and will be escorted by four F-108s. If the fighters come up, the F-108s will send them back down again.

"The remaining F-108s and RB-58s will hit assigned targets to assist the penetration of the B-52s. Unlike the Yaffo strike they will wait on Presidential authorization before executing their missions.

"Fly high gentlemen. But before that, get some sleep. Tomorrow will be a very busy day."

The Ruling Council Conference Room, Jerusalem, The Caliphate.

For the first time in more years than he cared to remember, Field Marshal Walther Model was frightened. That was just one part of his emotional mix, but it was the one he was unfamiliar with. He was, indeed, sick-scared but also furiously angry and seething with hatred for the morons whose bombastic arrogance and purblind stupidity had driven them all into this mess. The worst feeling of all was complete helplessness. He was here at this meeting by courtesy only, he didn't have a vote in its deliberations and his presence was simply to give information and take orders. Give information? To these brainless, arrogant, conceited, camel-humping offspring of a pox-doctor's douche-bag? They saw what they wanted to see and heard what they wanted to hear and woe betide anybody who disagreed with them.

They just didn't understand what was descending on them. They were now crowing about the fight on the beach, almost 36 hours ago. The Satrap of Egypt had worked himself up into a fine frenzy describing how the American Marines had poured ashore in their thousands to be defeated by a handful of gallant Believers. Lurid accounts of how the massacre of the invaders had been so complete that the infidels had left the water covered with their bodies packed so densely one could walk out of sight of land by stepping from one to the next and still see no end of them.

Normally, Model thought, that would mean one of the Marines had an ingrown toenail, but his own reports spoke of three burned-out American tanks found on the scene of the action. His own people had reported there had been one hell of a firefight there. One of his small mobile columns appeared to have been wiped out. How was a bit unclear, the battle scene didn't make sense. Call it a draw, Model thought, one mobile column for a Marine unit bloodied. As if it mattered now.

More talk, more chatter, more mindless bombast. The Satrap of Palestine, a short, plump man in green battle-dress fatigues and a black-and-white checked cloth on his head, had grabbed the limelight and was haranguing the Ruling Council. According to him, the American navy offshore had been smashed by the land-based missiles and fast attack craft. He spoke of ships exploding and sinking under the relentless attack, of the sea on fire with the destruction, of crew slaughtered to the last man, praying for salvation before their inevitable destruction. Model paused for a second there, did nobody think to ask how, if there were no survivors, anybody knew what the crews had done? The man was still ranting though

"To Washington, we are marching, martyrs by the million!" declared Yasser Arafat, as the Ruling Council roared its approval and chanted along with him.

Well, martyrs by the million they were certainly going to get. The newspapers, television and radio had all reported the bombers taking off from America hours earlier. The American press was crying out for vengeance against the people who had launched the attack on the American forces, the Northern Europeans were bewailing the impending end of the world. 'Can't we all just get along?' was the plaintive headline in one newspaper, from Manchester of all places. The Southern Europeans were speculating that whatever the Americans did, it would take the threat that was pressing in from the east further from them. The Russians were cheering the Americans on and publishing long lists of the atrocities committed by Caliphate-linked terrorists.

No matter what their position though on the events themselves, all the news was filled with doom and foreboding that was increasing as the American bombers swept across the Atlantic. They would have been half way over when this futile apology for a meeting had started and were now much, much closer. Three hours of mindless boasting and not once had the American ultimatum even been mentioned.

Model looked down at his copy of the American message. Couldn't these fools read? It was written and constructed to be unacceptable, written to be refused. It was nothing more than a transparent excuse for the sledgehammer blow that was to fall on the Caliphate. He scanned the demands. A full public apology by the Caliphate for the attacks on American units. Payment of compensation for the shot-down bomber and also additional compensation paid to the crew for the hardship and distress they had suffered. More compensation for the Marines killed and injured last night, payment for the vehicles and equipment lost and fuel and ammunition expended. Beneath his impassive expression Model raised his eyebrows at the latter amount, the Americans had thrown how much ammunition at his little unit? Then yet more compensation, for the fighting around the ships, for the missiles used, for the bombs dropped and rockets fired, even for the fuel burned by the jets and ships.

Then there were the non-military provisions, a full admission of liability for the attacks on defenseless refugees and the cessation of all such acts. The establishment of a neutral zone around Gaza for refugees who wished to leave the Caliphate, a zone to be administered by the Red Cross and maintained until all the refugees had been transferred to countries wishing to receive them. An end to the destruction of antiquities and the establishment of another international zone around the Pyramids and Valley of the Kings. Any attacks by anybody on either international zone would be considered an act of war by the United States and treated accordingly.

It ended with a reiteration of the American "Open Skies" policy and stated quite bluntly that any further interference with Strategic Aerospace Command flights would result in a response involving all US national resources. It was a vicious, calculating ultimatum., one intended to cause an infuriated rejection. And the only alternative on offer, the American bombers, were already on their way. The only way to stop them was to accept the unacceptable. Yet, these fools who called themselves Satraps hadn't even started to discuss it.

And they had to discuss it, they had to. Because, incredibly, unbelievably, this ultimatum offered him the one thing he had been looking for. For months he had racked his brains trying to think of a way out of this trap he was in, then the Americans had dropped it into his lap. All his people had to do was sit tight and the Americans would get them out for him. Model modified the thought, sit tight and remain unincinerated. He could read a map as well as anybody. His people were right in the middle of the ring of bases that had launched the attacks precipitating this crisis.

If nothing else, the Americans would destroy those bases, just to show what would happen to anybody who attacked Americans. They wouldn't, probably wouldn't deliberately target his people but it didn't make any difference. They would be collateral damage. The irony was overwhelming, after almost twenty years of trying to save his people, they would be wiped out by accident. Unless he could focus this meeting and persuade the Satraps to accept the American demands.

Cockpit F-108A Rapier "Wicked Stick", 68,000 feet over the Eastern Mediterranean

"Bandits. We have Bandits." Not Bogies, General Larry noted. Bogies were unidentified contacts, bandits were enemies. For this mission, for the Rapiers that were flying point, everything in front of them was an enemy. "Bandits are climbing fast on intercept course. Enemy count is twenty four in four groups of six. Tentative identification, tentative identification, Irene fighters."

So much for the pre-raid intel of 16 fighters. No matter, this was one of those occasions when added enemies just made for a richer target environment. Larry ran the threat over in his mind, the Irene was a point defense interceptor, very high rate of climb but with limited fuel reserves, poor armament and worse radar. If the intel was right, these were dash-fours with a pair of 30 millimeter cannon and a pair of Tanto-kai air-to-air missiles - heavy but infra-red homing and limited in range. No matter, the inbound groups were in the tight formations that had become obsolete with the introduction of nuclear-tipped air-to-air missiles.

"Revised raid count, enemy force is now 32 fighters in eight groups of four." That made sense, the old Luftwaffe Finger Four group. For a moment Larry pined for the old days when a pilot could see his wingman. Now, his wingman, *Maybelline*, was so far away that the aircraft was lost to sight, its translucent silver-blue finish lost in the glare of the sky. Even further out were the other pair of F-108s, *Midnight Fantasy*, and *Black Velvet*. Yet, visible or not, all four fighters were ready to concentrate a deadly volley of missiles onto the enemy fighters.

Larry felt the rotary launcher aft of his cockpit whirr as an AIM-47 was moved to the launching position. "Take them!" and his fighter lurched as the missile dropped clear. It was a weird sensation, the enemy fighters were still far below them yet the missile curved upwards, climbing for the thing air where resistance was less and its speed and range correspondingly greater. Then, at the fuel-optimum point, the missile turned over, its active radar guidance system snapped on and the AIM-47 started to dive on its selected formation.

At that point, two things happened. One was that *Wicked Stick* and her three sisters were able to lock their radars onto four more of the enemy formations, the other was that the enemy themselves suddenly realized the deadly threat that was already hurtling down from above. Their formations shattered as each aircraft tried to put as much distance between themselves and the initiation point as possible. The problem was, once again, physics.

In the time available, there was only a limited footprint that they could occupy given their speed and agility. The size and shape of that footprint were incorporated in the guidance system of the AIM-47 which plotted the aiming point to include as many targets as possible. The first wave of four finger-four elements had least time to react and, therefore, the smallest footprint. The rippling wave of nuclear explosions took down thirteen of the sixteen aircraft. The brief delay between the two missile salvoes gave the second group of four formations a greater chance of getting clear, eight of the sixteen fighters vanished in the fireballs. In less than two seconds, 21 of the 32 Caliphate fighters had been blotted from the sky. Of the remaining eleven, all had varying degrees of damage from blast and thermal pulse and their pilots were disorientated, in some cases blinded from the light flash.

General Charles Larry knew the rule; when fighter fought fighter, speed and altitude were everything. His four fighters were sitting 30,000 feet above the shattered enemy formation. What was more, the cruising speed of *Wicked Stick* was 300 miles per hour faster than the maximum speed of the enemy aircraft; when the Rapier went flat-out it was almost a whole Mach number faster. The F-108 may not be the tightest-turning fighter in the world but in this sort of fight it didn't matter. The Rapier pilots had a name for this final mop-up stage in an air battle, they called it clubbing baby seals.

He'd already picked his first baby, a cripple limping away from the nuclear inferno with smoke trailing from its fuselage. As *Wicked Stick* screamed down behind her victim, Larry caught a flash picture of the odd-looking aircraft. The designers had put the two engines one above the other, not side-by-side the way God had intended. And the wings, very sharply swept indeed with ailerons on the tips, just like a delta but with a piece cut out.

Then, flashes erupted over the cockpit and forward fuselage as the four 20mm cannon under *Wicked Stick's* nose raked the enemy fighter. Almost as he fired Larry broke right and climbed, taking him out of his own stream of shells, shooting oneself down tended to be frowned on. By the time his target exploded, *Wicked Stick* was already climbing hard, trading speed and energy for altitude while Larry and his RIO picked out their next baby seal.

The Ruling Council Conference Room, Jerusalem, The Caliphate.

The brilliant flashes of light lit up the conference room. Model instinctively counted the seconds between the flashes and the rolling thunder of the explosions. Almost 50 kilometers. That wasn't a thunderstorm, those were nuclear explosions, nothing else could be that bright at that distance. And the Satraps around the table were still wrapped up in their fantasy world of glory. Model's aide came in with a teletype report. He read it and his eyes widened. It confirmed both his guess and his worst fears. If the Americans were hitting this hard this early, they were holding little back.

"Your Excellencies. I have just received some highly disturbing news." That interrupted the conversation, a little anyway. "The leading edge of the American bomber formations have just reached our territory. The main body is still some hours away but the American strategic fighters and reconnaissance aircraft appear to have started the process of eliminating anything that may prevent their heavy bombers attacking whatever targets they choose.

"A small lead formation is approaching the coast of Palestine. The fighters based in Northern Palestine took off to intercept that formation and were engaged by American fighters which used nuclear weapons to destroy them. According to this report, there have been eight high-altitude nuclear explosions sighted and it appears that none of our fighters have survived the attack. There are casualties on the ground as well, how many this report does not tell me. There are no reports of any American losses. The Americans have sent us an ultimatum, have your Excellencies considered your response?"

The response from the Satrap of Syria was almost a sneer, one that made Model reflect on the virtues of old Heidelburg tradition of dueling with sabers.

"A few fighters, what are they to worry about? And some reconnaissance aircraft? What will they do? Photograph us to death?" There were guffaws of laughter from around the table and a few pounded their fists on the table with glee. "And our response to the American message? We should coat it with camel dung and send it back."

"Your Excellencies, you have all seen a handful of rocks thrown against a window. They do not arrive at once but first one then two or three more before the rest arrive in a mass and smash the glass as if it had never been. This brush is the first stone. The American fighters deal with ours, then their strategic reconnaissance aircraft move in to locate our defenses and eliminate them. Then, and only then, do their heavy bombers, their B-52s, come in to destroy us.

"What has happened in the last few minutes is just the start, the opening move. The situation is going to get worse, much worse, very quickly now. In 1947 it took the Americans less than an hour to destroy Germany. We may have less time than that."

Model looked at the assembled Satraps. Blank incomprehension and disbelief. They simply weren't getting it.

RB-58C "Tiger Lily", Approaching Yaffo

Some of the targets couldn't be missed. The harbor was one of them. When the ASG-18 was in mapping mode, it showed up clearly and the military part, the fast attack craft base, was easy to pick out also. It was impossible to punish the fast attack craft unit that had attacked the American fleet, the Djinns had all gone to the bottom under the lash of American naval air power so another FAC unit and its base was to suffer instead. *Red Sonja* had that duty and she was carrying a missile with a 225 kiloton warhead to do the job. That would erase the entire military facility. The town surrounding it would be collateral damage.

Another target that couldn't be missed was an airfield to the south of the town. That was where the fighters so summarily dispatched by the escorting F-108s had come from. It was scheduled to receive an AGM-76, one with its warhead dialed up to maximum yield, 65 kilotons. That airfield was one of three targets assigned to *Spider Woman,* the other two were coastal defense missile batteries.

Other targets revealed themselves. The surface-to-air missile bases for example. They had to turn their radars on to function yet the moment they did so, the threat location systems aboard the RB-58s would plot their positions and target them with AGM-76s. Taking down the SAM batteries was a relatively simple task, one for which the AGM-76 had been designed.

The warheads used were set to normal yield, 35 kilotons. *Tiger Lily* had three such batteries plotted and had her missiles ready to go. Her wing mate *Coral Queen* had three more. That left each of them with three more missiles for "targets of opportunity". *Tiger Lily* and *Coral Queen* were to open the show.

In their big belly pods, the rotary launchers clicked and the first of the ten missiles, total yield 630 kilotons were on their way to their targets. The rules had been quite simple to understand, attack SAC aircraft and the US would retaliate in a time, manner and place of its own choosing. This was the time, the manner and the place.

The Ruling Council Conference Room, Jerusalem, The Caliphate.

This time there could be no doubt about what was happening, the blinding flashes of light had created a rippling scintillation on the walls and ceiling of the room. Then came the thunder of the explosions, shaking the room and concluded with a big blast that brought down fragments from the ceiling. Model had felt the difference between the sky-wave and the ground-wave and knew these hellburners had been fired at targets on the ground. Out of the window, on the horizon, he could see the red, glowing mushroom clouds rising, one significantly bigger than the rest. West, he thought, probably the complex around Yaffo. Not Gaza thank God. There was still time but so very little.

His aide had slipped the message in front of him while he had been hypnotized by the mushroom clouds. "Your Excellencies, I have to report that that there has been a concerted attack on our facilities at Yaffo. The Americans have exploded at least ten hellburners on a variety of targets in and around the city. We can assume that all those targets have been destroyed. Civilian casualties, what the Americans call collateral damage, are likely to be very high, probably in the tens or hundreds of thousands."

"To Washington, we are marching, martyrs by the million!" The Satrap of Palestine repeated dreamily.

"Thy enemies plotted and they plotted well but Allah plotted also and Allah is the best of plotters." It was the Satrap of Syria, Model thought in despair, once they start swapping quotations, they'll be lost for hours.

"To Washington, we are marching, martyrs by the million!"

The Satrap of Palestine had the same, defocused, slack-jawed expression on his face. It struck a chord, years ago, before the Fuhrer had gained power in Germany, there had been a man who had hung around the outside of a town school, watching the children playing with the same, slack-jawed expression. The police had been unable to do anything, just watching wasn't an offense. So one day a group of local brownshirts, the SA, had dragged him away and beaten him. That lead to another thought, he'd been told that story by an SA man who had survived the Night of the Long Knives because he had taken a gun to a meeting where guns were not allowed. Model had given up his own P38 when entering this room but he'd never been checked for a back-up piece. Suddenly he knew how to get these people's attention. In a smooth action he drew the Tokarev from its concealed holster and fired a single shot into the head of Yasser Arafat. Blood and brains sprayed over the Satrap sitting next to him. Arafat slumped forward onto the Conference table.

"Do you have any idea what is coming? Any idea at all? In 1947 the Americans destroyed Germany with their hellburners and they killed 60 million people. Each bomb carried by a B-52 is four times as powerful as all the bombs dropped on Germany in 1947. Each bomber carries four such bombs and there are more than two thousand of those bombers coming to attack us. Do the maths. Four by four by two thousand. That means the American attack aimed at us is 32,000 times the strength of the one that destroyed Germany. Do the maths. 32,000 times 60 million. You claim Allah will protect you from the Americans? But who will protect Allah from the Americans?"

Model looked around. He was getting through at last, blasphemy had succeeded when logic and reason had failed.

"One of their planners was told that bombers could not kill a religion. He answered 'No, but we can kill everybody who believes in it and burn all their books'. When all the believers are dead and all the writings are destroyed, who then is left to follow Allah? What is left of his teachings?

"And remember this, those are bombers, not missiles. If there is anything left after their strike, they will just go back to their bases, get more hellburners and destroy whatever it is that they missed the first time. The Americans do not want you to agree to their terms, they want to destroy us. The only way you can prevent them from wiping you off the face of the earth is to do what they do not want. Accept their ultimatum."

The Satrap of Iran tore his eyes away from the spreading pool of blood on the conference table to the rising mushroom clouds on the horizon. Technically, he was only the first amongst equals but when he made a decision, it was final.

"I would rather drink a chalice of poison than agree to these terms. But the Great Satans have left us no choice. We must agree to these terms and set our revenge aside for another day. And we will have our revenge for this. Field Marshal Model, please leave and arrange to have the Great Satan advised of our compliance with their demands."

Model left the room, closing the door behind him. As he did, he saw the Caliphate Council continuing to discuss business. And he had no doubt his own execution was top of the agenda.

War Room, Underneath the White House. Washington DC.

The map showed the bombers gathering at their fail-safe points, just two hours from their targets. The strategic recon wings and the fighters were closer in, the 305th had already dropped the hammer on the Yaffo base complex. That was the indispensable bit, the visible penalty for attacking a SAC bomber.

"Mister President. Message from Switzerland. The Caliphate Council has agreed to our demands. In full. The Swiss Federal authorities have confirmed that instructions have been received from the Council to transfer the compensation amounts demanded from Caliphate reserves to whatever financial institution we specify."

LBJ looked at the map. "Turn the bombers around, bring them home." Then he paused. "I get a feeling this is a mistake, we should bomb them anyway. We're going to have to fight them some time or another, it might as well be now when we are so incomparably stronger." He shook his head. "We made our demands, they groveled. Its enough for now. Bring our bombers home." Another pause. "I'm making a terrible mistake aren't I?"

"Yes, Mister President."

Chapter Eleven
Clearing Up

Gaza-North Airfield, Gaza International Zone.

Father Andras Schneider doubted that this airfield had ever been this busy before. Just to start with, there were three big turboprop aircraft, American C-133 Cargomaster transports, over on the hard pad and an even bigger jet-engined transport, one of the newer C-141 Starlifters beside them. The C-141 had brought in troops from America, the C-133s were taking the refugees back to Germany. Some the latter were crying, some were silent, some were openly furious at the years they had wasted and the friends and family they had lost. But, they were going home. They had a home to go to.

It hadn't been easy to convince them. The Marines had landed first and they had come in hard and fast. Some over the beaches, others had been transported by rotodyne straight to the designated perimeter. It had been a terrifying display of power and force, backed up by the bombers circling overhead. The Germans would have fought even so but orders had come from Field Marshal Model himself, not a shot, not a blow. Not even a rude word. The Caliphate troops had taken one look at the massive force deployed against them and departed. Very rapidly. That had been the easy part. The tough part had been persuading the Germans that everything that they had been told for almost twenty years was a lie.

The survivors of the German armored infantry unit had told their story. They were alive, that had persuaded some that the story about immediate and universal execution wasn't true, but there were not many of them. What had happened to the rest? Destroyed by a tornado of light and fire? A likely story.

In the end, somebody had an inspiration, The head of the ICRC, Doctor Wijnand, had arranged for some of the women and children who had resettled in Germany after their expulsion from New Schwabia to be flown in. They were known personally by some of the Gaza Germans, known by reputation to others. They had told their stories, good and bad. The bad stories had been more convincing than the good, nobody, especially the women, would invent such things about themselves. Those stories had the ring of truth about them and they'd given credibility to the good news. There had been no great massacres, despite the nuclear bombing, there was a home to go to. It was not a home that the people here would recognize but, they were going to go there. As soon as they could be screened and those who were wanted for crimes against humanity isolated. That was taking time, but, over the years, enough refugee Germans had been screened that the procedure had been refined to the point of being a fine art.

So, the Germans had decided to go home and the Americans had provided the transports that would take them there. One of the Cargomasters had finished loading and was closing its rear ramp while Father Schneider watched. It's engines were already running and it started to taxi out to the runway, ready for take-off on its long haul to Warsaw. There, the refugees would be transferred to trains for the refugee processing center at Gorlitz, on the German-Polish border.

As the transport waddled down the taxiway, it passed a line of F-105 bombers and F-106 fighters that had been sent to cover the evacuation. Amongst the detachments of sleek jets was an equally sleek transport, a C-144 Superstream, only this one wore the markings of the Russian Air Force. That brought Father Schneider's mind back to the person standing next to him. And a question he had to ask.

"Field Marshal, why did you do it, why did you lie to them all."

Model looked at the Jesuit steadily for a moment. For that moment, he was about to crush the question with a wintry retort but he didn't. For all that he'd told himself that he didn't care what other people thought and didn't need to explain himself to anybody, he suddenly realized he did want one person to know, he did want one person to understand even if they didn't approve. And who better than a Jesuit, told under the seal of the Confessional?

"This is a Confession, understand Father? It will be covered by that secrecy and remain between us. Agreed?"

"Agreed."

"At first it wasn't a lie. Not knowingly at any rate. When we heard of the bombing it seemed like the whole of Germany had been destroyed, as it had been of course. Nobody could get news from there, communications were down, all we could get was that an immense fleet of American bombers had destroyed everything of value there.

"Some commanders sent back troops to find out what was happening, some troops deserted and tried to get back. The messages we got from them was that there was nothing left. Germany was a destroyed desert where nothing lived or would ever live again. We knew that Germany had "surrendered" but we assumed it was the surrender of a corpse "agreeing" to be buried. So we were trapped deep inside enemy territory with nowhere to go and nobody to turn to.

"Remember Father, the Russians might show mercy now but then they did not. Surrender meant slavery or death. Or both. Had there been something to go home to, we might have tried to fight our way back, to cut a path back home, but there was no home. Of course, now we know the worst news, the news that came back to us, was from those who hadn't made it back to Germany, the ones who had given up and exaggerated the stories to explain their dereliction. The ones who had made it all the way back, stayed.

"So we tried to make our own homes in the territory we occupied. We set up our own little states, ruled them ourselves and tried to turn them into new Germanies. I was fortunate. My Army Group had ended the war in a good defensive position and with enough people to make a functioning state. Enough but only just. The countries that didn't have enough people became nothing more than bandits hiding in the woods. I hoped that they would buy us enough years to become a new country, to become too strong for the Russians to defeat and they would decide to let us be.

"Then, after a few years, I began to learn the truth. That there were survivors in Germany, that a shadow of our home had survived. I knew if my people learned that, some, perhaps many, of them would try to get back. I knew that their chances of getting back were slight and in trying for that slight chance they would destroy the rest of us. Remember, we had only just enough people to create a functioning state. If any significant number left, we would also become nothing more than bandits hiding in the woods.

"So I kept the truth a secret, and once the truth was kept secret, it had to be guarded by a bodyguard of lies. I had to lie to prevent some jeopardizing the survival of all. Of course, once the lie was started, it couldn't be stopped, year on year it grew and took on a life of its own. As times changed and situations developed, I had to create new lies and invent new bodyguards to prevent the truth being told."

"Why did you not just tell your people, let them decide? Lay the issues out for them so they understood what was involved?"

"Because I was their leader, it was for me to decide, not to desert my responsibilities."

And that, thought Father Schneider was it. A leader either trusted those he saw as his people or he didn't. In the final analysis, Model didn't. However much they had deserved his trust, he hadn't deserved theirs. Now, he never would, for there were a group of Russians coming. Two officers and a pair of enlisted men.

"Field Marshal Model? Major Putin of the Russian State Security. I am placing you under arrest for crimes against the Russian People. Crimes, I might say, that are almost without number."

"Major, If I may get my bag from my office?"

"I think not Field Marshal. You will remain with us. One of my men will get your bags. We have an aircraft waiting to take you to Moscow for trial."

Father Schneider watched as the German was lead away. It was ironic in a way, of all Model's people, he was the one who would not be going home.

The Oval Office, The White House, Washington

"The South Africans have agreed Mister President. They'll be sending troops into the two neutral zones starting within a week. The ICRC will be the supervisory authority for the refugee zone around Gaza, the British have agreed to do the same for the cultural preservation areas in the Nile Valley. We should be able to pull the Marines out very shortly."

"How much is this costing us?"

"We're agreed to supply the South Africans with military equipment and some economic and trade considerations. Actually, they'll benefit us as much as them, there's a storehouse of raw materials down there and the South Africans have been out in the cold for decades. They're taking some of the refugees as well by the way, not all the Germans want to adopt the simple agrarian lifestyle. All in all, the economic impact on us will be pretty negligible. We got off lightly in that respect.

"Militarily, we've learned a lot. There's a lot of things wrong with the M60 that need fixing. It turns out there is a design fault in the hydraulics, the whole system is shock-sensitive and the fluid is inflammable. Colt have an urgent contract to rechamber the captured MG42s for our standard .276, the Marines are riding herd on that. They won't make the same mistake we did last time we tried to copy the '42. We hope to issue the new gun within a year.

"Politically? This one has cost us."

LBJ nodded bitterly and looked out of the windows. The anti-nuclear demonstrators were out again, their chanting could be heard faintly through the heavy glass 'Hey, hey LBJ, how many kids will you kill today?'

"I wish it was as easy to make decisions as they think. Damn, I wish it was as easy as I thought before I got this job. Sometimes there are no right decisions are there? There are only the less wrong decisions. And we made a lot of wrong decisions didn't we?"

The Seer sighed. "This hasn't been our proudest hour, no. We've made a lot of errors all of us. This whole story has been one of mistakes, made honestly and in good faith, but mistakes none the less. From the best of motives, mostly, from lack of knowledge, often, from making assumptions based on too little evidence and then treating those assumptions as facts, all too often. The old proverb says that 'the road to hell is paved with good intentions' and we've just seen a perfect example. If we could go back, make a few small changes in decisions, we could avoid this. But, we can never go back, all we can do is say to ourselves that this tale was one of mistakes and errors of judgment and try not to repeat them."

Ortega farm, Rosario, Surigao del Sur

A few miles away from Rosario, in the hills that overlooked the town, Graciella Ortega returned to her little vegetable farm. She'd taken a ride in a bicycle taxi this time, her stomach hurt far too much to let her make the long walk up the hill. Her doctors had been very firm, if she felt any sign of stress, she was to rest immediately. Her wounds had come within a hair's breadth of killing her and she would have to take great care of herself lest the job be finished.

But, she had to come. Her vegetables had been neglected and she knew the crop was lost. The jungle would be taking back the little field and she would have to weed and hoe with care for the snakes would also have returned. Then, she went dizzy with fear. There were men in her farm.

The fear went quickly for the men were big, Australians. And was replaced by relief, for her farm was beautiful, the rows neatly weeded, the ground between them carefully hoed. The plants had been watered properly, at dusk so the midday sun wouldn't burn their leaves.

"Missus Ortega? Good to see you up again. The boys here, we were all brought up on farms back home and we couldn't stand to see a nice field go to ruin. So we looked after it for you." The Australian soldier looked a little embarrassed. "Some of the produce was ripe and we didn't want to see it wasted so we took it for our unit."

He reached into a pocket and produced a grubby piece of paper. "We kept a list of everything and paid for it at market price. Your daughter has the money. Now Missus Ortega, will you look around and show us what we've missed. We'll get it seen to. Feels good to be working a field again."

B-58A "56-0213" On Final Approach to Carswell AFB.

0213 was a B-58A in name only, in fact she was a YB-58 that had been loosely upgraded to B-58A standard then used as a hack. She was tired and her controls were sloppy. This was her last flight, she was to be retired and broken up. Major Mike Kozlowski and his crew were bringing her back to Fort Worth so they could pick up their new aircraft, an RB-58F.

They'd picked her out off the production line a couple of weeks earlier, they'd been invited down by the Fort Worth management and given a VIP tour of the plant. That tour had ended with the final assembly area for the new RB-58F. They'd been invited to make their choice. The foreman had taken them around but when they'd stopped in front of one, he'd shaken his head slightly and led them to another.

267

"Odd thing about building these" he'd said "some of them are just right from the start, it's as if they want to be put together and fly."

He'd been right, this aircraft seemed to have an air of eagerness about her. "Can we have her?" Asked Kozlowski.

"Sure, Major. 64-9617. What you want to name her? *Marisol II?*"

Just as had happened six years earlier, the name just popped into his mind. Kozlowski shook his head. "No, she's *Xiomara*. Spelt like this." He wrote the name on a piece of paper and handed it over. "Its a Latin American name, it's pronounced Zomara."

As he taxied the old B-58 in, Kozlowski felt himself finally saying goodbye to *Marisol*. She wasn't entirely lost, Romano Mussolini had sent him a painting of her, with Sophia sitting in the cockpit and Kozlowski standing on the access ladder by the cockpit. It had come with an official sympathetic letter from the Speaker of the Legate and a much warmer personal note from Mussolini. Sophia and Carlo had also written to him, expressing sympathy and reminding him he always had somewhere to stay when he visited Italy.

The painting hung in his quarters now and sometimes, at night, he had spoken quietly to *Marisol*. A couple of times, he had thought she'd answered but it had certainly been a dream. But, for all practical purposes, *Marisol* was gone. SAC investigators had carefully collected every piece of wreckage from her crash site and reassembled it in a hangar at Nellis. They'd learned a lot from that and those lessons had been included in the design of the RB-58F. That program had been delayed by almost six months as a result. Once the investigation was over, the wreckage had been buried under the Red Sun test range, an honor reserved for aircraft lost in combat.

Now *Xiomara* was standing on the hard-pad waiting to be flown out. Complete, she looked quite different to *Marisol*. Oh, the shape was the same, if one ignored the new engine nacelles, and the new wing shape. The perfect delta of the earlier versions had been modified by extending the wing root forward so that the leading edge was cranked at the inner engine pylon. From the side, that wasn't obvious though.

What had changed was the color. *Marisol's* brilliant chromed silver had been replaced by a soft, translucent bluish-silvery white, the same color used on the F-108 and the B-70. The national markings were now a darker shade of the same color, the previous blues, reds and whites muted. Even the nose art was muted now, a soft black-and gray portrait, instead of the full color. That was another result of *Marisol's* death. Somehow, nobody knew how, SAC had got hold of full operational specifications of the electro-optical sights used to shoot down *Marisol*.

A study had shown that the system only worked well when aircraft had brilliant color contrasts and sharp reflections from highly-polished surfaces. Reduce those and the efficiency of the sight dropped dramatically. Hence the new paint scheme. The bean-counters in GAO had tried to use it as an excuse to end the custom of a single crew being assigned their own aircraft but their sally had been met by a virtual SAC mutiny. It had gone as high as SecDef who had ended it with a terse judgment. "If the crews want to keep their own aircraft, let them. Don't fix what ain't broke."

Kozlowski actually preferred the new paint scheme, it made the older chrome silver and full color markings look old-fashioned somehow. Like cars with too much chrome and exaggerated tailfins. But, the color was just a detail. The real secret of the RB-58F was those engines, unreheated J-58s that gave the aircraft more thrust cold than the older J-57s had on full afterburner. As a result, the RB-58F was a true supersonic bomber, cruising at Mach 2.8 and capable of dashing in at Mach 3.2 when needed. Even better, without the fuel-thirsty afterburners, the F model substantially outranged the older variants. Add in revised electronics that were more reliable than the older systems and a 30mm tail gun, the RB-58F was truly a new generation of Hustler.

It took an hour to get the acceptances signed then the crew mounted up. As the cockpit closed Kozlowski leaned forward slightly and patted the control console in front of him. "Hi *Xiomara*. I'm Mike, your pilot. Eddy is in the Bear's Den and Xav is sitting back there in the Electronics Pit. Welcome to the team."

Silence.

Retraining for the RB-58F had been fairly limited for Korrina and Dravar, the front end of the systems they worked with was virtually unchanged. Eddie's job was actually easier, the old layout of two radars had been replaced by a superior multi-mode adaptation of the ASG-18. Kozlowski's workload was also much less without the elaborate control systems for the afterburners. That didn't decrease the list of pre-flight checks of course, they got longer every year. Sometimes Kozlowski thought that if the Wright Brothers had flown for SAC, they'd still be doing pre-flight checks. Eventually, they started up and moved along to the taxiway, the undercarriage bumping as it hit the panel joins in the concrete. Soon, they were at the runway end, ready for take-off clearance.

"Just a shuttle flight today *Xiomara* so we can all get used to each other. We'll start real training next week."

"Where are we going?" The voice was different from *Marisol's* brash assertiveness. It was quieter, more mature somehow. In the Bear's Den, Korrina gave a thumbs up and aft of him he heard Dravar give a muted cheer. In the cockpit, Kozlowski relaxed slightly, he'd been afraid he'd speak to his aircraft and nobody would answer.

"We're taking you home, Bunker Hill Air Force Base. Isn't that long a flight, not for you. We'll be supercruising at Mach 2.8 and 75,000 feet most of the way. You're the first F-model in the 305th so you'll be getting a lot of visitors over the next few days. But, once we're home. I'll introduce you to your ground crew and we'll get to work. We've got a lot to catch up on. While we were away in Italy, a group of cowboys from the 45th stole our Angel Eyes Shield and we've got to get it back."

There was a chuckle on the intercom system. "We can't let them get away with that, can we?. Mike, take me home. I'm *Xiomara,* fly me."

EPILOGUE

Bang Na-Phitsan Palace, Bangkok, Thailand

"This place is beautiful, Madam Ambassador. I'd never have even guessed it existed or that we are in the middle of the city. How do you do it? Is this your home?'

"When we rebuild an area of the city, Mister President, we put modern high-rise buildings all along the main roads and we put them close together. This leaves areas in the center of each block that are screened from the noise and pollution of the city. They are shaded by the buildings and we use the old canal system to make sure they are watered. They give the city lungs, allow it to breath and permit us to get away from modern life, back to where we are comfortable. You perhaps noted that the way into this compound was unmarked and deliberately unobtrusive."

That, LBJ thought, was an understatement. The walled house had been reached through a battered and peeling wooden gate at the end of a sordid alleyway. He'd actually wondered what was going on until the gate had opened and he'd seen the exquisite garden within. Then he'd seen the complex of ornately carved and enameled teak buildings. They'd been modernized, inside they were wholly 1960s with air conditioning and electrical power, yet outside still looked like something from centuries ago. It wasn't really a single house, more a series of small residences interconnected by doors, paths, and passageways.

"This is my family's home, in a way, Mister President, and in another it is not. This is really a Royal Palace, a small one of course, that was loaned to my family for our use. Originally it was built for the Royal Family of Phitsanulok to use when they came to this city. But, once they had no further use for it, my family was awarded its loan as a mark of Royal favor. My family has served the Kingdom for many generations you see."

"May I ask how long have your family lived here?"

"About six hundred years Mister President."

Next to the President, Ladybird Johnson choked briefly on her drink. Silently, a maid moved forward, cleaned up the spill and replaced the glass with a freshly-filled one.

"In a way, the Palace predates the city. When it was first built, there was no city here at all, just a small river port on the other side of the river. But, you may have noticed, the way the Chaophrya curls around this part of the city, this is a very easy spot to defend. It has river on three sides and the fourth is narrow and fortified. So many members of the ruling classes built homes on the ground protected by the river loop. When the Burmese destroyed Ayuthya in 1792, the survivors gathered here and a new capital city grew up around their compounds. In this part of the city, there are still quite a few Palaces like this one, tucked away where visitors seldom go."

"Six hundred years." Ladybird Johnson was still trying to grasp the idea of a family that had lived in the same home for all those centuries. "And your family was always in Royal service?"

"Always First Lady, always. My own position is hereditary, handed down from mother to daughter." Unseen in the shadows, the Seer looked down and grinned broadly at that. "One day I will retire into privacy and spend my old age trying to make merit, to offset the price of some of the things I have done. Then, Sir Eric, I hope that you will give my daughter the same wise counsel and precious advice that you have always given me."

Sir Eric Haohoa started. He'd been leaning back in his seat, enjoying the cool of the evening. Now, he almost overbalanced backwards. "Your daughter Ma'am? I didn't even know you were married. Is she here? Does she look like you?"

"I'm not." The Ambassador gave him a dazzling, friendly smile. "And I am afraid my daughter is away, learning the things she must know if she is to take over my duties one day. But I am sure that she does look very much like me. All the women in our family have a close resemblance, I am told it is something to do with the genes in the female line of my family being very dominant. But tell me Sir Eric. How is the President's new Chief-of-Staff settling in?"

"Very well Ma'am, very well indeed. Sir Martyn taught him all he could and Sir Pandit Nehru has built upon his lessons. He has Sir Martyn's style even so. Sir Martyn is greatly missed but his legacy is safe and secure."

"And what a legacy." LBJ's voice was soft with respect. "In a single lifetime he rebuilt one of the largest countries in the world, turned it from a poor, undeveloped and ill-fed colony into one of the great countries of the world. I wish that I could be remembered in such a way. Instead I will be remembered as the man whose actions ended the Pax Americana. I'd never thought of it that way, not until I read one of the commentaries. There are people in my party who called the Pax Americana ruling the world by terror. Chalk was one of them, I think his long-term goal was to so tie us up in international treaties that we couldn't keep the peace by ourselves. Pax Americana, it had a nice ring to it. Now its gone."

"We had a good run Mister President, and it had to end sometime. As for us ruling by terror, that's a phrase for the terminally bewildered. The truth is, for twenty years we kept the peace and we did it with less overt use of force than any other nation in our position. Even the British had their small wars after all and they kept the peace as well. Give them credit, they did pretty well for a lot longer than we did. But it was a simpler world back then."

The Seer thought for a second. "We were unlucky, a lot of things came together, they interacted in ways that proved hard to predict and we made a lot of mistakes. But, we got off better than we could have. Nobody will challenge one of our bombers again, not for a very long time at least, and our position as hegemon is secure. We're going to have to work a lot harder in the future to stay that way, that's all."

"No matter Seer, its on my watch that the easy days ended and I'll carry the can for that. And, I'll always be known as the baby-killer now. That's a hell of a name to carry for posterity. Damn that moron Chalk."

Prime Minister Joe Frye grimaced in sympathy. He'd had more than his share of being dropped in it by subordinates whose ambitions exceeded their capability. "From what I hear in the newspapers, he's fairly well damned. What happened to him, I wouldn't wish that on anybody. Is he showing any signs of recovery?"

LBJ shook his head. "On a good day he sits in a corner of his room and gibbers to himself. On a bad day, its horrible to watch. Joe, your army is doing darned well down in Mindanao. My military advisors are impressed. By the way, why is a monkey drinking your beer?"

Frye looked at the small table beside him. Sure enough a small monkey with a sad face and eyes was holding his glass and had his lips on the rim, making drinking motions. It was strangely like a young child trying to drink from a glass that was too big for it. "Hey little fellow, having problems there?" Fry tilted the glass slightly so the beer ran up to the monkey's mouth. "There, feeling better now? Getting a taste for good beer a bit young aren't we."

Frye liked having high-level meetings in Thailand, the country's brewing industry had been founded by Germans just after World War One and the Thais still brewed a good beer.

"Willie. You bad boy. What are you doing? Come away from there immediately. I'm sorry everybody, he slipped out when I looked away for a minute. Stop disturbing these nice people and come home." The speaker was a plump, elderly lady, obviously embarrassed by her monkey's escapade.

"Lani, I would like to introduce you to Mister Lyndon Johnson, President of the United States and his wife Ladybird, Mister Joe Frye, Prime Minister of Australia, Sir Eric Haohoa, Cabinet Secretary of India and, hiding over in the shadows there is The Seer, American National Security Advisor. Everybody, I would like to introduce my Aunt Lani."

The Seer glanced across the courtyard at the Ambassador and lifted an eyebrow. She replied with an almost imperceptible nod. Meanwhile, Aunt Lani was standing on the grass, her jaw hanging open. LBJ decided a rescue was in order. "Lani, what a delightful little monkey. He's been no trouble at all, is he your pet?"

Lani was still standing with her mouth open, apparently in shock at the realization of the company she had suddenly found herself in. The Ambassador answered for her. "No Mister President, its not a family pet. Lani and her husband run an animal welfare and rescue service, they take in animals like monkeys and a few others that were being smuggled out of the country, get them back to health and release them in the wild. A few are too young to be released immediately so they stay here until they are ready."

"It's a terrible problem, Mister President" Lani had finally recovered her voice. "People take these animals and trade them as exotic pets or kill them to make Chinese Medicines. Not just monkeys but tigers, bears, birds, all sorts. Some of the things they do are horrible. Did you know they cut bears open and prevent the wound from healing so they can drain the bile out? My husband and I have been trying to get some sort of agreement to get the trade controlled and the worst excesses stopped but nobody will listen to us."

LBJ looked at the little monkey. If that monkey had escaped by accident, he was the Flying Dutchman. "Well, Lani, somebody is listening now. I will instruct our Ambassador here to speak with you about this and come to an agreement about controlling this trade. I'll also tell him the matter has my personal interest and I'll have his hometown bombed if it isn't resolved satisfactorily. After Yaffo, he'll believe me."

Lani triumphantly swept up her monkey and left. LBJ looked defensively at the group. "Have you any idea how many little old ladies cast their votes because they think a candidate is kind to little furry animals? Enough to swing a marginal my way. Anyway, I can't really think of a situation where I would order our bombers to take down an American city."

"I can." The Seer said idly. "Several in fact."

LBJ looked pensive for a moment. "Probably Seer, but a recalcitrant ambassador isn't one of them. I hope." He looked at the Seer and got a nod of agreement. A recalcitrant ambassador wasn't one. LBJ got a feeling he would find out later what were the situations, he wasn't certain he wanted to know though.

"Seriously, an agreement of this sort really will play well. Its the sort of thing we should announce when the Summit Meeting is over. The security agreements and trade accords will mean nothing to most people, but an agreement to protect little furry animals, that's something everybody who votes can relate to."

Joe Frye nodded. There spoke the master campaigner. When LBJ was in Texan geniality mode, it was easy to forget that the man was a politician without equal. He would speak to the Australian Ambassador as well.

"Have you seen Model's trial in Moscow Mister President? No matter how much we despise the man and everything he stood for, I think we have to respect his performance there. Stood up in front of the court, took full responsibility for everything that had been done and tried to exonerate all his subordinates on the grounds they were only obeying orders. Then stood mute."

"Doesn't work." The Ambassador grunted. "German Army Officer's manual, 1930. 'Officers are trained to receive commissions so they will know when to disobey orders'. Specifically states that an officer who obeys an illegal or criminal order has the same degree of guilt as the person who issued the order."

She looked around at her companions. "Our army was trained by German expatriates in the early 1930s and our Officer's Manual is just a translation of the German one. Anyway, we'll probably never know why he did the things he did. To be honest I don't think he knows, he's probably justified them so many times to himself he believes his own story. Mister President, how is the evacuation of refugees from Gaza progressing?"

"Very well Ma'am. We have our troops out now and the South Africans have taken over protecting the areas. There are some experts from the British Museum in the Valley of Kings, trying to repair the damage the Caliphate did to the relics there. They've got the fragments of the Sphinx and are trying to reassemble it, the FBI are helping them out, they have expertise in putting bombs back together that can be applied. The Caliphate tried to blow up one of the pyramids as well but they hardly scratched it. The paintings though, I am told, are defaced beyond recovery and, of course, everything in the Cairo Museum was burned to ashes."

There was silence for a few seconds, ended by the blast of a car horn from outside the gates. One of the servants opened up the door, letting in four Executive Assistants loaded down with packages from stores. The Ambassador got up to greet them.

"How was your retail therapy girls? Naamah, how did you get on? Redheads are really rare here, I was worried you might not be able to find anything to suit you. Lillith and Igrat wouldn't have had any problems of course. Nor would Inanna, now we have so many American tourists here."

"We did just fine Snake." Naamah held up her packages triumphantly. "Shinawatra Silk had every color and pattern you can imagine. What do you think of this?" She fished in a bag and pulled out a luminescent emerald green silk and held it up to her hair. "Got some dresses and office suits being made up for me. Lillith's having a dress made that'll bring Washington to a complete stop."

"Lyndon, that's beautiful. Will we have time for some shopping here?" Ladybird looked at the bags of silks with acute longing.

LBJ nodded agreeably. "Perhaps Naamah will take you tomorrow. Naamah, I've talked to The Seer on this and the Contractors are agreeable if you are. I have decided the Presidency ought to have an Executive Assistant from The Contractors, one independent of which party is in power. That'll help policy continuity and avoid communication gaps. I would like you to take that job, starting when we get back. You'll have an office in the White House."

"Why thank you Mister President. I'll look forward to that." Naamah thought for a second. "Does this mean I can charge today's retail therapy to Uncle Sam?"

LBJ looked at The Ambassador and the four Executive Assistants examining and comparing their purchases. "You little demons." he said affectionately.

Naamah looked at him, her head tilted a little to one side. "Mister President" she said curiously "How long have you known?"

The End

Printed in Great Britain by
Amazon.co.uk, Ltd.,
Marston Gate.